THE ANNUAL BANQUET
OF THE GRAVEDIGGERS' GUILD

THE ANNUAL
BANQUET
OF THE
GRAVEDIGGERS'
GUILD

Mathias Énard

translated by Frank Wynne

A NEW DIRECTIONS
PAPERBOOK ORIGINAL

Originally published in French as *Le banquet annuel de la Confrérie des fossoyeurs*
by Actes Sud in 2020. Published by special arrangement with Actes Sud in
conjunction with their duly appointed agent, 2 Seas Literary Agency

Manufactured in the United States of America
First published as New Directions Paperbook 1575 in 2023

Library of Congress Cataloging-in-Publication Data
Names: Énard, Mathias, 1972– author. | Wynne, Frank, translator.
Title: The annual banquet of the gravediggers' guild / Mathias Énard ;
translated by Frank Wynne.
Other titles: Banquet annuel de la confrérie des fossoyeurs. English
Description: New York, NY : New Directions Publishing Corporation, 2023.
Identifiers: LCCN 2023016478 | ISBN 9780811231299 (paperback) |
ISBN 9780811231305 (ebook)
Subjects: LCGFT: Novels.
Classification: LCC PQ2705.N273 B3613 2023 | DDC 843/.92—dc23/eng/20230410
LC record available at https://lccn.loc.gov/2023016478

2 4 6 8 10 9 7 5 3 1

New Directions Books are published for James Laughlin
by New Directions Publishing Corporation
80 Eighth Avenue, New York 10011

To the savage thinkers

"*In our former lives, we have all been earth, stone, dew, wind, fire, moss, tree, insect, fish, turtle, bird and mammal.*"

—Thich Nhat Hanh (quoting the Buddha)

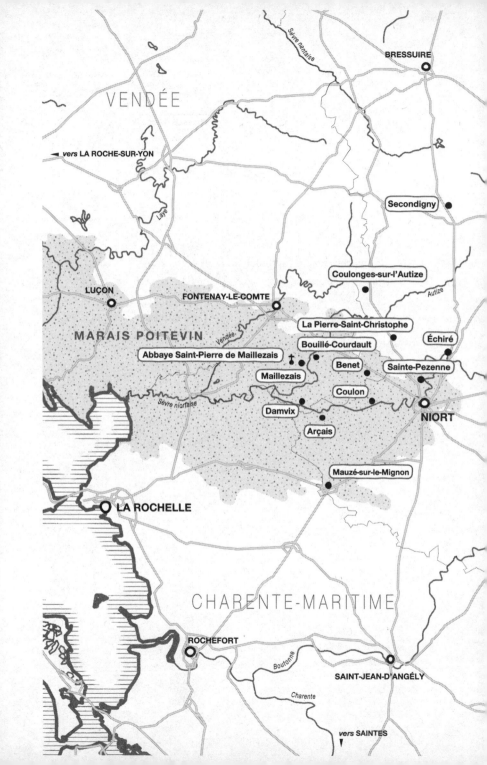

BRESSUIRE

VENDÉE

vers LA ROCHE-SUR-YON

Sèvre nantaise

Laye

Secondigny

Coulonges-sur-l'Autize

Autize

LUÇON

FONTENAY-LE-COMTE

MARAIS POITEVIN

Vendée

La Pierre-Saint-Christophe

Bouillé-Courdault

Échiré

Abbaye Saint-Pierre de Maillezais

Benet

Sainte-Pezenne

Maillezais

Coulon

Sèvre niortaise

Damvix

NIORT

Arçais

Mauzé-sur-le-Mignon

LA ROCHELLE

CHARENTE-MARITIME

ROCHEFORT

Boutonne

SAINT-JEAN-D'ANGÉLY

Charente

vers SAINTES

CHÂTELLERAULT

Moussais-la-Bataille

DISSAY

Dive

Thouet

PARTHENAY

Vouillé

POITIERS

Vienne

Vonne

Clain

SAINT-MAIXENT-L'ÉCOLE

Lusignan

LUSIGNAN

VIENNE

Sèvre niortaise

DEUX-SÈVRES

COUHÉ

MELLE

Tillou

Boutonne

CHEF-BOUTONNE

Nantes

Tours

Angoulème

20 km

CONTENTS

THE ANNUAL BANQUET
OF THE GRAVEDIGGERS' GUILD

I.

THE SAVAGE MIND

"Whichever way a man may turn,
his eyes alight upon Libourne."
—Onésime Reclus, *Le partage du monde*

December 11

Needless to say, I have resolved to name this place the Savage Mind.

I arrived two hours ago. I don't yet know quite what I'm going to write in this journal, except, well, impressions and notes that will make up an important part of my thesis. My ethnographer's diary. My field notebook. I took a taxi from Niort train station (heading north-northwest, fifteen kilometers, a small fortune). To the right of the road, flat open country, boundless fields, no hedgerows, a little cheerless in the gathering dusk. To the left, we were skirting the dark shadows of marshland, or that, at least, is how it seemed to me. The driver had a hell of a time finding the address, even using GPS. (Coordinates for the Savage Mind: 46°25′4″N 0°31′29.3″W.) Eventually, he pulled into a farmyard, a dog began to bark, I was here. The owner (sixty, smiling) is called Mathilde. I took possession of the premises. My house (my apartment?) is, in fact, the rear ground floor area of the main farmhouse. The windows look out over the garden and the kitchen garden. To the right, I have a view of the church; to the left, a field (I don't know what's growing in it—alfalfa? I often assume that all

3

fields of green low-growing crops are alfalfa) and, opposite, rows of what I suspect are radishes or cabbages. A bedroom, a kitchen–living room, a bathroom, that's all, but it's more than enough. My feelings, when Madame Mathilde said, Okay, there you go, this is your place, were mixed. Simultaneously happy to finally be in the field and a little anxious. I rushed to my laptop to make sure the Wi-Fi worked, using my article for *Studies and Perspectives* as a pretext. I was only fooling myself; there was nothing urgent. I mostly sent some messages and chatted with Lara. I went to bed early, reread a few pages of Malinowski and, in the darkness, was keenly aware of the aural environment. The muffled hum of some contraption in the distance (the boiler?), from time to time an even more distant car. Then I went to sleep on an empty stomach. I really need to sort out the transportation issue and buy some stuff to eat.

December 12

First day acclimatizing to my new terrain. La Pierre-Saint-Christophe marks the center of a triangle whose vertices are Saint-Maxire, Villiers-en-Plaine and Faye-sur-Ardin. So many fantastical names that give substance to my New World. Fifteen kilometers from Niort, ten from Coulonges-sur-l'Autize.

I left the Savage Mind shortly before 10 a.m., having realized that I was not alone in my ethnographer's quarters: there is a plethora of fauna. Doubtless, the toad is drawn by the countless insects and the cats by the toad. In the bathroom, equidistant from the shower and the toilet, is a colony of red worms, or rather living red filaments that look like worms. Quite cute, as long as you don't step on them. They slowly slither toward the door, so you have to spray them down the plughole before taking a shower. I easily managed to overcome my disgust, which is a reassuring sign for my ability to deal with the difficulties of fieldwork. After all, even Malinowski notes that insects and reptiles are the principal obstacles to the work of the ethnologist. (Since no one will read this diary, I might as well admit that I was pretty disgusted at the thought of worms in the bathroom and it was fifteen minutes before I steeled myself to take a shower.) There is also a handsome caravansary of dwarf snails, which is harmless enough. I assume that the humidity, together with being at garden level, are mostly to blame. So anyway, I left the Savage Mind at around ten o'clock and went to see my landlady, Madame Mathilde, to ask if there was some way of getting into town so I could stock up the larder, she looked tremendously surprised, Well, now, I have no idea, she had no idea, she had no idea whether there was bus service to the village. (Today, I discovered that it's possible to take the early morning school bus, but I'd look like a dirty old man and besides, I would have to wait a good two hours for the supermarket to open, something to note in the *Transportation* chapter.) Mathilde immediately advised me to buy a car: in La Pierre-Saint-Christophe, there is nothing except a café that sells basic essentials, which, around here, means fishhooks, cigarettes and fishing permits. But at least I won't have to fish for my breakfast: Madame Mathilde (or rather her husband, Gary, I'm keen to interview him) was kind enough to lend me an old moped belonging to one of their children (note for the *Transportation* chapter) and an old black helmet with no visor and threadbare padding decorated with a few vintage stickers (a frog sticking its tongue out, an AC/DC logo). As a result, I have a somewhat precarious but efficient means of locomotion. Toward midday, I went to the supermarket in the county town, Coulonges-sur-l'Autize (pretty name), and bought lots of things before it occurred to me that it wouldn't be easy to carry them on a moped: tins of tuna and sardines, frozen pizzas, coffee, a little something sweet (chocolate). The departmental road (number something or other) twists and turns on its way to the town, crossing quite a wide river. (The Autize?) A market, a post office, a church, a small château, two boulangeries, as many pharmacies, a clothing store, three cafés, there's not much to see. I bought a newspaper in order to look nonchalant in the Bar des Sports and drank tea while eavesdropping on conversations, my way of initiating contact with the place. The local dialect (officially Poitevin-Saintongeais—I wouldn't like to offend anyone) is probably dying (but let's not get ahead of ourselves: *Tongues* chapter, lovely title). I hope to have more luck at the market. After tea I headed back to the Savage Mind; thanks to a stray dog, I almost crashed into a low wall and totaled the moped (there's a sentence I never thought I would write) but, by some miracle, I managed to right the bike in time. Then I went over my work schedule. La Pierre-Saint-Christophe has six hundred and forty-nine inhabitants, according to the latest municipal census. Two hundred and eighty hearths, as old-timers would say. The demonym, according to Wikipedia and the mayoral website, is Petrochristophorian. Esteemed Petrochristophorians, ladies and gentlemen, I have decided (chapter: *Questions*) to conduct about a hundred interviews from among your number, choosing interviewees such that, by the end, I will have equal numbers for each gender and age bracket. This seems to me, empirically, a good idea. A year's work subdivided into two six-month campaigns. Great. I feel full of energy. I skimmed through the rough draft of my article for *Living Rural Lives* and immediately had my first intuition. Evidently, working in the countryside suits me.

December 12 (contd.)

It's two in the morning now, I'm finding the silence and the solitude distressing, can't get to sleep. I hear creepy-crawlies and I'm convinced that they're going to clamber over me in the darkness. Too late to call Lara again (she had a good laugh when I told her that my lodgings would henceforth be called the Savage Mind), and there's no one online, so I can't chat. Worse, the only books I have to read are Malinowski's *Argonauts of the Western Pacific*, his *Diary* and Hugo's *Ninety-Three*—not exactly great distractions. (Why did I bring *Ninety-Three*? Probably because I had a vague impression that it's set somewhere around here.) I feel a little cold, tomorrow I'll have to ask Mathilde if she can lend me a heater. What now? Play Tetris, that will take my mind off things.

December 13

Radio: weather report, Christmas approaching, etc., etc. Freezing rain, moped impossible. Buy anorak: important. First sorties into the village. I've discovered that at the far end of the field facing the Savage Mind, behind the trees (poplars?) and slightly downhill, a river flows. My landlady took me to visit the church. The key— at least two kilos of cast iron—is very impressive. The church a little less so. Cheap, rather banal furnishings. Pretty, all the same. Learned something funny: the mayor is also the local undertaker, or vice versa. Read an excellent article online about the inventor of Tetris, a Russian. The guy's a genius. They should award him a Nobel Prize—apparently, he hasn't been given one yet.

   Nothing to report.

December 14

Slept well. The cat has left another dead toad outside my door, a friendly offering, yuck. *Gallia est omnis divisa in partes tres*, Caesar wrote about Gaul, well the same could be said for this godforsaken place. I've divided the Ordnance Survey map into three sectors, the café district, the church district and the housing estate. Quite densely populated in the center, farms spaced farther apart around the church, and newly built houses in the estate. It's a safe bet that the residents living in Les Bornes are *rurbanites* who commute to town for work. (Note for the *Toiling* chapter, good title.) I've decided to go back to Paris on the twenty-third for the Christmas holidays, I have ten days of work to do before my sabbatical. First interview, Mathilde, since I have her to hand, so to speak, it makes it easier, she'll help me hone a list of questions that I can later refine. I explained to her why I was here, why I planned to spend a year in the village, she seemed surprised. You're going to study us, is that it? she said. I said, Well, um, no, not just you, which was hardly tactful. So I added, The goal of my thesis is to understand what it means to live in the country nowadays, an abstract I thought rather brilliant (note for the chapter: *Questions*). It just goes to show that it's through concrete contact that we truly formulate our goals. She seemed reassured, I think. In any case, we've arranged to meet again tomorrow morning. Right now I have to run, I have to meet the mayor at the Café-Pêche so he can introduce me to the owner and the regulars. The village potentate takes his responsibilities very serious, apparently. When he found out that I was coming from the Sorbonne (which is sort of true) he insisted on personally acquainting me with the village. His question is "Why us?" "Why here?" I can hardly tell him about the grant I've been given by the Deux-Sèvres regional council, it would be a little embarrassing (nor can I tell him that I found the name of the village amusing and that it's far enough in the ass end of nowhere to be interesting), so I tell him that it was my thesis supervisor, the famous professor Yves Calvet, who chose the location, it sounds more serious, as though the finger of God (or of the Sorbonne, in this case) had singled out their village, that way they feel valued, which is good. I wonder what Calvet would say if he knew. He most likely wouldn't give a fuck. Right, got to go, I'm already running late.

December 14 (contd.)

So it's done, I've been inducted into the key socialization space, the beating heart of the village: le Café-Pêche chez Thomas, which, as it turns out, does sell cigarettes, various items of fishing tackle, tinned food, water and other fluids, and a handful of newspapers and magazines. Thomas, the owner, is about sixty, and positively portly. Tables of faded red Formica, a bar fashioned from the same material, chairs with metal legs. TV. Pungent smells of wine, anisette and stale tobacco, which makes me think that smoking restrictions are not necessarily respected in public spaces. (First observation: countryfolk are rebellious.) Four men playing cards, two others at the bar, not a single woman. Kir, draft beer, Ricard®. I had a real job refusing a drink, and eventually accepted a bottle of Orangina® so ancient the pulp had congealed at the bottom of the bottle and the cap was rusted, which leads me to think that the people around here don't drink anything fizzy besides lager. I should probably have accepted a Kir or something like that, but I need to keep my wits about me if I'm to get a little work done.

I'm beginning to enjoy writing the journal. It's amusing, it feels like talking to someone. I am conscious of just how much I'm not myself with the people here. I feel like I'm playing a role. That of the observer attempting to subdue a hostile environment. I'm walking on eggshells. Perhaps I am being a little too wary. (*Questions* chapter?) The mayor seems to be a jolly old soul despite his funereal profession. Thomas, the café owner, said: Just park your ass here for a week and you'll meet the whole village.

A week of drinking antediluvian Orangina® and I'd have an

ulcer, was my first thought. Just then, as though to prove the owner's point, a young woman came into the bar. A little older than me, about thirty-five I'd say, with a hippie-hick vibe (well, at least *I* know what I mean), and without a smile, without so much as a glance in my direction, she planted herself in front of the bar and started yelling something I didn't quite catch about vegetables and payment. Thomas the owner wasn't going to put up with it: I don't owe you shit, and they started trading insults until the mayor intervened saying, Let's all calm down, let's all calm down now, then the virago stormed out and slammed the door, eliciting a sigh of relief from both the mayor and the café owner, a sigh that was followed by a series of offensive but apparently justified remarks.

"She just gets crazier and crazier."

I casually asked who they were talking about.

"A head case," said Thomas.

"A local farmer," said the mayor, "she grows vegetables."

"Is she from around here?" (I thought my question very apposite.)

"Sort of," I was told, which left me none the wiser. I knew one thing for certain: the village had at least one female autochthon in the thirty-to-forty age bracket.

And that was the end of the gossip. The nights are going to be very long here, unless I become a barfly at the Café-Pêche. Thankfully, I've got Tetris, the internet and Malinowski, fonts of pleasure and wisdom. As soon as dinner is over (as now: an omelet sandwiched between slices of white bread while staring at the screen) I start to get bored. I don't feel like tackling Victor Hugo. The Savage Mind is not a gloomy place, just a little spartan. I'll have to bring a few things from Paris, a couple of pictures to hang on the walls, some books, just to brighten the place up. After all, I'll be spending a year here. When I look at it like that, it's depressing; my third night in the village and already I'm bored stiff. Luckily, I've arranged a video call with Lara in ten minutes.

December 14 (contd.)

Webcams are intensely unsatisfying, in spite (or maybe because) of the powerful erotic tension. Lara was wearing pajamas made of some silky material, I think. Hmm ... that last comment was misjudged. It's impossible to imagine Lévi-Strauss commenting on lingerie. (Idea for an article: the sexuality of anthropologists while in the field. Discuss Malinowski's dirty fantasies while under his mosquito net.) The fact remains, I'm frustrated. I'm almost tempted to call it a day and head back to Paris right now, but that would mean twenty kilometers by moped through the icy darkness to get to the train station, then two and a half hours on the TGV, assuming there are even still trains at this hour, which I doubt. So, no go. I'm as isolated as Malinowski in the middle of the Pacific, since isolation simply means not being able to have what you want when you want it: whether civilization is two hours, two days or two months away makes little difference. Right now, at this moment, I'd like to be with Lara, but here I am, alone in the Savage Mind; as alone as Napoleon Chagnon among the Yanomamo people. Come, ye gods of anthropology, ye little gods of Savage peoples, come to my aid and bear me to Perfect Thesis.

Best to think about something else: let's continue with an account of my afternoon encounters. So, after the fulgurant appearance of the aforementioned Lucie, ranting about nickel and dime stuff, the mayor took it upon himself to introduce me to the cardplayers, who looked at me as though I were a Martian. In me they saw the mask of the Other, to use the term coined by Levinas. If I'd taken out a bag of glass beads and machetes and made ritual offerings, they would scarcely have reacted any differently. It will take some time before I am accepted. I gave them a smile, I even asked what game they were playing, just to give the impression I was taking an interest, for all the good it did, since they simply stared at me, wide-eyed, *'tis the coinche, what else?*, so, that will teach me. I've just looked it up in the Encyclopédie Le Robert: *coinche*: regionalism, West (so far, so good), a card game similar to belote involving contract bidding, which does little to enlighten me. I discreetly questioned the mayor, the cardplayers are village men who practice various trades, but all are avid hunters and anglers. Since I knew I would run into them again, I didn't bother to jot down their names.

A more stimulating encounter in every sense: Max. Fifty-something, leather jacket, black goatee, moonfaced, broad-shouldered, bit of a paunch, biker's helmet, motorbike parked outside the door, so blunt it almost made me think I was back in Paris—in Montreuil, to be precise. He had just dropped in to buy cigarettes when the mayor called him over and suggested he have a drink with us. Max is an artist; he settled here about a decade ago (in fact, he had lived in Montreuil—an amusing coincidence). From what he said, he now has a large farm just outside the village. He cordially invited me to visit when I have a moment. Max moved out of Paris because he needed more space to work, and because his ex-wife was getting on his ass, as he puts it. I'm keen to hear his thoughts about the locals. He's clearly not one to mince words.

So, a couple of pastis later, the mayor—now on his fourth glass, if I counted correctly—was a little tipsy. His cheeks were flushed, his eyes were bloodshot, and his speech had taken a noticeably local turn. Intelligible, but decidedly local. He was talking about politics with Max and the café owner, complaining that the prefecture had just overturned a municipal edict he'd issued the previous autumn forbidding outsiders from foraging for wild mushrooms in the local woods. This was a serious blow to his pride—but only his pride, joked Max, since no one had ever seen so much as a single cèpe in the little woods of Ajasses. There was a lull in the conversation when the local TV news came on, meaning that it was 7 p.m., time for me to head back to the Savage Mind; I thanked the mayor for his hospitality and his help, told Max (who now seemed in no hurry to leave) that

I'd call to arrange a visit, said goodbye to the landlord and set off home. It was a humid night; though starless, it was illuminated by the myriad strings of Christmas lights with which the locals had decorated their houses, like a competition to see who could have the most lights twinkling in the darkness and light-up Santas climbing through their windows. (Look into the origins of this curious custom.) At a normal walking pace, it takes precisely four minutes for me to arrive back at the Savage Mind (prompting angry barking from Gary's dog as I cross the yard—I'm hoping he'll quickly get used to me, it's a little terrifying).

Reading, then lights out.

December 15

Woke up having caught a cold. Subzero temperatures in the bedroom, must remember to ask for an extra heater. The worm colony in the bathroom is thriving (yuck), as are the dwarf snails in the living room—are the two things linked? Quick breakfast. Prepared my questionnaire, checked the digital recorder. Quick hello to Lara on messenger. Just spotted Mathilde crossing the yard, so she's obviously at home. Right, I'm out of here. Time to finally get down to work.

December 15 (contd.)

Two hours' recording and a lunch of rabbit in mustard sauce (couldn't bring myself to tell Mathilde I hate rabbit, so I ate rabbit—turns out it's pretty tasty. I really am acclimatizing quickly). Mathilde is very good-natured and full of surprises. First surprise: after we had coffee in her kitchen, she brought me into what she calls "the office." I need to revise my assumptions: not only does she own a state-of-the-art computer, but there's a printer and a pile of books about accounting and data processing. Mathilde manages the family business. Her career path (can't think of another way to put it) is impressive. The daughter of farmers, Mathilde married young and single-handedly taught herself business management. She "got into computers," as she put it, in the 1990s. Gary takes care of the actual farming, while she manages the business. Bills, investments, loans—she deals with everything. Not to mention the kitchen garden and the farmyard animals (poultry and rabbits), the farm's only livestock, raised mostly for domestic consumption. Mathilde recently took up breeding again (having given it up after her mother's death many years since) because, as she put it, she was sick and tired of eating revolting supermarket chicken. Once again, countryfolk and city folk agree on the subject of food quality. Her children went to the city to study and settled in distant places (suburban Paris, Bordeaux). They don't have the expertise, much less the desire, to take over the farm, so the issue of retirement is looming. (Mathilde is fifty-seven, Gary sixty-two.) In the past, Mathilde took care of the parish church and also helped the priest with day-to-day matters, until his sudden death (she seemed very moved when she talked about him) almost two years ago. From that I surmise that she's a practicing Catholic (I haven't yet drafted a "religious" questionnaire, but I plan on adding a chapter called *Faith*). She says that since the curate's death (is "curate" the right word? Shit, I don't know a fucking thing about Catholicism), there's no longer a village priest, only a locum who pops by for christenings, funerals and weddings. (So, the village has lost something of its centrality, ecclesiastically speaking. Are there any religious minorities here? Protestants, Jews, Muslims? Buddhists, who knows?) Mathilde is quite prudish, especially when it comes to anything to do with intimacy and sexuality (I need to review that section of the interview—my adultery question is absolutely hopeless, I couldn't bring myself to ask it, I need to come up with a more oblique way of exploring such relationships), and also on the subject of money, when the subject of earnings comes up, she is vague: We manage, there're good times and tough times, last year was very good. (I can always guesstimate numbers from the price of a ton of wheat.) On the other hand, on the subject of her childhood, I can barely get her to shut up. Her parents' farm, her sisters, the evenings with friends, the bonfires on the Feast of Saint John (a tradition I thought was chiefly urban, must investigate for the *Celebrations* chapter), roasting chestnuts by the hearth, forest walks, village festivals, the bakery ovens (she claims she can still remember the taste of piping hot bread on which freshly spread butter simply melted), the Saturday-night dances of her adolescence—I must have at least an hour's worth of tape. And the various people she knew as a child: her father, her mother, her sisters; how she met Gary, who initially wooed her elder sister, Because I was still little, she said, as though, had she not been, Gary would've immediately taken an interest in her; then the period covering their engagement, their marriage, taking over her in-laws' farm, etc., etc. I think she was happy to have someone listening. Mid-interview, we headed back into the kitchen, where she prepared the rabbit (which, thankfully, emerged gutted and jointed from the fridge). I raised the subject of relationships between neighbors in the village, and once again, she drew mostly on memories: how once upon a time, people had more opportunities to meet up, there were farmyard lunches, the good old days, and so on. More nostalgia. But she was completely unable to relate any recent social gathering she had attended, with the singular exception of the parish priest's funeral. From what she said, she is on friendly terms with her neighbors. Oh, and I also found out that my Savage Mind had been built as a tourist *gîte*, but given the work involved and the few takers, Mathilde found it more financially viable to rent by the year. (Note for *Work* chapter.) Then we sat down to rabbit, Gary joined us for lunch, having been out servicing a tractor. He asked no questions about the interview, just saying, So, how did it go?—as though out of respect for his wife's privacy.

Gary has a rather handsome face and piercing blue eyes, he looks young for his age. We chatted over lunch, and it was their turn to ask the questions. They were curious to know how someone goes about becoming an anthropologist and wanted me to explain why an anthropologist would be interested in their village. I decided to tell the truth: the grant from the département, my desire to write the definitive monograph on country life sorely lacking in contemporary ethnology, my sense (based on an in-depth reading of available sources) that the area might be emblematic of the current issues facing rural communities. I told them my previous field of study had been a tiny hamlet in the Ariège, and Gary said, Ah, the South, you'll be missing the weather, I expect, which proves he knows nothing about Ariège, which is almost as waterlogged as here. I thanked them for lunch and especially for the moped, which has literally saved my life, I got Gary to promise he would take me hunting someday, then I left. Back at the Savage Mind, I decided to postpone transcribing the interview (my transcription software has as much difficulty deciphering Mathilde's speech as it did the Ariège accent, I should have expected that, these things are programmed by Parisians for radiologists in Orléans) so I could quickly set down these events in the journal.

What I find surprising and genuinely promising is that, thus far, the village seems friendly and welcoming. Or maybe the little glass of red wine Gary insisted I drink has made me high-spirited (not so rotten, the local rotgut, as it turns out).

December 15 (contd.)

Late night. Lonely. Carnal thoughts. Lara everywhere. I wonder whether we should give up the webcam and move on to truly postmodern sexuality. I find the idea of jerking off in front of a computer screen faintly repellent. Never mind, just have to hold out for eight more days, it's no big deal.

Made an interesting discovery while tinkering with the calculator on the computer: the multiplicative inverses of 11, 22, 33, 55, 77, and 121 are all recurring decimals. $1/11 = 0.090909090909$ recurring, $1/22 = 0.0454545454545$, and so on. I wonder whether this formula might not be the hidden aspect of some important theorem on the multiplicative inverses of prime numbers.

Boredom and curiosity are the twin breasts that suckle science.

December 16

Fuck, today has started off badly. Just received the peer reviewer's notes for my article for *Studies and Perspectives*. The bastard. (Or the bitch, it's quite possible it's a woman, though there's something unspeakably *macho* about the sardonic comments and the dripping irony.) Who do they think they are, these officious little dickheads? First comment: *The meager results of this brief contribution on the Ariège are inversely proportional to its overweening ambition.* Scabby dogs. Besides, it's completely meaningless. Brief contribution, bullshit. Fifty pages, the core of my thesis. I despise them. And it goes on: *The methodology is so woolly that it further undermines the relevance of observations that are, at best, unexceptional.* A complete hatchet job, I'm sick to my stomach and my eyes are stinging. And, after a long paragraph of vicious vitriol, it concludes: *The title "Return to Montaillou" might elicit a wan smile from the reader if the subsequent text were not as far removed from Le Roy Ladurie as the thirteenth century is from the twenty-first.* This reviewer is really taking the piss out of me. To paraphrase Thomas Bernhard: "The distinguished editorial committee of *Studies and Perspectives in Anthropology* is an academy of talentless assholes." Add a well-worded quip, like "one cannot help but wonder whether the mediocrity of your journal is the cause or consequence of your interminable idiocy," and conclude, "I remain, Monsieur-le-fucking-peer-reviewer, yours with boundless contempt," which at least has the merit of being unambiguous.

I'm sick, I'm pissed off, so I'm going back to bed.

December 17

Too depressed to boot up the laptop for most of yesterday. Glorious weather today, an occurrence so rare it bears noting. This cheers me up. It froze overnight; the trees are wreathed in a glittering canopy of hoarfrost (a nice turn of phrase, I think). Mathilde lent me an electric heater, it's pleasantly warm. I started my day with a little housekeeping, forcibly evicting three dwarf snails, cleaning away the corpses of two I inadvertently crushed, dispatching a dozen red worms to hell while scrubbing the bathroom. Since I was fed up having to kick the cats out every time I opened the door, I've decided to adopt them, and truth be told their animal companionship is comforting. One restriction: they're not allowed in my bedroom. There are two of them, a friendly ginger tom and a slightly disturbing black cat straight from the pages of an arcane book on bucolic black magic. They rub up against my legs when I write. I've been here almost a week now and I still haven't seen the marshes, so I've decided to set off on an expedition. After my bout of depression, it will do me good to make the most of nature. Luckily, Lara was online last night, we were able to chat for a whole hour, and that cheered me. An academic career is clearly a long road paved with misery. Just thinking about the assholes at *Studies and Perspectives* I feel I could commit murder. I need to publish if I'm to have any chance of landing a job after my thesis, I can't keep being a student forever, begging for scholarships left and right. I'm about to turn thirty (aaaargh), so time's not on my side. Lara claims that *Ruralia* would happily accept my article, but I don't have the energy to send it to them right now. I could try storming the battlements of *Studies and Perspectives* again with a reworked version of the lecture I gave at the conference in Clermont-Ferrand (had a wild time, actually, wound up at fuck knows o'clock in some bar called the Viking, or the Drakkar, I can't remember, dancing with various women from the conference, particularly a research fellow at the CNRS who specializes in the history of agricultural technology—why am I thinking about her now?), but my lecture is too good for those shit-stain frauds, they don't deserve it. Right, time to unwind: I figure I've got enough fuel in my bike to cover about a hundred kilometers, I've stuffed the panniers with chocolate, biscuits, a bottle of water and an Ordnance Survey map of the area, I've got my wool scarf and my gloves, I'm all set.

Avanti, popolo.

December 17 (contd.)

Frozen, absolutely frozen stiff. Thought I wouldn't be able to get off the moped on my own, my knees simply refused to flex. Right now, I've got the heater cranked up to max and tucked under the desk but I'm still shivering. Still, it was a nice ride. When you cross the main road, the landscape changes so abruptly it's almost as though the road was put there intentionally, a physical border. On the far side, the marshlands roll away, with their leafless trees and countless watercourses—rivers, canals and narrow gullies called *rigoles*; the fields are grassy islands littered with dead tree trunks; there are flat-bottomed boats, propelled by men with long poles who stand in the stern; low-roofed houses with brightly colored shutters and, kneeling at the water's edge to wash their verdant tresses, the bowed branches of weeping willows. Your gaze steals through the layers of mist, surprising anglers lined up like poplars along a towpath; traversing pale, desolate villages nestled in limestone shrouds. I was struck by the area's extraordinary beauty and immense sadness, even in bright weather. Come spring, I'll take a boat ride, there are a number of piers that offer day trips. I can take Lara with me, if she comes to spend a few days at Easter. By then, I'll know the region like the back of my hand, which is certainly not the case now. Despite having a map and GPS, I managed to get lost twice—though, in my defense, I have to say it's not easy to check your phone, much less a map, while riding a moped, and the fact that the landscape is almost completely flat makes it difficult to find your bearings. By midday, I was freezing, so I stopped at a touristy village on the water with a souvenir shop and a real estate agent, though needless to say there wasn't a living soul to be seen on this glacial Thursday morning. The local shop sold curious regional specialties, Angelica liqueur (what on earth is Angelica?) and pâté of ragondin, some species of water rat (I imagine potbellied anglers in their flat-bottomed boats using their long poles to slaughter semiaquatic rodents before turning them into pâté—yuck!). A tourist restaurant offered a menu of local delicacies: lumas soup (a regional name for snails—double yuck!) and eels, I opted for a rather nice little creperie a stone's throw from the river (possible article: trace the southern frontier of the buckwheat pancake, which may be just as significant as the border that separates roof tiles from slates or granite from limestone—hypothesis: buckwheat pancake territory is a breeding ground for left-wing voters). There was a roaring fire, I warmed my bones, sated my hunger and resumed my expedition, heading north this time. Without realizing, I crossed the boundary into the Vendée and happened on an island, where, perched on the water's edge, stood the Abbaye de Maillezais, the abbey that inspired Rabelais's Abbaye de Thélème (now a ruin, no monks obviously, no kitchen garden and, of course, no vineyard—bought the complete works of this great man about whom I know next to nothing, it's good to know you're surrounded by eminent luminaries, it's heartening). Headed eastward again, passed through a series of picturesque villages, visited a twelfth-century Roman-esque church—cool—then recrossed the highway and once more found myself in flat open country, then cruised back to the Savage Mind, frozen to the bone, but pleased to feel better acquainted with my surroundings.

Right, it can't all be fun and games, I need to get back down to work, I've got Mathilde's interview to transcribe before meeting with the mayor at the café at six, which, in local time, is the hour of the Pernod. He's planning to introduce me to the oldest man in the village and help me arrange a time for an interview, before—as he put it—it's too late. Apparently, he is a very elderly gentleman. The mayor was so excited by the idea that I hadn't the heart to tell him I'm not a folklorist, and I've no particular desire to meet old geezers, but, anyway.

December 17 (contd.)

Lara, are you online? Are you theeerre? Nope, she's not online. Okay, so now what do I write? It turns out Rabelais is pretty unintelligible; I don't understand a fucking thing. But that's not the real problem. I've just lost miserably at Tetris in two minutes flat. What do I do? What would Malinowski do? I'm pretty sure Lévi-Strauss would have been a brilliant gamer. Anthropologist is a truly shitty profession. "Whichever way a man may turn, his eyes alight upon Libourne." A quote from Onésime Reclus's *Le partage du monde* that is particularly appropriate to these circumstances, Libourne is—what?—250 kilometers from here? Good thinking, Onésime Reclus. Not very fashionable these days. Booze agrees with me. I'm an eagle, I think swiftly, I think brilliantly. Ideas are flooding in, ideas are flooding in, just give me a second while I get you down on actual paper. I can scrabble scribble with one hand and tap type with the other.

December 18

Frozen stiff, bit of a headache. Too drunk to remember to close the bedroom door last night, slept with the cats, woken by rough sandpapery tongues. I've decided to leave that last paragraph rather than erase it, after all, it's an experience that has value. I need to try and remember how I got there, it's important. It's nothing shameful. (I only hope I didn't send an abusive email to the editors at *Studies and Perspectives*; apparently, I sent a blank message, luckily, after a long bout of paranoia, I probably decided that silence was more eloquently contemptuous than invective. As to my pornographic missive to Lara, it's certainly embarrassing, but of no real consequence.) It's disconcerting to see the twisted workings of alcohol-fueled memory—Onésime Reclus, Jesus Christ. But let's take things in chronological order.

I headed out at 5:55 p.m. yesterday to meet the mayor at the café, having transcribed an infinitesimal section of my interview with Mathilde, exhausted as I was by my marshland expedition. At the insistence of the assembled company (the usual suspects: Max, Mayor Martial and the landlord), and reluctant to repeat the Orangina® experiment, I accepted a Blanc-Cassis, and then another, while we chewed the fat. I told them about my little trip, and they gave me details about those places whose names I could remember. Max has a boat and offered to take me out for a spin whenever I feel like going. So far, so good. At this point, a picaresque character by the name of Arnaud showed up. This Arnaud is thirty-something, a round face, anxious eyes that constantly dart about and a curious tic: forcefully sniffing his forearm then scratching his head—in that order—every thirty seconds or so. Besides the snuffling and scratching, Arnaud, also known as Nono aka the Half-wit, has another peculiarity that makes him popular: he is a living calendar. Just give him a date (typically the current date, but it works with any date, I tried) and he launches into an astonishing litany: *December 17, feast day of Saint Judicael;*

birthday of Napoleon Bonaparte, Constantine the Areopagite, and Michael Jordan; death of Marie Curie, Michel Platini and I don't know who all else; December 17, 1928, so-and-so elected Président du Conseil; December 17, 1936, Léon Blum resigns; December 17, 1917, 2,157 killed during the Chemin des Dames ridge offensive; December 17, 1897, Paris premiere of Cyrano de Bergerac*; December 17, 1532, election of Pope Pius VI; December 17, 800, coronation of Charlemagne; December 17, 1987, death of the inventor of the spring mattress and of Marguerite Yourcenar,* and so on, rattled off pell-mell at top speed. The mayor told me every date was correct, that it was impossible to catch him out. Needless to say, I asked Nono, How do you come to know all these things, and he said, Uh, I just know 'em, is all. Nono is also obsessed with engines and works for the tractor mechanic on the outskirts of the village. I said May 1 to him and he reeled off, *May 1, International Workers' Day, feast of Saint Jérémie, May 1, births of Thingamajig and Thingamabob, death of What's-His-Name; May 1, 1955, brutal suppression of Oran protest marches; May 1, 1918, 1,893 killed fighting in the Somme,* somewhere-or-other, etc. He asked for another drink and Thomas, the landlord, chuckled and poured him one.

A few dates later, and Arnaud was a little the worse for wear—actually, to use Max's expression, he was plastered as a Polack. He was sniffing his skin more than ever, he was stuttering and only managed to stay upright by firmly gripping the bar. His diction was increasingly strange, he muttered unintelligible phrases to himself and tapped his oil-smeared sneakers against the bar, beating out the rhythm to nameless songs. A real rare bird, old Arnaud.

We were still chatting (specifically about the possible arrival of a saucisson delayed only, according to Max, by the bar owner's tightfistedness) while Arnaud was clinging to the countertop to keep from falling over when the woman known as Lucie (shock of long hair, denim jacket, red pants) swept into the place like a whirlwind. Instantly, I saw Thomas and the mayor look away, as though oblivious to what was happening; Lucie gently took Arnaud by the hand, shooting black looks at the assembled company:

"You're all fucking assholes. Come on, Arnaud."

Arnaud tottered after her, looking contrite; Thomas heaved a sigh; the mayor looked at his shoes while Max (from what I could tell) stared at Lucie's lower back as she walked to the door.

"That was a bit much, calling us assholes," Thomas griped as soon as she had left. "I mean, he's a grown man, her little Nono."

"She's his legal guardian," said the mayor.

"Even under guardianship, you're allowed to drink, far as I'm aware," protested Thomas.

"In the shadow of guardianship," chuckled Max.

"Maybe we took it a bit too far," Martial the mayor said regretfully. "We shouldn't have plied him with drink."

Later, he explained that Arnaud is Lucie's cousin. It's a tragic story: Arnaud's mother died young, then his grandmother kicked the bucket, leaving Lucie's ancient grandfather and her "half-wit" cousin living alone together. Some months ago, Lucie moved into her paternal grandparents' house. After a breakup, according to the mayor. While she was looking for a place to live, I suppose. I was beginning to understand the woman's foul mood a little better—having to live with her doddery old grandpa and her crazy cousin is no bed of roses.

I shouldn't have stayed at the bar, that much is certain, I was already starting to reel from the three Kirs I'd drunk, though it was—what?—half past seven? and outside it was colder than a brass toilet seat in the Yukon. Max bought me a drink, the bar owner finally produced a saucisson, and we continued talking, mostly about art. Max is pretty bitter, his career hasn't gone as well as he'd hoped, but he's planning his revenge, he tells me. A colossal exhibition, he says, I'll show 'em, I'll show 'em, five years' work, knock 'em on their asses. These works (he wasn't prepared to give any details, it's very hush-hush, apparently) will mark his comeback on the Paris scene and thrust him into the limelight, or so he says. At around eight o'clock, Max left, and I was about to do the same when the mayor said, You heading back? I'll come with you. I'll drop by Lucie's place. I thought this was very gentlemanly on his part, although probably not very wise, given the young woman's foul mood, an objection he brushed off, muttering, Bah, she's not so bad, despite her airs. I didn't really see why I needed to apologize, but I went along with him, mostly out of curiosity. The road was icy, the village utterly deserted, the only lights were the Christmas decorations strung on the facades of the houses. Martial told me that he and Lucie were related. I expressed surprise at the idea of showing up unannounced at such a late hour; he told me not to worry. We came to a ramshackle old stone house about two hundred meters away. We rang the doorbell and Lucie answered, looking about as friendly as she had been earlier. She wasn't exactly thrilled to see us, but she stepped aside and ushered us into a large room with a fireplace, a long wooden table, a sideboard, a television that was turned on. The walls were soot-blackened, the floorboards were filthy and warped in places, it didn't exactly radiate comfort. In fact, it reeked of smoke and a mixture of mildew, dust and food. An elderly gentleman in a hat sitting by the fire turned toward us, and a gray dog shambled over and rubbed up against my leg. Martial introduced me; Lucie shook my hand. On the oilcloth-covered table stood an empty crock-pot and some dirty dishes; in one corner there was a sink, a burner and a gas cylinder; directly opposite me was a flight of stairs, the whole scene poorly lit by an old chandelier dangling from the ceiling. Martial the mayor said, Lucie, I came by to apologize for what happened earlier. Next time we'll try to be more careful.

Lucie shrugged, a gesture that might have meant "I've told you often enough" or "go fuck yourself, you bastard." It was all pretty grim. I made my excuses and gestured to leave—kind of like, I don't want to intrude—but Lucie stopped me, saying, You're here now, at least have a drink, so I sat down. Lucie disappeared for a moment and came back with a bottle and three small glasses.

What is it? I asked. Ah now, this is the local liquor, she said. Plum brandy, added the mayor-cum-undertaker. The clear glass bottle with no label looked lethal, and so it proved. It's at moments like this that you become keenly aware that you have a tube called the esophagus and a pouch called a stomach—the booze sets them blazing like a string of Christmas lights, it reminded me of a childhood toy, Anatomie 2000, a plastic model of the human body, complete with organs. Either the glasses were minuscule or we were already shit-faced because Lucie kept refilling them (I think she took a perverse pleasure in doing so). Martial was flushed and stuttering in a way I never would have imagined.

I rather took to Lucie, maybe because of the brandy. She seemed interested in me, she asked questions, intelligent questions, about my thesis, my field of study. When I asked if I could interview her she reverted to her surly tone and brushed me off, Why don't you ask my grandpa, she said, he's got stories he could tell, haven't you, Pops? At the mention of his name, the old man dozing in front of the television woke with a start, turned to us and roared, I'll have a little glass meself, or something to that effect; seemingly he wasn't allowed alcohol, since his granddaughter paid him no heed.

She also ignored the undertaker, who was silently, assiduously getting hammered. In spite of the hooch, I was beginning to feel a little awkward, and to make matters worse the dog had started humping my right leg rather dangerously, adding bestial lust to the already charged atmosphere: I decided to make my exit, warmly thanking Lucie for her hospitality. I promised to come and interview her grandfather soon, she smiled and said, Whenever you like, he's always here. I got to my feet, the mayor didn't seem in any hurry to go, he was pouring himself another shot, so I left.

Either it was much less cold, or I was much too drunk to notice. Whatever it was, I couldn't walk straight, I kept veering to the left slightly, brushing up against the walls. I remember that when I got back, I was ravenous, so I wolfed down some leftover pasta. Then I tried reading Rabelais, but the print was dancing before my eyes, I couldn't understand shit, so I opened up the laptop.

I really need to talk to Lara, explain the whole weird evening and the porno message I sent, or she'll think I've gone insane, with my story of bitches in heat. None of this explains the whole Onésime Reclus mystery. Anyway, onward and upward, today's priorities: finish transcribing Mathilde's interview and start writing the chapter *Questions*.

Garçon, a couple of aspirin …

December 18 (contd.)

Napped with the heat cranked up to max and the cats purring next to me. I've named them: the black one is Nigel, the ginger is Barley. I don't know whether they're tomcats or female cats but it doesn't really matter, I've always found felines to be much more discreet about their sexuality compared to the polymorphous perversity of their canine counterparts. It's five in the afternoon, pitch-dark already. It's almost the winter solstice. No appointments scheduled for today, just me, my animals and my Savage Mind. The *Questions* chapter is coming along nicely: I think I've managed to come up with my central hypothesis, which posits that these days, the countryside is the true melting pot, the place where wildly diverse lifestyles coexist. Farmworkers, rurbanites and retired expats all share the same space; what I need to ascertain is how they relate, to each other, on the one hand, and to their surroundings on the other. (I'm eager to get Max's take on this. His keen outsider's eye will probably make him a valuable source of information, to say nothing of his taste for scandalmongering, which makes for the best sources, even in ethnology.) Started in on Rabelais—it's a lot easier sober. (Note: the local

dialect is a lot like the French of Gargantua. Martial the mayor reminds me of Pantagruel or Grandgousier.) Damn!—completely
forgot about the business with the oldest man in the village,
though it appears that he did too.

No news from Lara, I hope she wasn't offended by my drunken
pornographic ramblings.

December 19

Slept twelve hours straight. There has been a moderate increase
in the red worm population, perhaps due to the heater, so I've
declared chemical warfare—worms aren't protected under the
Geneva Protocol—sodium hypochlorite, enemy decimated.

Only four more days before I head back to Paris, and I'm
dreading it. Leaving fieldwork is always complicated; you take
with you your fears, your plans, your frustrations, you feel a nag-
ging desire to get back as quickly as possible, to continue with
your observations. Ah, how long it is, the path to the thesis! *How
long it is, the path that leads us home / Pleasure always follows upon
pain / Fear not, my friend, I shall come home again.* I've got a pretty
good singing voice, I think. *It is our travels that shape our youth,*
that would make a fine epigraph for my thesis. Despite my longing to spent time with Lara, I've moved my return date up to
January 2. Max has kindly offered to drop me off and pick me
up at Niort train station, which gives him the opportunity to do
some shopping, since, he tells me, he rarely ventures into Niort.
He buys his supplies online. The mailman is his best friend, he
jokes. I should spend a little time in Niort myself, after all it is
the administrative capital of the département, and the principal
labor market—especially for the service industries, apparently.
It's strange, but I'd dismissed it as a city like Nevers, Vierzon or
Guéret—the sort of place no one cares about and where no one

would want to live—but Max claims it's quite nice, and rather beautiful, boasting a château, a market and a river. (Thinking about it, that probably describes half the administrative capitals; the other half would have *a cathedral*, a market and a river.) *Sleepy* is the adjective most used to describe the city. Just like Foix, the main city in the Ariège: VERY *sleepy*. In fact, when I interviewed Mathilde, she said she almost never goes into Niort, or at least not into the city center. She just stops off at the strip mall on the outskirts of the city, thousands of square meters of lurid warehouses festooned with the logos of every chain store brand—the joy of living in the ass end of nowhere. You can buy anything and everything there, she says, from sporting goods (fishing rods, ammunition, hunting jackets) to cultural consumables (DVDs of stand-up comedians, American movies, wildlife documentaries for Gary), whereas there's nothing in the city center. To her, Niort is just one big supermarket. Nor is she interested in the entertainment on offer—she never goes to the theater or to concerts, and goes to the cinema very rarely: once a year, on Christmas Eve or Christmas Day. Mathilde says her multichannel TV package is a lot more interesting than whatever is playing at the Arts Center.

For his part, Max says he's disappointed that there's no strip club, since that would give him a good reason to go into town.

Personally, I prefer my Savage Mind to an apartment in a sleepy, nondescript prefecture, even in the center with views of the château.

Lara has accepted my apology for my libidinous misdemeanor. Thankfully, she's anything but a prude and she understands that fieldwork isn't always easy.

Today's agenda: Coulonges market, then a quick, informal interview with Martial the mayor and his team of undertakers.

I've found the perfect name for my moped: *Rocinante*, what else?

December 19 (contd.)

Relieved to have avoided getting drunk or, worse, having a traffic accident—a miracle. I was able to stick to just two drinks, but I need to be careful or I'll wind up a certified alcoholic instead of a PhD in social sciences. And I won't even mention the dangerous handling of my moped. The undertakers' is located midway between La Pierre-Saint-Christophe and Coulonges; I stopped by on my way back from the covered market, which, it turns out, is fascinating. A small but elegant building where local market gardeners work side by side with itinerant butchers, artisanal producers of goat cheese and honey. I was flabbergasted to spot the infamous Lucie behind a vegetable stall—selling her own produce, I think. I said hello and bought some potatoes; such a pity she refuses to be interviewed, I thought. I was also a bit disappointed by the local dialect (Poitevin-Saintongeais, why do I find it so hard to simply call it that?). From what I can tell, not many people speak it anymore. On the other hand, the regional accent (Rabelaisian? I need to speak to a linguist who works with *Idioms*) is absolutely exquisite. Here and there you hear English spoken. (I need to find data on the number of British expats who've settled in the region—possibly from the prefecture?) With Christmas fast approaching, the poultry farmers' stands were burgeoning with fat ducks, geese and turkeys, and there were whole stalls selling oysters from Marennes. The atmosphere was festive. Bought some eggs, because there were downy feathers still stuck to the shells—I thought it looked rustic. In the city, it's easy to forget these small, nutritious oviform things emerge from the cloacae of hens and are intended to produce chicks. All around the market, vendors were hawking cheap clothes, discounted CDs and DVDs; I tried to find a present for Lara, no luck, so I mounted Rocinante and headed back to the village to see Martial. I've never visited an undertakers', although you see them everywhere, and the profession—as far as I'm aware—is universal. It must be the oldest profession, predating even "the oldest profession." Or perhaps they emerged simultaneously. Martial has a flourishing business, employing three staff. It's a highly regulated profession, one that involves considerable technical sophistication, and requires genuine skill as well as the human touch (*dixit* Martial). The coffins, needless to say, are not made on-site, but ordered from a catalog. There are three broad types approved by the government (decidedly the legal system pokes its nose into EVERY aspect of our lives): the Parisian, the Lyonnais or the American. The thickness, quality and water resistance of each is regulated by law—which clearly has nothing fucking else to do. The various models have evocative names: *Repose* (solid pine, the cremation special), *Eternity* (oak, a Parisian model with brass handles), *Emperor* (handcrafted from walnut with gold-plated handles) and a whole raft of names that evoke luxury and beauty: *Venice, Florence, San Remo*, with a range of colored quilted linings. Martial was in his element as he showed me all this. He has a brand-new hearse. The appearance of the hearse is of paramount importance to clients, he tells me, it must always be immaculate, glossy black (and indeed, when I arrived, his employees were buffing the bodywork, singing a dirge that was anything but funereal). Undertaking is a profession usually passed on from father to son; it rarely attracts those from outside the congregation. These days, a qualification is required. From what I could tell, authorization to transport and dispose of corpses is like an explosives license or a permit to own military-grade weapons: it falls within the purview of the prefecture. One of the peculiarities of France, explained Martial the mummifying mayor, is that ambulances are not permitted to transport cadavers: in cases of sudden death (after the emergency services have been called, said Martial), it falls to the undertakers to transport the mortal remains using a special "First Response Vehicle" before placing the body in a coffin. As a result, they are often called out when the deceased has the good sense not to kick the bucket in a hospital. Some people still prefer to die at home, in fact, explained Martial, it's considered trendy these days. Home births, but also home deaths are a booming market. *O tempora, o mores!* I mean, it's not exactly a cheery business, he added, but, well, we're used to it. The mayor, then, a registered embalmer and owner of a nationally affiliated funeral parlor, was scion to a family-owned funeral parlor and grandson of a gravedigger—quite the career path. His role as elected representative is very useful to the business, since he is tasked with signing death certificates in the region (a rare combination of roles, he admits with a smile, but one permitted by the powers that be). Thus, the village has three main trades: carpentry, engineering and the disposal of the dead—three trades that, it seems to me, used to be interrelated. (Curiously, the backyard of the funeral parlor is itself a cemetery, not for humans but for broken-down vehicles: he showed me the remains of a "horse-drawn funeral hearse" straight out of a song by Brassens, and a model dating from the Second World War powered by a gas generator. What can you do? said Martial, people die all the time, even during a war, a comment that struck me as both preposterous and fascinating.)

His three assistant undertakers are cheerful fellows, which, depending on your point of view, is unsettling or reassuring. Ruddy-faced, gap-toothed, of uncertain age. Always with a glass in their hands, they seemed half-drunk when I showed up and they spent their time making fun of my moped—that ain't no Paris model, they said (Martial the mayor seemed to find their attitude toward me completely normal). They might be three brothers. The kind of guys you can easily imagine breaking the legs of a corpse to fit it into a small coffin. (Funeral rites: in the *Faith* chapter?) The Three Graces alternate their roles as drivers, coffin bearers, gravediggers and monumental masons—carving by hand or machine, they said with a chuckle. I imagined them dressed in black suits and ties, their faces masks of sympathy and commiseration: creepy. Flanked by this company, Martial took on a disturbing aspect; his bonhomie seemed out of place. I have to admit, the place scared me shitless, it's not every day you have an aperitif in the back room of an undertakers'. Actually, what I found most horrible were the three black suits in translucent garment bags that hung over an open (thankfully unoccupied) padded coffin. So, I made my escape as soon as I could, explaining that it was late and that I needed to get lunch—but not without being forced to down another shot of pastis. (I've just realized that the huge fridge from which they fetched the ice cubes was probably stocked with things like formalin, antiseptics and other pharmaceuticals used in postmortem surgical procedures—yuck.) Martial the mayor, whose personal life I know almost nothing about at the moment, seems to have become fond of me: he wants to invite me to dinner before Christmas. His wife, he assured me, is a splendid cook. We settled on the day after tomorrow, since tomorrow I'm having dinner at Max's. (So far, I've made absolutely no progress on my thesis, but my social life is improving by leaps and bounds.)

So, I mounted my white charger with its twisted handlebars and headed back to the Savage Mind and, as I rode through the center of the village (about a kilometer from the undertakers'), I almost drove straight into a car—though it was an accident, I have to admit it was my fault, I turned left without signaling just as the car was about to overtake me. Hearing the horn honking, I panicked, slammed on the brakes, lost control, skidded and found myself sprawled in the road—thankfully the car wasn't going very fast, otherwise it would have sent me to kingdom come, which would have been tragic, but rather droll, when you think I'd just come from a funeral parlor. A rusted little red delivery van, not exactly in the first flush of youth. A bit of a fright, no bones broken and it had two positive consequences: one, I immediately took out an insurance policy, something I'd completely forgotten to do, and two, I got to interview Lucie, who apologized for almost running me over, even though it had been my fault. She helped me to my feet and checked that neither I nor the moped had suffered any lasting damage. By a stroke of luck, she was on her way back from the market; I got off lightly. I'm pretty proud of the way I reacted, having the balls to ask her point-blank to invite me round to her place. She laughed. Well, aren't you quick off the mark, eh? she said. Thinking about it now, maybe she assumed I was trying to pick her up—fuck, I hope not.

December 19 (contd.)

One o'clock in the morning. As the great Malinowski says on page 122 of *A Diary in the Strict Sense of the Term*: "Resolution. Eliminate potential lechery from my intercourse with women." I suspect such resolutions are easier to make after one has achieved orgasm. I swear, this was the first and last time. I feel overwhelmed by a terrible shame. Not Lara, apparently. On reflection, there's nothing shameful about it. People do this stuff all the time, it seems. The internet is made in our image: Angels and Demons. A camera. I'm the one who asked her to unbutton her blouse, I'm to blame for things getting out of hand. At first, it was just a game. A deceptively puerile game, I knew precisely where I wanted it to lead, I admit that, *I had an idea at the back of my mind*, as Blaise Pascal would say. (Italic is a magical invention for emphasizing important terms.) *I had an idea at the back of my mind*, deep down, I knew what I wanted her to do, what I wanted us to do, I passionately desired her. It was *my desire* that led the dance, she had only to acquiesce, because she is *loving* and *tender*, and if she ended up with her hand down her pajamas, *I was to blame*, I have to acknowledge that, out of sheer magnanimity— the shame! Or not shame, perhaps, but guilt. When I think about it, it's not so much the shame associated with the curious sexual practice of synchronized onanism by high-speed broadband as it is my *guilt* at persuading her to do something *that she did not want to do*. I had manipulated her in order to achieve my goal, and if she allowed herself to be overcome by my desire and my lechery *in order to please me*, it's logical that she would feel no guilt. So I must make a resolution: *eliminate potential lechery from my intercourse with women*, if only now, after achieving orgasm, while the images of Lara are still burned into my retinas. I could have made a screen recording. I should have made a screen recording, stolen that scene and thereby transformed virtual reality into a low-rent porn movie that can be played, endless and unchanging, on a loop.

I wonder what Walter Benjamin would have thought about cybersex?

The first and last time, I solemnly swear.

But I miss Lara, so what can I do? An anthropologist's life is hard, having to spend long periods far from home. Then again, the reason I was able to leave Paris was because Lara wasn't *available*, being caught up preparing for her civil service exams. She works 24/7, last year she blamed me (somewhat) for her setbacks, accusing me of *distracting* her with my dilettantish PhD student antics (which mostly entailed reading and writing index cards) while she was *beating her brains out*, as she put it, cramming administrative law, English and her general knowledge. True, I was always the one calling up and inviting her for a drink at Bastille or to the cinema, so she was almost happy when I got a grant for this fieldwork, I say "almost happy" because (and this is a minor example of her capriciousness) when it came time for me to leave (two months later than planned, it should be said; consciously or unconsciously I deferred my departure by two months so I could stay with Lara) she was sullen, jealous and anxious, she was constantly finding excuses not to sleep with me, which made me hurt and anxious too. Happily, distance has brought us closer. (A curious phrase.) Every day, I think about her every day; every day, I talk to her and long for her, and I can't wait to see her again three days from now.

Weird fact: I had to put the cats outside during our webcam session, I had the unbearable impression that they were watching and mocking me.

Right, bedtime. Tomorrow I've got an interview that should be interesting.

December 20

That cow! Lucie is absolutely odious. She conned me. I fell for it, and wasted half a day. As Malinowski memorably writes: "On the whole my feelings toward the natives are decidedly tending to 'Exterminate the Brutes.'" I spent the first part of the morning with a senile old geezer, and the second part with a senile old geezer *and* a basket case—she got me good, the bitch. I'd barely arrived at her place when she popped out, supposedly for half an hour while I interviewed her grandfather. The backstabber didn't come back for four hours. I was so furious I said nothing, not a damn thing except *thank you, goodbye*, and hopped on my moped. *Dignity, above all, dignity*. Best to treat the incident with the contempt it deserves. When I think that, just yesterday, she almost killed me with her rusty, shit heap of a vehicle, my blood boils. I should have gotten up and left after the first hour, I should have, I'm an idiot, I'm too nice for my own good. That'll teach me. Hoodwinked by a savage. Manipulated by a native. Just goes to show—you don't need to visit the Nambicuara or the Jivaro tribes. The Deux-Sèvres département is far enough. I hate this shithole. I felt so humiliated that I launched a vicious kick at Nigel, who was meowing by the door; luckily, I missed. Once again, it's all my fault. I loathe myself for this innate kindheartedness that borders on weakness. Three hours struggling to make sense of the grandfather's answers to my questions before the cousin, Arnaud, showed up in oil-smeared overalls. He had come back for lunch. I was delighted to see him, thinking that here, finally, was my salvation. He didn't seem surprised to see me there, he planted himself right in front of me, vigorously sniffed his fore-arm and scratched his head. He was staring at me, seemingly waiting for something to happen, so I got up from the chair and held out my hand, he stared at it as though he had no idea what to do with it. Today is December 20, the feasts of Saints Abraham, Isaac and Jacob, birthdate of so-and-so, birthdate of What's-His-Name, world events various and diverse, which prompted a bestial laugh from the human wreck in the armchair, the grandfather was literally doubled up with laughter in his chair, yelping and squealing—it felt like being in an asylum.

I am motivated by rage. It's essential that professionalism prevail over all else. There were some interesting things about my misadventure. First, the house. I had all the time in the world to study the ground floor. What I saw was rather ramshackle and confirmed my first impressions the other evening. Something out of Victor Hugo, you might say. A large, murky room, a fireplace, a kitchenette, the sink filled with filthy dishes, a small bathroom—well, more of a utility room with a washing machine and a bathtub set bizarrely on the bare concrete in the midst of a mind-boggling tangle of rusty bicycles, bottomless saucepans and old gas stoves, towers of empty bottle crates that rose as far as the shelves that groaned under the weight of canned food and full bottles. The bog is at the far end of a neglected garden where a mangy mutt prowls, barking at cars. Paradise! On a wooden sideboard stands a small television that is permanently blaring; on a shelf, a dust-covered radio is flanked by a couple of ornaments from the 1970s: a blue, plastic Butagaz™ bear, a yellow Ricard® jug; so much for the decor. The electrical cables are ancient fabric-insulated flexes, the light switches are prewar ceramic. The wallpaper was probably white, I think, about thirty years ago; these days, the best you could say is it's piss yellow; as far from the fireplace as possible, the only other source of heat that I spotted, the gas boiler next to the sink looked much too small to heat radiators (of which, in any case, there are none).

The Thénardiers' hovel, without Cosette to do the housework, though mercifully the wood fire does a little to mask the musty smell. I was dying to take a tour of the upstairs, but since I was convinced that Lucie would come back at any moment, I didn't dare. One way or another, it's a far cry from Mathilde's spotless, well-equipped farmhouse. In vain, I looked around for a book or a magazine, but I didn't open the cupboards or the drawers. At first glance, the only sign of the written word was the pile of free newspapers next to the hearth for lighting the fire. But all in all, I wasn't too uncomfortable, settled in my armchair next to the old man, watching the dancing flames. I stopped recording after two hours. On several occasions I put more wood on the fire. Determined to make the best of a bad situation—I was keeping the old geezer company, a good deed in itself. How to describe his manner of speech? It appears that his false teeth make it impossible for him to speak normally. *Me braynz all tirn'ta mish*, he kept saying, which I interpreted as "me brain's all turned to mush," or, in other words, "my memory's failing me" or something of the sort. As for his former profession, he kept saying (approximate translation) *fahma* (at least I know what that means). I'm fairly sure he said he was ninety, so he's not that old. Looking at him (haggard face lined with broken bloodred veins, huge honker, ears that are elephantine but thin and tremulous) you'd swear he was older. He finds it difficult to walk, but he can walk. I think he had four children, including Lucie's father, children he refers to as *striplings* and *fillies*, I've no idea whether the words are intended as pejorative. Anyway, it's going to be a complete pain in the ass to transcribe, I'll need the help of a linguist. I thought I'd found my first Poitevin-Saintongeais speaker, it was no joke. Arnaud, the cousin, says little aside from the interminable lists of dates but at least, despite his highly parochial phonetics, I understand him perfectly. The more time passed, the more my anger surged, so I rather lost my patience with the boy, something I regret, since it wasn't the poor guy's fault. I watched him eat—something I could well have done without. Face down in his plate, gripping the handle of the spoon like a hammer (a Mexican farmer in a Sergio Leone Western was what came to mind), he gobbled up a can of cold ravioli in two minutes flat. He continued snuffling at his forearm, thereby jerking the spoon, causing splatters of tomato sauce to fall on his left biceps, though he didn't seem bothered. Once he had wolfed down the ravioli, he let out a satisfied belch, a beatific smile on his face, and wiped his mouth on his right sleeve. Then he stared at the door and said, to no one in particular, I was really hungry. The splotches of tomato merged with the oil stains on his overalls; it was impossible to say which was which. Astonishing. Then he sat in front of the fire and muttered to himself, rattling off his dates: *May 6, Feast of Saint Prudence, May 7, Saint Gisèle, May 8, Saint Désiré*, until the litany finally lulled him to sleep, chin on his chest, mouth open, tongue lolling. The grandfather kept saying *fuhin hahwit, fuhin hahwit*, laughing so hard his false teeth almost fell out, which seemed to me somewhat uncharitable, but left Arnaud completely indifferent. Despite the importance of these observations, I was starting to feel seriously exasperated and was preparing to abandon this happy breed when Lucie casually showed up—just rolled up, as they say—and casually said, All good? Still here? All butter-wouldn't-melt, as though I was the babysitter and she had just come back from the cinema. *Dignity, above all dignity,* I thought. I cloaked myself in fury and took my leave. Not a word of apology, nothing. I won't fall for that again.

Hey, it's snowing. It's quite pretty, the snowflakes whirling over the fields and the church. I hope it doesn't settle, because otherwise I won't be able to go to Max's place for dinner tonight.

December 20 (contd.)

Napped with the cats, since their presence prevents me from descending into lechery, they are a frequent feature of my postprandial siestas. It snowed all afternoon and into the night, then the temperature suddenly plummeted: minus six degrees Celsius according to the thermometer. It's seven o'clock, I'll phone Max and tell him I can't risk going out on the moped, I'm not yet skilled at riding over frozen snow.

I've just realized I'm spending more time writing this journal than I am working on my actual thesis: after a good start, the *Questions* chapter has not progressed so much as a line in the past two days. Is it too early? Perhaps I should wait until I have more data before settling down to write. What a disappointment, I had such high expectations for my interview with Lucie, and my dinner with Max looks like a washout too. Black dog. Gave the cats some food so they don't have to go out in the cold. Sent a communiqué to Calvet, so he doesn't think I've turned into an Inuit. It's important to allay the fears of your thesis supervisor.

December 20 (contd.)

In the end, Max was kind enough to come by in his truck and drive me over to his place. The roads were covered in snow and the main road was a sheet of ice. (Magnificent scenes of trees glittering in the headlights and opalescent fields shimmering in the moonlight.) His house is stunning, an old U-shaped farmhouse not far from the river. To the right, in the old stables, his studio; in the middle, set out over three floors, the living quarters; and, to the left, the former barn is a garage big enough for God knows how many cars. He did most of the restoration himself. Max told me that, ten years ago, he earned a lot of money but now he had fallen on lean times. When the farmyard automatically lit up, I was greeted by snow-covered metal monsters, grotesque and terrifying creatures fashioned from old farm tools—wheels, carts, plows, scythes—attached to wooden posts. These are my giants, said Max, my army against the rank fatuity of my neighbors. He created these sculptures with the things he found in the barn when he bought the house. I couldn't say whether these fantastical bucolic creatures are dreamlike or demonic.

The interior was entirely in keeping. A bizarre sculptural group stands at the entrance to the cavernous main room: a stuffed gundog (a cocker?) mounting a fox, also stuffed; the artist's sole contribution being the superposition of these two beasts and the—undeniably clever—substitution of a rusty old rifle for the dog's prick, muzzle buried deep in the fox's ass. (I suppose if you take away the fox, you'd have what they call in heraldry a "stuffed mutt rampant.") I couldn't bring myself to ask Max whether this was a hunting allegory, a pun on "cocksmanship," "cocking a gun," or all of the above, though it should be said that, as a work of art, I found it particularly loathsome and vulgar. Seeing me contemplate his work, Max remarked, Bit of a mindfuck, isn't it? I didn't disagree.

The canvases by Max adorning the walls are not in the same humorous vein. Scenes of women being tortured in concrete basements; chiaroscuro studies of public urinals in which, by the faint glow of a single bulb, it is just possible to make out a skeletal hand on a man's penis; prostitutes dripping with flesh rubbing panties that are yellowed at the crotch. The sort of thing you might get if Lucian Freud and Caravaggio had hung out in the brothels and back rooms of London. Nothing remotely pastoral. Max gave me a tour of his living room and, every time he passed one of his works, said, Sick, yeah? or, Now that's a banger, yeah? Truth be told, his painting has a brutish intensity, it's undeniable, one matched by a strong technical ability. I found one that immediately appealed to me: a small portrait of a woman, fragile, almost abstract, in simple tones. I couldn't help but say: Now *this*, this is a masterpiece, bravo, which made Max chuckle, No, that's not one of mine, I bought it at a garage sale. I felt mortified, but he didn't seem to take offense.

Since it was a little chilly in the great room, Max had set up a table "in the oven," as he put it. It was a little room with an old-fashioned bread oven, which he had preheated for the occasion. The menu, pizza to start and a main course of roast beef, all cooked over a wood fire, delicious, amply washed down with a red Anjou from the north of the département. His house is really very pleasant.

As I expected, Max proved to be a precious font of information. He's been living in the village for a decade. He knows everyone in this godforsaken shithole (*sic*). I heard some pretty racy stories about everyone, I was sorry I hadn't brought my recorder. Max makes a distinction between those who *live* in the village and those who merely *reside* here, the people you never see: those who own houses in the new development; the city folk who work mostly in the service sector and whose principal preoccupation is fencing off their land so they can go skinny-dipping in their pools three days a year without being seen; the garden gnome collectors seen riding their bicycles on Sundays, who spend the rest of the week polishing their mobile homes and longing for summer—a rogue's gallery of cruel but hilarious verbal portraits, I thoroughly enjoyed myself.

Max didn't allow me to see his studio, his famous magnum opus is still a work in progress, It's too early, he said. I don't know why, but I'm in no real hurry—I imagine something truly *monstrous*, in keeping with his talents.

Under the influence of wine, I told him my stories of the Ariège and rural ethnology; I confided my doubts and my qualms about the French university system that was being demolished, piece by piece, by absurd reforms brought in by moronic right-wing professors. He agreed wholeheartedly: his brief tenure as a professor at the École des Beaux-Arts had put him off teaching forever. The pretentious, empty-headed students who are cosseted by Young Masters—more apparatchiks than artists—to mask their own mediocrity; the Regional Contemporary Arts Fund buying up local artists' installations left and right and leaving them to rot in some basement where no one—not even the cleaning staff—ever took them out of their crates, etc., etc. All in all, a fun, enjoyable evening tinged with bile and bitterness. As Max drove me home, the thermometer in his truck read minus eight; thankfully I left the heating on at the Savage Mind. The night is cloudless, the frosty fields glitter and the icy church bell glints in the moonlight. I hope this cold spell doesn't last, otherwise I'll find it difficult to get around.

Right, time to hit the sack.

December 21

Last night it froze hard enough to split the stones. Minus ten, according to Gary. It's minus six now—*brrr*. Faint, hazy sunshine. I really need to google whether there's some connection between the red worms in the bathroom and the dwarf snails in the living room. The former could be the larvae of the latter. Are gastropods oviparous? Do they have a similar life cycle to insects? Is there such a thing as a snail pupa? Who knows? It's amazing how little we know about the things around us, even the most common things. I think I'd like to have been a naturalist. A nice little expedition to the Galápagos sounds idyllic in weather like this. A naturalist, or maybe a mathematician: I've been continuing my investigation into recurring decimals. They are tireless toilers, drilling through the numerical floor with a barrage of decimals, one foot on each arithmetical unit, on to infinity. Obviously, they are not as mysterious as their cousins, the irrational numbers, though they're just as abstract: like the hamster in his wheel, or man in his world, they spin in endless circles, toward nothingness. Magnificent.

This morning, a surprise: a letter of apology. Gary delivered it, with the weather forecast. Made the most of it to gently make fun of my cats, You've adopted them, I see. (I should say they were serenely stretching on my bed when he showed up.) Hope you don't feel unduly deprived, I said. He looked like he didn't understand, so I let it drop. I was surprised to get a letter, given that, besides Lara, no one has my address here. For a minute I thought she'd forwarded a bill, but no, it was a folded piece of paper—no envelope—with my first name in ballpoint, *For David*. It was a brief apology from Lucie: *Sorry about yesterday morning, you left before I could explain. I would of phoned but I don't have your number, I called round but you're not in. Come see me whenever you like. See you soon, Lucie*, it was written in an elegant cursive, though here and there the ballpoint had gone through the paper (she probably wrote it on her lap, or her handbag—something soft in any case), and her spelling was flawless. Well, not quite flawless, she used *would of* rather than *would have*, but still, pretty good. Initially, I was irritated, she's got a nerve, I thought. But it was okay of her, at least she doesn't take me for a complete fool. And I'll show her the length that an ethnologist will go to in his quest for information: I'll be on her doorstep this afternoon, recorder and questions in hand, in spite of the icy north wind, right after I've bought fresh supplies. (All I've got left is one frozen pizza and one freeze-dried shepherd's pie, that's two meals sorted out, but there are four before I leave. Is it really worth going shopping? I could just ration myself.) I'll have to bundle up like a German postboy at the siege of Stalingrad to get to the nearest branch of Super U. I just hope I can get the moped to start in the cold. Does gas-oil mix freeze more quickly than gas? One more environmental mystery to solve.

Coffee, Tetris, shower, resisted my lustful urges, exterminated some creepy-crawlies: I'm starting to settle in.

It's half past ten. Sometime around 1 p.m., when the sun is at its zenith and the temperature outside has reached its peak, I'll see where things stand.

Right, two hours of problem-solving.

Back to the grindstone.

December 21 (contd.)

Idea for an article: *On the deleterious influence of the internet on the productivity of the intellectual.* Googled details about gastropods, nothing terribly interesting, not widely studied, apparently—weird. Hung out for a bit in the group chat of fellow PhD students scattered all over France: seems to be freezing everywhere for once, even Marseille. Messaged Lara; arranged to talk tonight at zero hundred hours, no webcam. Reread my five pages of *Questions*—dismal. Skimmed through a brilliant thesis on the history of crop rotation in Bas-Poitou—nice to see some people getting results. Sorted out my virtual bibliographic records. Played with the cats. (Think about buying a litter box, it's tiresome having to open the door for them, and more food, the kibble has almost run out.) The sky clouded over. Got an unfathomable message from Calvet: "Thanks for the update, glad to know the cold hasn't numbed your brain, because time is fleeting: I'm waiting for your problematics." Such rigor, such a great man.

Twelve forty-five, the outside thermometer reads minus four; I'll attempt an expedition. I'm happy to ration my food, but I'm not about to send Barley and Nigel out hunting for victuals in this cold.

December 21 (contd.)

Disaster. The moped won't start. I pedaled long enough to ride ten kilometers while it was still on its stand, but nothing doing. It sputters a bit then cuts out. Gary isn't around, so I'm a little at a loss. I wheeled Rocinante into the hall of the Savage Mind to warm him up a bit and see if he might agree to work again. I could call Max, after all he did offer yesterday, but I don't dare.

December 21 (contd.)

In the end, Mathilde drove me to the supermarket, since she was going anyway, so I helped her with her shopping—it was fascinating. Jotted down her shopping list for *Eating* chapter. She's very attentive to the ingredients and provenance of products. Noted this interesting phrase: "We're sick and tired of eating garbage." Observation: Super U has a whole aisle of British products; bought a load of baked beans, shortbread, ginger jam and salt and vinegar chips—finally, civilization! So lucky to have all these Brits in the area. I really must meet some.

The weather forecast is not exactly glorious, to put it mildly: there's a blizzard forecast for tomorrow, heavy snowfall and glacial winds. Disruption to train schedules. I hope everything's running again on the twenty-third so I can leave as planned.

December 21 (contd.)

The latter part of the day proved more productive than the morning: arranged two meetings, conducted half an interview and took part in a very enlightening dinner. Max grudgingly gave me the number of his British neighbors, and I phoned them; they were a little surprised, but not unfriendly, and agreed to meet with me tomorrow at 5 p.m., for afternoon tea, I assume. The woman who answered speaks pretty good French, certainly her phonetics are no more unintelligible than some of the locals'. I also managed to arrange to interview Gary at midday tomorrow—the one advantage of this abysmal weather is that people stay home in the warm, and are more inclined to receive a researcher. Gary also suggested I leave Rocinante in the garage and sort out some other means of getting around, Otherwise, he said, in this weather, we're likely to find you in a field, frozen stiff, or wrapped around a plane tree. I suppose he's got a point.

I set off for Lucie's place on foot and arrived there chilled to the bone, shoes full of snow. Her car was parked outside the house; the beast was in her lair. I rang the bell, there were hurried footsteps inside, then Arnaud opened the door, said hello, put out his hand, pulled it back, sniffed his arm, then proffered it again. I shook it, he smiled, I said, Hello Arnaud, what's the date today? December 21, winter, feast of Saint Peter Canisius, birthday of so-and-so, and so on, he looked happy, but he stood on the threshold and showed no sign of inviting me in, as though he thought it was completely normal for me to drop by just to hear his ephemera, it was quite funny. I heard Lucie ask, Who is it? and Nono said, I don't know his name, and I said, *May 10, 1990, esteemed anthropologist David Mazon born in Paris; May 10, 1981 François Mitterrand elected President of the French Republic, protest marches on the Place de la Bastille,* this made Arnaud laugh, he said, *May 10, feast of Saint Solange, patron saint of the Province of Berry, death of Napoleon Bonaparte,* etc., I was freezing my balls off, I could hear Lucie shouting, Well, let him in or go outside but shut the fucking door, for God's sake, Arnaud asked whether I wanted to come in (or, more precisely, *whether I needed to come in*) and finally ushered me in, though only after asking me to take off my shoes, so I found myself in my socks on the parquet floor, which was pretty mortifying. Lucie was decorating a Christmas tree that stood next to the fireplace, but, aside from the tree, nothing had changed: the old man slumped in his armchair, the grime, the smell of the wood fire. I greeted the forebear, who recognized me—or at least I think he did. Lucie flashed me a smile, she seemed in a good mood, You got my note? I'm sorry about yesterday, making you wait. I had no desire to revisit this lamentable incident, so I said, It doesn't matter, forget about it, do you think you could spare me an hour or so now? She glanced at the pine tree, Do you mind if I just finish this? My cousin is really excited, he wants me to put on the fairy lights, and indeed Arnaud was planted next to her, sniffing at his arm as he watched.

I wondered if he still believed in Santa Claus. I waited patiently while she hung the Christmas lights and plugged them in; Arnaud instantly set a chair in front of the tree and sat, staring at it; I suppose it gave him something to do besides staring at the fire.

The dog was indoors and padded over to greet me. (I don't know why, but I loathe the mutt, maybe because it reminds me of Max's hideous stuffed thing.)

Lucie and I sat down at the table (crusts of bread, sauce stains) and talked for a while. Unfortunately, I didn't have time to get through the whole of my questionnaire, but she said we could pick up after I get back from Paris. I'm keen to transcribe the results. Max was right on one point: Lucie is a deeply political animal. Not like Mathilde the royalist (not to say conformist). Lucie is very much a committed activist (well, I know what I mean), though her dialectic isn't marked by ideological dogma. She is appalled by the brutal injustice of the times we live in, the growing inequality between rich and poor; she's concerned about the environmental disasters that are routinely covered up to serve the vested interests of Big Agri-Tech. She loathes the thoughtless local farmers who ripped out all the hedgerows and went on to impoverish the soil in pursuit of a bumper harvest such that you can't grow so much as a blade of grass now without tons of fertilizers and pesticides; the farmers who are indebted to the seed companies who sell them products so toxic that the local tap water is now undrinkable (shit, that's a little detail I forgot; up to now, I've been downing liters and liters of weed killer, pesticides and nitrogen fertilizers, I need to buy some bottled water); she hates the developmental model, which is the root cause of climate change and the imminent Apocalypse. Contrary to what Max told me, I think this is the limit of her activism. No longhaired hippies, no Citroën 2CV, no artisanal goat cheese.

Lucie expresses herself fluently. She grew up in a village outside Niort. She studied at an agricultural college and lived near Le Mans for a time before moving back here. She and her partner started a market gardening business, some of it organic, they do direct sales, and work with community-supported agricultural associations like AMAP and the whole gamut of modern bucolic acronyms. Vegetables, soft fruits, apples, pears, plums. The land and the high tunnels are the legacy of her ex-partner. She offered to show me around the farm and to introduce me to Franck, her ex. Financially, things are not great, especially since they split up—what was enough to support them as a couple isn't enough to support them separately. The problem with organic farming is that the transition period is long and yields are lower. Alright, you can get slightly higher prices, but, as Lucie says, no one around here is going to pay €6 a kilo for organic carrots at the market. I'm embarrassed to say I have no idea how much a kilo of carrots should cost.

Lucie has few dealings with the people in the village. She's convinced that they all hate her, she says, because she doesn't live the way they do. I can't help but wonder if she's not a bit paranoid. Most of her friends live in Niort. She's the one who does the farmers' markets: Coulonges on weekdays, Niort on Saturdays and the Marais Poitevin on Sundays.

Lucie radiates a strange energy, a curious mixture of sorrow, melancholy and irrepressible joie de vivre. She terrifies me a little. I decided to leave my questions about sexuality until later; I was afraid she'd tell me to fuck off, and besides I still haven't revised that section of the questionnaire. (What the hell are you doing with your days, aside from writing this diary for Christ's sake? A field journal is important, David, but the most important thing is your fucking dissertation, I wonder whether I'm coming down with writer's block.) Anyhow, I've gleaned some interesting information for the chapters on *Work* and *Faith* (Lucie's answers have borne out my idea of including political issues in *Believing*).

Back home, I considered canceling my dinner with Martial the mayor, I just wanted to stay in the warm with my cats and read (and, I admit, stuff my face with microwaved baked beans), but I didn't have time: there was a knock on the window; for a second I thought I was going to die of fright, but then I recognized the face of the mayor-cum-undertaker, who had had the brilliant idea (the bastard) of coming to pick me up. So, I had no choice but to go to his place for dinner (he even drove me back). It was an experience. Small ignominious detail: I couldn't bring myself to eat the main course. Fricasseed chicken's blood, Jesus wept, if Maman had seen it, she'd have fainted on the spot. A smooth, dense, purplish crepe, I had one mouthful, it tasted very metallic. (I couldn't stop thinking about my host's line of work and the things he kept in his fridges—*yuck*.) Eating blood—just the thought makes me shudder. Long story short, this primitive ancestor of the modern black pudding is known locally as sanquette, and made me miss Ariège. It's very easy, Monique explained, you slit the chicken's throat, you collect the blood and then you cook it. *Voilà, voilà.* Martial and his wife, Monique, were a little disappointed, having hoped they could introduce me to some regional specialties, but I made up for it by doing justice to the delicious pâté d'herbes, which around here they simply call *farci*, "stuffing" (Swiss chard, sorrel, spinach, eggs, a few lardons and four spices—I need to remember the recipe), and to the famous mogettes, as haricot beans are known in the Marais Poitevin. (Passed up my baked beans for mogettes, which is pretty much out of the frying pan and into the fire. Dangerous territory for those with a propensity for flatulence.) Not particularly refined, but seriously hearty. If you'd been here last week, we had some very tasty song thrushes, said Martial. But no one goes out hunting in this cold. I clearly had a narrow escape. It reminded me of the little lamb in Montaillou, the one I inadvertently condemned to death—the shepherd asked me to point to one of the flock, and I picked one I thought looked sweet and gentle, not realizing that I'd see it the next day being spit-roasted for lunch.

Their place is a vast, opulent bourgeois house with a lovely garden; they have three children, though only one still lives locally. Martial explained how much he loved being mayor, since it allowed him to get to know everybody and to make himself useful. You see, in my line of work, he said, we don't get much cause to laugh, so it makes a nice change. He is also very active in his chosen profession, and every year he organizes an undertakers' conference, or something of the sort. Bet that's a laugh, I thought. He had just come back from burying a young married couple who had died of carbon monoxide poisoning from the fumes of their wood-burning stove. Poor things were just lying there in bed, said Martial. Luckily, they hadn't had time to have children, he added, and his wife nodded compassionately as she served more beans. Curious profession. I learned a few things about the Three Graces in his employ. He was amused by the fact that I'd thought they were brothers. They're bighearted guys, he said. Monique carried on nodding, apparently agreeing with every word that came out of her husband's mouth. I decided to change the subject and ask how the village had changed over the past decade—the population has almost doubled, mostly thanks to the building of the new housing development. *Luckily*, he said, the only foreigners we have are three retired British couples who bought up big farms in the area. I tried not to sound annoyed. After all, it's simply a resurgence of the age-old animosity between the sedentary and the nomad. I must reread Ibn Khaldun's *Muqaddimah,* and a couple of pieces by Maffesoli. (*Notes on postmodernism: the gastronomy of chicken blood.*) Martial, meanwhile, was upping the ante, We put a stop to the Arabs round these parts a long time ago. The conversation moved on to the subject of immigration. Martial is a firm supporter of assimilation, or enforced integration. Immigrants, he said, should *abide by* French customs. They've no respect for anything, he said. Not the Republic, nothing. This, he considered a form of *ingratitude.* Soon we'll have to ask their permission to eat pork, he said. They come over here, they exploit the system, but they won't make an *effort* to integrate. Our whole way of life could collapse, you know, the social security system, education, these things are fragile. We need to be vigilant. Though he can hardly have been talking about his village, unless he's unaware that the Brits are very partial to a little roast pork.

I asked Martial whether he was a member of a political party and he immediately interrupted, No no, absolutely not. I'm apolitical, as they say. You know, being mayor of a village, a small agglomeration, has nothing to do with politics. (I like the word *agglomeration*. It really describes this place. Note for *Questions* chapter.) What matters is getting to know the people, and finding out what it is they need. (This reminded of a city councillor who proclaimed that sewers were neither right-wing nor left-wing.)

Martial is more interesting and less reactionary when talking about changes in farming, though even then he has a tendency to throw the baby out with the bathwater. The situation of small landowners is appalling, especially those in animal husbandry and market gardening. Anyone without the means or the resources to invest in organics, which offer better margins (not that Martial believes in organics either), is doomed. The area manages to survive thanks to cereal farming, principally wheat. The dairy industry that was once the pride of the region of Deux-Sèvres (Échiré butter, goat cheese, etc.) is also badly affected. In the short term, Martial predicts that small farmers will be wiped out by vast Bayer™ agribusinesses on one saide and rurbanization on the other. Prefab houses and more prefab houses filled with poor bastards (former farm laborers, tenant farmers or small landowners) living in poverty, a somewhat sinister image, but one that is sadly du jour.

I'm keen to get Gary's opinion tomorrow.

Naturally, red wine flowed freely, as did the brandy served with coffee: I think I'm starting to get used to it.

It's snowing again, large, heavy flakes. I wish I had a fireplace.

I wonder if Lara has her phone with her; it's just after midnight.

December 21 (contd.)

Didn't manage to fend off my lustful urges, but at least it's better without a webcam. The written word is erotic, arousing, imagination is a fantasy factory, a private film studio. Over the course of brief messages, passion gradually settles in. Freed of inhibitions by alcohol, phrases and passions are set loose. Decidedly, the undertaker's plum brandy is an aphrodisiac. I dared to confide my fantasies to Lara, in graphic terms; I had a vision, I sent it to her:

(.)¡(.)

She immediately understood what the glyph represented. (I'm quite happy with the realism of my cyberbreasts.) She typed back:

Your "¡" !!!!! You really make me laugh, but it's quite a sexy prospect.

Seeing that she and I were on the same wavelength, I posted something more risqué:

Then you'd lie on your belly and, I'd gently)o(you

She correctly guessed what this represented:

Ow, ow, no way my little jackrabbit, you can make do with),(

Lara is so intelligent, so sharp. She is the perfect woman.
I can't wait for the day after tomorrow.

December 22

Hangover and electric blackout when I woke up this morning, no heating, everything is frozen solid. Acetaminophen. I have an hour's battery life left on my laptop, the Wi-Fi isn't working and my phone is only half-charged. The forecast was right, blizzards, icy winds. I'm worried that I won't be able to leave tomorrow as scheduled. According to the radio, the whole of the west of France has been plunged into chaos: trains canceled, roads impassable, etc.

From what Gary told me, the substation that supplies the whole area had a meltdown.

December 22 (contd.)

Gary managed to run in a line to power the lights and the laptop using one of the two generators he has on the farm. This means I can continue with my work. On the other hand, the temperature in the Savage Mind has plummeted to dangerous levels, and there's not enough juice to power the heater. The ungrateful strays have already sought refuge at Mathilde's. I think the glacial wind is getting in under the door. Even wrapped in two blankets I'm freezing, completely freezing. The indoor thermometer reads fifteen degrees. I should pack up my things and try to get to Paris today, but in this snow, it's like *Mission Impossible*. Unless electricity comes back on sometime today, I'll have to seek asylum from my landlady, otherwise it's hypothermia.

I mean, how difficult can it be to repair an electrical substation?

Though that's assuming that engineers from EDF can make it out here.

December 22 (contd.)

Phoned Lara; being pessimistic by nature, she's convinced I won't be able to get to Paris tomorrow. I hope she's wrong. Already I could hear a tinge of accusation in her voice, as though I didn't want to leave. I'd like to see how she'd cope, snowed in, with no heating. I get the impression she doesn't believe me.

With a bit of luck, I might be able to prove her wrong and show up on rue Saint-Antoine at 6 p.m. tomorrow. I need to call Max and see if he's still free at noon tomorrow to drive me to the train station in his pickup, if not, I'll ask someone to give me a lift as far as the main road and I'll hitchhike. Just twenty-four hours before I leave the Savage Mind for ten days. That thought warms me a little.

Just heard from Gary that we won't have electricity before tomorrow, or maybe even the day after. According to received wisdom (which in this case means gossip at the Café-Pêche, I assume) it was an act of sabotage, which seems highly unlikely to me: Who would want to sabotage an electrical substation on a freezing cold night in eight inches of snow? As far as I know there are no alpine chasseurs in al-Qaeda or Daesh. Even the Resistance fighters in Melville's movie *Army of Shadows* would stay home huddled up by their radiators. And it's not 1942 anymore.

Today's agenda: transcribe my interview with Lucie, interview Gary at midday, then go visit Max's British neighbors at five o'clock—which (once again) poses the problem of transportation. Right, down to work.

December 24

So, after writing the foregoing, I decided to get moving because my hands and feet were starting to freeze. I dropped by Gary's to make sure he was still happy to do the interview, that would have been at about noon. (I also nurtured the secret hope that he'd invite me to lunch—everything at the Savage Mind is electrical.) I was still pressing the doorbell (moron! With no electricity, it wouldn't be working) when the door opened and Mathilde (baggy cream anorak and rust-colored Wellingtons) looked extremely surprised to see me. I was just about to come fetch you, there's a phone call for you. Automatically, I fished my phone out of my pocket, it was working and I had no texts and no missed calls. Mathilde looked taken aback and said, No, they called you here, on our phone. What disaster could have happened: I immediately thought about Lara, about Maman, I imagined car crashes, fires. No one had Mathilde's phone number, only a God as omniscient as the police or the emergency services could ferret me out here, I went to the telephone and said, Hello, my voice suddenly hoarse. Mathilde stood right in front of me, almost close enough to touch. I didn't recognize the person on the end of the line, only my name, David? I said, Yes? I had to clear my throat.

"David, it's Lucie."

I said, "Hello? Hello?"

"Can you hear me? It's Lucie Moreau."

"What's happened?" I said. "Is it something serious?"

"No, no. I'm … I'm in Niort. I'm planning to stay here until tomorrow."

I sensed a little weariness in her voice.

"Would you mind taking a few minutes to drop by and check on my cousin and my grandfather if you've got time? Just to say I won't be home tonight. They're not answering the phone. And Arnaud's already left the garage. Sorry to call you at Mathilde's like this, but I haven't got your number. I'm so sorry, you'd be doing me a big favor. Could you … could you give me your mobile number?"

"Hang on, I'll jot yours down, it'll be quicker."

I took down her number and even before she had hung up, I'd sent her a text: "?"—an undeniably terse message but one that, I think, well conveyed my confusion.

"Let's talk later. Thanks, goodbye, and thanks again, it's really nice of you. Even five minutes would be great. Bye."

Mathilde had not taken her eyes—or her ears—off me.

I passed her the receiver.

"She's got some nerve, doesn't she?" said Mathilde.

We were still on the threshold, and Mathilde suddenly remembered the door was open, Come in, come in, have some lunch, you must be cold over there with no electricity. It was true, I was cold, and I was hungry—I went into Mathilde and Gary's place. Why had Lucie called me? Surely, she had friends, she knew everyone in the village. Like a zombie, I followed Mathilde into the living room, where a glorious fire was burning in the woodstove.

"Some people are just full of themselves," said Mathilde.

"Yeah, well, I'm not sure, there must be something wrong."

I was dearly hoping this was the case. That Lucie wasn't just taking me for a sucker. But I had my doubts.

Still, it was weird that she should call me.

After lunch (terrine with cornichons, Swiss chard au gratin) Gary was busy, so we decided to postpone the interview until later and I headed back to the Savage Mind.

I'm not sure why I suddenly decided to do a favor for a woman I hardly know, maybe I feel a little sorry for her, and I'm quite fond of Arnaud. Besides, her house is only a couple of hundred meters from mine. I'd needed to postpone meeting the Brits to another time, with the snow and the cold there was no way I could get there, so I called them to reschedule. (The woman who answered sounded relieved I wasn't coming, which wasn't terribly encouraging. Look, we'll see how things go.)

So, at around four o'clock I headed round to Lucie's place, it was still snowing and the village was swathed in a pale half-light, I didn't pass a living soul. There was a smell of woodsmoke and winter on the breeze. The shutters on most houses were closed; here and there I glimpsed a flickering orange glow behind a window, everyone was using candles. It felt like being in a Christmas fairy tale.

When I reached the house, I knocked and Arnaud immediately opened the door. The large living room was dark, there were no lights; no fire in the hearth. Nono looked very agitated, he kept sniffling his arm and he asked three times when his cousin would be home. I had to admit that I didn't know, but probably tomorrow. Why don't we start by lighting a fire, alright? This idea seemed to amuse him. I went over to the fireplace while he watched. Among the ashes, I found a few live embers, added a little kindling and used a bellows to get it going; when the fire caught, I waited a minute or two for the flames to grow, then added a log; I was rather proud of myself I have to say, despite the fact that ashes were flying pretty much everywhere, the result was there.

At least no one would die of hypothermia.

Night was drawing in; it was getting increasing difficult to see. I asked Arnaud whether they had any candles. I had to repeat the question three times before he said, No, I don't think so. Well, that's a fine state of affairs, I thought. In the pitch-darkness, the evening promised to be entertaining. I found a flashlight on the sideboard and the remains of a melted candle in a dish; I rummaged through the drawers and the chaos of the scullery (I wouldn't call it a bathroom), without success. So, no candles then. Alright, Arnaud, I'll go out and buy some candles, okay? He didn't reply, I think he'd fallen asleep in his chair.

I walked toward the Café-Pêche in the hope of finding some candles, having hesitated about whether I should just borrow some from Mathilde, but I wasn't sure that she would approve of my good deed. I arrived at the café, white as an iceberg, the bar was open, the purr of a diesel generator came from the yard, a chink of light filtered through the curtains—when it comes down to it, the countryside can be very resourceful, technologically speaking. I pushed open the door, the place was thronged, mostly with men I didn't know—apart from the cardplayers I'd met the other day, though this time they were at the bar. They were all involved in heated conversations, complaining about the power outage, Spent three fucking hours hand-milking the cows, said one; My piglets are freezing to death, said another (I didn't realize sties had central heating); I need to find another generator to save the freezer, muttered a third, then he added, If I got my hands on them bastards, I'd give them a good beating, can you imagine, I mean pulling a stunt like that so close to Christmas. The gendarmes nabbed them, said Thomas, which did not placate the assembled company, quite the reverse. And anyway, we don't give a shit about nuclear energy, I mean, for Christ's sake, what's with all the wind turbines they've put up around the country, if the fuckers still aren't happy, I'll give them a piece of my mind. I didn't dare interrupt, but Thomas turned to me, Want a drink? I said, Yeah, why not, I came to see if you had any candles, but yeah, a little Kir might warm me up a bit, one of the guys at the bar found this hilarious, only thing that'll warm you up in this weather is hard liquor, or Viandox®, or a cocktail of both. I ignored him. Thomas poured me a Kir, You'll be hard-pressed to find any candles, there's none to be had between here and the Vendée, the supermarkets are sold out. There's not a gas lamp, not a candle, not a generator to be had since we heard the electricity wouldn't be back on before the day after tomorrow. So, what exactly happened? I said. The question triggered a tsunami of comments, Bunch of stupid little bastards fucking things up for everyone else, it was a terrorist attack, that's what it was. A terrorist attack? Bah, yeah, the substation was blown up, for Christ's sake.

I pictured a crack commando team of snow-clad Islamic fundamentalists coming down the slopes of the Hindu Kush, with bricks of Semtex under their arms, to heroically blow up an EDF substation in the Deux-Sèvres, and I couldn't help smiling and saying, That's ridiculous, it can't be a terrorist attack ... There was a general outcry. Well, they said on TV that the gendarmes have arrested them. Antiglobalization activists. Tree huggers. Terrorists. I mean what the hell have we got to do with globalization, tell me that? The little shits have no respect for anything.

I didn't want to sound as though I were defending alleged terrorists, so I mumbled an innocuous "Oh, really..." So, no candles.

I downed my Kir, paid up, thanked Thomas and headed out into the blizzard.

My only option now was Mathilde, but that would be complicated. How could I explain that I needed candles or a lamp when I had electricity at my place thanks to Gary's generator? Option one: bring the cousin and the old man home to the Savage Mind. I think I'll pass on that one. Option two: ask Mathilde for some candles. Option three: there is no option three. Huddle with Lucie's family in the dark for a while, then calmly get up and go home. Hardly a very chivalrous solution.

So, Mathilde it is, I thought. I have to say I found the idea a little embarrassing, for no particular reason.

Maybe it was the word *crime* flickering into my mind that gave me the inspiration, or maybe in each of us there slumbers the black soul of sacrilege, but as I came to the crossroads where, by right, I should turn left to go to Lucie's place, a thought occurred to me. I knew a place where I could find candles, big, beautiful candles. In the church, obviously. I'd seen tons of candles there when Mathilde took me on a tour. And I knew where to find the enormous key, hanging on a nail in the shed with various others; I had only to borrow it, open the church, take the candles (I couldn't bring myself to say *steal*) and that would be that. After all, needs must ... I mean, I'd be doing it to bring light to the old man and the orphan, wouldn't I? The closer I came to the Savage Mind, the more brilliant I found this idea. Risky, granted, but brilliant. Assuming the chapel hadn't been looted already, in ten minutes I could be basking by the fire reading Hugo's *Ninety-Three*, and keeping Arnaud company. I was already feeling rather proud of myself. What cunning! What resourcefulness! What magnanimity! To bring the light of God back to the common people!

Of course, I should have realized that criminal undertakings are never as simple as they first appear. First, I had to find a way to get into the shed; it was pitch-dark now and I couldn't see a thing. I remembered I had Lucie's flashlight in my pocket. It gave a feeble glow, but at least it was light. Taking no trouble to conceal myself (but having surreptitiously checked that Mathilde's shutters were closed) I crept into the shed. Thankfully, the dog didn't bark. Thinking about it now, I realize the dog hadn't barked at me for days, which was a stroke of luck. What excuse could I give Gary if I ran into him? That I was just checking the generator was working, that's it. A perfect excuse. The hum of the generators drowned out the sound of my footsteps. I knew exactly where the big rusty nail was. Despite my dread (Oh, I was scared; my heart was hammering) I moved deftly and precisely, a first-rate burglar. I even switched off the flashlight before stepping out again so as not to attract attention. I had the key, it was heavy. Now all I had to do was cross the street. Not a living soul. Pitch-darkness, the wind had eased a little, it was still snowing. I walked over to the church. Minor hiccup: the door was clearly visible from the street; if a car happened to pass, I was done for. I remembered hesitating for a moment. This is stupid, I thought, here I am about to loot a church, what a fucking stupid thing to do. I'm putting my fieldwork here at risk. I'm an idiot. For a minute, I stood stock-still; the situation was absurd. Oh, that fearless thirst for adventure will get you in the end, I thought. It'll give Lara a good laugh when I tell her the story, I thought. Alright then, once the bottle's uncorked, you have to drink the wine, as they say.

I mounted the church steps quickly, no sound of a car, I had to fumble blindly to get the key into the lock, it took two or three attempts but eventually the door creaked opened in an endless excruciating shriek of rusty hinges; people could have heard me at the far end of the village; my goose was cooked. I stood, petrified, before the yawning doorway, I could imagine Mathilde already racing over to defend her sacristy and catching me red-handed. Urged on by panic, I ducked inside, pressed myself against the wall and waited. Nothing; silence. After a moment, I decided to gently close the heavy door and switch on my flashlight. A shadowy Christ contorted in pain scared me half to death. A dimly lit church is incredibly eerie. I didn't hang around, I could feel the eyes of the saints and martyrs boring into me, I took a sharp left to where I remembered seeing the candles, and there it was, the treasure: armfuls of wax candles, some half-burnt, others pristine, some thin, some thick, some long, some short. Without thinking, I grabbed half a dozen of the thickest candles and raced back to the entrance. I thought about leaving the door open and fleeing, but that would simply call attention to my crime; in the end, I decided to risk easing it closed, millimeter by millimeter, while still inside, then slipping through the narrow gap, to avoid being seen outside. The lock turned effortlessly; I took to my heels, the spoils tucked under my arm, panicking, then slipped and went sprawling. I could already see the headline in the local paper:

UNBELIEVABLE!
UNDER COVER OF DARKNESS
ETHNOLOGIST PILLAGES CHURCH!

How could I have gotten myself into this situation, I thought with my face in the snow. Be brave, I thought, be brave; I gathered up the plunder and crossed the street, my heart in my mouth. I left the candles outside my door and quickly put the key back on its hook. I stashed the corpus delicti in my anorak and headed back to Lucie's place filled with remorse but also, I have to admit, with pride.

As I walked through the dark night, I somewhat recovered my composure.

In times of need, you have to be resourceful.

I had proved myself to be swift and shrewd.

We all have it in us to be criminals; I was living proof.

By the time I got to Lucie's, I was my old self, proud as the Good Samaritan of my feat. Arnaud and the old man—who had woken up in my absence—looked dumbfounded as I set four of the candles on plates and placed them at the corners of the table. I hadn't noticed that the sacred candles were emblazoned on the sides with little blue Virgin Marys. It looked bizarre, like a funeral wake for the basket of fruit.

I hadn't noticed, but it was already half past six: my endeavors had taken more than an hour, but at least we had light. I put the flashlight back on the sideboard and sat in front of the fireplace, exhausted.

Well, clearly ethnology can lead to anything, I thought as I listened to Arnaud reciting his ephemera, December 22, feast of Saint Francis Xavier, etc., ethnology can lead to anything, even larceny. Like Jean Valjean and the bishop's stolen candlesticks. This reminded me that I'd brought my copy of *Ninety-Three* with me; I fished it out of my pocket. Strangely, neither Nono nor the old man asked what the hell I was doing there, as though I were family. In the firelight, the old man's face seemed longer and gaunter; his sempiternal cap cast a baleful shadow on the wall. Nono had his hands in his lap. All things considered, I was happy to be there.

Arnaud did not let me read for long, which was just as well, since reading by candlelight is pretty exhausting. We played historical dates. I drew up a little list of events missing from his collection, he was thrilled: April 7, 1884, Bronisław Malinowski born in Krakow; November 28, 1908, Claude Lévi-Strauss born in Brussels, etc., not to mention June 11, 2015, the eminent anthropologist David Mazon passes the first year of his MA *summa cum laude*, and so on. The speed with which he can learn things is remarkable. It's impossible for him to categorize information except by date. Asking "Arnaud, what date is Saint Martial's Day?" elicits no result, whereas simply saying "June 30" will set him off: June 30, feast of Saint Martial, etc., I checked his replies against an old post office calendar I found lying around. I also discovered that Arnaud can barely write; it takes him hours to trace four letters. I admit, I was a bit disappointed he's terrible at mental arithmetic, nothing like *Rain Man*. A simple two-number addition leaves him flummoxed. I was getting a little bored with the litanies of ephemera, so I suggested we play a game; Nono was very excited. He was hopeless at checkers, but pretty good at ludo. The thrill of the game, of imminent victory or defeat, triggers a similar reaction to the one alcohol had on him the other day: he starts to pant, flushes brick red, he can't talk or else talks a mile a minute, it's like he's about to choke. Anyway, we had fun; it had been years since I played ludo.

It was after eight o'clock, the grandfather had eaten his dinner (hunks of bread soaked in milk—ugh). I asked Nono if he was hungry, he said, What about Lucie? When's Lucie coming home? I said I don't think she'll be back tonight. He looked upset.

I foraged for something I could make for dinner—winging it in the role of babysitter. In the kitchen, I unearthed a box of pasta and a saucepan, which I filled and set to boil. Nono triumphantly yelled, Noodles! Noodles! At least he's not a fussy eater. Time was starting to drag. I had stuff to do before heading back to Paris, I needed to pack my suitcase, call Max to check he could still drive me to the station, assuming the trains were running.

Arnaud wolfed down his buttered coquillettes as though he hadn't eaten in weeks; it was a pleasure to behold.

The grandfather headed off to bed; his bedroom (actually, more of a wardrobe) is accessed through a tiny door I hadn't noticed before in the shadow of the fireplace. Arnaud kissed him, said good night, and seconds later he was snoring.

Wee-wee, brush teeth, Arnaud said.

When the door to the yard was opened, the dog took the opportunity to slink inside, I didn't have the heart to put him out, and he curled up by the fire.

Arnaud went upstairs and, out of curiosity, I followed; on the
first floor were two rooms bathed in shadows. Arnaud's room
seemed to be cluttered with things made from Lego and Meccano; he undressed in the dark, put his pajamas on and climbed
into bed. I felt embarrassed and self-conscious, so I crept out—
you could barely see a thing. As I headed back downstairs, I've
no idea why, I felt a wave of sadness mingled with shame; I paced
the room for five minutes, put some more wood on the fire, made
sure there was nothing nearby that could catch light, left one of
the stolen candles burning just in case, pulled on my anorak and
went back to the Savage Mind.

January 3

So I'm back.

It wasn't easy leaving Lara this morning, even if we did spend
a lot of the last week arguing, I think she's stressing about the
exams. She's decided to come and spend a few days with me at
the Savage Mind at the end of the month. I'm not keen to leave
the terrain before early March, not even for a weekend (hence
all the arguments). I need to make some progress.

Unpacked suitcases, put my stuff away, cleaned the bathroom—the lack of heating hasn't stopped the creepy-crawlies
from thriving—yuck.

The snow has melted. It's not as cold (six degrees), the electricity is working again, the moped starts up, what more could
you ask for?

Today's agenda: food shopping in Coulonges, visit to Mathilde's, then a drink at the Café-Pêche.

My grant money has finally come through, so I've decided to
buy a car, which would be less temperamental than Rocinante. A
convertible—why not? It would be perfect for taking long drives
through the country on fine days.

66

January 3 (contd.)

I said happy New Year to the mayor, Thomas, Max and the cardplayers, drank a couple of Kirs (I have to admit, I've missed Kir—I think I prefer it to champagne) while we chatted away. Max spent Christmas alone, *all on my lonesome*, as he put it. When I asked about the substation, what had actually happened, no one could give me a straight answer. Thomas had spoken to one of the EDF engineers who said it was a complete mystery—that it had almost definitely been sabotaged but they couldn't work out how. The substation had been charred to a crisp. What mattered now was that justice be done—this quip made Max snicker. Don't forget "innocent until proven guilty." Not that that's stopped the EDF from playing the victim, joked Max. No way, said Thomas melodramatically, the victim in all of this is *me*! Remember the ten kilos of pike and eel we had to eat? That was the upside, said the artist, I'm happy to be the victim of a terrorist attack if it means eating quenelles de brochet every day—this brought gales of laughter from the mayor: But given how cold it was over Christmas, you could just have buried the eels in the snow, they'd have been fine.

In a nutshell, everyone's in good form and they all drink as much as ever.

Got back to the Savage Mind at eight o'clock, had dinner (mackerel with tomatoes and pasta), wrote up some notes, sent some emails. At five past eleven, something strange: a distant explosion, like a giant firecracker or a gunshot. Immediately thought of a terrorist attack, which is ridiculous. No police or ambulance sirens, nothing; the village is silent once again.

Looked at the online classifieds for used cars, convertibles are rare as hen's teeth and very expensive. Don't have it in me to chat with Lara online. Lights out now, at 12:17 a.m.

January 4

Dug out my thesis, reread the twenty pages of the chapter *Questions*. Let's not mince words: it's utter shit. And you can't polish a turd. The only thing is to start from scratch and change my methodology: I'm going to wait till I have much more material before writing. Lowering sky, heavy rain. More melancholic than depressed. Had a chat with Gary, which lifted my mood a little. I have to say, I really like the guy. We talked about his winter schedule; he said things would be pretty quiet until March. Spreading fertilizer, fixing farm equipment ... He showed me his new GPS-equipped tractor—it's amazing. The layout of his land is stored in the onboard memory, and all you need to do is choose a particular function (plowing, sowing, crop spraying, etc.), make sure it's in the right field, and set it going—you don't have to touch the steering wheel or the pedals. Mind-blowing. Obviously, you have to stay on the tractor in case there's a malfunction, or something unexpected happens, otherwise everything's automatic. The march of progress never ceases. On flat ground, it's very, very practical, he said. I believe him. Mathilde uses the tractor too, something I didn't realize. She occasionally does the crop spraying or takes a turn on the combine harvester. Gary says they've always shared the farmwork, though he readily admits he know nothing about accounting or management software. The history of family farming encapsulates how agriculture has evolved in France: early twentieth-century mechanization, steam-powered threshers, etc., gradually leading to the introduction of intensive farming in the postwar years, combine harvesters, tractors, artificial fertilizers; the increase of acreage during the 1970s mostly through the consolidation of lands from in-laws, uncles, neighbors, and so on, whether inherited farms or tenanted farming; the 1980s farm crisis of agricultural overproduction, increased yields and greater debt, all the way to now, when global grain prices had put a lot of money in the coffers, much of which goes to service huge debts racked up ten or twelve years ago. Gary acknowledges that they are doing better than the beef and dairy farmers; the principal advantage of cereal farming, he explains, is that you can bide your time, keep the harvest in a grain silo and sell it for the highest price. His cousin, who fattens beef cattle on a factory farm a little farther north, is having trouble making ends meet, the investment is huge and the margins are very low—farmers sell to large chains at high discounts, and the price per kilo for beef cattle on the hoof is derisory. The only way to make money, says Gary, is to stake everything on quality: grass-fed beef, rare and heritage breeds bring in greater profits, but the investments (in livestock, in time and especially in grazing land) are greater too. It's a vicious circle.

Gary's offered to take me out hunting on Saturday or Sunday morning. Bring your Wellingtons, he said, it'll be pretty muddy.

January 4 (contd.)

I forgot to mention yesterday that I phoned Lucie to wish her a happy New Year and to ask after Nono and the old man. Somewhat surprised by my call, she thanked me for "the candles"—without going into details; she was extremely touched that I'd stopped by to reassure her family. I didn't ask her any questions about her odd behavior. I asked how Nono and her grandfather were. We're getting by, she told me. Weirdly, although I didn't have anything much to say, somehow, I couldn't manage to hang up. Agreed to pop by sometime this week so she could show me the farm.

January 5

Just back from hanging out with Max: Wellington boots, a hunting jacket with padded shoulders in khaki, matching pants with large pockets on the thighs: I'm all set. I like the brand names of hunting gear in the big stores: the names of lustrous hardwoods, expensive rifles, magnificent regions; my sweater is "Périgord black," my pants are "Guy du Berry."

When I asked if he was planning to go into town, Max sighed that he had to go into the Zone to find a new mattress because his was too soft. "The Zone" refers to the shopping precinct east of Niort: a bunch of garishly painted aircraft hangars with designer logos, a blight on the landscape of every European city. Acres and acres of discount shoes, gadgets, sporting goods, furniture, outlet designer stores, sprinkled with fast-food stalls and cheap pizza joints. You could live there and never see daylight, said Max, which is probably a grim version of hell. Wedged between a couple of four-lane bypasses, in the shadow of high-rise buildings housing a large insurance company, it would be a fine place to pitch a tent. Even so, the sheer ugliness has its advantages: I have my hunting gear, and Max has his mattress. (I suspect there's a woman involved, since Max also bought new sheets and a duvet, but I didn't dare ask, it's none of my business.)

On the subject of women, I need to face facts, my relationship with Lara is fucked. We somehow manage to argue even when we're texting. I've changed ever since I've been out in the field, I'm more aware of what is truly important: the planet, climate change, nature, life, death, whereas she (forgive me, Lara) is a pampered, cosseted Parisian with no idea about the challenges facing humanity. I'm sorry, but yes, we need committed environmental activists more than we need armchair diplomats in designer blouses. I'm sorry, but the whole ecosphere is quaking, from everywhere we hear the dull rumble of the end of the world: fire, flood, plague—the four horsemen of the Apocalypse, basically. (What was the fourth horseman, again?) They are bearing down on us, and the only people who can save us are the people who work the land, not politicians. Alright, maybe I'm laying it on a bit thick, but I can't see international law and geopolitics doing much to feed the ecumene, amen!

Alright, okay, maybe I'm getting a little carried away, I mean, I've been here—what?—two months? Maybe it's a bit premature to be discovering the meaning of life somewhere between Mathilde's radishes and strip malls. It's the burden of writing a thesis that's got me wound up. Maybe I'm jealous of Lara, she has her career all mapped out for her, all she has to do is follow the Primrose Path of Civil Service Exams. But there's no point sitting around feeling for myself, I need to make progress.

Right, a little tinkering with the bibliography and a quick email to Calvet.

January 7

Finally, a good day's work! Lucie came over to the Savage Mind this morning. (First time I've had guests—realized I have no cups, so we had coffee in Duralex® tumblers.) She brought a box of Chocolats de l'Ambassadeur as a New Year's gift, which I thought was touching, I could have one now, but I'm too lazy to brush my teeth again, so I'll try them tomorrow. This time, it was Lucie conducting the interview, pretty much: I told her the story of my life (well, my professional life), sheep farming and transhumance in the Ariège, Montaillou, Prades: my domains. The bears, the vultures, the wolves. (Alright, maybe I was a little overdramatic about the wolves.) The challenges faced by young sheep farmers in the Pyrenees. Lucie seemed really riveted. Then it was her turn: she told me how she spent December 22 in a police cell after a protest march in Niort that went sour. This was why she wasn't around the night of the power outage. It's completely unfair: when industrial livestock and cereal farmers protest in favor of higher subsidies, they can lay waste to the city, burn down the prefecture or use fire hoses to bury it under shit tons of slurry, and they're never arrested. Ever. In fact, they're given what they want. Meanwhile, ecoactivists protesting against the vast reservoirs in the Marais Poitevin (a multimillion-euro outrage attempting to shore up an unsustainable agricultural model and give control of publicly owned resources [water] to a handful of maize farmers in the pockets of Dekalb™ and Bayer™) get a taste of police batons and a night in the cells. The whole world is going to hell. Lucie told me that two of the green protesters the press refer to as "zadistes" were charged with "terrorist-motivated sabotage" over the EDF substation. Two close friends, she said. Never been radical, never been violent, she said. She's asked if I'll help her draft an appeal for the national media. I think it would be a good idea for me to be committed to the environment. I'll ask Lara what she thinks.

January 8

Big day out: went hunting for the first time in my life. Even fired a rifle. Up at five in the morning to be at the hunting ground before dawn. Hunting ground: right in the middle of the flatland, in the tangle of paths left after land consolidation, a few kilometers outside the village, between Ajasses and La Taillée, or to be absolutely precise, next to a little patch of woodland ringed by fields, with Gary's dog, Gary's rifle and Gary himself. We parked his battered Nissan Patrol on the edge of the woods. You find yourself wreathed in light without being able to determine the source; it seems to radiate from trees and stones, to flare from the shrubs; the morning mist begins to glow; the dog pants eagerly, its breath tracing vaporous dragons. It yaps but doesn't bark. The cold nips at my nose and my cheeks. Gary took the rifle from its case. It's a smoothbore double-barreled shotgun fitted with a choke (I had to do some googling to work out why you would want to constrict the bore—apparently, it's to regulate the shot pattern: I'm as ignorant about ballistics as I am about electricity). A flexible shotgun and various types of ammunition—just in case, according to Gary. Even if all we're likely to shoot is a pair of crows. In the dying breath of the bitter night, Gary explained "game drive hunting," which involves moving across the flatland with a spaniel ahead "quartering the field" until it scents game; at this point the dog will stop and point to indicate the location of the game and wait for the hunter to catch up, never losing sight (or scent) of the pheasant—assuming it's a pheasant—then, when the hunter is ready, the dog flushes out the bird, which takes to the wing, the moving target is shot down, and the spaniel goes and retrieves the spoils, so to speak. That's how it works in theory.

In practice there are a number of hurdles: the hunter's main enemy is barbed wire. I nearly left my balls hanging like Christmas ornaments on the first fence, until Gary laughed and said, It's easier to slip under, or between two rows, that way your pants don't get snagged. Obviously, I didn't say anything while we tramped through the mud and the barbed wire with a rifle, but it reminded me more of the Battle of the Somme in 1916 than the Deux-Sèvres in the twenty-first century. As it happens, this year is the hundredth anniversary of our Victory. The second great danger for the poilu (or the hunter) is the mud. It envelops your boots and creates a powerful sucking action that imprisons your boots for a moment; when the aforementioned boots are slightly too large (as mine are), you risk losing them with every step. O future ethnographer, O gentle reader of this field diary, whatever you do, never attempt to run, or you will suffer my fate and find yourself on your belly with your face being licked by the dog, one foot booted, the other bootless, and the green plastic tube of your Wellington behind you sprouting from the earth like some hideous shrub, as though you'd been made discalced by the blast of a mortar shell. I'm sure Gary's still pissing himself laughing, as is his dog. Moving swiftly along . . .

Aside from that minor humiliation, what a morning! A streak of orange along the horizon heralds the day in a clear sky, between wisps of fog that hug the rolling plain. Everything trills with the desire to trill, from dog to birds, from lowliest shrubs to the highest treetops. Nature quivers—you walk silently into the north wind on the outskirts of the woodland; the spaniel "quarters the field," rapidly zigzagging back and forth, muzzle pressed to the ground. This is the hour of the partridge and the pheasant, according to Gary. And wood pigeons. And rabbits. The wild pheasant is wily and refuses to show itself if it hears the slightest sound—the pheasant is cunning, unlike the rabbit, which always flees, racing into the open field and ending up full of lead shot. The pheasant has its bolt-hole, its carefully prepared refuges. Gary told me that when farm-reared pheasants are released for the hunt, they wander aimlessly along the roads and invariably (as is their life's goal) end up plucked.

We had been walking for about half an hour when the spaniel first stopped and pointed. Near the ruins of a windmill, where the road forks toward La Taillée, just behind the patch of woodland, the dog suddenly stopped about twenty meters ahead, its muzzle pointed. Gary cocked his rifle and strode over; when the dog sensed his presence, it ran forward and flushed out a fat bird, framed black against the daylight; Gary raised the rifle but did not shoot—a magpie, he muttered disgustedly, and scolded the dog. The common magpie is the garbageman of the plains, as I understand it, they will eat anything. They're related to crows— in the springtime, they can be caught using nets or from blinds, according to Gary. But it's hardly very noble.

The idea that hunting has a concept of nobility (and one I am beginning to glimpse) and that Gary, a farmer, should use the word, was something I found very pleasing—the privilege of killing, once the preserve of the few, is now accessible to all—or almost all. It is one of the rights gained by the People during the Revolution.

A second point in the broad field that slopes down to the river, before the pastureland. It was at this point that I went sprawling, and so Gary could not shoot, busy as he was laughing, helping me to my feet, retrieving my missing boot and helping me put it on while I hopped on the spot. (Even the dog seemed concerned, and licked my face; these animals show great compassion, though their breaths reeks.)

Walked alongside the riverbank by the meadows for at least an hour (which is where barbed wire almost divested me of my manhood). First shot, a miss: the rabbit darted into the hedge-row; not enough visibility to fire a second shot. Things weren't looking promising: it was almost eleven o'clock and our bag was still empty. Gary suggested we take a break (I think he felt sorry for me, I was dragging my feet and despite my sweater with its padded shoulders, I was shivering, and covered in mud). A fallen log on which to sit, a thermos, two plastic cups and a piece of saucisson. Before us, the valley slopes shone greener near the plains; the winter sun, remote and orange-hued, caressed the damp grass; I glanced at the shotgun Gary had unloaded for safety, and at the dog, sitting nearby, hoping (clearly knowing the routine) for something to eat; suddenly, I thought of the Native Americans, the Comanche, the Cheyenne: it was a beautiful day to die, as they say in the West. Gary poured a steaming cup of coffee, cut some slices of saucisson. We sat there for about twenty minutes. I took some photos. Then we carried on.

I must admit, I found the second part of the morning a little long. (It has to be said that I was trailing fifty meters behind, struggling to pull off my sweater when the spaniel stopped and the successful shot rang out, so I saw nothing, I just heard the bang. Having started out shivering, I was now boiling after a long trek in three layers of clothes.) Gary had shot a hen pheasant. By the time I caught up, the spaniel was retrieving it. Gary fussed over the dog and gave it a treat. As the name suggests, the kill (the prey?) looks like a hen, but the feathers are brown streaked with black. So it was that, from a distance, I witnessed the death of this creature with the long, lifeless neck. I felt neither pleasure nor disgust, I felt nothing. Humans are probably more sensitive to the death of mammals than birds. Or maybe I've grown used to

it. Gary was satisfied. Which was hardly surprising, I thought—
if we're out hunting, our aim is to kill. Otherwise, why tramp
around with a rifle and a dog? Speaking of a rifle, a little later, just
as I was starting to resign myself to the long trek back to the car,
Gary asked if I wanted to take a shot. I felt a surge of childlike joy
and instantly agreed. Gary set up the "shooting range": a gentle
slope down toward a meadow to limit the dispersal of the lead
shot, and the target, a rusty tin can (jammed on top of a fence post
to stop it rotting away). Gary called the dog to heel to prevent any
accidents; he showed me how to shoulder the gun. I found the
shotgun heavy, difficult to aim. Gary told me to relax, but that
was impossible. I gritted my teeth and clenched my buttocks as
though facing a Versaillais platoon during the Paris Commune.
(Why Versaillais loyalists, when I was the one holding the gun?)
I did precisely what Gary said not to do: I closed my eyes as I fired.
Huge bang (my ears were ringing), acrid smell, slight recoil, but I
was so tense that the rifle barely moved.

Shit, I thought immediately, forgot to get a photo for Lara, so
we did it over, with Gary as the paparazzo and me as Tartarin.
The dog was yapping and running in circles, probably thinking
I was shooting at invisible, scentless animals. I was a little less
nervous taking the second shot, but I still squeezed my eyes
shut—the proof is in the photo, though it came out pretty well:
my lowered eyelids, my cunning expression, my furrowed brow,
the spurt of yellow flame flaring from the gun barrel.

It was almost a two-hour walk back to the car, and then home,
starving but elated, exhausted but content.

Next time, Gary said he'll get me to be the beater and flush
out big game.

I can't wait.

After lunch (black pudding and mashed potatoes with Gary and
Mathilde—I'm a long way from turning vegan), which we spent

relating our game-hunting exploits (I suspect the tale of the boot in the mud will get around the whole village), I texted Lucie at about three o'clock to see if she had some time free that afternoon; she texted back to say she had to pick cabbages and leeks for the Sunday market, and suggested I come along. I have to say I thought long and hard—it's all very well tramping about in the mud, with or without a dog, but you need to make progress on your thesis, David, so you have to make sacrifices. I put on my Nikes™ (I'm done with boots), straddled Rocinante and roared off to Maupas, on the Marais Poitevin road, where Lucie's land (well, technically it belongs to her ex, I think) lies on the border between the Deux-Sèvres and the Vendée. (Remember to ask her whether there's any difference in terms of soil, regulations, subsidies, etc.) A twenty-minute ride later, I was learning to cut cabbages and pull leeks—a very agreeable activity. Such joy to be in a large field sheltered from the wind by hedgerows, feet planted in the cool, dark soil speckled orange by a few discarded carrots, cloaked in the vivid green of cabbages (*Brassica oleracea capitata*), with your hands among the leeks! It feels like being in an enchanted land. Lettuces peacefully overwinter in high tunnels, safe from the frost. Heads of kale are lush and curly. Swiss chard—in white, yellow and red cultivars—blooms in glorious sprays. It didn't feel like it, but we worked for at least two hours; I must have pulled about forty leeks and twenty cabbages. Lucie truly has the body of an athlete. She offered me a basket of vegetables, I didn't dare tell her I hadn't a clue what to do with them (it's insane that I have a degree in rural agriculture and I don't know how to make a soup, but then again, what are we taught in our seminars? How many pages did Bourdieu devote to soup? There might be one or two in Jean-Pierre Le Goff. Victor Hugo, on the other hand, is constantly writing about soups. About food. That's the example I need to follow. I'll get cooking. And write to Calvet to ask if he's got a recipe for garbure). I can't just throw the vegetables out. I suppose I could give them to Mathilde.

Or I could get off my ass, download a recipe app and learn how to make fucking soup.

Found a recipe in *Ninety-Three*: "A soup made from water, oil, bread and salt, a little lard, a small piece of lamb."

Alright, I give in, I'll give the vegetables to Mathilde.

January 9

I've decided to spend less time at the Café-Pêche so I can discover the rest of the village: the people who don't live there. Door-to-door is the only solution; Martial the mayor wrote me a letter of introduction in his inimitable style that begins "Dear fellow citizens" and basically offers a broad outline of my work and his high esteem for the ethnologist David Maçon (*sic*). A bona fide safe-conduct. Just in case the inquirees (*sic*, bis) wish to know why I'm asking all these questions. The first step is to make contact and arrange the interviews. So, this morning (the advantage of buttonholing people on Sunday in the dead of winter is that they're usually home), I met seven: François B., dark hair, glasses, forty-five, married, two children, legal adviser for a big insurance company in Niort. Old house, rather pretty. Initially, not particularly forthcoming, but curious to know what sort of questions I would ask. Slyly ironic, reserved the right to choose whether to answer, which is logical. We'll see how it goes. Christophe C., divorced, much the same age, three children, huge motorcycle, property developer. Small company that mostly builds modern detached houses. Can't accuse him of being a hypocrite, since he lives in the same kind of house. Cheerful and quite friendly. Arranged an appointment for next week. David S., roughly the same age, two children (this will simplify my statistics and give me a hypothesis about the rurbanites living here), divorced, teacher in training center for young apprentices in the Marais Poitevin. He is an ideal subject. Very garrulous. He can tell me about his students, and maybe even let me interview a few of them. Not so much luck with Jean-Pierre B., sixty-something, who sent me packing and told me to write if I had any questions, because right now he was ironing, and ironing requires focus and precision. I think he was mocking me, but whatever, you can't win them all. Florent F., computer analyst, fifties, quite affable, but nonetheless thinks that it isn't necessarily—and I quote—a good idea to answer my questions. Sylvie P., forty-something, married, lawyer husband, two kids, also works for an insurance company. In a hurry, speaks very quickly, but friendly enough, arranged an appointment. Alain B., tall, debonair, a shock of white hair, a retired farmer, his wife is a retired teacher, three married children: another excellent subject. He used to own the land on which the housing development was built. To recap: six meetings arranged for this week, brilliant. Just hope none of them cancel.

Good to see things moving forward. Not sure about writing to Calvet—probably better to wait a bit.

Note: urgently need to buy a car. Got caught in the rain twice this afternoon, and although the village is not very big, it's not ideal to show up on someone's doorstep looking like you've been out with a fork when it's raining soup (ha! Back to soup!)— though sometimes they take pity and let me in. Foul weather we're having. Max said Thomas is trying to sell off his old van, which would make a great rustic vehicle—must check it out. Besides, around here, convertibles are like swimming pools: perfectly fine, but useless most of the year.

January 11

Nothing new to report. Two frustrating days watching the rain fall. Fast becoming a Tetris champion. Did a little more investigation into rational numbers. Disappointed to discover that there's apparently nothing new to discover.

Finished *Ninety-Three*, wonderful novel. Have to admit that Victor Hugo has talent.

Don't know why, but I don't feel much like chatting online with Lara. I'm even tired of webcams, my libido's a little flaccid.

Wonder if I've got latent depression.

Got a New Year's card from good old Calvet: "Wishing you a happy pastoral idyll" with a photo of a steam-powered engine in a farmyard, dated 1922.

I've been thinking about phoning Lucie to offer to help out, given this weather, but I'm not sure she's still going out to the farm. I could stop by for a chat. As for Max, he seems to be billing and cooing with some mysterious lady friend. He doesn't even pop into the Café-Pêche for an aperitif. Actually, the place is pretty deserted these days. Apparently January is good for nothing but thunderstorms and ennui. January, mournful plain.

January 13

Alright, okay, I have to admit I'm bored shitless. It's Friday, and I'm thinking about taking the train back to Paris, but I don't want to admit defeat just yet, and besides I've got appointments this weekend. It's been raining the whole week, there are frozen-pizza boxes strewn outside the Savage Mind and the place is starting to stink of cat piss.

Jesus Christ, David, get a grip!

January 13 (contd.)

Here's a thing: I read an entertaining article in the local paper, *La Nouvelle République*: a murderous zoophile has been raping and strangling goats near Melle. Police and goat farmers in the southern Deux-Sèvres are on tenterhooks. It's a weird word to use about a goat, "rape." According to a vet (interviewed by the local rag) it's possible for the goat to take pleasure in the act although—and I quote—"the male member of humans is pretty small in relation to a goat's vagina." Maybe our local zoophile mounted the nanny like a billy goat. Shocking, obviously, but very funny. It lifted my spirits. It's insane the things you find in the local newspapers. I should borrow them from Mathilde more often. Right now, clean the house and go round to Thomas's place for an aperitif, that should take my mind off things. And also, I need to talk to him about buying the van.

January 13 (contd.)

Just back from the café, the Savage Mind is clean as a new pin, which makes me feel better. Good news: Thomas is happy to sell me his crappy Renault for a symbolic one hundred euros. Even better, he'll sort out the MOT and the registration, all I have to do is get insurance. It's not a bad minivan, it's no spring chicken, but it still moves. Bright yellow, which is nice. Dent in the front bumper, a little rust here and there, but for what he's asking—hey … It's a two-seater, but it's not as though I know anyone to take out on a day trip. One drawback: it absolutely stinks. It's weird, but the back seat smells of rotting flesh. Thomas laughed and said it's probably a dead field mouse or something, don't worry, it will go away. I've no idea what it is, but it reeks. There are disgusting black stains on the floor—blood? I can't exactly picture Thomas engaged in satanic rituals and slitting the throats of animals in the back of his van. Oh well, a few bottles of bleach should do the trick. Two days from now, I can bid Rocinante farewell and take a day trip to the seaside. La Rochelle, maybe. Or the Vendée. It will give me something to do, because, let's be frank: I haven't so much as looked at my thesis in the past ten days.

SONG

As he did every morning, Antoine was looking, not simply at Rachel, but at her everyday ritual: the crinoline dress, the parasol in her right hand, the basket in her left, the smile on her face, the song from her lips. Her dazzling beauty. Her everyday ritual, because, in early summer, Rachel invariably appeared at precisely the same time, in precisely the same manner; she would walk slowly from the square next to Les Halles to the Hôtel de Ville, pass the headquarters of the learned society, greeting the scholars—if by chance she encountered any—with a flourish of her parasol; she would turn onto the rue des Tribunaux, stroll past the Palais de Justice, turn left onto the rue du Tourniquet toward Notre-Dame, which she would circle before taking the rue de la Cure, past the barracks of the gendarmerie on the rue de la Motte-du-Pin to the corner of the road heading west toward Ribray. She would walk down to the river and amble past the gardens of the prefecture and the château to the rue Brisson and the covered market, where she would greet the butchers, the dairymen and the customers, before taking the rue Civique up past the town hall, and so on. This peregrination, undertaken with the elegant gait of a young lady, pausing to greet every person she met, even crossing the street to do so, took at least three-quarters of an hour. On market days, Antoine noted, she would continue walking from nine o'clock until midday, or, in other words, according to Antoine's calculations, six or seven circuits in a single morning.

Sometimes, she would walk along the river Sèvre as far as the Jardin des Plantes in the late afternoon, when the bourgeoisie emerged to take the air; it was a lovely walk, the rippling reflections, the roses and the wisteria, the daffodils and lilacs. Rachel was a flower seller; beautiful sprays of fresh flowers in summer, magnificent dried bouquets in winter.

Antoine's shop stood on the corner of the place des Tribunaux, so he could watch Rachel's progress at his leisure while he repaired wooden clogs and punched holes for ladies' boots. Antoine was unfamiliar with Halévy's aria from *La Juive*, "Rachel, quand du Seigneur ...''; had he not been, he would have sung it all day long as he worked. Antoine dared not speak to Rachel beyond a curt "hello" as she passed his workshop. He was happy simply to watch. He knew everything about her—her slender waist, her ample breasts, the little black boots that hugged her ankles like gloves, eyes that you might see in a picture gallery set into a perfect face. But more than her sublime body, what drove poor Antoine crazy with love was Rachel's voice. It had a unique timbre, a fullness, a huskiness that was so melodious. Antoine would sometimes hear her hum as she passed his window; he longed for her to sing for him, every morning, every evening, and he cared little what she might have to say since, with such a voice, she could say anything she pleased and Antoine would listen, spellbound.

Of course, Rachel was entirely unaware of the passions she stirred in Antoine; she had noticed the cobbler's gallantry whenever she crossed the place des Tribunaux, but all the good citizens of Niort were chivalrous to Rachel—they bought her flowers; while the bourgeoisie, the merchants and the dignitaries purchased other favors for a moderate fee, and, they believed, far from prying eyes. Unsurprisingly, Antoine was blind and deaf to those things that, had they reached his ears, he would have dismissed as ugly jealous rumors; but, in truth, no one knew—Rachel paraded her beauty throughout the city; from time to time, she could be seen in a phaeton or a cabriolet drawn by a pair of thoroughbreds next to an immaculately dressed gentleman, heading, no doubt, to picnic at La Roussille in the shade of the great plane tree by the river, an innocuous day in the country, all pretty fabrics and rakish hats. That all these suitors were already married did not trouble Antoine, since he did not know. Not that he was credulous, but he was blinded his tender, heartfelt love for Rachel. He spent his days working with awl, needle and scissors; Saint Crispin, patron saint of cobblers, looked kindly upon him, and his business was thriving. Excellent, inexpensive leather was to be found in Niort, a city of tanners. Pigskin and calf leather made beautiful shoes, with fine hardwood heels. Ah, had he but dared, he would have suggested that Rachel come into his shop, where he could measure her delicate feet, and for her fashion a splendid pair of little boots. But he had never dared. Many a time as he watched her pass he would say to himself, Tomorrow. Tomorrow, without fail, I shall speak to her ... but when tomorrow came, he would merely greet her politely, as he had done yesterday and the day before, cursing the march of the seasons and the looming autumn bleakness that would deprive him of the quotidian pleasure of Rachel's smile.

One early September day shortly before summer's end, when Niort reeks of sludge and fish oil, when the waters beneath the bridges ebb, when it seems the Marais marshland, with its gnats and dragonflies, has risen to engulf the town, Rachel stepped into Antoine's shop for the first time. It took him all the strength he could muster to mask his agitation. He listened as she spoke (or rather allowed himself to be lulled by her singular voice, a little husky, almost injured) and spluttered some inanity in response. He was shaking. He swiftly took the proffered shoes. This is the design? Yes, that is the design. Let me just measure your left foot. Often the left foot is the larger. Please don't laugh, a person's feet are never identical, as any cobbler will tell you. Even Antoine had begun to despair of his inanities. He wished he might be witty and charming. Rachel was gentle, and redolent of cinnamon and forget-me-nots. She was smiling. She wore a white dress trimmed with red, whose swooping neckline afforded a glimpse of her bosom. Antoine had to let her leave. He wished that he might marry her. She will come back to collect the shoes. I shall make the most beautiful pair of boots the world has ever seen. Antoine was eager to set to work. For Rachel.

He heard two loud, sharp cracks, like timbers falling from a height. Puzzled, he raced outside; Rachel lay sprawled across the steps of the Palais de Justice; an orderly was struggling to overpower a woman who was waving a revolver and howling, she looked distraught, her mouth was vast and monstrous. Antoine recognized the vulgar, hateful face of Gabrielle, the wife of the court clerk. The orderly had managed to wrest the gun away and was staring at it incredulously, like a tomfool. Antoine sank to his knees and took Rachel in his arms; her breath was faint, the ghastly soft hiss of a ball deflating; a sticky warmth spread over Antoine's belly and his thighs. Antoine held Rachel and crooned: *my love if it pleased you, we could sleep side by side ... My love if it pleased you. Until the world should end. Until the world should end.*

II.
THE HANGED MAN'S TOE

"What can a man who believes in reason
scream? There is only one thing he can
scream: no matter what happens or what he
observes, it has to be for a reason."
—Gilles Deleuze on Leibniz

Two years earlier, when the wild boar, the vessel for the soul of
Father Largeau, was born, at the very moment when the noble
beast whimpered against the pink teats of its mother in a cleft
between two roots, in the mossy hollow of an oak, minutes after
the old priest had peacefully breathed his last, his heart stilled,
Mathilde discovered the body empty of its soul, she wept hot
tears, she knelt before him, took his hand, realized that he was
dead, and she prayed.

Mathilde cried and prayed inconsolably for a long moment,
long enough for the newborn shoat to be licked clean by its
mother, long enough for it to suckle its first teat and, fortified by
maternal nectar, take its first stumbling steps, urged out into the
world by the sow's snout, quickly forgetting the circumstances
in which it had departed its previous life.

When Mathilde stopped crying, she realized she had to do
something; reverently, she laid out the corpse, a difficult task
since, despite his leanness, the man was heavy, and she thought
that perhaps it was bone that gave the man his weight rather than
fat or soul, since he no longer possessed either. She folded his

arms across his chest, pressed his eyes closed, blessed herself and cried again, distraught with grief. She was a staunch Catholic and could not imagine that the old priest was gamboling now beneath the leafy trees, hesitant and stumbling, not like the drunkard he had occasionally been, but like the young boar he had become: she consoled herself by picturing him in Heaven, among the Angels.

The burial, three days later, was a qualified success.

The mourners were disappointed that the dead man, with his gift for the funereal, was unable to deliver his own eulogy; all the more so because, being accustomed to his sermons, the sound of this strange priest in the pulpit preaching in a singsong accent that was clearly not local gave the solemn rite a curious, light-hearted air, a carnival atmosphere that had the sanctimonious sobbing even harder; meanwhile, this unanticipated sense of permissiveness prompted the few secular souls to nudge each other and quietly speculate about the circumstances of the priest's death; then came Holy Communion; finally, the mourners had one last look at the deceased through the small glass window in the coffin, and the gravediggers, mercifully sober that day, went about their business. Once the coffin had been interred, some headed off to the café, others to work. Mathilde rejoined her husband as he climbed down from his tractor. Her husband never went to church, not that she reproached him, because she sensed in him a faith that was profound and sincere, the faith of a man who works the land, lives according to the seasons, so close to the daily miracle of nature that he cannot help but respect the Creator, even if this meant choosing to sow seeds rather than attend the funeral of Father Largeau, who, despite being a man of the cloth, was no saint, however much Mathilde might have wished him so: her husband had spent many nights playing cards with Father Largeau in the Café-Épicerie-Pêche, which sold fishhooks, leaders and pale, fat, white maggots wriggling in sawdust that turned into beautiful silvery flies if left forgotten at the bottom of a tackle bag. Mathilde's husband drank, though not as much as other men; he had beaten his children, though not as often as other husbands; he never cheated on his wife and left the family home only to fish or hunt, thereby precipitating other suffering souls into the Wheel: perch, pike, pheasants, partridges or hares that were, perhaps, vessels for the souls of intrepid explorers or valiant soldiers, no one could know, certainly he was completely oblivious to the idea. He could often be seen with his dog at daybreak, on the plains, his break-action shotgun over his arm, his cap pulled down over his ears, his nose and cheeks red with cold, and people would call from a nearby hillock, Hey, Gary!, since this was the nickname given to Mathilde's husband's, a nickname from the mists of childhood whose origin no one could remember, everyone knew him as Gary, especially the regulars at the Café-Pêche, so much so that, when he was appointed secretary of the hunting association and filled out the forms, everyone was surprised to be reminded that his name was actually Patrice.

So, Mathilde kissed her Gary as he climbed down from the tractor, then she went into the kitchen, feeling melancholy: she would no longer cook Father Largeau's meals, the soup to which he liked to add a glug of red wine on winter nights, sipping it slowly before taking the bowl in his fists and lifting it to his gaping mouth, keeping his eyes closed to the end, adieu; adieu to the contented sigh of a man who has held his breath for a long time, and then pours another glug of wine into the bowl, crumbles another hunk of bread and leaves it to soften, his eyes shining. Mathilde never dared linger. She would gruffly take her leave of the dear priest, the better to spy on him from the yard. When the soup had been finished and the farmer's wife had left, the priest would invariably move on to hooch, and Mathilde believed that the saintly father had all the vices of his virtues; he forgave himself that which he forgave his flock, as steeped in alcohol and indulgence as others were in sin, but so beneficent that—charity begins at home—he would allow himself, in solitude, a large snifter of plum brandy, the bounty of his orchard, distilled in secret under the noses of the gendarmes by an accommodating neighbor, who levied only a quarter of the clerical harvest for personal use.

No, Mathilde would no longer bring the priest the dregs of her soup, or the leftovers of the Sunday chicken or guinea fowl since—God have mercy—he was dead; he would no longer have his little snifter, he would no longer say, Ah, dear little Mathilde. She was overcome by a great melancholy, and her husband, seeing her sob, took her in his arms; this show of affection so touched her that she almost forgot the priest and his tragic death, even the moment when this story truly begins, the moment when the young boar that is vessel to the soul of Father Largeau encounters his first sow, in a copse, after several heedless months spent foraging for food, eating fledglings fallen from nests, over-turning rotting carcasses and gnawing on them, over on the edge of the marshlands by the soaring poplar trees, in the few dense hedgerows the cereal farmers have purposefully spared, a few hundred meters from the presbytery abutting the Romanesque church where Abbé Largeau departed this life to join the swine.

In the meantime, the old priest's role had been taken by a young man in his forties who lived in town and ministered to several parishes. The sacristy was shut up with the memory of Abbé Largeau; the church was reduced to opening only one Sunday a month, and even then at an ungodly hour since the priest's complicated schedule required him to leave straight after service to get to the regional capital for midday mass; his parishioners' unwillingness to adapt to this early hour only served to confirm the new priest's belief that the parish was not worth his time; in short, he succeeded in emptying his own church, thanks to the fierce jealousy his female parishioners nurtured toward the sur-rounding villages, since they had already been deprived of both a post office and a bakery.

Mathilde devoted herself to her accounts and to skinning rabbits without the help of the Almighty, with whom she was no longer on speaking terms, because He had taken from her the only man, apart from her husband, whose desire she had never felt, despite her in her chaste plaid skirt.

*

The village extends from a river to a Christ crucified, a roadside cross marking the boundary with the Vendée, its mysterious neighbor: west of here, the lands that stretched down to the ocean were occupied by royalist Chouans, and although this was a modern boundary—two hundred and thirty years old at most—it accounted for the fact that the villagers rarely went to the seaside, preferring to paddle around in canals and rivers when they felt like a swim, which was far from being the case on this particular morning, since it was autumn, the tail end of a wet, chilly autumn, when the mist-slick days are so short and the evenings so propitious for a hanging. Just as the young boar carrying the soul of Abbé Largeau was eagerly mounting his first sow in a nearby copse, Lucie opened eyes as gray as the dawn she could see through her window, barren elderberries and leafless hazels; she shivered, briefly considered lingering in the animal comfort of her own warmth beneath the heavy eiderdown, where the long night had left her insensible to the smells of dog, sweat and charred wood, closed her eyes and rolled over; the spaniel licked her forearm, she pushed him off the bed with her knee, her bare leg emerged from the refuge of the duvet, the cold rushed in, she whimpered like the wounded dog, it was too late now, the womb-like comfort of squalor and sleep had been broken, she brusquely threw back the eiderdown, spreading panic among the invisible dust mites, slid her feet into her slippers and raced down the stairs while, a couple of kilometers away, the young boar was beginning its endless ecstasy, its forelegs on the shoulders of the sow.

The temperature downstairs was more clement, some embers

still glowed in the hearth; the grandfather in his armchair listening to the radio took pleasure in watching the nightdress, the bare legs and the underwear flash past: reflexively, he gripped his penis through his pants, two fingers held what was no more now than a length of lifeless flesh, the way it might hold a piece of bacon; Lucie sensed (or thought she sensed) the old man's concupiscence and flushed with anger; she locked the bathroom door, since the old man sometimes shuffled over and spied on her. She splashed water on her face, sniffed her clothes and decided they would be fine, dressed and, thinking it was not cold enough to piss in the bathtub, slipped on her Wellingtons and headed to the outhouse. The dog followed and disappeared into the long grass and the flower beds, oblivious to the fact that many years earlier, it had been he, in the body of Lucie's grandmother, who had hoed, planted and weeded here, tended the same kitchen where he now enjoyed hunting field mice and moles, though they proved much too swift for him. Lucie stepped out of the outhouse, shivering, a kick of her boot sending a sickly spider into the Wheel where resided, waiting for flies, a former local schoolmaster killed in action in 1916, whose name featured prominently on the war memorial by the former town hall now converted into a village hall. Heedless of the dismembered arachnid, Lucie quickly sought out the warmth of the house. Her grandfather (face gaunt, ears interminable and cartilaginous) was bellyaching; she graced him with a clip around the back of his head, which further infuriated the old geezer, since the clout knocked his dentures forward and he had to put it back in place, like a slippery bar of soap, forcing him to move his right hand from the crotch of his trousers. Lucie heated some leftover coffee in a pan. She stared at the pile of cracked plates in the sink, at the mold scaling the rim of a forgotten saucepan; she gazed in wonder for a moment at the pretty garlands of green-gray fungi adorning the clotted red of some primeval sauce, little realizing that her compassion promised these creatures reduced to the state of fungoid a nobler reincarnation when the dish liquid consigned them to the abyss. The grime, the dishes, the trash, the lascivious old man weighed on her shoulders like the weight of the world, she sighed and put a log on the embers. The coffee in the pan was boiling now, she swore and raced over; the thick, gurgling liquid had boiled over, creating a dark pool on the stove, an oil slick that slid over the layer of grease that covered the enamel. Lucie sighed again, turned off the gas, tossed a wet dishcloth at her grandfather who had started to laugh, or bellow, or bawl, before cursing and swearing when he was hit in the face by the damp dishcloth that smelled of death.

On the radio, the forecast promised snow, one piece of good news for the day, though her elation was short lived when she suddenly remembered that she had to go into town to do bureaucratic paperwork, which she hated. Niort, the only prefecture in the département, was some fifteen kilometers south; if left alone and free for too long, her grandfather would sometimes shuffle over to the Café-Pêche for a few swift shots, or climb onto a kitchen stool and take down the bottle of brandy he was forbidden to drink on account of his diabetes and his advancing age. Not that Lucie cared much if he dropped dead, but she had not yet dealt with the idea of being responsible for his death—a sign of her complicated relationship with the forebear. At the moment when the young boar, formerly Father Largeau, was forsaking his sow to return to snuffling among dead leaves, bristles still stiff with pleasure, the young dark-haired anthropologist was parking his moped outside Lucie's house, removing his helmet and clumsily taking his papers from his saddlebag; he exuded youthfulness, the vigor and the confidence of youth. Lucie had completely forgotten that, the day before, she had agreed to a meeting, compelled by circumstance; she did not trust this guy who talked like a textbook and, from what she could tell, had already forged an alliance with the gravedigger-in-chief—but now here he was, outside, so she opened the door, smiled, took little pleasure in lying to him, and left him in the company of her grandfather who was surprised but delighted to have someone take an interest in him. With what little freedom was afforded him by his dentures and his faltering memory, the old man did his best to answer the anthropologist's questions; he confusedly recalled his childhood, the school he went to on foot, the fields he went to on foot, the farm laborer's life that had been his, working from dawn to dusk for the grandparents of Mathilde who, even now, was mourning the death of the priest, at the far end of the village, and while Lucie was pulling up in front of the government building in which she would squander several hours of life she would never get back, the ethnologist was sweating blood attempting to transcribe the old man's tale, to decipher his ancient, savage tongue, the vernacular of the earth and the violence of the land little heard these days, since it makes people feel ashamed, just as once they were ashamed of those hands black with grime they hid behind their backs when approached by the schoolmaster and his cane, who spoke such elegant French. Had he been more perceptive, or more curious, the young investigator might have heard the story of the old man's parents—the mother impregnated in a pleasureless coupling, her head against a tree stump, in a glade where the pale buttocks of her rapist glistened in the spring sunshine, to an ever-faster rhythm leading to the irrevocable; the mother beaten until she bled by her father, who howled with rage as he whipped her, inveighing against God, life, women, all the humiliations against which man is powerless, until his arm ached, before drinking himself into a stupor and sobbing, alone, since he believed this shame would forever exile him from the company of men. The man whose gleaming sunlit ass so fascinated the blackbirds swiftly disappeared, and the former virgin, whose whipping had made her forget the pain of the copulation, did not denounce him—indeed, in time, she retained fond memories of the coupling, the smell of onions in the shed often reminded her of the oily sweat that had dripped from the anvil-like brow of the man who had first taken her. She had been married off to a poor man with no land who saw an opportunity to gain some when all the decoctions of esoteric plants, the moonlit rituals, the prayers and hours spent wielding the thresher proved vain, the little bastard was well attached and her father, for all his shame, did not expel it with the toe of his boot as promised, but instead sought out a son-in-law, a lackland called Jérémie, to whom he promised fields, fields and cattle; the priest had glowered but hastily celebrated their union, the two pimply altar boys had giggled, sparrows had fluttered from the steeple, and that was that, until Lucie's grandfather was born. The Wheel rewarded him with the soul of a notary public, a former resident of La Pierre-Saint-Christophe, who had died like a bourgeois of a heart attack and been buried the following Monday. The gravediggers had been upbraided for their drunkenness by the widow, who used this pretext not to pay the customary tip; their mournful faces fell without complaint but spat plentifully on the coffin when all the mourners had left, then filled in the grave and returned to the serious business of drinking. The eldest of the gravediggers was the grandfather of Martial Pouvreau, the village mayor who, just as the anthropologist began to tire of the old man's colloquial peregrinations, was pulling up in front of the Café-Épicerie-Pêche for a lunchtime aperitif. He was in excellent spirits. As every year, influenza had scythed down the elderly villagers; the winter looked to be promising, though it was chiefly the poor popping their clogs, those who did not indulge in caskets from the *Venice* or *San Remo* range, but no matter, a corpse is a corpse, it must still be dressed, transported, buried or cremated, rich or poor, and for the destitute, the government pays, and the undertaker pockets the money. Not that Martial delighted in the deaths of others, on the contrary, he grieved for them, but sooner or later everyone kicks the bucket, including him, and suspecting that his children would prove tightfisted in this regard, he had long since made arrangements for his own funeral with a fellow undertaker in the town.

Martial, then, was in excellent spirits as he pushed the door open and greeted Thomas; Thomas cheerfully returned the mayor's greeting, reached across the bar and shook his hand, then turned away to prepare the anisette aperitif Martial favored, which had first appeared in these parts back in the 1960s, to judge by the yellow-and-blue plastic ashtrays and water jugs that sales reps had liberally distributed at the time, just as they supplied liberal quantities of alcohol to village fetes and soccer teams. Time was, the villagers drank their own concoctions, their own liquor, their own sloe wine, or other tipples now forgotten, whose peeling painted advertisements flaked from village walls: Fernet-Branca, Dubonnet and Byrrh, liqueurs that only the incorrigible nostalgic or the intrepid explorer would imbibe now. The mayor was not averse to a little gentian liqueur on occasion; sometimes he poured a little into his anisette, producing a country cocktail known to connoisseurs as "tractor fuel" because of its curious color; but such extravagances were generally reserved for evenings; before lunch, and then only on days of rest, he limited himself to one or two drinks to whet his appetite, and he could often be heard to joke that he was "sober as a gendarme," something he did not say that morning, since there were two gendarmes standing at the bar sipping black coffees to which Thomas—who knew them well—had added a little Calvados; they appreciated the gesture since persnickety regulations forbade them from drinking in public while in uniform, thereby forcing them to have aperitifs in the privacy of the police station. These two were examples of a dying breed. While their young colleagues were muscular, efficient and restrained, these veterans were paunchy, bone-idle and cheerfully corrupt: for many years, they had gotten drunk on the bottles of pastis and whiskey offered in exchange for their leniency with regard to minor driving infractions, and for their clemency in matters of illegal stills; they obligingly turned a blind eye to poaching in exchange for a promise not to reoffend and a share of the spoils, since deep down, these miscreants were fine upstanding men, not crooks or immigrants, and so did not warrant the full force of the law. These two were neither the keenest nor the meanest of cops; they were not locals, one of them hailed from near Ruffec, the other from Thouars, in other words the ends of the earth, but they had pounded the beat here for so long that people had all but forgotten this detail, since most of their colleagues and fellows officers came from all over France: the chief of police in Coulonges, for example—a real TV news cop with a singsong accent—was originally from Pyrenees-Orientales; being the son of a smuggler, he had always known he would have a close relationship with the forces of law and order, though for a long time he did not know on which side.

There was talk of cold and the coming snow, of hopes for a white Christmas; the gendarmes drained their coffees and climbed into their van to resume their idle wanderings, in no hurry to return to the station.

The mayor (handsome, ageless face, gray slicked-back hair) gave Thomas two new hunting notices to post behind the bar, notices he had received from the prefecture that morning. He had already posted them illicitly outside the town hall, but rightly assumed it would be more expedient to post copies behind the bar, where everyone could benefit from them. A number of fortunate species would enjoy a winter truce. Thomas glanced vaguely at the posters and pinned them willy-nilly on a bulletin board already crowded with more or less out-of-date notices about eel fishing, minimum landing size for anglers, and quotas for big game determined by the accredited communal hunting association, which had its headquarters at the Café-Pêche, as did the local soccer and pétanque clubs (as evidenced by the trophies on the shelf above the liquor bottles, and the pallid banners that had hung for eons from the aforementioned shelf). An observer possessed of a keener eye than the young anthropologist would have spotted Thomas himself, already a little tubby, in a faded photograph taken forty-five years earlier, standing to one side of his teammates, wearing a goalie's uniform and gloves; it was a photo that had been taken to mark the village team's victory in a junior subdepartmental tournament, where they had played brilliantly. Trophies were invariably provided by the local Crédit Agricole, as were the playing cards, the board games, the posters for belote tournaments, the pens used for scoring and all the prizes with the exception of pork products, which were extorted from Patarin, the local pork butcher.

All these people (tubby Thomas, Martial, Patarin, Gary and the others) had known each other since boyhood and no longer knew, after so many years, whether they thought of each other as friends; together or apart, they had tramped the fields with slingshots hunting birds, and despite their playground boasts of dozens of kills, most of them had only ever hit one, a fat tired crow that had languidly flown away after the outrage; they had half-heartedly used poles to shake walnuts from the trees in autumn; built secret hideouts in haystacks, to the despair of their mothers, since they came home covered with bruises and scratches, as they did when they slid off their bikes freewheeling down the quarry slopes. Every one of them had felt the sting of the strap and some the crack of their father's belt, which was a more effective deterrent. They had spent summer nights dozing in the cabs of tractors, and, when they were older, steering the trailer behind the harvester; as soon as they sprouted pubic hair they started hunting, and would forever remember the smell of their first shot and their first girl, neither a great success; together they had smoked the filler tobacco grown by the fathers of the luckier boys and got drunk for the first time at some distant cousin's wedding, earning them a vicious beating from their fathers. None, other than Martial, had studied after high school; all had grown up to be what their parents had been: farmers, bartenders, butchers and even undertakers.

The mayor downed his drink and was heading home just as

the bored anthropologist, with mingled delight and dread, saw Lucie's cousin, the pudgy simpleton Arnaud, arrive; he had come from the garage where Jucheau, the local mechanic, employed him—if the word is appropriate, since he was not paid any wages, or only a few coins that he hoarded like treasure in a box (his vault) fashioned from flat Meccano plates screwed together. Arnaud was a godsend to Jucheau: he never tired; if properly supervised he could do the work of two or three men in a day. Tire changes, oil changes, assembling and disassembling gearboxes and crankcases, these were his specialties. He knew nothing about the workings of engines, brakes or electricity, but put a wrench in his hand and he was king. That morning, he had rebuilt the engine of tubby Thomas's van and changed the fan belt; he felt very satisfied. That afternoon, he would change the oil, and feel just as satisfied; then, at home, he would gaze at the fire, at his cousin and his grandfather, eat his dinner, brush his teeth, pee, go to bed and be back at Jucheau's garage the following morning, and so on. The routine filled him with joy; there was nothing he loved more than repetition. Often, he had strange dreams, which he quickly shrugged off come morning, dreams in which he was sometimes an insect climbing a blade of grass, sometimes an owl haunting the night, sometimes a knight riding across the plains; when he woke, he would shake his head to dispel these images, the way people shake themselves when getting out of the water, and, inexplicably, all that lingered of these dreamlike escapades into the secrets of his past and future lives was an endless list of dates, dozens of recent or far-off events that he reeled off without understanding, but which earned him a few more coins and a little drink at the village café. Arnaud loved his cousin and his grandfather more than anything, and at the moment when the young boar vessel of Father Largeau's soul was grunting and foraging for food on the edge of a field, Nono was missing Lucie terribly; for a time, he had stared at the young man he had seen before, though he could not remember where, and made himself lunch, which in his case meant opening a can of something, pouring its contents into a dish from the sink, *his* dish, after carefully wiping away the existing food debris with his sleeve.

Then he ate greedily, because he was extremely hungry.

Then he belched, because he was full.

Then he went about his business, as the young ethnologist watched in dazed astonishment, and slept like a log in front of the fire.

*

Once upon a time, on the very spot where Lucie's grandfather's house is now, stood the château of the lord of the manor, the residence of mud-caked country squires whose coat of arms—gules three wolves, heads erased argent armed and langued azure—dated back to the Crusades and, according to family legend, had been granted them by Louis IX himself: it was, in truth, their sole fortune. They liked to claim they were kinfolk of the Rohans and the Lusignans; they owned a few serfs, a windmill, an oven and a patch of woodland. Some of their ancestors were buried in the local church, the others were buried around the grounds: the digging of cesspools sometimes saw these remains unexpectedly resurface from their eternal rest, and Lucie's dog, vessel of her grandmother's soul, often gnawed on the remains of patrician bones, knights and provosts marshal, bailiffs and seneschals, those whom history had forgotten after their castles were destroyed during the Revolution. The castle had been almost razed two centuries earlier during the Wars of Religion, when Protestant forces led by Louis de Saint-Gelais marched through on their way to occupy Niort, but the inhabitants had since recovered—the angry peasants in 1789 then succeeded where the Huguenot rabble had failed, and the building was burned to the ground. Little is known of what became of the family or its descendants thereafter; they had long since abandoned the castle by the time of the blaze, and would have been unaware of

the peasants' decisive victory; their goods and chattel were sold
together with those of the émigrés in 1794, and, aside from the
name "rue du Château" (where stray visitors would vainly look
about for some distinguished building), all memory of their time
here had disappeared. Lucie's house had been acquired in 1932
by her forebear, Jérémie, lackland farmer and protector to the
newborn bastard and its mother, together with the two adjoining
barns, which were later sold off and demolished. Jérémie was
eager to prove his manhood, to ease the wounded pride that, despite this money, still burned within him; he regularly mounted
his female, hoping, by an agonizing birth, to erase all trace of
the previous *membrum virile*. He labored at this task a year, then
two, but in vain. He brutally beat his wife, convinced that her
unwillingness was to blame, then abruptly changed his strategy,
stopped beating her, relieved her of all manual labor, all the while
redoubling his passion, but to no avail. The bastard child was
almost three years old. The very sight of this child, who called
him *peupâ* or father, saddened him; little by little this sadness
gave way to disgust, and eventually to virulent hatred. His wife
no longer knew which saint to beseech; she burned devotional
candles; she, who had never prayed before, would pray; like
many women in the village, she had visited the Standing Stone
by night, there to leave an offering to fairies and magical beings;
one August evening, at the full moon, she had even managed
to lure her husband to the river's edge, on the advice of a local
woman who attributed magical powers to celestial bodies and
shooting stars. She consulted Pélagie, the bonesetter, known to
everyone as the Witch, who, despite her spinsterhood, flaxen
hair and crooked nose, was not a witch. All in vain. Four years
passed. Still, Jérémie did not flag. He stubbornly persisted; he
became resentful. Rightly or wrongly, he believed himself to be
the laughingstock of the village; he no longer went to the café,
preferring to get drunk at home, since hard liquor was the only
thing that cheered him, hard liquor and cheap wine, which he

drank by the cask. His wife, Louise, would tremble when she felt her period coming on, and more than once was tempted to hide the cotton rags that betrayed her and earned her a vicious beating: Jérémie would end up in tears of rage and impotence at this flow of blood about which he understood nothing, except that it was the color of misery, reddish brown.

He began to beat the living daylights out of the bastard.

One night, weary of her husband's frantic assaults, terrified by the marks on her son's body, tired of the blows and the guilt, one night after a particularly difficult coupling, Louise sighed and said, There, you did it right, which was a comfort to Jérémie, who indeed felt he had done it right that night. She said nothing more. Two days later she smiled and whispered in his ear, you know, I think he's in there. Jérémie was surprised that she could feel it so soon, but she dismissed his questions, women know these things, and Jérémie, though he knew much about the wombs of cows, sows and the beasts of the field, wanted to believe her. Perhaps Louise believed it herself. Whatever the case, from that day, she refused his advances, it was important not to unsettle the newly attached babe, she would say, which sounded wise to Jérémie, who lavished attention on his wife. She experienced dizzy spells, nausea, weakness, Jérémie a trepidatious joy. Louise ate and ate and ate, she began to swell; not much, but she swelled nonetheless. She would cup her little belly, complain about her breasts which, she said, were getting larger; they seemed larger to Jérémie. The much-feared blood did not come; at least, Jérémie did not see it. Jérémie headed back to the café, proud as a pope; he bought drinks for the Chaigneau brothers; he bought drinks for Poupelain, the blacksmith; he bought drinks for Chaudanceau, the postman, and for the gamekeeper. Joyously, he drained a great number of snifters, a smile playing on his lips, telling no one the secret that was no secret to anyone. Being a good farmer, Jérémie was telling himself that hard work and perseverance always paid off in the end when, on February

17, 1940, an official from the prefecture, or perhaps the town hall, posted a conscription notice for agricultural laborers.

There, under the letter *M*, was the name Jérémie Moreau.

He was to report to Poitiers, where an infantry regiment was waiting.

They would have to face down the Krauts again; it was hardly surprising, his father had done it twenty years before; Jérémie remembered the day he left in 1917: the boy he had been back then had felt proud, proud and terrified. Needless to say, for some months, Jérémie had been vaguely aware that France was at war; a number of village men had already marched north—old man Patarin, Bergeron, Berthot—but he had not heard all the news, because the Maginot Line and Poland were far away, because he was having trouble with the cattle, and because his father-in-law had been working him like a dray horse. His wife's parents had a wireless that played pleasant music, but he had not heard a single news bulletin. The bastard was now at school, and would go until he turned twelve; Jérémie had only dim memories of his time there. He could read a little, and write a little too, having been taught during his military service, the same military that had now called him up to do his duty.

Louise was pregnant. Jérémie was supposed to leave the following Monday. So, he went to explain to the mayor that he couldn't because his wife was expecting; the mayor said that was not how things worked, that he would be granted a furlough when the baby was born, but he had to report for duty in Poitiers or the gendarmes would come for him. No one knows why the mayor did not inform Jérémie that he could justifiably claim to be his family's sole support and thereby avoid conscription for a time; the military authorities did not inform him either, perhaps because Jérémie, despite bearing the name of a prophet, was not much liked either by those who knew him or those meeting him for the first time.

Louise probably pretended to be sad, but not too much, since she did not want to panic her husband and drive him to desertion; she tried to reassure him, her parents would look after her, and he would soon be back on leave, when the child was born. She even found stirring words—defending his country, motherland, honor—words she had heard on the radio, words that gave Jérémie courage.

With a heavy heart, after one last monstrous drinking binge, he set off from the village with the Chaigneau brothers.

Louise felt relieved, somewhat, and also helpless; without a husband near, it was easier to feign pregnancy, but in the absence of the person most concerned, the pretense was pointless; she resolved to persist in her lie for a while, then lose the child. In the two months that followed, she slipped a small bag of oatmeal under her dress, and padded her brassiere; she had her photograph taken and sent it to the Ardennes, where Jérémie had been posted; he leapt for joy, showed his wife's new curves to the Chaigneau brothers, and shared his wine ration with them. It occurred to Louise that, in theory, she was now six months pregnant; she no longer knew how to shake off her deception. She avoided her mother, who was astonished by her behavior; she hid her body from her son; every morning she would tell herself that the little visitor had to die, but she did not know how, what excuse she could use, what she would have done with the fetus; the doctor would visit, what would she tell him, she could not sleep for thinking about it, she prayed for a miracle; in the north, the Phony War showed no sign of ending; Jérémie might come home on leave at any time; she was lost.

She had just turned twenty-five.

Twice a day, she forced herself to walk through the village to show her face; she would stop at the Café-Épicerie to buy something small, talk for a few minutes with the postman, then head home.

The only solution she could foresee was death. If she died, she would be buried before Jérémie came home, and no one would be the wiser.

A month passed and still she could not decide; her mother was increasingly worried about her, she was ashen, her eyes dark-ringed. Jérémie wrote to say that, at last, he would be coming home on leave the following week. I can't wait to see my little wife. Louise began to consider ways to die. Poison or drowning seemed most apt. Spring was glorious that year; shimmering sunlight caressed the trees.

One afternoon, she walked down to the river with a basket on her arm. She did not really know why she had brought the basket, so she would look self-assured, perhaps; on the way, it felt as though her belly really was heavy and hampered her progress, and she thought about how she truly wanted to have a second child. She pictured Jérémie as he was, a brute, a stone, or rather a bull. As she came to a line of trees along the riverbank, a ray of sunlight blazed through the leaves, caressing the carpet of rushes, duckweed, the bloom of algae; a few fish gulped at the surface sending small ripples spreading across the water; Louise sat on the bare ground, a stone's throw from the bank. She felt as never before the life force all around, the great Wheel of Suffering in which all living things were immersed, birds, dragonflies, the gnats buzzing at her ears. For a long time, she sat, motionless, her mind a blank.

Then she got to her feet and walked toward the river's edge.

*

When the young boar vessel of Abbé Largeau's soul first smelled the noisome odor of the human being—a mixture of vanity, cruelty and detergent—he was so scared that he ran to seek refuge in a bramble thicket so dense even he found it difficult to enter, and there he stayed, hiding, trembling, until he chanced to catch the scent of a dead squirrel and began to feed, and in doing so forgot the danger. The man whose stink he had smelled down-wind spotted him, and stopped, bewildered: what the hell was a young shoat doing in a field so close to the village; he thought he had been mistaken; it had probably been a dog, but he was sure he had seen a snout and a pair of tusks, bloody hell, this needed clarification, the possibility that such an animal would venture so far he put down to the bitter cold and the snow that had begun to fall. And so, Gary resolved to come back later with his shotgun and his dog and flush out the truth—wild boar for Christmas, that would be tasty—and continued to the Café-Épicerie-Pêche, where he had a coffee and chatted about the weather; tubby Thomas was waiting impatiently for the home hairdresser, whom he would ogle shamelessly as she ran the clippers around his ears, her heaving breasts right under the poor barman's glasses like the temptation of Tantalus. Thomas would allow himself to be lulled by the rasp of the metal and the jangle of the professional's bracelets; then he would give her an exorbitant tip, as he had done every month for years. The hairdresser was called Jacqueline, a name she hated, so she had renamed herself Lynn; she cut the hair of elderly men devoutly, performed a shampoo and set for ladies with kindness and humility, and organized get-togethers selling cosmetics—girls-only afternoons, she called them—where the neighborhood women painted their nails and tried different creams. Lynn dedicated the greater part of her intelligence to money, to getting it and spending it; the villagers would have been astonished to know the scale of her bank balance, which compared very favorably with that of the miserly Thomas or the funereal entrepreneur Martial. Everything went right for Lynn, or almost everything: the fickleness of men was her one cause for grief. She took a pained comfort in her profession and was happy to listen to the many middle-aged women who promised she would soon meet a Prince Charming, being so young and beautiful; she lied about her age, and no one other than her doctor and the taxman knew that she was thirty-five.

For Lynn, tubby Thomas would have sold his soul.

Around her, he was sometimes a slavering puppy, sometimes a strutting cockerel. He dreamed of suddenly being widowed, getting down on one knee to declare his love, offering her a handsome Peugeot convertible, taking her to a hotel by the sea where together they would feast on oysters and lumpfish caviar and drink champagne, all the things he associated with sensual pleasures.

Together, Lynn and her cleavage managed, in spite of themselves, to sustain Thomas's desire. Whether the hairdresser knew of her talent for seducing lechers, or the effect she had on the village men more generally, is impossible to know. A number of ladies in the area had long been deeply suspicious of this husband-thief, but as the years passed, they were forced to admit that Lynn had not stolen a single one. Indeed, she was quick to put those same husbands in their place with a sharp rap on the knuckles if they became too fresh; she would irritably button up her blouse whenever she caught old perverts, their eyes lewdly following her, their mouths gaping, leering at her breasts; but she forgave them, because at heart she enjoyed these harmless games which reassured her about her seductive charms. That old age could be seduced by youth, ugliness by beauty—what could be more natural. Even so, she avoided the more persistent offenders, like the old man with the big ears who groped himself through his pants whenever she approached, despite a clip around the ear from his granddaughter, who, as it happened, had been her best friend since primary school.

Gary was just finishing his coffee when Lynn arrived; behind the bar, Thomas was quaking; the hairdresser was dressed to the nines and in a particularly good mood, since that night she was meeting her secret lover. Lynn leaned across the counter, and kissed Thomas on both cheeks, then smiled when she saw she had left a trace of lipstick near his mustache, a trace she hastily rubbed away with a finger. This produced a fiery exhilaration in the proprietor, which he did his best to hide. Lynn politely greeted Gary, whom she did not know as well. Thomas managed to find the words to offer Lynn a cup of coffee, before she set to work; she accepted, and produced a surprise from her metallic gray briefcase: as every Christmas, she had printed up a calendar to give to her customers, a piece of folded cardboard that could be easily set on a desk or shelf. The photo depicted a traditional local boat known as a punt with a man standing in the prow propelling himself along a duckweed-covered river fringed with trees; Lynn didn't care that there had been no duckweed in the Marais Poitevin for years, probably a casualty of pollution and climate change. Below the photograph and the name Lynn Guérineau in cursive gold lettering, was her profession, "Beautician—Home Hairstylist," and her phone number. She gave calendars to everyone, a little pre-Christmas gift; Gary thanked her warmly and resolved to leave the calendar in a drawer, finished his coffee, set a coin on the counter and left the proprietor to his affairs; Thomas was preparing to retire to the back room to sacrifice his mane to Lynn. Lynn did not have many male clients; generally (she did not dare say "fortunately") men either visited barbershops or entrusted it to their wives who, armed with clippers or a pair of scissors, scalped them with scant ceremony. Lynn liked working in the countryside, she liked the narrow roads, the villages; she loved to see a deer on the edge of a forest or a rabbit hopping through a meadow, to surprise a snuffling hedgehog at night, to catch a glimpse of a carp at daybreak in the river Sèvre. Whenever she walked along the towpath running behind the old tannery near her house in Niort, which wound past mills and kitchen gardens, between two islands, two crumbling drystone walls, two weeping willows, where the city was quickly diluted by countryside before completely dissolving in the waters of the Marais, she reveled in nature's perpetual movement, felt part of the riotous illusion of the world: she loved this place for its fragility born of uncertainty, this rustle of indecision between the beautiful and the commonplace; she loved this city which was as one with the surrounding lands she drove through in her Renault sedan from dawn to dusk, Sainte-Pezenne, Saint-Maxire, Saint-Florent, Saint-Liguaire, Saint-Maixent, Saint-Rémy, Saint-Pompain, Saint-Pardoux, Saint-Christophe, Saint-Symphorien, Sainte-Macrine: a long succession of miracles that, to her ear, comprised a beautiful geographic poem, the map was a great reliquary, the GPS a hymn, even someone oblivious to the stories hidden behind such names could not help but sense that it was a region suffused with sanctity. Here, even more than the Romanesque churches that dotted the Poitou, the names of saints, male and female, conferred grace by the scattered confetti of their syllables. Lynn thought the hamlets and villages formed a farandole, an endless song: Taillepié, Pied-de-Fond, Fond, Fonderie, Riz, Riveau, Veau, Volière, and on, and on. Lynn loved Niort (that said, she had little point of reference, having never lived anywhere else) for the gentle undulation of its landscape, for the weather and other more mysterious reasons that she and the tourist office called "quality of life." Coulonges-sur-l'Autize marked the northerly boundary of her working area—Max's farm was perilously close to the border with the Vendée, which it was foolhardy to cross, since all the road signs on the other side pointed only to mysterious Chouan towns—Fontenay-le-Comte or Maillezais—so the unwary traveler was bound to go astray.

Outside, snow was still falling; Gary thought the snow was good for the soil, that it promised a temperate spring and an excellent harvest. He had no idea whether this was a scientific fact or stemmed from traditional wisdom, but it hardly mattered. Gary passionately loved his work. So ingrained had the work been since childhood that he did not think of himself as having a profession. True, as a teenager he had had dreams; dreams of high adventure, of airplanes, outlandish hunting trips, faraway safaris and wild beasts, but he had shrugged them off with no regrets; all that remained was a vague interest in wildlife documentaries and the programs on a cable channel that specialized in the exotic. Gary had never pushed his children to follow in his footsteps. He knew that his way of life, the one he shared with his parents, was dying out; that time was permanently changing customs and the countryside. Not that he felt nostalgic, but sometimes, like this morning, as he tramped the plains, keeping close to the hedgerows, between the fields brought low by winter, he could feel the irrevocable change more keenly.

Gary shook himself and shuddered, dispelling his somber thoughts; he pushed his cap down over his ears and hurried toward the house before the strengthening blizzard could turn him into a snowman.

*

Needless to say, Abbé Largeau, the last parish priest to live in the village, had no idea he would be reincarnated as a wild hog, just as he had no idea that he had previously been a frog, a crow, a boatman and many other things; he believed in heaven and hell, gardens of dead souls that went about their business, in ecstasy or agony, while they waited for the Resurrection of the Body, but no one can know whether the old priest truly believed in the existence of heaven and hell, or whether he accepted it as one more fact, a job lot with the Father, Son, Holy Spirit and the rest of it, renouncing reason for faith since childhood in the shameful fear of divine wrath. He had been born in the marshlands to a family of dairy farmers some thirty kilometers from here, in a vast, dark, dank house. Every spring, his father would take the cattle to pasture by boat, and Largeau remembered seeing him standing in the prow, using a long pole to punt the boat groaning a little under the weight of a docile old milker that placidly watched the passing trees, accustomed as she was to making the journey. Father Largeau had taken the boat out himself on summer evenings to milk the cows in fields ringed by water; he would come home, the small boat weighed down by milk, careful not to capsize by trying to moor too quickly. He remembered the first time he had been allowed to navigate alone through the creeks and ponds aboard a boat that, to him, seemed huge, and he had felt—God forgive him—like the king of the world. He owed his Catholic education and his steadfast faith to his mother, and to a priest from Damvix who ruled the village school with a rod of iron; the mysterious Vendée—even more than the other surrounding regions—was as steadfast in its Catholicism as a roadside cross carved from granite. As an altar boy, Father Largeau had been fascinated by catechism—he loved the stories, parables, scriptures, the martyred saints and holy relics—and so, after Catholic school, and despite the misgivings of his father—who privately felt that these religious trappings would turn his son queer, but dared not simultaneously defy his wife, the priest and God Almighty—the boy was admitted to Poitiers seminary, where, at twenty-five, he was ordained on the feast of Saint John, 1962. Father Largeau had an excellent memory, an ecclesiastical demeanor and an extensive knowledge of Sacred scripture; when celebrating mass, he sometimes committed the sin of pride by reciting rather than reading the Gospel, while staring his congregation in the eye. He could have aspired to a career in the church, a bishopric, a cathedral, a crosier set with amethyst—had he not completely lacked ambition. His one desire was to find "his little niche," as he put it; and so, he moved into the handsome presbytery adjoining the Romanesque church in the now familiar Deux-Sèvres village where, almost fifty years later, he would die, before scampering through the thickets as a young boar, the same boar that, having feasted on the squirrel's carcass, was now playing in the wet, cold snow. The boar thought he was encountering snow for the first time, not remembering that, for years and years, he had trudged these fields in an entirely different form, on two legs; he did not know that, in 1954, he had seen the marshlands so hard-frozen that he could have walked across the pods without wetting his feet; he knew nothing of the taste of eel or snails, the smell of incense, the nature of the Eucharist when taken from the ciborium, white and smooth as snow; still less the harmony of liturgical chant and the emotion that filled the priest's chest when he sang them on his first day. His was a small parish, but large enough for him. Father Largeau celebrated the baptisms and marriages of most of the characters in this story; he had known them as children; had buried many of their parents and made them weep for the memory of those they had lost, all of whom he addressed by their Christian names; he had allowed Mathilde to hold the monstrance when she was seven; he had fetched Gary and Thomas from school for last-minute funerals when they were altar boys: the teacher had always assented with a grave nod, not troubling to wonder whether this was in accordance with the tenets of the Republic; Largeau had been remunerated for special masses, when that practice was still common, and received many gifts of food and drink and money for the upkeep of the church, whose door he never locked, though no one had ever sought refuge there from the cold or the police. He had buried hanged men with a compassion that earned him the respect of the long-faced gravediggers; he had inspired parents to persuade their offspring to study at secondary school and even at university; he had loved his flock, forgiven drunkards and comforted their wives; in short, he had completely fulfilled all the obligations of his ministry. He might have been a saint, had he performed miracles, and had he not spent so much time frequenting the Café-Épicerie-Pêche on the pretext of encouraging his parishioners to spend less time there; had he been more abstemious, and, above all, had he not been possessed of an overwhelming passion for the mysteries of the bodies of women. All women, not simply the Virgin Mary; this was his tragedy: the vow of chastity he had taken at ordination still burned like a white-hot branding iron, but being reverent and devout, he had never once succumbed to the sin of lust. Largeau believed that this obsessive curiosity would fade and disappeared with time; this he had been assured of by his confessor, who advised him to seek strength in prayer, which he did; despite his best efforts, Largeau son of the Marais often remembered the only female body he had ever seen naked—not his mother, obviously, but a movie actress in a magazine shoved under his nose by a classmate at Catholic school, a picture he had quickly pushed away as though it were Satan himself; despite all his efforts the images of the starlet's round breasts, the glimpse of pubis between her slender legs had haunted him for years, and, at night, in the solitude of the presbytery, when Satan beckoned, he would have to pray for a long time, a very long time, before he managed to fall asleep. He had to replace his television with a radio to free himself of images; he dared not open the mail-order catalogs regularly pushed through his door for fear of stumbling on pages of scantily clad young women; in this way, he managed to impose on himself an iron law, to ward off sin and keep the devil at bay. He tried hard to forget that, as a boy, he had already been touched by the demon, in the person of a priest who was more affectionate than appropriate, of a soutane perhaps rougher than necessary, by a smell that was wilder and more feral than a pond at night; a memory so powerful and so troubling (a primal soup of memory and desire) that only his clammiest dreams, his most terrible nightmares dragged him back and, though no images appeared, forced him to relive the stench of suppressed violence and the devastating gasp of being forced to orgasm—Largeau would have struggled to tell anyone what he'd spent so long pretending not to remember, just as he would never have allowed himself to become close to a boy, even if he had wanted, a boy as young as he must have been at the time, in a terrifying confusion of bodies frozen in mingled fear and surprise, and such insinuations—which he heard from time to time on the radio, about other priests, other parishes—plunged him into a towering rage in which he railed against idle talk, against the profanities that sullied every impulse toward sanctity, tarnished faith with lurid innuendo whose noise drowned out the deep bass song of the divine. Everything was filthy, desecrated, and despite the confused memories, when he walked through the fields, keeping close to the blackthorns, the dog roses and rowans rustling with birds, or through the patch of woodland near La Pierre-Saint-Christophe among the ash trees and the field maples and the roadside cross on the chemin d'Ajasses between the twin oaks of Les Bordes, and Christ—the tree of life, a lone human figure amid all this vegetation—suddenly appeared, consoling the walker with his downcast gaze, Largeau, whom long years of day-to-day routine had not inured to this epiphany, would experience an instant of hope greater than he did during mass or when at prayer, would glimpse the fleeting glow of salvation and, for a moment, God was that invisible hill, that almost imperceptible curve of the plain before it disappeared forever from the walker's sight.

Years later, when Mathilde regularly came to the sacristy and devotedly tended to him, made his meals, and did his housework, when, helped on by age, he believed he had rid himself of his private turmoil, the devil returned, more handsome than ever, but in a very different form. Largeau would gaze at Mathilde, caress her with his eyes, he knew the beauty mark on her forearm, the rustle of stockings against her skirt, the curve of her breasts beneath her sweater, and as soon as she had left, he would pour himself a large brandy and pray that it might pass, Our Father who art in heaven, but alcohol did not help him shake off his concupiscence, quite the contrary, it lulled him into a sleep that he thought was dreamless since, the following morning, he was utterly unaware of the tricks played on him by desire during the night. From the wisps of fragmentary reality that dreams are made of, shame and flesh danced and twined; Largeau knew nothing of the journeys, the witches' sabbaths, in which his soul participated, the Baphomets and dragons upon which it rode into clouds haloed with moonlight. There, the priest would have recognized people from his childhood and, behind the myriad masks, the unchanging face of the eternal Enemy, despite the names he is given or the features he takes on.

By night, Largeau swam though this dark matter, and by day he was tormented by guilt and desire. Oblivion came only during masses and services, when he put on the white alb and the chasuble, or when he read the Sacred scripture, alone or in public, *And Simon Peter answered and said, "Thou art the Christ"; And he began to teach them, that the Son of man must suffer many things, and be rejected of the elders, and of the chief priests, and scribes, and be killed, and after three days rise again*, the Name has been spoken, everything has been said.

Mathilde could sense the priest's shame, and it made her sad. She was insightful, she could imagine Father Largeau's crisis as he struggled with desire; the love and devotion she felt for him were so unselfish that, had it been possible, she would have relieved him with her own hands, as one might help a child be sick or blow its nose, but she was held back by modesty, respect and, more especially, what she could discern of Largeau's deep faith. Mathilde understood; her empathy and kindness were such that she sensed and shared Father Largeau's sufferings, though she did not call them Satan, the devil, the Enemy or any such thing, she called them body, needs, passions, even temptations: those things that urge you into weakness. Mathilde wondered why Catholic priests could not simply marry, like Orthodox priests and Protestant ministers, who though heathens were Christians nonetheless. Never had Mathilde been faced with such meaningful looks, never had she been as aware of her body as through Largeau's eyes: as an outline appears only through the ink of the pen that traces it, so Mathilde was aware of her breasts, her shoulders, her legs, when Largeau's searching gaze brought them to life.

Father Largeau, who was sixty-five at the time, could feel his strength was waning. Not physically, but spiritually; he spoke to his confessor, who suggested a monastic retreat, or even taking

permanent retirement at a home. The priest elected to do neither. Courageously, he faced his demons alone, even if he now
prayed less and drank more and more plum brandy to numb his
senses. He would spend his days waiting for Mathilde to arrive;
he would say, Ha, my little Mathilde, how are you today, and
Mathilde would smile. He would study her from head to toe, and
each time he would see the picture of the naked actress from his
teenage years, perhaps because Mathilde's figure was somewhat
similar; then he would turn away and take another gulp of red
wine, or brandy, sometimes without even waiting for the object
of his passion to leave. Then he would pick up his book of hours,
or lives of the saints, and try in vain to take his mind off things.

Then he would go out for a walk, wander through the countryside while reciting Sacred scripture to the crows in the fields,
the dark murmurations of starlings against the clouds, and as he
wandered through the orchards near the river he would think
of the miracle of flowing water from the book of Ezekiel: *And
it shall come to pass, that every thing that liveth, which moveth,
whithersoever the rivers shall come, shall live: and there shall be a
very great multitude of fish, because these waters shall come thither:
for they shall be healed; and every thing shall live whither the river
cometh ... And by the river upon the bank thereof, on this side and
on that side, shall grow all trees for meat, whose leaf shall not fade,
neither shall the fruit thereof be consumed: it shall bring forth new
fruit according to his months, because their waters they issued out of
the sanctuary: and the fruit thereof shall be for meat, and the leaf
thereof for medicine*, a passage he had read so often in church,
and he would pick a few familiar leaves to make a tisane, then,
at length, having made a tour of the village, wondering how all
things could so sweetly sing the praises of the Creator and yet
also be the mark of His abandonment, he would head back to
the presbytery, there to surrender to the gathering night, to dereliction and to hooch.

God remained silent, leaving him alone to suffer his ordeal.

*

The Gypsy pushed his hat back from his brow, smiled and, through gritted teeth, spat the most terrifying curse in Serbian: of the four languages he spoke fluently, it was the one with the most terrible, graphic and frightening curses and imprecations, and if the young French gendarme had known what these strange sounds portended for the corpse of his mother, he would probably have beaten the shit out of the Gypsy (Gypsy, Romani, Traveler, Pikey: the gendarme in his ignorance fumbled for the correct nomenclature, since they were very different peoples, though all the same) and taken immense rage and considerable pleasure in doing so. But, misled by the young man's smile, he merely repeated his question, which was perfectly simple: Where d'you think you're going like that? The senior officer was standing to one side; you could never be too careful, he'd had his fair share of curious customers—he remembered one time, some years ago, when a particularly diabolical light-fingered Gypsy had relieved him of his own wallet out of sheer bravado—and of all the peoples he had encountered in his career as an officer (French, Italians, Arabs, Africans, even Corsicans), none were more volatile and mysterious than this people whose origins were so vague and undocumented that he barely knew what to call them. To a gendarme accustomed to the notion that every man had, at the very least, a country in the form of an area of land, an identity and the corresponding documentation (whether these papers were in order was a different matter), these elusive tatterdemalions represented the greatest possible danger, chaos, to such an extent that he was hesitant (except in cases of force majeure, i.e., a crime other than the simple fact of being there) to ask any question other than the one his experience had just whispered to his junior officer—Where d'you think you're going like that?— when within arm's length of the suspect. The Gypsy was so used to hairsplitting with the forces of law and order that he considered offering a more pointed insult, but he could see that this young gendarme was a greenhorn, eager to do the right thing, and in the presence of a superior, three things liable to make cops vicious. So, he stammered *thank you, thank you*, and slowly took a Romanian passport from his gray jacket. With a nod of his head and a casual air, the gendarme signaled to him to put his papers away before repeating his question, Where d'you think you're going like that? The Gypsy felt a faint dread, and began sweating under his hat, what did this man want from him, then he said, *home, home*, since he knew very little French, and doubted that the gendarme spoke Italian. The gendarme glanced at his superior, who discreetly signaled that the answer was satisfactory; so, they thanked the Gypsy, wished him good day and Merry Christmas and continued their tour of the bustling market, the last before the holidays: the local farmers were out in force and there were a few stalls selling stewed eels and the legs of frogs whose passports, had anyone thought to ask, were also Romanian; the appealing scent of garlic and fried food drifted through the covered market, mingling with the maritime fragrances of the fish stalls where crabs gaped and a few lobsters dribbled next to resolutely tight-lipped oysters, blind in their shells, and unaware that their days were numbered and that, soon, burned by lemon juice or shallot vinegar, they would end up in the great dark tube of acid from which none returns. Here, hundreds, indeed thousands of souls to which no one gave a thought lay waiting in fridges, on beds of ice, in baskets, to be returned to the abyss only to be reborn, again and again, in one form or another, while the fishmonger, grabbing fistfuls of shellfish to stuff into bags, or the farmer's wife, pulling live rabbits from cages by the ears, paid not the slightest heed to these living creatures, or to the fact that they had once been humans, insects or birds. The two gendarmes gave no thought to this either; they were making their rounds, as they say; the senior officer saw Lucie at her stall selling fruits and vegetables and, in a low voice, said to his partner, We know a thing or two about her, and the junior officer gave him a knowing look, though obviously he had no idea what was meant; the senior officer also jerked his chin at a beekeeper selling honey, a friend of the aforementioned Lucie, who was known to the police. On a neighboring street, the two gendarmes stopped to study a stall selling belts and handbags, paying no attention to the young ethnologist David Mazon, who was vainly looking for a Christmas present for his paramour.

The Gypsy had kept an eye on the two uniformed officers to make sure they were no longer following him, and once he decided they were far enough away, he took from his hat the sign written for him by a kind friend: *No money, six young children, please help*. In fact, he had only three kids, and they were no longer very young, but he assumed, albeit somewhat naively, that this slight exaggeration would earn him public sympathy. So he moved through the milling customers and, holding the hat like a bowl in his left hand, and the cardboard sign in his right, he began to beg; the women sent him packing with a scornful sneer, folding their arms over their shopping baskets lest Émir should steal a lettuce or a radish, which filled him with a furious desire to do precisely that; he forced himself to smile, to say thank you, thank you, to those who gave him nothing; a comical greengrocer thought it would be funny to give him a huge carrot that was more of an inconvenience than anything, but Émir thanked him profusely and slipped it into his jacket pocket. Half an hour later, he had collected one euro and seventy-five centimes, a carrot and two apples—not great pickings for a Christmas market. Refusing to admit defeat, he wandered through the adjoining streets lined with stalls selling various wares, passed David Mazon, who gave him another euro and was tempted, out of professional curiosity, to ask the beggar where he was from and how he'd ended up here but bit his tongue for fear of offending or frightening the Romani; the Gypsy thanked him and continued on his way, until he saw the gendarmes, doggedly persistent, reappear on the corner. He sighed, donned his hat, decided that was enough for the morning; though he had only three euros, two apples and a carrot, he had no desire to end up in the cells. Since a pogrom had chased him out of a makeshift camp on the outskirts of Milan, where his children were attending school, he had passed through an assortment of grim places; he and five other families had been driven out of the Lyon suburbs where he had wound up, having crossed the Alps and sojourned briefly in Grenoble; he had traveled north to Paris, only to be forcibly ejected from the less-than-welcoming suburb of Seine-Saint-Denis, where he had been temporarily living on a patch of wasteland—the Gypsy had grown up on the banks of the Vršac Canal in Serbia, near the Romanian border; he had spent time on the outskirts of Belgrade and later Timişoara, but when Romania joined the European Union, he had decided to head west with fifteen other families. Little did he imagine that he would end up so far west that he was separated from the Atlantic only by a stretch of marshland. He had endured segregation, racism, violence, but in the end, despite the determined efforts of the gendarmerie and the hostility of the locals, he decided that he liked this region, flat as the back of his hand, which reminded him of Vojvodina, though the river Sèvre didn't look much like the Danube. In previous lives, the Gypsy had been a horse, a woman and an eagle, an eagle that flew over the mountains between Greece and Albania, a fact of which he was unaware, except for moments in the depths of his dreams when great cliffs would rise up and he would soar above them, carrying tremulous rodents snatched from the ground whose blood filled his sharp beak before they were ripped apart by hungry eaglets in the shelter of two rocks near the peaks. These images would haunt him for a time when he woke—the agony of childbirth, then the pleasure of being born; galloping through the smell of hay; gliding high, borne up by the heat of summer crags—and then they would fade, as dreams do in everyone but the mad and the illuminated.

At that very moment, David Mazon, rural ethnologist, was

deep in conversation with Lucie at her vegetable stall, which was poorly stocked since it was the end of December, so there was little aside from some Swiss chard, turnips, carrots, potatoes, cabbage, a few heads of lettuce and some leeks. Still, that morning, she had had lots of customers buying trimmings for their Christmas chickens, guinea fowl and capons. Lucie also sold white mushrooms, or rather those white agarics called "champignons de Paris" because they used to grow in the catacombs over the bones of the dead (Lucie bought hers near Saumur, a dozen crates of manure seeded with mycelium harvested from the deep, labyrinthine caves carved into the chalky banks of the Loire by water and time), she sold dried onions, plaits of beautiful pink garlic and bouquets of herbs (a few sprigs of thyme wrapped in two bay leaves and tied with a strand of pretty colored wool, a bouquet garni whose price per kilogram, as Lucie was the first to admit, eclipsed the price of Alba white truffles, or very nearly). David quickly realized he could not keep hanging around pestering Lucie with questions about the use of fertilizers and pesticides in market gardening, since there was a growing line of impatient customers and Lucie herself had started to irritably drum her fingers on the brown paper bags she used to pack up purchases. Lucie had a weighing scale that also served as a cash register, weighing, reckoning, tallying and printing a receipt on which, in addition to the weight and the price of the produce, was a nice little message, *Bee & Bean Ltd. wishes you a Merry Christmas and a prosperous New Year*. But, aside from David Mazon, endowed as he was with the perspicacity of the high-level academic, few customers noticed this philosophical play on words. So, the young student of ruralism reluctantly brought to a close his conversation with Lucie, from whom he was considering buying a few vegetables that might provide a healthier diet than the frozen pizzas and tins of Heinz™ baked beans that he feverishly consumed, but decided against the purchase on account of his culinary incompetence, and resumed his tour of the market—he liked the little redbrick markets with their cast-iron pillars and carved stone pediments mounted with the sort of clock one might see on a train station, where they still posted bylaws relating to "the allocation of market pitches and the levies imposed on measured goods," according to which the sale of a small basket of eggs incurred a levy of twenty centimes, as did the sale of blackbirds, thrushes or larks, while the levy for a kid goat was one franc: David Mazon was astonished that people were permitted to sell (and, presumably, *eat*) blackbirds and larks—why not crows or starlings?—and would have been surprised to learn that, when plucked and marinated, such birds were used to make perfectly acceptable kebabs and pâté en croûte.

*

When Lucie's grandfather, at thirteen, found his father hanging from a joist in the barn, eyes rolled back, neck snapped, face slightly blue, arms rigid and fingers splayed, he stood in the door-way, frozen with grief and terror, unable to scream, unable to tear his eyes from the levitating corpse but without noticing some-thing that would later amuse the gendarmes and gravediggers, the hole in his grandfather's left sock through which a fat, accusatory toe pointed at the door, at least a meter above the clogs that had fallen onto the straw. Lucie's grandfather did not come to his senses, any more than he fainted or ran away. He simply stood there, bolt upright, his mind blank, emptied suddenly by shock and terror, and later, when the gendarmes had cut down the body and the gravediggers had done their drunken business, he would have no memory of his discovery or what he had seen, nor who had called for help, since his brain quite simply refused to imprint these images on his memory, just as his mind refused to accept what everyone knew, namely that he was not the son of Jérémie Moreau, the poor bastard who had hanged himself. He cried a lot at the burial, and people took pity on him, but the priest—Father Largeau's predecessor—did not and refused to

celebrate funeral mass for a suicide, and entrusted the corpse
to the drudges of the sorrowful countenance who hurriedly
bestowed it in the corner of the cemetery where his wife had
been laid to rest, here lies Jérémie Moreau, 1911–1945, before going off to drink and to celebrate Victory after their fashion, for
it was May 1945, spring had come, the wheat was high and the
Germans defeated. The Teutonic troops had retreated from the
region some months earlier, triggering a spontaneous rallying of
young men to the French Forces of the Interior and the Resistance more generally. They made the most of this to plunder the
properties of collaborators, rape some pretty women and tramp
across the plains with guns and white ribbons on their sleeves;
they'd had their fun, but now, gradually, order was being restored
and, with it, routine. The elder of the Chaigneau brothers came
home from a POW camp to learn that his brother had died two
years earlier; he wept with rage and shame, then visited his grave
in Niort with Chaudanceau, the postman, and together they had
gotten drunk in a little bistro near the market. They also talked
about Jérémie the hanged man but did not dwell on the subject,
as though they feared his dismal fate might somehow rub off
on them, particularly the elder Chaigneau brother, whose conscience was anything but clear and who was already distraught
to learn of his brother's death; as they downed their shots, he
chanted, My God my God my God—he knew no other form
of prayer. Then, passably inebriated, they got a ride back to the
village with Patarin the butcher in his truck.

And so Lucie's grandfather was an orphan; he began to work
the land; his family nurtured a hatred for him that was unspoken but effective. Without knowing why, the young man grew to
adulthood in bitterness and fear. The barn where he had found
his father with a rope around his neck was sold off, then demolished; the death of his mother was a constant rupture that he
thought he could repair by marrying. He wed a girl named Marie,
about whom we know nothing beyond the fact that she bore

two children, one male, one female, and, after a wretched life, was reborn as the dog we have already encountered. Meanwhile, the recently appointed village schoolmaster, Marcel Gendreau, a graduate of the École normale and a native of Échiré—in other words, an alien world some fifteen kilometers away—a lover of literature and poetry, got wind of Louise's story and Jérémie's terrible fate; how he did so, no one knows, but there is never a shortage of tongues to spread stories of misfortune. The schoolmaster, having heard the story, felt sorry for the child; he pitied Louise and Jérémie, the hanged man with the hole in his sock; he discreetly questioned the surviving Chaigneau brother, who shared his memories of the Ardennes over one, two, numerous glasses of white wine. Marcel Gendreau also spoke to the gendarmes, who were more forthcoming than the tight-lipped gravediggers. He questioned Pélagie, whom he, unlike the rest of the village, did not dare call the Witch; she told him of her own troubles, the violence she had suffered, prescribed herbs to relieve his aching knees. He even spoke to Louise's son, in whose home he spotted a small black wooden frame containing the photograph of his round-bellied mother, pregnant, the young man told him, with his stillborn younger brother. Gendreau began to set down the story of Louise's misfortunes, a tale he considered edifying, since she had been the victim of the calumny of simple souls. He had previously, in 1948, published a number of poems in a now-forgotten magazine; he loved the land and the people of the land. In his book, he described the countryside, the harvests, the steam-powered threshers, the cattle, the milk collections, the cooperative dairy; he depicted the miserly farmers and the profligate, the scandalmongers and their spite; he tried to portray the animality of desire and the burden of duty. What is certain is that he spent hours in the lamplight, struggling to find the right words, sketching customs and characters, striving for accuracy and truth, and, within a year, he had covered seventy pages in a neat, elegant hand with no crossings-out, since he had twice recopied the manuscript. Marcel Gendreau did not intend to publish at someone else's expense, so he went to Chiron Printers in Niort, who printed a hundred magnificent copies on heavy cream laid paper in an elegant typeface with engraved drop capitals. The compositor who set the text was moved to tears by the story, and therefore made a few errors, but nothing serious; the cover bore the title *Nature Compels* ... with three portentous dots, and the legend "Published by the Author." Proud and excited, Marcel Gendreau treated himself to a taxi to transport the ten carefully wrapped bundles back to the village. The following day he entrusted three copies to Chaudanceau, the postman: one to be sent to the inspector of schools, since Gendreau respected hierarchy and bureaucracy; one for the Niort public library, since he wanted everyone to be able to read this story; and one for the local newspaper, because he deludedly hoped it might be worthy of review. Then he personally delivered copies of *Nature Compels* ... complete with courteous dedications, to the mayor and the local vet, and awaited their reactions, somewhat nervous, but satisfied.

*

As David Mazon the pretentious anthropologist poured half a bottle of bleach over the red annelids taking over his bathroom, he was unaware that he was returning to the Wheel the black souls of murderers whose vicious crimes had condemned them to many generations of suffering, blindly slithering in the damp; cheek by jowl were Marseil Sabourin, sent to the guillotine in 1894, and little Chaigneau, sent to the guillotine in 1943, together with their executioners, the infamous Deibler and Desfourneaux: having been dissolved by the bleach, they were almost instantly reincarnated in precisely the same form, and the young ethnologist was most surprised the following morning to find the same wretched creatures and their threnody of silent moans; one of the local murderers had killed his own sister, the other the gendarmes who had caught him poaching, now both were slithering toward the faint light, together with their accusers, the Lord High Executioners and the prosecutors responsible for their sentencing, doomed to endless suffering, since no one yet had shown compassion for these tiny worms, certainly not the two cats adopted by David who now watched with a discreet smugness as he poured poison on them. The Felidae were artfully licking their paws and dreaming, unaware that two years earlier, they had been a drunken writer and an inveterate liar of an actress who died together in a car crash on the nearby highway, an accident caused by the former's drunkenness and the latter's tantrums—their mutilated bodies had been pieced together after a fashion by the gravediggers, saddened by the youth and beauty of the actress, whom they knew by name; the writer's head they replaced upside down, his sticky hair against the blackened neck, out of revenge, since they did not know him and blamed him for his own death and that of his companion, but also those of the local family who had been quietly driving home when he drove into them at top speed.

Of these previous lives, the cats retained a supercilious demeanor and useless indolence, forced to beg for their food and rub up against David for a little warmth, as once they had rubbed up against journalists and benefactors, and, contrary to the ethnologist's notions, they looked at him only to earn a rain of kibble or a soft bed, and deeply disdained his shameful activities in front of that box of flickering blue images on which the appearance of a young woman in lacy negligee did nothing to hinder their night vision.

Having sluiced the murderers and their executioners into the abyss, David shuddered, took off his dressing gown and took a long shower; beneath the scalding spray he fashioned fevered dreams of glory, leading, twenty years later, to a chair at the Collège de France, and to various honorary doctorates (ideally Oxford, Harvard and Chicago) and a well-deserved

Nobel Prize, the first awarded to an anthropologist, and a place in the Académie française, the seat formerly occupied by Lévi-Strauss, obviously, the only seat appropriate to the overweening pride of its young occupant. He was happy and smiling as he emerged from the warm mist of the bathroom and dressed before reluctantly setting down to work for a good ten minutes before diving into the rabbit hole of internet sites devoted to the natural sciences; he was spellbound by the perverse sexuality of gastropods, the reproductive cycle of invertebrates, principally earthworms; he carefully avoided porn sites and, proud of his moral fiber, embarked on a virtual conversation in cyberspace with other doctoral students, and emerged from the liana of data communications faintly depressed, feeling that others were more advanced, more determined than he was, and would beat him to the finish line of academic honors, a competitiveness that paralyzed rather than stimulated him. In vain, he tried to return to his work, only to become lost in lascivious contemplation of the photograph on the desk of his girlfriend, this woman he believed that he loved passionately because he passionately desired her, then he got up, stroked the cats and fed them, glanced at the outside thermometer, wrote a few lines in his field diary, paced around, made a quick inventory of his foodstuffs, looked at the thermometer again and left.

He mounted the ancient white Peugeot 103 moped, pedaled furiously to no avail while it was on its stand, scratched his head and returned to his apartment before reemerging and wheeling the moped as far as the gate.

David Mazon was reasonably slim, with dark hair and eyes, something he attributed to his father's origins in the Vaucluse, though he knew very little about the Vaucluse. His arrival had been the subject of much gossip and speculation in the village; people wondered whether they should be flattered or offended by the sudden interest of scientists in their region. I mean, come on, we're not savages, grumbled tubby Thomas; on the other hand, Martial, the mayor, was delighted: this might stop Brussels from making stupid decisions, he argued, though no one knew quite how one related to the other, which was hardly surprising, since everything relating to the European capital (and capitals in general) seemed obscure and arbitrary. Gary's comments on the subject were a vote of confidence in favor of David Mazon: one would be hard pressed to find someone more upstanding and re-spected in the village than Gary, so if he said that the young man was trustworthy, and did not look down on anyone a priori, quite the reverse, the village toed the line. David was an outsider, and fell into the category of outsiders who are not straightforwardly despised, like the English, who, when all was said and done, paid in sterling and had some claim to the land since, eight hundred years before, Richard the Lionheart reigned over the region, as attested by a number of plaques and signs erected by the depart-mental tourist authority determined to keep the manna from En-gland (from moving further south), signs emblazoned "Route of the Kings of England." That the Kings of England had passed this way was indisputable, but unlike James and his wife Kate, they had paused only to groom their horses, and indeed James con-stantly reminded his wife that he was not some medieval fucking monarch, pleading for them to move back to Britain as soon as possible, where there was a pool table in every bar and a friend at the bottom of every pint of ale. Kate would reassure him, en-courage him to be patient, insist that the plumber would come eventually, the roofer would find an opening in his schedule, the tanks in the attic would soon be repaired, that everything would be fine and they would be happy, which, all things considered, they already were, despite the minor problems, especially after 5 p.m., gin o'clock, when James and Kate silently repaired to the whitewashed wicker chairs on the veranda, each with a book in hand and their first drink of the evening.

In the late afternoon, when David Mazon phoned to request an interview, they were already savoring their first G&Ts and engaging in one of their favorite arguments about the comparative merits of the kingdom of France and verdant Albion, an argument that, as we know, invariably began with an advantage to the latter, followed by a dangerous challenge by the former, thanks to a gastronomic-climatic counterattack by Kate, and ended in a last-minute draw due to James's bad faith and some fallacious arguments involving climate change suggesting that vineyards and date palms would grow as far north as the Scottish borders. Kate had been surprised by the phone call, and her initial reaction was wary: the young man claimed to be a friend of their uncouth neighbor Maximilien, which did not augur well. But the young anthropologist had one cardinal virtue, honesty, a candor that was instantly apparent; so Kate allowed herself to be persuaded by the scientist's disarming sincerity and agreed to meet with him, which of course prompted a furious response from her husband, though only on principle, since in fact he felt rather flattered: it was novel for France to take any interest in him other than to collect some obscure local tax.

For now David was running a hair dryer over his moped in an attempt to deice it. Outside, snow had begun to fall again, much to the anthropologist's despair: he pictured himself starving to death in the blizzard; having eschewed remote expeditions precisely to avoid the vicissitudes of the weather and the repulsive fauna, he now found himself caught between the two. He thought about Paul-Émile Victor, about *Apoutsiak, the Little Snowflake*, a favorite childhood book which had inspired his vocation for ethnology, and he steeled himself; come on, cheer up, there are people in the world who hunt seals by making holes in ice. He returned to his digital journal, where he'd already set down his thoughts about his dinner the previous evening with Maximilien Rouvre, the Parisian artist, who was also feeling cold that morning in his vast atelier, very cold, as he worked away, tackling the nine hundred and ninety-second photograph of his magnum opus, cursing and swearing in his eagerness to immortalize this instant. He connected his camera to the umbrellas, the flash reflected off the white porcelain. One more, he thought with satisfaction, one more, meaning one more step toward the end, the end both of the work and of his own life. Max brought up the photo on his magnificent screen: nothing special; he zoomed in to focus on the material, the texture, increased the contrast a little, looked for clues that might suggest a color, found an area of the shot where reds (at least according to the software) were more present and boosted them further; he then printed off the photograph at 24 × 32 cm on special paper, took his paintbrushes and subtly enhanced it with small touches of a dark purple, the color of beet. Then he studied the results from a distance; perfect; he placed a small bead of special paste on the back, took out the stepladder and affixed the photograph next to the others on the vast wall of the former byre. He had only about two weeks' work left before it was finished; there would be precisely twelve photos per square meter, almost six hundred in total. Naturally this number, and his time frame, were arbitrary, dependent as they were on the size of the gallery. All the photographs were digital so, if need be, he could enlarge the size of his work for a truly vast space. Indeed, he had already selected a dozen of the most impressive shots (such as those taken following the ingestion of methylene blue) for an unlimited series to be exhibited (and sold) separately. Maximilien was convinced that *The Bristol Scale: Autobiographical Droppings* would be a howling success. No one else had yet seen the work; he kept it hidden from everyone, from his art dealer, his friends and his occasional mistresses. Only Lynn had glimpsed the as-yet-unknown masterpiece: she had felt so completely distraught, so tainted, so besmirched, that she ran out of the studio, her stomach heaving in her mouth. Like the young woman and the secret room in the tale of Bluebeard, she had taken advantage of Max's absence—he had headed off on his motorbike to buy croissants—to have a look at this work he kept hidden from her. By the time Max came back, she had

already absconded, taking a small byroad in order to avoid meeting him.

Max had not understood the reason for Lynn's sudden disap-
pearance and, without knowing why, had felt a little bruised—he
had supposed that he did not care about their relationship. True,
Lynn had already been shocked by the subject of a number of
Maximilien's paintings that hung in the living room; she had also
been a little terrified by the artist's sexual fantasies, which she
had so far refused to gratify, but she was quick to forget the fail-
ings of men, especially men who were sophisticated and really
knew how to live, as she put it, meaning that they would happily
open a bottle of champagne for an aperitif and lay a sheepskin
rug in front of the fire. (When she naively remarked to Maximilien, during the boozy dinner that preceded their first coitus,
that there was no rug or animal hide in front of his hearth, Max
smiled; he said, don't worry, I'll slaughter a heifer tomorrow, I
promise, and when Lynn had returned two days later, she had
been surprised to see not a cowhide, but the lush white pelt of
some sort of alpaca, bought from a secondhand shop, that sen-
suously reminded Max of certain Swedish films from his youth
and which, his painterly eye considered, would perfectly complement Lynn's ample curves and colorful underwear [sea green,
blood orange]: he immediately suggested that they christen it,
she blushed.)

But the studio was beyond the pale. Max was a pervert of the
kind that required a shrink: discovering the secret chamber of
Bluebeard with its thousand horrors prompted Lynn to flee,
trembling with rage and revulsion, and to decide that she never
again wanted to see this man whom she had believed, for several
weeks, was her long-awaited prince.

*

Louise, who was Lucie's great-grandmother, spent a long time
on the riverbank; she stood, motionless, boots in the mud, a

few inches from the water, contemplating the teeming life that surrounded her. She did not know how to swim. She imagined herself drifting downstream with the current, her floating hair like a prow, to the swamplands where carrion feeders would devour her body before it was found, bloated and purplish, stripped half-naked by the waves, some days later. Recalling the huge carcass of a cow she had seen pulled from the canal, a great balloon of putrefaction, she made her decision: she would not die today.

She hiked up her skirt, took out the little sack of oatmeal and emptied the contents into the river; the seeds would be carried away by the current, she thought, or perhaps the fish would profit from her dissemblance. She wept with relief, put the burlap sack in her basket, dried her tears and walked home, happy that the drama was finally over. She would seek refuge with her mother and tell her everything; she would send her father to talk to Jérémie, who would be forced to face facts, and that would be that. She felt ready to face the sly looks of the scandalmongers, the smiles and the mockery—never mind.

Her mother made a dreadful scene, but took her in. Her father slapped her, hugged her, slapped her again, and cursed the man who, ultimately, was responsible for this new shame.

Over in the Ardennes, holed up in one of the wide meanders of the Meuse, Jérémie was preparing to leave at dawn the following day; he was supposed to take the first truck to Reims, then a train to Paris, and another to reach Niort. He slipped the photo of the pregnant Louise into his pocket with his military papers, packed his kit bag, shared the remains of his wine ration with the Chaigneau brothers, who did not have his good fortune and would have to freeze their asses off in the forest, sitting on logs, waiting for a spring that seemed as though it would never reach these parts.

Jérémie was about to climb aboard the military truck heading for Reims via Charleville when the news broke: the German army had invaded Belgium as part of a fearsome offensive toward the south: all leave was canceled.

Nothing is known of Jérémie's actions and gestures in the en- suing six weeks, aside from one or two incidents; no one knows, for example, how he became separated from the Chaigneau brothers, one of whom was later taken prisoner and the other discharged in the summer of 1940, nor how, given that he was posted in eastern France, directly in the path of the German ad- vance on Sedan, he found himself in Dunkirk where he, together with members of his company, boarded a boat for Dover; he nar- rowly missed being burned to death or drowned with the eighty people aboard when the vessel was hit by a bomb; he was shiv- ering with cold when, by some miracle, he was pulled from the channel by a British minesweeper; he spent three days feverish and in a state of shock before coming to his senses in a make- shift camp for French soldiers some miles from the coast. In a blind panic, arrangements were made to send the soldiers back to France—perhaps in the belief that they could keep fighting.

Three weeks later, France signed an ignominious armistice in the very same train carriage where it had humiliated Germany twenty years earlier; finding himself in unoccupied France, Jérémie did not hesitate. He resolved to go home. He had fought, he had seen others die around him, by chance he was not among the hundred thousand corpses that military and civilian grave- diggers put into the ground. His country had been defeated; what more could he do; Louise and his unborn child were wait- ing, it was time to head back to the village.

Like most soldiers who had not been taken prisoner, Jérémie was discharged; in Limoges, he returned his rifle and his uni- form, but was permitted to keep his underwear and his gloves as a souvenir. He found it very strange to see German soldiers standing guard outside the prefecture and the train station when he eventually caught a train to Niort a month and a half after his promised furlough. He was gaunt, tired, and his eyes were dimmed by the wild shadow of those who have seen action.

Louise was secretly praying that he was dead; the chaos of those weeks was such that it was impossible to get news about anyone. Here and there, refugees camped out in strange, somber holiday; some had mattresses, clothes, provisions; others had nothing, slept under the stars and wandered, lost and aimless, unsure whether they should head for their homes three or four hundred kilometers away.

In La Pierre-Saint-Christophe, the people were surprised one morning to see a coach arrive full of orphans from northern France; the children had been traveling for two weeks, the bus smelled worse than a chicken coop; the driver had long since been overtaken by German troops, which might have lent a comical air to the flight but for the war, fear and devastation all around. The villagers received the children with good grace, promising to send them home when the hostilities had ended, and the driver headed back, with numerous claps on the back for his pains and some saucisson for the journey, though no one quite understood why he had elected to deposit his boisterous cargo here—then they realized the orphans were nothing of the sort; to hear them talk they all had families, in Charleville, in Rocroi, in Auvillers-les-Forges, so many remote, exotic locations. The imperiled youth of the country were shared among the families of La Pierre-Saint-Christophe and the surrounding villages like a precious commodity, just as, a year earlier, people had taken in exiled Polish soldiers when their country was invaded by the Germans: several thousand men and countless horses had set up camp near Parthenay, before heading off to rejoin the fight near Belfort and spending the rest of the war billeted in Switzerland.

By the time Jérémie reached Niort from Limoges via Poitiers, it was very late; much too late to travel onward by public transportation. But he was determined to get home that night, so he visited some of the taverns he knew around the market and had a couple of drinks; no one knows whether he encountered a familiar face; all we know is that, with scant regard for the curfew, he arrived back at the village around midnight, after an hour's ride on a borrowed bicycle. The scents of the harvest filled the night spangled with bright, ominous stars. Jérémie could feel his heart pounding. He was about to see his wife again, particularly her belly, which by now would surely be very swollen; he hoped this birth would blot out the humiliations, the suffering and the terror, not just the vicious gossip, but also the memory of fighting, of the English Channel ablaze, of the bombs; he hoped that, in the morning, he would set out to the harvest with the others, reap his father-in-law's grain and store it in the barn while waiting for the threshing machine, as he had done the year before and the year before that; then, his son (he knew the child was a boy) would be born and that would be that. The little stone cottage in which Lucie would live seventy years later was sunk in darkness; Jérémie was hesitant to knock or call out; in the end, he did not dare; he went around the other side so he could go through the barn, whose door was always open, and not startle Louise and the bastard, who were probably asleep.

The heavy wooden latch was obviously in place because, try as he might, he could not open the door. But, after all, there was a war on. It was sensible for Louise to barricade herself in. He went back to the front door and resigned himself to knocking, gently at first, then, getting no response, more and more loudly. He finally pounded the door with his fists for a moment, suddenly feeling ashamed to be standing outside his own house, knocking like some stranger, as though he had been gone for years. At a loss, he imagined all manner of catastrophe; he who had become so familiar with corpses pictured Louise, dead, carted off by the gravediggers to the next world. Of course he considered heading straight to his in-laws; he could hardly bear to humble himself, to play the man who comes from afar to find his wife is gone, but in the end he resigned himself, he had no other choice. So, he walked up the rue du Château toward Louise's father's farm, passing the three village shops which were closing up; the son of Poupelain the blacksmith was standing outside, enjoying the warm evening air with Chaudanceau, the postman; they had obviously had a lot to drink since, despite the lateness of the hour, they hailed him loudly, Jérémie, Jérémie Moreau, and they welcomed him like two puppies, dancing around, grabbing his sleeve and dragging him into the bar where old Longjumeau was wiping down the counter: he shot them a black look, then, recognizing Jérémie, said, So y'er back, then, They say ye lost the war, ye bloody fool; Jérémie's face froze, Longjumeau added, Come on, then, I'll stand you a round, one more the Krauts won't get to sup. Jérémie was tense; the three men bombarded him with questions, about the front, about the rout, about the Chaigneau brothers whom no one had heard a word from since the Ardennes, which now seemed an eternity ago; they filled him in on village events, on those who had already come home (old father Patarin, posted to Limoges, discharged without seeing a single Nazi; Lebleu, wounded during the winter, one foot frozen solid, discharged; Bergeron, in a stalag; Belot and Morin, dropped off yesterday by a truck, and even Marchesseau, the vet, called up to tend to mules for an artillery regiment, who had managed to find his own way home) and those who were still missing, including him, Jérémie, who naively attributed the three men's awkwardness to their guilt at not having fought, while in fact they were pestering him with questions to avoid talking about Louise and the make-believe child, which they all knew about since they had wives, mothers and sisters to paint the picture. They did not ask Jérémie where he was going, or what he was doing here at this hour when he could be home with his wife, and, while Jérémie was not particularly intelligent, he was shrewd enough to guess that something was wrong; he had the first pangs of shame, he felt half-drunk, drunk and exhausted; he drained his third glass and, whereas, according to universally acknowledged custom, it should have been his turn to buy a round, he made his excuses, said his wife would be waiting for him, and slipped away, leaving the three men so dumbfounded they dared not say anything to keep him there.

Jérémie was reeling a little in the summer night, he grabbed his canvas kit bag and set off for his in-laws' farm. His disjointed conversation with the three men had at least reassured him on one point: Louise was alive, and Jérémie imagined that she had moved in with her mother where she would be more comfortable, which was logical.

At the farm, a faint glow still filtered through the shutters; perhaps they had stayed up, or come home late from the first day of harvest. Jérémie crossed the yard, some chickens cackled, a dog growled but did not bark, he walked over to a window whose shutter was a few inches ajar; by the light of an oil lamp, he saw Louise button a nightdress over her perfectly flat stomach; he did not even look at her face, he stared at his wife's fingers as she fastened the buttons over a navel that left him in no doubt, he would not be a father, not in September, not ever, and the realization left him paralyzed, he stood there, his face pressed to the glass, until Louise glimpsed a shadow in the window and shrieked: she had thought she saw her husband's face, she doubled up in terror and screamed for help—Jérémie was stung, the scream was like a slap in the face, and he, who had endured the rain of shells and the German planes without flinching, turned and ran, he fled through the fields like a chicken rustler and eventually collapsed a couple of kilometers away, felled by shock and disbelief, amid the rustle of ripe wheat.

*

So, Jacqueline Guérineau known to all as Lynn was (secretly; she had told no one) the mistress of Maximilien Rouvre, the artist exiled to the countryside, and had been for some weeks now, and had they known, the villagers would have been astonished by their affair; they would have considered it against nature, or very nearly so, just as Max's Parisian friends and acquaintances would have been astonished, to say nothing of tubby Thomas, who, if he heard of their trysts, would have secretly spat in Maximilien's drinks out of jealousy (or so the artist claimed, with a depraved little smirk). Only the anthropologist David Mazon would have studied this affair through a more objective eye, and come to the conclusion that, beyond the apparent class differences, both partners were comfortably well-off and worked in the service sector, both were freelance, and artists in their own ways, so their relationship was fiscally likely, if culturally surprising. Lynn saw things differently: Capricorns like Max were naturally drawn to those born under Cancer, it was a powerful, solid attraction of astrological opposites, like magnets brought together by a stroke of chance and impossible to separate. As for Maximilien, he did not trouble to analyze things; he liked Lynn, her stunning body, obviously, but also her simple presence, her company, her generosity and her unique worldview, qualities that his chauvinist carapace dared not call altruism, subtlety and intelligence. Lynn had a difficult time because many people considered her profession and those who practiced it frivolous— Max had never made cruel remarks about her work, which he compared to sculpture. In Lynn's eyes, Max was the perfect man, a little childlike, granted, but a "good man at heart," as she put it; as for Max, he considered himself powerfully virile during the sexual act and tender afterward, something he believed essential. They had been lovers for several weeks, and Lynn secretly hoped—without giving it too much thought, and certainly without saying as much to Maximilien—that the affair would last: and so when she was confronted by the vast studio wall plastered with horrors, she was not only shocked but disappointed, because the revelation meant the end of their affair. If need be, she would have tolerated the vast collection of pornography stored on Max's laptop, his penchant for huge breasts and overweight women—Rubenesque, he would have said—whose dugs and rolls of flesh bounced to the relentless rhythm of professional porn-star thrusts, but the atrocities that hung in his atelier defied the imagination. What she could not understand was Maximilien's motive in taking so many grotesque photographs. It was clearly related to some depraved fantasy that she would be expected to gratify. Just thinking of Max as she sat behind the steering wheel made her retch; two tears welled in the corners of her eyes. Fucking hell, she thought, because her disappointment was as great as her conjugal expectations and, when she got back to her house in Niort fifteen minutes later, she took a long shower, changed her clothes, sent Lucie a series of text messages littered with crying and vomiting emoji, then got back into her car (she would be just in time for her appointment with the pervy bar owner) and buried herself in her work to forget the hideous vision of that morning.

*

Martial Pouvreau locked the door of the funeral parlor where, in a pair of modest Parisian coffins, lay the young couple who had died the day before, quietly suffocated by the carbon monoxide fumes of a poorly installed stove, died without realizing, in the midst of a dream that ended with a permanent fade to black; they had been unaware of passing through heat and cold, of the shifting colors that preceded the Bright Light that they did not see, of their subtle bodies being propelled—after a brief sojourn in the Bardo, the world between worlds—toward immediate reincarnation in the bodies of twins, boy and girl, born in a Niort clinic, caught by a skilled obstetrician and handed to a father who was at once spellbound and repulsed and who could not tear his astonished eyes from his wife's parted labia, unable to believe that such an orifice could allow the passage of two whole bodies, albeit frail and bloody: his wife's brow streamed with sweat, her eyes with tears, she held out her arms to the babes she had just delivered in terrible pain, and whom the eternal gravediggers would one day carry to their graves, just as that same afternoon they were preparing to bury the young dead couple who now lay in the adjoining room, so they quietly drank in the workshop, perched on marble headstones yet to be engraved, while they waited for the appointed hour; they swigged hooch from the bottle that they passed back and forth—if one of the three kept it longer than he should, the other two grunted impatiently, since time was short, time is always short despite the unvarying task of burying mortal remains or consigning them to the flames; the long-faced gravediggers chatted as they got drunk, they talked about the Banquet, which would take place soon, in three months, in the spring, as it had every year since the creation of the world, where they would have a few laughs, drink dry and eat hard, and for three days there would be no corpses, because, as is well known, no one ever dies during the Banquet of the Gravediggers' Guild, for this is the Grim Reaper's gift to the Guild, these three days' repose, these revelries far from death are the Christmas of the baleful, the Feast of Saint Nicholas for the men with long faces. Three months may seem like a long time but, for the gravediggers, winter was a season of impatience, when they drank more than usual, because of the cold, because the coffins' handles were frozen, the marble icier than usual, and the earth difficult to dig even with the little bulldozer that was their only plaything, so they warmed themselves with the thought that the Banquet was approaching and everyone would come—the gravediggers, the cemetery keepers, the undertakers in their black ties, the drivers of luxury hearses—that the ritual words would be spoken and they would fall to feasting and drinking, telling tales and philosophizing, and for two nights they would forget that the Wheel was turning and that every human would one day end up on their shoulders, since none escapes it: whatever becomes of the subtle body, the body is always delivered into the hands of the gravediggers.

They talked little about the circumstances of death; they sometimes mourned the graceful curves of a woman, gently caressing them with a fingertip; they laughed at clubfeet, at the desperate shriveled or twisted forms the male member can take; they always counted the toes and giggled like children if they found one extra—a happy omen and a sign of abundance. They left the watches and stole only baptismal lockets, chain bracelets and signet rings that had been forgotten; sometimes they purloined a handsome shirt or a tie, which was not dishonesty, but respect. Modern wristwatches kept ticking around fleshless wrists for a long time in the graves, two years or more, no one knew, and, at the Banquet, the cemetery keepers always explained that this soft ticking that stirred the ground was pleasant company for them and the alarms of quartz watches reminded them to take their lunch if perchance they forgot.

The third and youngest gravedigger stared at the bottle as he waited his turn, his eyes shining and his hands trembling; he dared not say anything just yet, but he watched as the level of hooch dropped dangerously in the bottle, which so irritated his elder brother that he resolved not to hurry, and suckled the bottle lengthily to enrage him, until the youngest man, unable to stand it anymore, growled, are you passing the hooch or what? This mark of disrespect angered the eldest, who was a mean drunk— if that's your attitude, you don't get your turn—and took the bottle that the other now seemed willing to let go. The youngest scowled, stood, swore, spat on the ground as he watched the first gravedigger gulp down the mouthful that was his by rights—this was no way to behave—and the other two, by now half-wasted, laughed at his frustration: he was magnanimously offered the dregs of the hooch; he grabbed the bottle like a doll, like a young girl at a ball, and hugged it close, brought it slowly to his lips and drained it in a single swig. Then he sadly threw the bottle across the workshop into a large green plastic bin where it exploded with a hell of a racket among its sisters, prompting the sempiternal joke, "Careful now, you'll wake the neighbors," and all three laughed heartily. The time was approaching; soon they would have to dress, put on their black suits and white shirts, ensure they were freshly shaven; then they would perfume their breath by taking a little sip of *Russian Leather*, an expensive perfume they used to gargle, which burned their mouths even more than the hooch, then they would swallow, give a little *aaah* of relief, breathe into their cupped hands to check that they smelled alright, and then, suited and ready, they would wait for their boss to return. Only then could the actual work begin, four twists of the screwdriver at each corner of the coffins, after verifying (there had been a number of unfortunate oversights that had led to convoluted measures) that the corpses were inside; the hearse would be brought around to the front door, with or without the family present; the rear door of the vehicle would be closed after a single wreath (or several wreaths, depending) had been placed on each of the coffins. Finally, they would argue (discreetly, if there were mourners present) over who would get to drive this time, since that was the most enjoyable part of the job, where you could sit in the rather luxurious cab listening to the radio while the undertaker in the passenger seat took a little nap, and the two other gravediggers followed behind (discreet, as ever) in a busted-up old banger containing the necessary tools to fill the grave that they had dug that same morning. Once at the church, Martial, the undertaker, would become Master of Ceremonies, his official designation; it was he who allocated roles, had a little word for each of the mourners; the flowers would be brought into the chapel, and, if they were lucky, there would be volunteers to help carry the coffins, so that the tipsy gravediggers would not have to lug the corpses inside and set them in front of the ringside seats for an ageless spectacle that they would not witness. Then they would repair to the cemetery, Martial would give a little peroration to the confused congregation explaining that, if they wished, they could touch the coffin or throw a little earth on it as a final gesture, a last farewell; at this point, the crying would grow louder and the gravediggers, being hopeless romantics, would avoid looking at the mourners as they lowered the deceased into the grave with ropes. They would wait impatiently for the onlookers to leave and then, as they shared the bottle traditionally offered by the cemetery keeper—if there was a cemetery keeper—they would fill the hole with large, somewhat insolent shovelfuls, or close up the vault, as circumstances dictated, and the business would be over, they would go home, and would not speak of it again.

*

Lucie answered the young ethnologist's questions honestly, despite her reluctance to put herself in the light, since she considered her life of little interest. David listened attentively, making a few notes; the grandfather, as always, was sitting in the battered cane chair in front of the fire, mentally rehashing his grim life story; once again he saw images of his mother, Louise, of Jérémie, of all those whom the gravediggers had long since put into the earth, and in the old man's mind the faces blurred; he could no longer quite tell his daughter from his wife, his granddaughter from her mother, all these female figures merged into one, they swirled before the grandfather's eyes like flickering ghosts, and, looking at Lucie in her chair, he felt a glimmer of desire just as flickering as the flames dancing in the hearth, and instinctively rubbed his crotch through his trousers, a gesture that would have shocked the young scientist had he noticed, for despite his erotomania he was curiously prudish, an apparent contradiction—while Lucie was telling him about her life, her childhood, her studies at the agricultural college in Sainte-Pezenne near Niort, her early years as a farmer, David was staring into the open neck of her blouse, between her breasts, almost in spite of himself, pretending that he was checking that the recorder he had placed in front of Lucie's bust was working. In fact, David Mazon was thinking (while Lucie continued to recount memories of her first dealings with the land, her parents, her family, her childhood friends) that her assets were more amply proportioned than they seemed at first glance, which was—to put it delicately—a pleasant surprise, and David allowed his mind to wander while his gaze remained planted like a flag or a pen between these twin folds of flesh—his imagination in such matters was boundless. Or almost. Of course he could not imagine, any more than Lucie herself could, that in the course of her previous lives, she had been a Protestant victim of the Dragonnades of Louis XIV, a zealous revolutionary executed by the Comité de salut public during the Terror, a French soldier obliterated by a shell during the First World War, and a host of farmers, some of whom had died quietly in their beds, some in childbirth, some from disease or drunkenness, some in horrific cart accidents or from grisly wounds, most of them without medical assistance but almost all piously, regardless of their concept of religion. Lucie and David's paths had perhaps crossed an infinite number of times in previous lives and would perhaps cross again in the course of their future lives, and they would have no memory of it beyond the strange feeling of déjà vu Lucie sometimes felt when she caught the young ethnologist blatantly staring at her breasts—but she carried on recounting her childhood in a village a few kilometers south, at a bend in the river Sèvre, Sainte-Pezenne, named after a beautiful, forgotten virgin whom Christians called Pexine, Pezenne or Pazanne, a devout Spanish woman, according to the legend, who fled the Saracen hordes and came to lose herself in these marshes sometime around the year 726—this Pechina (named after the shell carried by Spanish pilgrims), went to live with two maidens, Macrine and Colombe, in a convent near Niort, where the three beauties attracted the lascivious eye of a nobleman called Olivier: Olivier sought to take for himself that which belonged to the Lord, forcing these unspoiled flowers to flee the men-at-arms who came to take them away. After seven days of arduous trekking through the plains and the marshlands, Pexine-Pezenne died of exhaustion, leaning against the shoulder of her friend Macrine. Her remains were brought to a village known at the time as Tauvinicus, which in time adopted the name of a saint about whom Lucie knew little or nothing; she did not know, for example, how the relics of Saint Pexine ended up at El Escorial near Madrid in Spain; she knew nothing of the "return" of one of the virgin's fingers in 1956, which was posted to Poitiers in a box of kitchen matches branded *La Golondrina*, then wrapped in purple velvet and lined with cotton, until a beautiful gilded reliquary was found, a glass shrine that was placed in the church, where Lucie might have seen it when she took her first Communion. She had, of course, completely forgotten about the awe-inspiring piece of bone, which was rarely displayed, only on June 26, when the saint of the shell was celebrated shortly before the harvest.

The church and presbytery of Lucie's childhood, a stone's throw from her school, was a venerable building with a slate roof and wooden benches whose playground overlooked a grove of chestnut trees that sloped steeply down to the river—the chestnut grove provided both the weapons and the perfect theater of war for childhood battles; the sheerness of the slope and the proximity of the river did nothing to prevent titanic clashes with branches, sticks, stones and rubber bands. In fact, Lucie still proudly bore the mark of one such skirmish right in the middle of her forehead, a scar made by a chestnut fired from a slingshot with such force that it broke the skin, and her eyes, as in Homer, were veiled with crimson before they were veiled with darkness. David had not noticed the small scar between two wrinkles, a memory of valiant battles: blood streamed from Lucie's wound; she was sprawled among the dead leaves, her head resting on a root, having passed out not from shock, but fear, the fear of a brain hemorrhage, while her friends stood around, as pale as she, not daring to touch her while a Sioux warrior (headdress of pigeon and chicken feathers taped to cardboard; tomahawk a heavy rusty Peugeot hammer filched from a father's toolbox) strode back up the slope in search of help in the person of a woman from the library opposite the school, who laddered her tights on a branch before smearing herself with blood when she picked up the girl, who instantly regained consciousness—despite having been hit on the forehead, Lucie escaped the gravediggers, being more fortunate than giants of old. Thereafter, she was forbidden from playing in the small, steep copse, forbidden from hoarding schoolyard chestnuts that might be used as instruments of vengeance, and, in the end, the chestnut trees were felled, having been found guilty of providing ammunition for generations of dunces, and replaced with maple trees, whose keys would flutter onto the playground pavement like downed helicopters.

The farm owned by Lucie's parents was a few hundred meters to the northwest, where the flatlands plunged into the wide meanders of the Sèvre, a patch of land built over by houses of all shapes and sizes but which, almost thirty years ago, was still home to a few small farmers with broad fields and no hedgerows who piled up stacks of hay or alfalfa, and built pyramids of old tires where children built forts and tunnels, dislodging colonies of field mice so vast that the cat did not know which way to turn. Perhaps it was because her father was a farmer that Lucie chose horticulture and market gardening, away from animal husbandry, from the folds of life and death, the smells of disinfectant and curd, of shit and blood—but also far from the miracles of childhood, from the first calving when her father had come to drag her from bed in her pajamas, clutching her teddy bear, wearing slippers in the matted straw, a birth so difficult that everyone had forgotten it, when, despite the calving aid (two straps attached to the calf's legs and a lever mechanism), the animal was wedged against its mother's pelvis and it took a vet and the help of some neighbors to shift its position: by the time the slimy newborn had been doused with a bucket of water, had yet more icy water poured into its ears to stimulate it, and finally started to breathe and move, no one could have torn Lucie's teddy bear from her, or persuaded her that what she had witnessed was beautiful or miraculous; necessary, of course, but a far cry from the magical event she had been promised; she had felt the pain and sensed the sheer banality of the act, one soul succeeding another in a body that, although newly born, already bore the blood and mucus that were the signs of death.

Lucie had an innate awareness (one she could never put into words) of the movements of the Wheel that takes living beings from death to birth, rebirth to death, always in great pain, from the bloody hands of midwives to the shoulders of long-faced gravediggers and on to the dirt or the flames with no means of escaping Fate, and she daydreamed as she answered David Mazon's questions; just as her forebear, the grandfather in his chair, staring at the fireplace, hand on his crotch, lost in his memories, could not know that he had only a few months to live, that he would die in spring, just before the Annual Banquet of the Gravediggers' Guild: he would get up one morning at dawn and find, neatly laid out on the dining table, a huge bottle of brandy and a box of Belgian chocolates with a pretty red ribbon; the old man would scratch his cap in disbelief, glancing around in an attempt to work out the reason for such a gift, but there would be no one to explain; he would hesitate a moment, turn the chocolate box this way and that, run his finger down the bottle from the neck to the bottom; with a little grunt of pleasure he would eat a first sweetmeat, the ganache would be sumptuous, the sugar would start to spread in his stomach; unable to stop himself, he would quickly, too quickly, gobble up the whole box for fear that someone might come, but no one would come, then, racked by a boundless thirst, standing, bolt upright, a frail tree, he would grab the bottle of brandy as he used to do, as he had always done, rip out the cork with a sure hand, bring it to his trembling lips, open his throat and drink the illicit bottle in great gulps, with great speed, drain it, drain it so fast and so greedily that an onlooker would have said it was a miracle, *Montjoie! Saint Denis!*, then the grandfather would puff, then belch, his dentures would shift forward one last time, his eyes would roll back and he would collapse, overcome by oblivion, in a thunderous crash of dead flesh and shattered glass.

*

Marcel Gendreau, schoolmaster and writer, had been waiting impatiently for comments from the various notables and journalists.

Their reactions far exceeded his expectations.

While the mayor recognized most of the characters and was greatly amused by some of the pen portraits, the same could not be said of his wife, who saw herself portrayed as a spiteful scandalmonger responsible for many of Louise's misfortunes; she instantly complained to her husband and demanded, if not the total obliteration of the book, then a total rewrite, which put the mayor in an awkward position.

The only character that the vet recognized was the mayor's wife, but this was enough for him to laugh like a drain, until his own partner, out of solidarity, endorsed the jeremiads of Madame le maire and put him, too, in an awkward position.

The local journalists were indifferent to literature, but partial to scandal; they tried to work out how much truth there was in this grim story, conveniently decided that it was all fact, and published a résumé of the book in a long article entitled "A Village Lady Macbeth"—which had nothing to do with the content but made for a gripping headline—carefully neglecting to say that the work was a novel.

The inspector of schools praised the schoolmaster for his impeccable spelling and syntax, but urged him to be wary of publishing the work more widely.

Chiron, the printer, who was mentioned in the local newspaper, found himself inundated with so many orders that he contacted the author to suggest a small reprint, this time at his own expense.

The mayor's wife, supported by the spouses of the vet and the blacksmith, was more vituperative than ever and took her revenge by spreading all kinds of vicious rumors about the schoolmaster.

A dismayed Marcel Gendreau locked himself away at home.

He no longer emerged except to cross the yard that separated his house from the school; for a time, he stopped playing ninepins and shuffleboard; he no longer visited Poupelain the blacksmith, though it was in fact here that he had first gleaned the story that inspired his novel; he no longer visited the café, the rifle club or the adult education classes; he categorically rejected the entreaties of Chiron the printer, and did his utmost to stem the torrent of rumors with silence and solitude.

It was futile.

The goddess with a hundred mouths is a hardy thistle.

The villagers were dimly aware that something was going on, that there was some scandal brewing, but, since they rarely if ever read the newspapers, they were content to accept the version given by the three vipers, according to which the schoolmaster had been accused in the press of vile deeds that they were careful not to name, since, honestly, they were too ghastly. Since there must be a grain of truth in every rumor, they added, in a hushed whisper all but poured into the hollow of the ear, that the grisly affair had something do with poor Louise's death, with her bastard son, that it concerned a disgusting book perpetrated by the aforementioned schoolmaster, a book that, what's more, almost no one had read. In the evening, the village women would repeat these stories to their husbands, adding details of their own, details which they assumed were self-evident but which other women had simply neglected to mention; at the blacksmith's yard, the men did likewise, although they avoided discussing certain aspects, because among themselves they were prudish; more so than their wives.

Marcel Gendreau's sudden absence from the same black-smith's yard at pétanque or the card games played over an aperitif was proof that something was very wrong, and his absence was noted as an unspoken admission of some appalling misdeed, whose very ambiguity greatly increased its horror.

People took their children out of school.

Concerned by this turn of events, the mayor spoke to Marchesseau the vet, who thought the situation preposterous but difficult to resolve; he promised to talk to his wife, who told him a very different story than the one he had read in the novel, but one that left a great impression on him. He made an ineffectual attempt to reason with his wife while, simultaneously, as much from cowardice as laziness, giving her the benefit of the doubt.

Louise's poor son found himself the focus of a prurient curiosity, alternating between mockery and anger with a touch of guilty sympathy, the sort of collective guilt that quickly turns into resentment; the young man had no idea what was meant and simply shrugged and spat on the ground, which was taken as a sign of his bitter hatred for the schoolmaster.

When Marcel Gendreau saw that the number of absentees in his class was increasing exponentially and noticed that no one now showed up to his Thursday afternoon soccer practice, he realized that he had made a mistake and decided to adopt a new strategy. The respect inspired by his university degree and his position was mingled with fear, after all he was not from here, his education and his refinement could easily become a yawning chasm between the villagers and him. Having little idea of the rumors and the gossip being spread, he decided to tackle the situation head-on, and went back to Longjumeau's café one evening for his aperitif. The regulars were playing trut over a little drink when the schoolmaster made his entrance; cards froze in midair, mouths gaped; they watched in incomprehension as Marcel Gendreau took off his coat and his cap and hung them on the rack; Longjumeau set the bottle back on the bar though he had not finished serving. Marcel Gendreau swallowed hard and steeled himself to walk up to the bar.

Everyone stared at him in silence.

A log crackled in the hearth; the floor creaked under the schoolmaster's feet.

He walked to the middle of the room and mumbled good evening to the company, which he instantly found ridiculous.

Longjumeau glared at him; Marcel turned away, seeking a friendly face in the crowd, and finding none.

He stood motionless for a moment, waiting for something to happen, some answer to his greeting, a smile, a wave; he recognized Patarin, the butcher, and Bergeron, who both quickly looked up at the ceiling; he saw Poupelain the blacksmith and the elder Chaigneau brother, who abruptly slammed their cards down on the table.

Suddenly overwhelmed by shame, Marcel Gendreau turned on his heel, quickly grabbed his overcoat, pushed his cap down over his face to hide the tears in his eyes, and walked out without closing the door.

*

When the two gendarmes left tubby Thomas's Café-Épicerie-Pêche, reinvigorated by their clandestine nip of Calvados, they climbed into their van and took the longest possible route to Coulonges, chatting, as they usually did, about their looming retirement and the parties they would throw when it came; one of them had already seen a boat and trailer in a catalog that he planned to buy for this unique occasion—he already had a small fishing hut on the banks of the Sèvre, in the Marais; he had always wanted a nice little boat, and more than that, the free time to enjoy it; he was holding forth to his fellow officer—another great angler of gudgeon, carp and roach, for want of perch or pike—about the incredible catches he would be able to make with his boat, all the while carefully steering the police van along the narrow paths of reclaimed land. Snow was falling heavily, something that peeved them both, since it would no doubt generate work in the coming days, checking the state of the roads, rescuing road accident victims, and so forth, the only advantage being that they would be able to warm their insides in the company of the maintenance men driving snowplows and spreading salt, who always had a good stock of hooch. They had just reached the brow of the very gentle slope and turned west toward the town, chatting the whole time, when the officer driving spotted a shadowy figure moving swiftly across a field, bent double like a soldier, trying to blend in with the hedgerow. He quickly asked his fellow officer whether he'd seen anything, the other said, What? no, nothing, but guided by what might be called a professional reflex, the driver decided to investigate and took a left turn onto an even smaller road, to the exasperation of his partner, What the hell are you doing, there's nothing there, I'm telling you; the officer driving said, I'm not in the habit of seeing things, I'm sure I spotted someone; through the car window and the dense snow, he scanned the hedgerow, never taking his eyes off it; his partner sighed and watched over the driver's shoulder. The young boar, vessel of the soul of Father Largeau, was frolicking between the hedgerows, and, contrary to his habit, in broad daylight; he felt frisky that morning, the thickets smelled of sleet and winter, of dead birds and bitter cold, and, snout pressed to the ground, he darted for the cover of the trees—he had heard the drone of the engine, seen the blue flash of the police van, felt its vibrations and quickly decided to take cover; he resolved not to be caught abroad in daylight again; there were too many people in the area, he needed to move away, to the little patch of woodland with its watering holes, the mud baths in which he could enjoy a wallow and, most of all, the sows, because December was rutting season, a season of fierce fights between boars, and, for the victors, the long pleasure of mating: the young boar vessel of the priest's soul was a *ragot*, a lone male, who would soon join the much-desired sounder; fear and desire had given him the powerful haunches he needed to reach cover without being seen by the two cops that morning; the same cops who, seconds later, would howl in terror as a brutal crash hurled them against the windshield of the police van; they cursed and copiously insulted each other, not knowing what could possibly have happened, but they had to face the fact that the front axle of the van seemed to have fallen into some kind of hole. Warily, they climbed out; there, cut into the road, was a trench about a meter wide and about as deep; the van was stuck fast, the bumper jammed, the front wheels spinning in the void. It's your fault, you dumb bastard, said the second officer. Hold up, now, this has nothing to do with me, said the first. Fucking idiot, the least you could do is watch where you're driving, said the second. I could hardly keep an eye on a suspect running toward the electrical substation and guess that there'd be a fucking unmarked trench, could I? Yeah, well, a fat lot of good that's done us, said the second, philosophically. What exactly is the point of this trench anyway, said the first. It's designed to immobilize police vans, said the second sardonically. It's an antitank trench. Snow speckled their navy-blue sweaters; they were cold and pulled on their regulation greatcoats. So now what do we do, asked the second officer. We get the hell out of here, said the first, climbing back behind the steering wheel. Try giving it a push, said the second. Yeah, yeah, are you blind? I can't steer and push at the same time, said the first.

It was futile. Despite their valiant efforts and various changes of position, the gendarmes barely managed to keep their jackets clean of the torrent of mud churned up by the wheels.

They could at least have given us a four-wheel drive, fumed the first.

They didn't know you'd be driving, laughed the second.

We're going to have to call it in, get them to send someone out, said the first officer with a sigh.

We'll never hear the end of this, prophesied the second.

SONG

A man always sways a little when he hasn't set foot on dry land for almost six months.

The port of La Rochelle smells of pitch tar, wood fires and memories. It had been drizzling since they passed the Île de Ré and now that the frigate is in the fairway, the stevedores are starting to swing the hoists preparing to fill the holds with provisions, timber and gunpowder; a feeble sun polishes the paving stones of the quays and the rubblestone of the two rickety towers that flank the harbor, one short and squat, the other taller and more formal, standing to attention. The morning is already well advanced and, as soon as the bell clangs to set him free, the sailor takes the first launch ashore, in a peacoat and a tricorne, together with twelve other sailors; it seems to him that the jetty is heaving like a crude wooden pontoon. Six months since he has been ashore, five years since he was last in La Rochelle. Home. Until now, his home has been the flimsy frigate *La Marseillaise*, the cannon he loaded, the halyards and the sheets he sweated blood to hoist, his shipmates, his neighbors in the hammock. The battles. The blood that seeped into the deck. The sawdust. The smell of burning that lingers in the nostrils as much as the stench of the La Rochelle harbor. He feels himself jostled. Ho, you're a son of La Rochelle, you surely know some inn, some tavern, let us all go empty a few jars! I am, but Aimery's from La Rochelle too. Aye, but yon clodpoll is naught but a lad! At length, he agrees to show them around. After all, why not? Draining a few jars of pot is traditional. Being in company will make his homecoming easier, he thinks. Aye, I know a decent tavern. With a pretty serving wench and white wine. It's not far, just the other side of t'harbor. The sailors whistle through their teeth and throw their hats in the air. The lad from La Rochelle will guide them. All the others are from Brittany, save Pimbeau and Gantier, who are from Normandy. He remembers taking leave, five years earlier, on this very same quay, the farewells, the embarkation. The promises to write letters, he who cannot write a line. The *Saint-Jean*, his first ship, a little corvette scuttled by the English fleet off the coast of Gibraltar six months later. The flames, the screams, the wintry sea blackened by smoke and swell. Rescued by *La Marseillaise*, where he stayed aboard to replace a fallen sailor. The steerage, the weighty companionship of the guns. The war is still raging. The navy is all but wiped out, there are few ships left, but still the fight goes on against the accursed English. But for him, it is over. He will not reembark. Tucked into his waistcoat is his passport bearing the seal of the imperial eagle. King, Republic, Empire, none of these things matter to him. Ho, lad, ain't you happy to be home in La Rochelle? It feels a little strange, is all. He smiles. He looks around, nothing has changed; he recognizes the houses, the sentry barracks that seal off access to the port; the clock tower that overlooks the city; the clouds scudding as fast as the seagulls hovering between the towers; three fishermen, creels of glistening fish, dragnets hug out to dry on the edge of the quay; women with baskets on their arms in headscarves, bonnets, who take a quick look at the contents of the creels before going on their way; children caked in mud crushing green crabs with their heels to use as bait on makeshift fishing lines in the hope of catching the large mullets they can see circling in the depths of the harbor; the toll of the noonday bells from the Church of Saint-Louis as they ring out, and ring again, reflected by the walls, as though they were adrift at sea, between

Ré and Oléron. No doubt about it, he's home; once he was that boy playing in the mud at ebb tide until his mother screamed and grabbed him by the collar and tossed him into a drum of icy water to sluice the muck from him; once he was that young fisherman despairing of his meager catch, that soldier strutting and peacocking to beguile a girl who is no man's fool. He begins to laugh; he gently elbows his companions, oh, it will be grand, you'll see, a jug of white wine at the Auberge de Pertuis. They join in his laughter, they are happy for him; they too would one day like to return to Brest, to Roscoff or Fécamp, where their wives and children are waiting. Ho, lad, ain't you got a wife and babes? Where do they be awaiting?

You'll see it's good, the jug of wine at the Auberge du Pertuis!

The bells and the familiar city sights dispel the fears of homecoming and make way for the pang of anguish. Time enough for his wife and babes to see him. First the jug! The wine! Then he'll leave his comrades to sup their grog in the shadowy city taverns. His wife. His babes. They must be all grown up.

They have only to cross the channel at the far end of the port. And the barrier. Heading toward Saint-Nicolas.

The inn sign has not changed. He does not recall the curtains in the windows. The door feels heavier, more colossal; the host of sailors rolls into the empty tavern, laughing, and settles around a long oak table. The smells are familiar. Stew, fish soup, sour wine. On the wall, a portrait of an old man with a pipe.

The tavern keeper is pretty, she looks happy to see so many sailors. She gives them all a broad smile, paying him no particular heed. He endeavors to look deep into her eyes. She pours wine into a wooden goblet and he drains it dry as she watches. He doffs his tricorne and looks up. He thinks he sees her shudder. She averts her gaze.

The sailors quaff the wine in long drafts, a little sad that they are not in Paimpol or Morlaix, that they are not fortunate enough to be home.

Damn your eyes, lad, here you are home!

They drink the health of the sailor, who has eyes only for the pretty tavern keeper.

They elbow each other and jerk their chins.

The mistress of the house serves them again, asks what ship they came in on. The frigate *Marseillaise*, by Jove! Pulled into quay this morn, we did.

A warship, then, like my poor husband. The sailor looked down. Gantier, Pimbeau and the others gaze at her, dumbstruck.

My poor husband. Many's the sad letter I received to tell me he was dead, his ship destroyed by fire.

You have a look of him, Monsieur, the landlady said, a sob in her voice.

A child has just appeared, he has barely learned to walk and reels like a drunken cabin boy, coming to cling to his mother's skirts to keep from falling; tenderly she strokes his hair then takes him in her arms.

The sailor now is gazing at the portrait of the old man, with his stubby clay pipe; this is how he too will look, should he live to be old.

He thanks her for her hospitality.

Don't trouble yourself, she says as he fumbles for his leather purse, I'll not take a sou. Happy it is I am to stand you all a drink in memory of my late husband.

It is one of the Bretons who asks the question, The child, he is yours, m'lady?

Indeed. She gives him a wan smile, After my man died, I married again.

He listens; gets to his feet, leans against the table for fear that he might fall; his eyes are filled with tears, he mumbles a farewell, staggers as he pushes open the heavy wooden door. The sailors trail after him; two among them throw their arms about his shoulders, a man always sways a little when he has not set foot on dry land in an age. They all fall silent, now they carry him away, bear him off and lose themselves in the alleys and the hostelries of La Rochelle; they will say not a word, nor utter the name of the Auberge du Pertuis, which strikes fear in all; tomorrow, still half-drunk, they will go with him to the harbormaster's office where he will once again make his mark, a scrawled X at the foot of a letter of enlistment.

III.
AND WE SHALL PLAY A GAME
OF CARDS . . .

After the life force of Lucie's forebear, Jérémie the hanged man, departed his body, and following a fleeting passage in the Bardo, an infinite causal sequence returned him to life more than four hundred years earlier, for there is no time in Fate, an infinite skein of invisible threads in which everything is connected; he cried out as breath and consciousness returned to him in the year of our Lord 1551, in the biting February cold, not knowing his soul had crossed paths with that of his new mother, who had been immediately returned to the Wheel, having died in childbirth, her thighs streaked with blood, blood that the humble gravediggers would carefully wash away before swaddling her remains in a pristine shroud and consigning them to the corruption of the flesh-eating coffin, fare thee well, mother, beautiful and gentle as are all mothers, and indeed for a hap'orth he might not have been born in this place, in this time, in this wintry manor of Saint-Maury near Pons-des-Charentes in the reign of Henri II, for his father had long hemmed and hawed on the matter: when the doctor murmured into his ear that the Lord, in His Great Mercy, would allow him to save one of the two suffering souls, only one of the two, his wife or his unborn child, he was compelled to choose. The boorish Huguenot, having had the greatest of difficulties in acquiring a questionable nobility,

resolved that the child should be allowed to live; that his line
should continue: what mattered was that his newborn heir go
forth and multiply; had the wife survived, it was far from certain
that she would bring forth another child, yet if she lived, he could
not wed again—so he sacrificed the parturient for the fruit of her
womb, and so Lucie's great-grandfather howled once more in
the great cold of the world, and soon forgot the hangman's rope,
the endless fall, the snap of vertebrae that had ended his previous life four hundred years before and fifty leagues away. He was
bathed, dubbed Théodore, but also Agrippa, which means "the
child born in pain," so that, for the remainder of his life, the child
would never forget what he owed to the murder of his mother.
He was entrusted to the prudent care of a peasant girl who had
given suck to the babes of others since her own first confinement,
a human milk cow, gentle and plump, who tenderly stroked the
newborn's hair, and would feel a pang of melancholy when he
was taken from her, as she always did; so it was that this mother-
less babe, from this borrowed teat, thought to taste the maternal
tenderness he would never know—his green-eyed young step-
mother would ensure that the heir from the first marriage was
swiftly banished, thereby ensuring he would know nothing of
paternal tenderness either; from his father, he inherited a fiery resolve, a rare energy and a Reformation education in the Calvinist
tradition, which, despite itself, would lay the region to waste over
five reigns, and, with peace between the Loire and the Gironde
established for a meager fifty years, would reawaken the agonies
and pleasures of war. Agrippa studied Latin, Greek, Hebrew and
the Holy Scripture before leaving the region that had nurtured
his soul and his conscience, a region to which he would return a
soldier: this evangelist of the Holy Writ would have been startled
to discover that he had previously been a peasant farmer ignobly
hanged some four centuries later. It is said that, as a young child,
Agrippa felt a presence draw near his cradle one night and glide
into the river of the bed; a pale, ashen woman who placed upon

his cheek an icy kiss. So disturbed was he by the vision that he kept to his room for a fortnight, and though he never dared call it a specter, he never forgot its cold and final alien caress, any more than he forgot the severed heads in Amboise that hung from the gibbet teeming with flies and filth; he had been eight years old, and perhaps all the cruelty of which he would be capable, the terrible vengeance that he would pitilessly wreak, forsaking the Gospels for bloodlust and death, stemmed from these two child-hood scenes, a gentle ghost and a dozen severed heads hung by their hair, slowly bloating in the balmy Angevin sun—Théodore Agrippa d'Aubigné will make work for the gravediggers, he will revel in battle, kill with pleasure, loot and plunder, besiege for-tresses, villages and farms, blindly following the dark path of his previous incarnation, despite the schooling and his books; he and his henchmen will raze the hamlet where Jérémie will later hang himself in a violent fury, without realizing that all things are con-nected and that evil perdures, that it settles in the soul with each transmigration like silt upon a riverbed—Agrippa, blinded and ensnared by hatred, will persevere in the war and in vengeance for this Protestant sect that doubtless would not have survived had he not taken up arms in its defense; d'Aubigné, the greatest poet of his age, a devout Christian, spent his youth fighting with the lost children, from Jarnac to Orléans; he was equerry to Henri de Navarre, whom he spurned when his lord recanted and sided with the Papists; he will be a poet to expiate the sins of a youth in which he will have suffered more than any other, suffered and rejoiced, in his liberty, the great liberty of reading the Holy Book in French, this new and savage tongue he will come to love above all others, reading in French the pamphlets Calvin had printed in Geneva, where the young Agrippa will study. There, too, he will be wretched, abandoned, without means, he will leave Geneva for Lyon, where he will think of throwing himself in the Saône, consider self-destruction to escape his misery, just as Jérémie, the ancestor, hanged himself—or rather will hang himself—to escape his remorse; but perhaps stirred by his previous life, Agrippa will step away from the parapet, climb down from the bridge: in that moment, through the sort of happenstance that Fate alone contrives and which invariably holds a meaning, whether it be called portent or augury, sign or omen, he will meet his guardian, come to Geneva to bring his subsidies, a man who could not know that he had unwittingly just prevented the young Agrippa from taking his own life and was about to propel him into the delights of warfare. To avenge the beautiful martyrs of the Protestant cause, those from Amboise, those from Saintonge, from Paris, those burned at the stake, those buried alive, Agrippa enlisted with the troops of Condé and Coligny of calamitous fate: clad only in a shirt, he fled by night from the room where he was held precisely because he feared joining the men-at-arms. He is seventeen, the age of folly; he obtains his first armaments in an early skirmish with the Papists. *I cannot blame the war that it has ruined me, since I could not come out less well equipped than I went in*, he wrote on his debt certificate. A harquebus, a helmet and a cuirass purloined from a dead man, and lo, he goes to war.

*

Marcel Gendreau, the author-schoolmaster, was forced to leave the village. He requested a quick transfer and was sent to teach in the village where he was born, Échiré, a region of butter and fine castles, seven leagues to the southeast; all in all, he found his classroom near the Sèvre, and the short-trousered, scab-kneed schoolchildren much the same as those he had just left—he traded his writer's pen for a fishing rod and, well into his dotage, he watched the river shimmer, the carp mouth and the cows graze, leaning against a poplar tree, perched on a folding chair, facing the hills of Chalusson and the sunrise, and, despite himself, every time he folded away his rod, every time he put his disgorger and penknife into his wicker tackle box, he thought of the dead woman, Louise, and her bastard son, may God help her, may the angels help them, and he tried to take an interest in other things, other mysteries, like the invisible mucous slime that covers the scales of fish and makes them hard to grip, or the razor-like dorsal fins of perch that can cut your fingers to ribbons. He tried to forget he had ever written a book: sometimes, on Thursdays, being market day in Niort, he would run into Chiron the printer who would greet him with a friendly pat on the back and buy him a glass of white wine from a stall. But when Marcel Gendreau arrived home, troubled by the encounter, and took out a copy of his book and thumbed through it with an air of disgust, he discovered that the words were no longer his, had never been his, as though he no longer remembered the long hours, the sentences, the characters, the village where he had lived and worked for almost twenty years, lost in the plains like a coin that soundlessly falls through a hole in a pocket. Marcel Gendreau took to composing sonnets while he fished, poems that he set down as he headed home, his bucolic verses, *omnia vincit amor*, love conquers all, *paludum Musae*, O Muse of the marshlands, let us sit and sing in the cool of the beech, in the drowsy shade of the elm, let us sing these lines of tragic love, verses that would have reminded the observant reader of the fate of Jérémie Moreau, the hanged man with the big toe poking through his sock: Jérémie Moreau, fresh home from war, prostrate in the summer night, his eyes filled with tears and August stars, confessed his pain and humiliation to the dark sky, how he had survived the slaughter only to see, through a half-open shutter, his wife with her swollen belly gone—no baby, no child in her womb, and it now seemed clear to him that he had been the victim of some hex, some dark magic, to what end he did not know, but now he understood the suppressed chuckles of Longjumeau, the grimaces of Chaudanceau, the knowing smiles, they had all made fun of him, and he wept with rage beneath the stars as he imagined the ringleader, the man responsible for this deception, his father-in-law, the cursed man who had exploited him from start to finish, and so exhausted was Jérémie by rage, fear, disappointment and the glittering darkness of the stars that he closed his eyes on his tears, a man's tears, those drops of mingled shame and pride burning at the corners, and he fell asleep.

When morning came, he would have to face the snide glances and remarks, to put words to his rage; sounds, blows and howls to his loss; to endure the village snickering, to confront Louise, his father-in-law, to scream, to wield the axe, the hoe, the sickle, to drench with blood the memory of this family, this village; but he would not. He would do nothing. Jérémie broke into his home and moved back in, leaving the shutters open to signal his presence in the white stone house now occupied by his son, Lucie and Arnaud, a hundred meters from the farm of Louise's father-in-law, who was harboring the traitor and her bastard, and had been for some time, to judge by the dust on the long oak table and the cobwebs between the rafters.

During the Occupation, he barely spoke to anyone. He no longer walked past the cafés, no longer played trut or belote; he drank on his own, swilling down barrels of local wine stacked in his cellar and feeling sorry for himself, a husband with no wife, a father with no son, a farmer with no land. Louise, her bastard and her parents pretended not to see him. He was invisible to them. To everyone. When he went to the town hall to turn in his shotgun in compliance with orders from the occupying forces, the mayor was in deep conversation with some Kraut who could not be more than twenty, blond and very pale, in a green uniform; he was handing the mayor a sheaf of papers. The mayor did not even take the time to say, Hey, Moreau, what brings you here; Jérémie waited five minutes, ten minutes, still the conversation dragged on; politely he tried to attract the mayor's attention, Hey, Monsieur le maire, to no avail, Jérémie got nothing for his pains but an angry glare, so he slung his rifle over his shoulder—the rifle his father-in-law had given him as a dowry—and went on his way. He was an ugly drunk, everyone knew that; for an instant he considered discharging both barrels, one into the mayor's chest, the other into the Kraut's pale blond head, the sons of bitches deserved it, thirty-six grams of lead at point-blank range, that would put some fresh air into Fritz's brain, that would put some fresh air into the mayor's bronchial tubes, thought Jérémie as he walked through the village, his right hand gripping the shoulder strap of the rifle as though it were a weapon of war, and after all, there's a war going on, a war that robbed him of a wife and child, he thinks, he knows that he has been bewitched, he has been cursed, he has attracted the evil eye; he knows that his wife visited a witch in order to be rid of him and almost succeeded; the war almost killed him, and now misery and evil are about to put an end to Jérémie Moreau, the power of the Evil One let loose upon him like a rabid cur, the power, he will become an outcast, a hermit in the woods, he will run, relying on the power of hatred to flee far away, beyond the plains, into the impassable marshlands, beyond Benet, toward Coulon and Damvix, where no one will ever find him.

Back at his house, Jérémie packs his bag, the military rucksack he has been lugging around since verdant England. In midafternoon, he takes his bike from the barn and heads west, toward the Vendée, to lose himself in the Marais.

Omnia vincit amor, love conquers all, *paludum Musae*, O Muse of the marshlands, let us sit and sing in the cool of the beech, in the drowsy shade of the elm, let us sing these lines of tragic love, in Latin, the language of Messalina, of guilty passions and of the invincible Christ, the language of forgiveness, of desire and of medicine: so mused Marcel Gendreau, the author-cum-schoolmaster, as he sat with fishing rod in hand on his folding chair at a bend in the Sèvre, there where the valley sloped gently through lush green fields before the willows, the poplars and the limestone cliffs—a little farther away, the setting sun gleamed on the slates of the Château de la Taillée like the back of a perch, toward the slightly lumpen Romanesque church of Échiré, with its octagonal bell tower whitewashed by various renovations, firmly embedded in the soil of Poitou by the Middle Ages and the Plantagenets, where soon, in the waning light, would come the drone of vespers and the folding of fishing rods. Marcel Gendreau knew of the deeds of Jérémie the savage in the Marais, knew of those long dark years, years spent among the angry dragonflies, the frogs in springtime, the silence and the cheerless mud of winter—he had even located the hut where Jérémie the madman had nurtured his hatred of his fellow men for three years, receiving just two visits, both equally tragic: the first from the gendarmes who were looking for the young Chaigneau brother, the second from the younger Chaigneau brother himself, panicked like a sparrow trapped in a barn, his eyes wild, so terrified he refused Jérémie's hospitality, while Jérémie tried to reassure him, calm down, for God's sake, the bastards have already been and gone, they haven't seen you, they won't be back here anytime soon! But it was no use; the younger Chaigneau brother plunged into his fate as slimy and bloody as the marshland itself.

Jérémie loved his life as a hide hunter; a life as dull and free as the blow of an axe, a life of clay and elder, of comfrey and nettles, a life of roach and snails—from daybreak every morning Jérémie would roam the Marais (never leaving the cover of the tall trees, the refuge of the calm, quiet intertwining waterways) to forage, to gather, to fish for what he needed; he would spend the afternoons chopping wood, hoeing the few rows of vegetables in the black soil, snaring a rabbit or a partridge, which he would barter for wine, brandy and other essentials—string, matches, canvas; the first winter was dark and bitter, until Jérémie salvaged the old cast-iron stove from his house in the village. The following years were spent in the company of the flames that danced across the logs like shameless witches that sometimes moaned according to the breeze, and he would imagine the hoarse breath of fantastical animals, of griffins or fire dogs. Whenever he returned, the area around his hut smelled of burnt wood and this, together with the damp cold, immediately took him back to his childhood, to the smell the moment before it snows, and indeed sometimes it did snow. Often, as he stared into flames, he would think about the hex that had been put on him, that curse, that farce, and he would be seized by rage, fury, hatred; he would grab the axe and exact his revenge on the thick elm branches. He often dreamed of Louise, often glimpsed her in the mist, when fog danced over the marshes. Rarely, in despair, he would take the shotgun from its hiding place and put both two barrels under his chin, pressed against his Adam's apple, or take them in his mouth; more rarely still, he would squeeze his eyes shut and, arm outstretched, would pull both triggers with his thumb until he heard the click of the hammers echo in the void and imagine his body, brains blown away by force of the blast, lying lifeless in a pool of blood.

At night, Jérémie Moreau would nail toads to doors to jeer at Fate; he was filthy, his beard was long and he reeked of rotting fish and mud; everyone thought Jérémie was mad, mad and a warlock, especially his wife, who so feared him that even in her dreams she imagined him chasing her, with his evil spells and his prophet's name.

Jérémie Moreau the brute had become someone else, someone different; as water and ice shatter stone and over time give it a distinct shape, so Jérémie was a gargoyle carved by rain and time on the machicolation of a ruined castle—a grotesque shape, with a face contorted by hunger and hatred: he had grown through his ordeals, grown in malice and in cunning.

Jérémie Moreau waited for war to end to avenge himself. He waited for the first ball celebrating the Liberation, which was held while there were still Germans around La Rochelle, some sixty or eighty kilometers from the village; he waited while he fed on mugwort and hatred, on fury and the wind in the white poplars. Summers were joyful, violent, vibrant with grain, the threshing machines moved from yard to yard, from farm to farm, the tanks and cannons of a hundred and fifty Germans took revenge on the towns of the northern Deux-Sèvres; the stars wheeled in the sky like omens or airplanes; the air was redolent with curd and cordite. Not a ripple disturbed the waters of the Marais, the Nazi troops in the southwest fell back toward the front lines, for a time the roads teemed with soldiers in green uniforms, then once again silence returned—and with it the berets of the Forces françaises de l'intérieur.

On September 2, 1944, Jérémie went back to the village. Poupelain's son told Gendreau the schoolmaster that he spotted him hiding in the shadows with a bundle in his arms, while everyone was dancing; he was the only one. No one else saw him, not the café owners, the dancers, not the grocer or the baker. Above all not Louise, her son or her parents. After so many months, Louise had almost forgotten Jérémie, except in her nightmares. The war, it seemed, was over, the bastard was now tall and strong, she loved him with all her heart, this boy now fleeing toward adolescence. At the ball, she had danced with young people who proudly wore the armband of the Resistance; a singer and an accordionist sang fashionable tunes in patois—they no longer feared the Krauts, they were eager to sing of their defeat,

> For a time there, lass, they was crawlin' about,
> Thick as vermin in late summer heat,
> We'd steal around, always fearin' a clout,
> As we tended the beasts and the wheat.
> But now, all's changed in the lands hereabout,
> The Krauts have gone, in a thunder of feet,
> And there's joy now in life with no Jerries about
> And the air on the byways is sweet.

And the retreat of occupying forces, scarcely seen in the village, provided an excuse—like any battle, won or lost—for celebration; Louise didn't care; she loved the music and the dancing, she paid no heed to the song. Of course, the poor man's piano screeched louder than the village pump and Caruso croaked like a crow in a field, but for the people of the village there was the simple pleasure in coming together at the crossroads outside the town hall, instead of huddling at home with a wireless, even if the music on the radio was better. And besides, the Liberation, France, deserved to be celebrated.

Louise headed home with her son, the same son who would find Jérémie's corpse hanging from a beam in the barn, his boots lying in the straw, an accusatory toe poking out of his sock, the son who would die in the twenty-first century after guzzling a box of Belgian chocolates and downing a bottle of brandy, the son who would have children and grandchildren, but who, tonight, would quietly go up to bed while his mother slept downstairs— Louise was on the ground floor in that corner of the courtyard where, three years earlier, Jérémie had watched her undress; now, here he was, standing in the same spot, in the shadows beyond the gate, his beard was long, his eyes yellow with grief, passion and madness—Jérémie watching his wife through the lace curtains and the half-open shutters; she was wearing a bottle-green dress taken in at the waist, with short, puffed sleeves, a red Claudine collar and buttons down the front; the dress fell to just below her knees, and Jérémie gazed at her calves sculpted by high heels, the slender ankles. He remembered Louise's body, their embraces, her breasts in his cupped hands, the clamminess of her sex around his fingers as he readied her, the intensity of orgasm, the taste of perfume when he had licked her throat lengthily, like a dog licking pig's blood from the ground until its tongue was red raw, and these memories served to fuel the hatred, the madness and the desire of Jérémie, who cradled his accursed bundle in his arms and groaned, he was waiting for Louise to open the window and close the shutters, he trembled as he waited; for months he had been waiting for this moment, for the liberation, not of France, but his own liberation, and at this thought he caught a glimpse of war, the dragon's maw of war, Come on, Louise, open the window to close your shutters, it's time, open the window and poke your head out, bend down and raise the bolt; all the while Louise stood in front of the wardrobe mirror, admiring herself in her pretty dress, whistling, she lowered her chin as though about to unfasten the first button, then suddenly remembered that the shutters were still open, and Jérémie felt his heart lurch and then explode like a chestnut in the fire, like a machine gun ripping bodies in half; Louise turned the window latch, pulled the shutters and leaned out into the darkness.

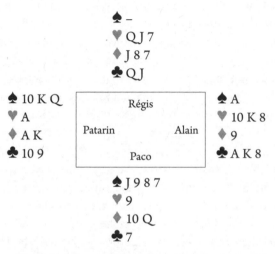

♠ –
♥ Q J 7
♦ J 8 7
♣ Q J

♠ 10 K Q
♥ A
♦ A K
♣ 10 9

Régis

Patarin   Alain

Paco

♠ A
♥ 10 K 8
♦ 9
♣ A K 8

♠ J 9 8 7
♥ 9
♦ 10 Q
♣ 7

*No declarations; West to deal; Paco has accepted
the jack of spades; Régis, miserably, opens.*

Tubby Thomas moodily watched them play belote; he felt a freshness on the back of his neck, a coolness that meant he would not see Lynn again for a month. Tubby Thomas had watched Lynn's buttocks jiggle as she left the Café-Pêche, had copiously rinsed his eyes, goodbye to tears, now he was following the game with great interest: Régis opened with diamonds, which is curious since Paco had accepted spades, if Paco called spades as trumps, why open with a small diamond, it's a mess, and it doesn't bode well, a misery of trumps matched by a drought of aces, Régis knew how to play; Thomas would have liked to see Paco's face but couldn't as he was sitting with his back to him: when you're playing for fifty cents a point it's nail-biting, you get a rush when you go all in, well, you got what you deserved, you jumped on that upturned jack, you went all in on the jack of spades and your partner hasn't got a single fucking trump or ace in his hand, which must mean Patarin has the spades, since otherwise Alain would have pounced on the tantalizing jack—unbelievable. A couple of guys letting a solid twenty trickle through their fingers doesn't happen often. Life's a bitch.

Thomas likes card games because he revels in other people's misfortunes; he enjoys watching them lose rather than win, and on the occasions when he organized a little game of Texas Hold'em, what he most enjoyed, aside from his own winnings, was watching the poor bastards circling the pot. Now that everyone played online, there were fewer people in the café, but Thomas could rely on a handful of regulars: the Café-Pêche was the only bar in the region, since there were none in the surrounding villages. It's the lighthouse of the plains, said Thomas, and mayor Martial Pouvreau would boast to the mayors of neighboring villages, We've got the Bar-Tabac-Pêche; in fact, everyone in the region was happy to drop by, to fill in a lottery ticket while sipping a Petite Côte or a Blanc-Cassis, or to buy maggots, Mystic™ lures in red, yellow, green or white in what look like tubes of glue, or Dudule™ bait in every color of the rainbow (to one side of the cream Formica counter, there was an advertisement dating back to the days of tubby Thomas's father, a promotional decal enjoining customers to "make love but check she's on the pill, let Dudule™ help you catch those brill") drop nets to catch crayfish or keep live ones cool, reels, leaders, weights—in short all the basic necessities for roach fishers. Thomas kept up his ichthyophilic trade despite the fact that it didn't bring in much money because he was as keen an angler as he was a cardplayer; every Sunday he would set up two or three fishing rods near Magné on the banks of the Sèvre where he had a little cabin—he would spend the day fishing for roach, bleak and tench, and in the evening, as night drew in and the river grew dark in the shade of the willows, he would fish for pike-perch using live bait he had pulled from the water that same afternoon: indisputably, Thomas was an expert; not only was he familiar with the current and the meanders of the Sèvre, he was intimately familiar with every tarn, canal, waterway and gully in the Marais.

Paco kept hold of his ten and tossed out the queen of diamonds with a long-suffering air; Thomas could see the looming danger, the pass, and Paco's ten being taken by the ace on the next trick: Patarin smiled as he took the queen with his king, and then Patarin led with the ace of diamonds: if Régis doesn't trump him, this is going to be a massacre, thought Thomas; he leaned both hands on the counter, the better to watch the game. It was going to be a massacre to rival Austerlitz: Régis has the eight of diamonds so can't trump, not that he could anyway, since he doesn't have a single trump card in hand—if he had a trump or an ace he would never have led diamonds and gotten his partner into this shit show. Paco was Napoleon, watching the points rack up like syphilis on the lower clergy: when troubles come, they come not single spies, Alain managed to off-load the ace of spades by trumping his partner. Thomas, ever magnanimous, could not help but roar— Thirty-two points for a single trick, that'll teach you! A turn on the jack, you've got jack shit! And, since he had the eight and nine of spades, Paco knew that his partner had no choice but to take the trick, he also knew, like Napoleon in Moscow, that his partner had, as they say, a shitty hand: otherwise Régis would have called the jack of spades himself. What he didn't understand was why Alain hadn't decided to pocket the jack; it must because he had been dealt the ace of spades later and, with Régis in the gutter, thought that the ace would end up, like many other trumps, falling in his favor, which had proved to be a particular mistake. Régis knew that he would have to finish this round as best he could by following the suit and attempting to discard (or, in vulgar terms, to piss away) the meager points he had to Paco's trumps, feeling sorry for himself since, in all his years playing belote, this was the first time he'd come close to having four jacks. But this was a five-hundred-point hand with no declarations, at fifty cents a point, and after a first-round loss, they were down 140–22, which meant they were in it for twenty euros apiece. Régis was the Marshal Ney of this Russian campaign. The Prince of the Moskova, weary and resigned, looked Napoleon in the eye.

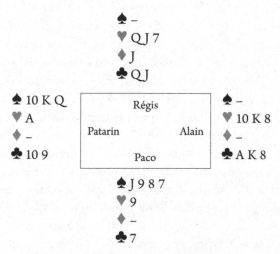

*After the pass to the ten of diamonds. Paco is sad
that he missed a possible capot.*

Play moves to Alain who, having trumped his partner, leads with the ace of clubs; Paco follows, sighing like a parturient; he is still hoping that all the trumps are not in the same hand. If Patarin has belote and rebelote, this won't be Austerlitz, it'll be Waterloo. Here comes the ten of clubs, *ouch*, Régis sacrifices his jack; Alain hesitates for a second then plays a small heart, a suit in which, again—as if by some miracle—Patarin has the ace. Régis makes a face and tosses out the seven of hearts.

Halfway through the game, and Paco hasn't taken a single trick, having thought he'd take them all.

*

The first sound imprinted on Patarin's memory is the squeal of the pig being slaughtered, and the first smell, its bristles being burned off with a blowtorch. Patarin the pork butcher was the son of Patarin the pork butcher who in turn was the son of Patarin the pig farmer, killers and butchers from father to son, until over-zealous legislation decreed that pigs should no longer be bled in farmyards, strung up by their trotters from the fork of a tractor; business had changed beyond recognition; Patarin still made sausages and pâtés, rillettes and stuffing, but using pigs from neighboring Gâtine that arrived dead and butchered in refrigerated vans; he traveled the countryside with his mobile shop, one day here in La Pierre-Saint-Christophe, one day in Coulonges, one day in Parthenay, one day in Coulon, and a day in Champdeniers or Cherveux. Patarin had his truck painted with his armorial bearings, as he called them, which he blazoned as follows: argent, two boars affronted gules; on an arched fess, vert bearing the name Patarin Fils, known throughout Bas-Poitou for the quality of his products, his boudins or his roast chickens, whose flavescent juices trickled out onto potatoes that were slick with goose fat and pleasure. Patarin was glad he had invested in a wood-burning rotisserie, the aroma attracted customers at least as much as its gleaming container, his impressive brand-new truck. Patarin had been playing belote since his teens, often with the same partners; he enjoyed taking part in tournaments he heard about on his travels through Deux-Sèvres. He would have been extremely surprised had he been told that, when he died, he would come back as a greylag goose; that every autumn, in a great flap of wings, he would fly thousands of kilometers from his native Poland to wintering grounds in the Marais and the salt meadows of the Bay of Aiguillon. Needless to say, Patarin was also unaware that, in previous lives, he had been countless factory workers and farm laborers, mendicant monks, a knife grinder, an innkeeper and even a horse—a small barbarian horse with a broad chest and a bay coat, in a far-off time when the plains between Tours and Niort teemed with miracles and wandering saints, around the year of our Lord 507; the horse that would become Patarin carried on his back a warrior, his sword and his francisca axe, a Frankish warrior king come from Tournai to conquer the lands of the Visigoths ruled by Alaric, king of Aquitaine and Hispania. The warrior has recently abjured idols and demons, he venerates Saint Martin and Saint Hilaire, though less than his throwing axe, his seax and his mount, which form a very different Trinity—how complex He is, this God in three Persons who has set about conquering the world by converting pagans like himself, forcing them to bend the knee the better to anoint their powerful foreheads with chrism. Worship that which you have burned, burn that which you have worshipped, Chlodowig worshipped trees and wellsprings, mares, wolves and the sound of a shield as it breaks; he worshipped gold and silver, forests and monasteries; he feared Remigius of Rheims as a saint, even as a god, and, more than anything, he loved the thick of battle, the howling, the valor and the danger. When he reached Tours, the man who would later be known as Clovis tells his men to take nothing from the lands of Saint Martin but water and grass; with his own hand, he slays a soldier who dares violate this order—the horse shies; the man falls to the ground, his helmet and his skull split open by the axe. Alaric held the South; his hordes were waiting somewhere near Poitiers, accompanied by their allies, the Arverni led by Apollinaris, son of Sidonius from the dark city of Clermont. Clovis is not afraid; he knows that if he does not displease the saints, then victory is certain. He is the lance against the enemy charge. Sometimes he can still feel the old gods breathe carnage in his face—and in the thick of battle it is not Christ's love that gives strength to his arm but Woden's fury or Yngvi's power, and after each battle he repents himself, kneeling before the altar. What has Chlodowig left behind him in embracing God? What forest sprites, what enchanted necklets, what amulets, what songs?

The bay horse that will later be a monk, and later still a knife grinder, calmly grazes on the misty grass of the valley in Vienne; Poitiers is still some leagues distant and already a first miracle is nearing. Vainly searching for some ford where they might cross this unfamiliar river, swollen by floodwaters, they ride along the bank fringed by dark forests, trailed by an army of thousands; despairing of finding a crossing, resigned to waiting for the spring rains to end and the waters to ebb. Suddenly the bay horse rears, Chlodowig looks up; a large, magnificent doe has just stepped out of the forest; it flees along the river; the bay horse feels Chlodowig brutally dig his heels into its ribs, the bit slack in its mouth, and takes off at full gallop in pursuit of the animal—a dark, moving blur—up ahead. A few strides farther on, the doe plunges into the river Vienne and crosses, the waters rising to its chest—this is the ford that the army has been vainly looking for. Chlodowig gazes at the doe as she races down the southern bank, while from behind, he hears his lieutenants cry miracle. Clovis recognized the goddess Freya; Freya or the intercession of some saint; he is bewitched by this omen, which he will take with him into battle—through to his conquest of the cities of Aquitaine, which will further enlarge the lands of the Franks.

In Vouillé, the plain has the gentle undulation of a woman's belly. The fields are glades in a forest bordered to the south by the wide meanders of the Auxence. The Visigoths are waiting. Countless cavalry horses in close-knit groups are champing at the bit. Under cover of night, the Franks make camp on the outskirts of the forest. Clovis grooms his horse himself. He chooses a broad, sharp seax with a shining silver ring set into the pommel, and a solid lance with its blade fashioned like a laurel leaf; he sleeps among his men, close to his mount, in the cool of spring. During the night, Clovis wakes to find himself bathed in a magical glow coming from the basilica of Saint-Hilaire some leagues distant. His troops witness this miracle and are spattered with bravery; long before dawn, while mist fills up the furrows and creeps between the warriors' legs, they are on their feet, chests bared, in the thousands; in groups, they advance onto the battlefield, in the sporadic glow of the moon setting in the west. Dawn is a gray-fingered old crone who brings with her the bloodcurdling howls of the Goth outriders, the first charge; the Frankish soldiers raise their weapons, a lethal fog of franciscas, a forest of lances, they stop them in their tracks, slaughter the wounded horses and unseated riders—Clovis remains in the background with his own horsemen, hidden by the outskirts of the forest; beneath him, he feels his little horse stamp the ground; he whispers to the animal, strokes his neck and reassures him. Clovis wants a speedy victory. He wants to face down Alaric and kill him. He waits for the King of the Visigoths to appear before sending his horsemen into battle. A bloody slash through the melee, a raw wound through the flesh of men, a gash of blood, a trough of brute violence to bring himself, like a burning spear, to the feet of the enemy king. Clovis's little horse snaps the limbs and shatters the skulls of fallen warriors as though walking through a field of gourds. Alaric is close at hand. Alaric *Gothorum Rex* is lord of all from the Loire to Africa. The little horse does not see the approaching rider, but bites Alaric's horse near its mane, then rears up; Clovis leans forward, the outstretched seax like an extension of the arm, and thrusts the weapon into the guts of the Visigoth—the blade reappears, a glistening black spray, above the shoulder blade, next to the neck made rigid by imminent death; Alaric is lifted bodily from his saddle, his howl doused by the gurgle of blood rising in his throat, his mouth—for a moment he hangs, suspended by a double-edged sword at the miraculous extremity of an outstretched arm, above a standing horse, its hooves forward. Alaric's eyes are fixed upon the skies above the plain; Clovis's little horse steps back as the Goth falls from his mount and Clovis pulls the sword from his body in a rasp of bone against steel and brandishes the purple sword foaming with enemy blood high above his head—Alaric is dead! Victory!—

as the king crashes to the ground in a clatter of bronze and the dull daze of defeat. In a final furious rage, the Gothic horsemen try to break free of the pincer movement about to crush them, and savagely tear themselves from the threat of the short swords slashing their legs, slicing through thighs in sprays of blood, fracturing faces from nose to neck—taking their king's mortal remains, they flee to his two sons, Amalaric and Gesalec, before retreating toward the south.

A few hours later, when he dismounts the bay horse, Clovis bends one knee in prayer, gives thanks to Woden and Yngvi; thanks the Christ who flutters around them like a raven on the battlefield. Thank you for the Last Kingdom. Thank you for the Dead. Thank you for the Miracles. Glory to Saint Martin! Glory to Saint Hilaire! Glory!

He strokes the horse that has served him so well (could it be a messenger of the Lord? an emanation of the forest god?), then, all but alone, accompanied only by a handful of warriors whose savagery has given way to numinous dread amid the pall of fog and death, he leaves the dead to the priests and the jackdaws and, as evening falls pearl gray over the blackened earth, he goes to the abbey of Saint-Hilaire where Maixent the Pious awaits, to give thanks for his prayers and tell him the result of the battle, the great victory won through his intercession—and to ask forgiveness for the help of the false idols, which he sought and which was granted. Shortly before nightfall, Clovis and his men (in a grove where a fragrance blue as snow drifts) suddenly come face-to-face with a snarling wolf, teeth bared, blocking their path. A wolf with a broad chest, yellow eyes, dark fur; the affrighted horses snort and whinny; the wolf seems to bow low, staring Chlodowig in the eye, seems to lie on its belly, then roll onto its back before leaping for the cover of undergrowth bushes and disappearing—now that is a miracle, a true and veritable miracle, proof of the pact between Christ and the old gods, a victory after the battle, a chalice in which the future of the world is reflected, and Clovis's little horse does not understand, of course, the meaning the Frankish king ascribes to this wolf, for him as for all those who fear, the true miracle is life in every moment, every second; the little bay horse that will later be a host of women, men and a greylag goose shakes its head before carrying King Clovis to the abbey, Saint Maxentius and his fate, the destiny of a candle flame, a personage in books, between the memory of baptism and triumphant battles.

Of course, in that moment, if someone had whispered the name of Zama or even that of the Catalaunian Plains to Patarin, it would have made no difference—Patarin was a simple man who dreamed of pigs, women and cars, for whom the name Vouillé did not evoke memories of Clovis's glorious battle in 507, but rather a village of the same name outside Niort, on the road to Limoges. Unlike Lucie's cousin, Arnaud, Patarin was unaware of his previous lives even in the depths of his dreams, and whether he was slamming a jack of hearts down on the table or plunging his knife into a pork loin, he did so with the same conviction: he held the ten of trumps, the third after belote and rebelote. As he put down the nine of clubs, his last discard, he imagined for a moment the torments Paco was suffering, the calvary, the Gehenna he must be going through: there were still seven spades in play; Paco probably had four of them. Who had the other three? By this stage, it was all but certain that Patarin was hoarding them, in which case Paco would have to be shrewd, very shrewd, or he would lose even the *dix de der*, not that this would make much difference to the score (they had already won, barring some miracle, and there are no miracles in belote), but it would influence morale. Now Paco knew how to play (as Patarin himself often said), indeed he played well—sometimes luck was against him and the Fates of the cards cut the game short, but Paco's decisions were never to blame, only a tragic misfortune in the order of the cards.

Paco was one of the few villagers of foreign origin, along with

Manuel the Portuguese painter and Yacine the Harki; his father had moved to the area in the late 1930s, when republican Catalonia fell into the hands of the nationalists and the republican soldiers had been forced to flee across the Pyrenees: France, ever magnanimous, locked them up in a series of rather ghastly concentration camps scattered between Roussillon and the Atlantic and later pressed them into forced labor, building fortifications during the Phony War and eventually—since, in the end, these men were merely useless mouths to feed—delivered many of them up to the Nazis. After all, the Germans had won the war; they promptly put the Spanish republicans in camps, principally Mauthausen, where more than half of them died—Paco's father had managed to escape this terrible fate and settled near Niort, in the more hospitable West, where he drove a truck, collecting milk for the Pamplie cooperative dairy; Paco, too, was a truck driver, traveling the length and breadth of neighboring départements for a logistics company based in Saint-Maxire. From Spain, he had inherited a shock of dark-brown hair, a love for paella on Sundays and for soccer every other day—he considered France a beautiful country, one that he loved deeply, but when a round leather ball was in play, it was a different matter, Spanish teams were vastly superior, an opinion that earned him many beatings and ripped pants in the school playground; he still remembered a pounding after Nantes lost 4–0 to Valencia in the semifinals of the Cup Winners' Cup; heading home, his hair glistening with spittle, his pants slashed, his eyes filled with tears, he had a broad smile on his face because "the Canaries" had been humiliated at least as much as he had—not once but four times in a row—and all the Maxime Bossis and Baronchellis could do nothing about it.

Paco looked at Patarin's nine of clubs, at Régis's queen of clubs and, from behind him, heard the coarse cackle of Thomas, reveling as ever in the misfortunes of others; Alain discarded the eight of clubs, he knew Paco would trump with the seven of spades; the son of the Spaniard took the hand, he had two master trumps and

the eight, Patarin had three trumps, ten, belote and rebelote—
Armageddon, Apocalypse, call it what you will: even with Régis
as Marshal Ney, the retreat was beginning to feel like a stampede.

*

In the winter of 1588, d'Aubigné, warrior poet and vessel of the soul
of Jérémie the hanged man, considered retiring to the Château de
Mursay, two leagues from Niort, at a beloved bend in the Sèvre,
there to hang his sword on a nail above the hearth, to stow his
breastplates, pistols and harquebuses in a trunk and finally devote
himself to rest, to his family and to his writing. Much as he loved
the fray, after months fighting in Bas-Poitou and Aunis in the service of Henri de Navarre, d'Aubigné needed some peace. Despite
relentless attacks by the Catholic League, the Protestants were
not faring badly, in no small part thanks to the military energy
of leaders like himself and Saint-Gelais, who had made Poitou
and Saintonge their playing fields—a battle in Melle, a battle in
Brioux, a battle in Brouage, a drawn-out defeat at Angers, granted
they had been forced to retreat before the Duke of Mercœur, the
scourge of Poitou, but had won a final victory over Anne de Joy-
euse, a *mignon* of Henri III, despoiler of the provinces, who in his
turn had been slaughtered at the Battle of Coutras in October of
the previous year. All these warlords rivaled the plague for the
terrible fear they inspired in the populace, Catholic and Protestant, many thousands of whom had died of the disease, before the
survivors were put to fire and the sword.

D'Aubigné feels safe in Mursay, in his château hidden among
the reeds in the depths of the Sèvre valley, protected by its high
turrets and its broad moat. His children, Louise-Artémise, Constant and Marie are happily growing up. Suzanne de Lezay, dame
de Mursay, his wife of ten years, fears for her husband's life; some
weeks ago, seeing a train of pack mules arrive in the castle courtyard, one of them bearing d'Aubigné's headdress and arms, his
sword and belt, she had instantly pictured him dead—but no,

the merry prankster was simply heralding his imminent arrival to avoid, he said, his wife becoming too upset. Much as he likes to take up arms, d'Aubigné also likes to lay them down—the horses, the night and the desert know his name; sword and spear, paper and quill know him too. During long months of repose, when a thin sheet of ice covers the canal by the leafless ash trees, he composes verses; verses that betimes are sad and furious, betimes witty and ironic. He seeks to bear witness to his times—to these brutish times, to the lies, the massacres, the peaceful endeavors doomed to fail, just as man is doomed to suffer. He already has a title, a simple title for this epic poem, this vast tirade against the ugliness of Fate; he calls it *Les Tragiques*. This year, 1588, he postponed his arrival at Mursay; in late December, he was with Henri de Navarre in Saint-Jean-d'Angély, where they learned that the Duke of Guise had been assassinated at the Château de Blois; doubtless, they drank to the death of the leader of the Catholic League. On the evening of December 27, d'Aubigné was to head north to meet with his comrade Saint-Gelais in a village called Sainte-Blandine on the edge of the forest of Chizé, to mount an assault on the headquarters of the Catholic League's troops in southern Poitou: Niort, held by Lieutenant Général Laurent and, more importantly, by Malicorne, governor of Poitou. They had marshaled several hundred soldiers, crossbowmen, harquebusiers, artillerymen, had secured gunpowder mortars to mine the city gates, siege ladders to scale the battlements, and heavy artillery: at least five cannons and culverins. The night was cold and moonless. The sentries on the ramparts of Niort are more concerned with protecting themselves from the bitter wind than from possible Huguenot attackers—they believe Protestant troops are marching on Cognac. The city's fortifications are formidable: walls some ten meters high, more than twenty turrets, a keep with a doubly fortified enclosure, protected to the west by a redoubt overlooking the river port, thronged with boats and barges. But the Protestants know which gates are best defended.

The first ladders are silently installed at the bottom of the ditch, north of the barbican that defends the Échiré gate, before the Souché tower. On the other side of the town, sappers set mortars to attack the Ribraise gate. They begin to scale the ramparts—the Huguenots gain an easy foothold on the walls, slit the sentry's throat before he can sound the alarm, then, as a group, they climb down into the city to open the Échiré gate. There ensues a brief skirmish during which d'Aubigné and Valières kill a number of the Albanian mercenaries who make up the watch. The alarm is raised and troops are dispatched to the north to rescue the besieged soldiers. Meanwhile, when they hear the alarm, on the far side of the city Louis de Saint-Gelais and a second group of assailants led by Jean d'Harambure detonate the mortars beneath the Ribraise gate and race down the streets to the Place de la Halle. The surprise is absolute; the Catholic troops and Albanian mercenaries are swiftly overwhelmed, so much so that they hesitate to retreat behind the castle walls—doubtless fearing the powerful artillery of Saint-Gelais. In the confusion on the Place du Marché where defenders have constructed a barricade, soldiers led by d'Aubigné are greeted by a harquebus salvo—Valières falls, mortally injured; d'Aubigné's men return a hail of lead and crossbow bolts; they hear the cries of the enemy—too late!—they recognize the voices as the men led by d'Harambure, who is blinded in one eye. The Huguenots wreak more damage to each other ... In any case, they inflicted a serious defeat on the Papists, who sought refuge in the castle, to which Saint-Gelais laid siege, installing his own artillery and that of the city, which the Papists had not had time to take within the walls. It was almost 5 a.m. D'Aubigné engaged in undertaking negotiations with the governor of Poitou. The city is to surrender to Henri de Navarre in person when he arrives from Saint-Jean-d'Angély later in the morning; and Jean de Chourses, Seigneur de Malicorne, together with his wife and chattels will be escorted to Parthenay. In the meantime, Saint-Gelais has postponed the looting of the town by a few hours, perhaps to allow those who can to take shelter; perhaps because it is too dark and cold to plunder—whatever the reason, the sacking of the city was brutal. Priests were disemboweled and their entrails tied around their necks; statues were smashed and candlesticks seized; the burghers were manhandled until they handed over their money in recompense for the pain and ills suffered by their besiegers since the laws of war dictate that the loser must pay; the body of Laurent, who fell during the battle, was hung from the same gibbet where Jamart, said to be the richest man of the city, was hanged.

The long-faced gravediggers carried off Vilpion de Valières and many others, Huguenots and Catholics, Protestants and Papists; some were quartered, burned with quicklime and tossed into the river; others repaired to the cemeteries—souls were reincarnated while bodies rotted; Valières is reborn as a crow that caws between the turret and battlements of Maillezais where d'Aubigné and later his son Constant are governors, the crow lives thirty years, tasting human flesh many times before dying and being reborn (while its corpse is eaten by a magnificent red fox) in the body of a captain's dog, a sleek greyhound belonging to François de La Rochefoucauld, which participated in the siege of La Rochelle with its master; later, it will become a seagull that, for twenty-two years, escorted ships from the tower at La Chaîne through the narrow channels between the islands; a number of sailors, one of whom, an important slave trader, will die on Île Bourbon and be reborn a baker from Sainte-Hermine who settled in Mauzé-sur-le-Mignon, and who will end up in prison and die in Rochefort penal colony on February 27, 1808, at the age of forty-six without ever having known his son René, the first European to set foot in Timbuktu and return alive—this same René Caillié, when he dies, will be reborn a gentle and determined Chouan lady married to a Breton nobleman whose tiny estate has survived both Revolution and Empire; a staunch Catholic, she died in terrible agony in 1878 when a pair of horses bolted, sending the carriage over the guard stone and crushing her against the gate of her own home—she passed through the interval of Becoming before being reborn as a girl to a family of poor starving cowherds near Fontenay-le-Comte where she died of a mysterious fever at the age of three: since her father had not the means to pay the gravediggers, he dug one more wretched hole behind his hovel, next to the grave of the stillborn child who had been consigned to the Wheel, the World between Worlds, having never felt the air scorch his lungs, and who was reborn far in the future, in the twenty-second century of Great Drought and desolation, where everything was dying, everything was vanishing and burning, before the renewal of Times, the era of the Maitreya, the future Buddha, the Buddha of tolerance and love, when this dharma will be no more, though the illusion of samsara and of consciousnesses precipitated into the Wheel will carry on, seeking enlightenment as a newborn seeks the air and a plant the light.

D'Aubigné spent the day with Henri de Navarre in Niort, then set off again at the head of a detachment to conquer other lands for his friend; on the first of the Year, the future Henri IV wrote to Diane d'Andoins, his "beautiful Corisande":

Shall I ne'er send you aught but captured forts and citadels? Last even, Saint Maixent and Maillezais surrendered to me, and I hope, by month's end, that you will hear of me. Everywhere, the King prevails: he has had the Cardinal de Guise garroted in his jail cell, then hanged the President de Neuilly and the provost marshal of the merchants in the public square for twenty-four hours, together with the secretary of the late Monsieur de Guise and three others. The Queen his Mother beseeched him: "My son, grant me this request that I make unto you.—I shall, if it be meet, Madame.—It is that you give me Monsieur de Nemours and the Prince de Genville. They are young, one day they will do you service.—I would fain do so willing, Madame (he said), I shall give you their bodies, and keep only their heads." He sent to Lyons to capture the Duc de Maine. It is not known whether he has succeeded. There is fighting at Orléans, and close at hand, in Poitiers, where by morn I will be but seven leagues distant. If the King wills it so, I shall put them in agreement.

I sympathize if the weather be as foul with you as it be here, where it has not thawed these ten days past. I wait upon the hour to hear that the former Queen of Navarre has been throttled. This, coupled perchance with the death of her mother, would have me sing the Nunc dimittis.

'Tis a too-long letter for a warrior. Good night, my soul, I kiss you a hundred million times. Love me as you have cause. 'Tis the First of the Year. Poor d'Harambure is one-eyed now, and Fleurimont a-dying.

Navarre immediately appoints d'Aubigné governor of Maillezais, an old fortified abbey and Catholic bishopric on an island in the middle of the marshlands; a few weeks later Agrippa returns to Mursay, to his quill and his family, where, as is his wont, he spends the last of winter.

Poor d'Harambure is one-eyed and Fleurimont a-dying.

The next year, Henri de Navarre would sing the *Nunc dimittis* on the death of his mother-in-law Catherine de Medici—she is reborn a moth, a plump, pale larva wriggling through shadows and the pains of metamorphosis, then a suffering chrysalis until it pierced the cocoon with its wings to finally become a noctuid dazzled by a lantern in the courtyard of the Louvre, about which it fluttered and circled a long time before burning itself hideously, dying, to immediately be reborn as another shadowy larva, for one does not easily escape the most heinous reincarnations that are the recompense for lifetimes of vile crimes and corruption.

*

When Kate and James, the retired English couple living on the edge of the village, agreed to be interviewed by David Mazon, the neophyte ethnologist, they were, as we have seen, at once suspicious and oddly flattered that their daily lives were of interest, not merely to science, but to French science—since France is known to be boorish when it comes to peoples other than their own. James had an inkling (or so he told his wife) that this interview would concern the decision of British citizens to leave Europe and the consequences for expats like themselves. Kate, for her part, was sure she had heard the phrase "ethnological investigation" and was expecting an elderly man in jodhpurs and a pith helmet. So, when David canceled the first appointment on account of the cold, she had felt a little relieved. As every year, their children had traveled by train from London (a six-hour journey to Niort station) to spend the Christmas holidays, when they had feasted on fattened duck, smoked trout, oysters, crab and lobster. Kate and James's house was spacious, it was an old farmhouse, though perhaps a little smaller than the one owned by their neighbor Maximilien Rouvre the erotomaniac artist, but it boasted a very pretty wrought iron veranda, a beautiful glass canopy above the front door and a pleasing garden of roses and hydrangeas, crisscrossed with gravel paths that crunched underfoot, in which there was a well, a birdbath mounted with a metal cherub and a large aviary of twined bars containing two white doves. All of these additions dated to the early twentieth century, and, since James was busy with other things, bills and court cases, Kate alone had had the rust removed and gotten them repainted. The house had cost, as they put it, a pittance, what on this side of the channel was called a "bouchée de pain," and so they had been able to keep their little London house in Hammersmith, where their children still lived, a home whose proximity to the Thames made it both pleasant and extremely damp, especially in winter—sometimes the fog was so thick, James would say, that it was impossible to hear each other from one room to the next.

When David Mazon, the intrepid anthropologist, arrived on January 14, he rode his moped into the yard, took off his helmet and his gloves and admired the garden, which, despite the winter, had lost none of its charm. He checked that he had the tools of his trade, his notepad and recorder, and was preparing to ring the bell to the right of the front door, but did not have time—Kate immediately opened the door for him. James was waiting in a squat mottled armchair that he had found over the summer at a flea market in Coulonges-sur-l'Autize, like much of their furniture, as David discovered: antique wardrobes and sideboards of tobacco-colored fruitwood, an art deco billiard room, and lastly the small sitting room, where James got to his feet—a glorious winter sun streamed in from the veranda, a sight that, on the banks of the Thames just as on those of the western Deux-Sèvres, was rare enough to be noteworthy. James inwardly marveled at David's youth, and his near-perfect English—British, for once, rather than American; David explained that he had lived in London for a number of years, and it was there that he had begun his studies—soon they were discussing pubs, bubble and squeak, and scotch eggs, which left David feeling nostalgic and James feeling hungry. They sat around the pretty green baize card table Kate had set up in the conservatory, and David turned on his recorder.

In the mid-2000s, they had moved to Deux-Sèvres, initially to a house they had often rented in the heart of the Marais near the village of Saint-Hilaire-la-Palud—which had a particularly fine butcher's shop and a Sunday market, James remarked—before going on to buy this farmhouse, and, although there were no local businesses other than the Café-Pêche, they had been won over, not to say entranced, by the house. Besides, the Marais was even soggier than the Thames. Better to live on the plains. A lot of British people had sold after the financial crisis, but they had stayed. Yes, they had a few English friends in the area. Yes, for the past three years, since James retired, they had been living here all year round. Of course with the indoor swimming pool they had installed in their barn, the golf course only a few miles away, the occasional trip to the beach and the fine wine, they were perfectly happy. Or they would have felt terrible to admit that they weren't. And besides, this is a little bit of England, said Kate in a curious non sequitur. These lands were English up to the late fifteenth century, said James, maybe that's why we feel at home here. England with vineyards—paradise, in other words, he added. David laughed heartily as he meticulously noted the couple's answers. Hobbies, health-care professionals, shopping, he asked them about all the things that made up their daily routine, and about what they thought of the region. Did they feel part of a community? What did the word "village" evoke for them? What about the word "countryside"? They did not entirely agree—Kate wanted to be more socially involved in village life, while James preferred to be left the hell alone. He ventured out as seldom as possible. For James, countryside was about peace and solitude, whereas for Kate it was about the relationship with nature, the flora and fauna and the prospect of establishing close relationships with the local women and men, in sharp contrast to the anonymity and the mistrust of other people in big cities. She liked to speak French, to go to Coulonges market once a week, to attend the patchwork classes in the town hall on Tuesdays, to chat with Lynn, the hairdresser, who visited once or twice a month (David decided it would be a good idea to interview Lynn, although it seemed that she did not actually live in the village, she was one of the few people, apart from the farmers, the gravediggers and tubby Thomas, who worked there, so he asked Kate for her phone number and she gave it to him), being a member of the committee for the annual village rummage sale; all these things meant that Kate got to know almost everyone in the village without having to spend time at the Café-Pêche, which James and Kate readily admitted to loathing, they found it depressingly grim and preferred to drink their G&Ts and their bottles of red wine at home instead of braving—as James put it—the putrid stench of the place. James, for his part, was not about to confess to David that he was bored out of his mind and was on the lookout for any excuse to spend time in Britain—birthdays, funerals, rugby matches; he mistrusted the French, he thought them arrogant, unreliable and utterly lacking in a sense of humor. His main occupation, as he put it, entailed waiting for the plumber one day, the electrician the next and the roofer the day after, then doing it all over again since they never actually came—you had to wonder whether they really existed.

Conversation moved on to the EU, and the British decision to leave; Kate and James honestly believed it would make no difference to their situation in France or that of French people living in England; as for the rest, they would surely find common ground. After all, the UK was an island. And not being part of the EU had not stopped Norway from prospering. Rather the reverse.

David was thrilled with his interview, he had plenty to chew on and plenty of rash conclusions to draw. Kate offered him tea and shortbread, which almost made him weep with joy; then he decided to take his leave, but not before accepting a formal invitation for the following week for an aperitif—one of James's favorite French words—and a game of billiards followed by dinner, which David already found himself looking forward to; he packed away his equipment and climbed back on Rocinante, which, for once, in honor of his hosts, immediately started up, belching a beautiful cloud of blue smoke into the Poitou sky.

*

After the ball, when Jérémie Moreau, Lucie's great-grandfather, saw Louise reach out to close the shutter, leaning into the darkness as though bowing down before him, as though bowing down before her Fate, he stepped from the shadows and stood in front of her, a muddy mask of hatred and fury, eyes glittering with vengeance, a silent howl cleaving the night with a stormless thunderbolt: Jérémie did not say a word, he clutched his package, and all the energy of this man who had survived the war, fire, water and the long months of solitude in the marshes was distilled into this moment when Louise saw him, only inches from her in the darkness—the black of his black beard, black eyes, black eyebrows, long black hair glistening with filth, a face that seemed carved by a knife from the shadows themselves, and Louise twice thought that she would die of fright, the first time because there was a man outside her window, the second because she recognized Jérémie and sensed that he had come to take revenge.

Frozen in shock and disbelief, screaming silently, mouth open, heart about to stop, chest tightening, Louise felt as if she were falling backward; she brought her hands up to shield herself, Jérémie took his accursed package, tossed aside the unbleached linen, the pouch reeked of blood and of abomination, Jérémie held aloft the baleful curse, and in the instant Lucie lost her balance, in the second she foundered beneath the weight of the horror, Jérémie hurled at her the foul, fetid thing—death, Jérémie hurled death at her, death still in the womb, still slick with blood, the black, rotting placenta still clinging to the belly, the greenish-white skin, the closed eyes, and Louise falters and falls, blood on her face, on her chest, cadaverous sections all over her face, the terrible stench, stillborn, a stillborn thing, a child, Jérémie has just thrown a stillborn child at her, Louise's arms flail, flail in helplessness and revulsion, she whimpers, whimpers so that she does not have to open her mouth to the murk streaming down her face, lying on the floor she cries and shakes as she pushes it away, this white creature with its closed eyes in its pouch of blood and mucus, Louise moans in horror through clenched teeth, she howls in the hideous silence before she faints, faints from fear and revulsion as Jérémie disappears into the night.

It was Louise's father who found her the following morning when, having knocked on his daughter's door several time to no answer, he decided to go in—still wearing the green ball gown, she was sitting on the floor, her back against the mirror, her face smeared with a blackish substance, her eyes open and staring, with what the father guessed was the fetus of a dead calf savagely ripped from the belly of a cow with the uterus; the sight was so terrifying, so incomprehensible, and the stench so overpowering that the father had to grip the doorframe to keep himself from turning away—he crept close to his daughter, softly whispering her name, Louise, and kicked away the sickening thing next to her, Louise was staring into the middle distance, she was somewhere else, somewhere far away, and he took her in his arms like a child.

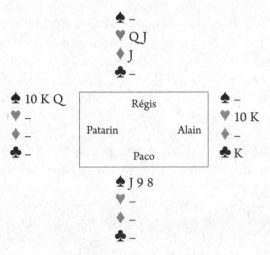

Sometimes all is lost but honor.

Paco had the lead and a bitter taste in his mouth. He could see only one solution if he was not to lose the *dix de der*, the ten points awarded for the final trick, and that was to play his lowest trump first, the eight—Patarin played his ten, Régis discarded the jack of hearts and Alain, shrewdly, discarded the ten of hearts, another twenty points stolen from under Paco and Régis's noses—he threw down the *trente-quatre*—the jack and nine of trumps, thirty-four points; Patarin, as the rules required, said in a whisper *belote et rebelote*, the king and queen of trumps; Paco picked up the last eight cards and perfunctorily glanced at

them, Barely fifty, we've barely scraped fifty points it's unbelievable, and Patarin couldn't help but agree, everything has worked
in his favor. Four trumps including the *trente-quatre* and we're
in. I have to say, you had nothing, Régis. You said it. Not a single
trump or ace, it was disastrous!

Tubby Thomas was delighted. He loved disasters and ignominious defeats; his family had been bar owners and farmers,
farmers and bar owners since the world was made; he, of course,
was unaware that his lustfulness, his lies, his massacre of small
game and fish would see him reincarnated as a hedgehog, one of
the last in the village, a hedgehog that would be unable to escape
the tires of Patarin's mobile butcher's shop, now run by his son;
Patarin's grandson would squash the hedgehog, though it had
curled up in a ball, the hedgehog that had been tubby Thomas,
sending him back to the Bardo to be reborn as a bedbug two centuries earlier, in 1815; a female bedbug, *Cimex lectularius*, which
after five weeks as a nymph reached adult stage, dark brown in
color and a few millimeters long, born in early June on the first
floor of the Auberge de la Boule d'Or, a large inn situated on
Avenue de la Quintinie in Niort, between the main Paris road
and the street then known, by a sort of onomastic metonymy, as
the rue de la Boule d'Or, with a view of the Champ de Mars then
called the Place de la Brèche, an inn run by a certain Lagrave that
boasted handsome stables, two dining rooms, kitchens, a large
cellar and about thirty bedrooms, making it one of the largest
establishments of its kind in the city. The bedbug *C. lectularius*,
being hematophagous, would feed upon the bodies of the inn's
guests at night; she lived in a small hole in one of the bed's slats
and had only a few decimeters to travel to find a sleeping foot,
crawl forward to the ankle, or to the calf where the skin was softer
and, between two hair follicles, plant her rostrum in the sleeper's skin—she would gorge on blood, return to her hiding place
to digest, then start the process again. Sometimes she would
encounter a male who would rush to pierce her abdomen with

his needlelike penis to inject his sperm directly into her with no coitus, a curious rape so brutal that sometimes the female was killed; if she did not die, disemboweled or infected by pathogenic bacteria, she would lay several hundred eggs not far from her hiding place, eggs that, following five larval and pupal phases, would become so many brand-new *Cimex lectularii* that would feast on blood, welcome in the male's sexual stiletto in their belly, or males, ready to pierce the titillating abdomens of female bedbugs; and all of these arthropods contained souls wandering through the infinite number of reincarnations according to the whims of the Karmic Wheel, and always in pain.

On the evening of July 1, 1815, the inn was in a frenzy. It had been a sweltering hot day and it had been a surprise to see Napoleon Bonaparte appear in person, with his generals, armaments and baggage, just as the sun was starting to set. He had set off from Malmaison on June 29, passed through Rambouillet, Tours and finally Saint-Maixent, where he found himself in grave danger because of the Whites there, and arrived at the Auberge de la Boule d'Or in Niort somewhat gloomy and taciturn. The people of Niort were Blues, in no small part because of the imperial troops billeted there to fight against royalist counterrevolutionaries; rumors quickly spread that the Emperor was in the city; crowds of people gathered beneath the windows of the Auberge; soldiers, burghers, citizens of every stripe, all came and shouted *Vive l'Empereur!* to the man who, since June 22, was no longer Emperor. These cries were as a balm to Napoleon's heart; "the Eagle" appeared at the window and thanked the multitude. It was the second time he had visited the city; he had passed through in 1808, and had a vague but pleasant memory of the visit.

On the evening he arrived, Napoleon dined with Generals Beker and Gourgaud in the company of the préfet. The following day the crowd was so clamorous that he resolved to spend the day of July 2 in Niort before reluctantly leaving for Rochefort on the third, having been warned that the English were likely to block the channels. Napoleon considered leaving France and seeking refuge in the United States; he hoped that a warship loyal to him might get him through the blockade and across the Atlantic.

The bedbug that had once been tubby Thomas and a crushed hedgehog could not possibly know that the city was decked with flags that evening, and the imperial standard had been taken from the wardrobe and fluttered over the Place de la Brèche; she knew nothing about the city, its geographical location or even the sleeping human bodies she fed on, as on the two nights when she feasted on the legs of the squat Corsican—island and imperial blood was as wholesome as any other, if not more so; *Cimex lectularius* did not notice the blue uniform with its gold buttons neatly draped over a chair next to the escritoire, nor the sword in its scabbard (a weapon that Napoleon would keep with him aboard the *Bellerophon* on his journey to Saint Helena) nor the celebrated bicorne that he kept with him until summer. Shortly before dawn on the morning of July 3, the bedbug scuttles over the imperial calf, then over the thigh, bared because of the stifling heat; the bug navigates by body temperature and carbon dioxide emissions; the bug prepares to feed again, a blind and pleasureless meal. Some hours earlier, she laid about a dozen eggs in a hole in the mattress. Having reached a suitable spot behind the knee where she bit the previous night, in the hollow between the thigh and the joint, she pierces the skin with her needlelike proboscis which has two stylets; one she uses to suck blood, the other to inject anticoagulant and anesthetic. She ingurgitates a milliliter of warm blood. She is oblivious to the twitch of the imperial hand, itching from the previous day's bite; she cannot comprehend the movement of those fingers inadvertently crushing her; she feels her body envelope burst, the blood she has just sucked spills out on the sleeper's skin, she feels a pain similar to that of mating, when a male pierces her abdomen; she does not understand death, does not understand the passing of her ability to sense hot, cold, tepid; she does not understand the Bright

Light, she melts into unconsciousness; she does not understand her reincarnation in the Wheel and her rebirth in another body, a mere moment in the cycle of continual existences.

SONG

Foulques Valère de Coëx is captured in the thick of battle, on 22 Nivôse, Year 2, not far from his home, the castle of Brétignolles-sur-Mer, after a skirmish at a place called La Chaize-Giraud, in the company of some thirty peasants, while attempting to join the army led by Charette, which has won a valiant victory at the Battle of Saint-Fulgent.

He has just turned twenty. Since the man from the Vendée has a deep wound to the thigh, Republicans are hesitant to summarily execute him, for, although he has left them with twelve dead and as many wounded, Coëx's youth and his valor command respect: the Republican officer stares at him; Coëx is ashen, close to passing out, but holds himself erect though he has only one good leg. His face is handsome, his features delicate and harmonious, his fine eyebrows are coal black, and he has an air of gentleness that starkly contrasts with his formidable skills as a warrior. A shame, he thinks, to draw and quarter the youth. Pack him off to Nantes—they'll string him up there, or blow his guts out with a cannonball. Pack him off with the rest of yon rabble. Slit the throats of two or three, bleed 'em like pigs here on the highway, like as not t'will keep the others cowed. Come, let's go.

It is done according to his word. As the cart pulls away, four peasants are still thrashing on the ground as their lifeblood drains away. It is a day's ride to Nantes, allowing a stop at La Roche. Barely conscious, Foulques de Coëx lies slumped in the back of the cart being drawn along the rutted paths by a pair of granite-gray Breton shire horses at a painful pace. By the time they reach Nantes, he is at death's door; the enemy warriors are dispatched to the former coffee storehouse, now a prison; Coëx, the handsome warlord, is sent to the prison at Bouffay. Curiously, the jail he imagined would be teeming seems all but deserted. He is confined to a cell on the first floor; it is bright and airy, the straw mattress is fresh and does not stink unduly. No sooner has he arrived than Coëx sinks into unconsciousness; he is as pale as a winding-sheet. Bled white. His jailers tend to him. The dressing on his thigh is changed for one of lint and strapping. He is in great pain. Foulques wonders why the prison guards show him such compassion. Is he not fated for a swift death? See how they bring him broth. What do they desire of him? Even the jailer's daughter comes to visit. She and he are much of an age. She has a beauty spot on her cheek and a pair of green eyes. Aqueous eyes, smoldering, almost blinded eyes, or so it appears. Foulques sups his broth, is there then a dearth of Christians to imprison, else why is the jail empty? Where are my comrades? Your comrades have been taken to the coffee store, Sire. What is this prison, then, my comely jailer? 'Tis the Tour de Bouffay, Sire. The most far-famed in all of Nantes! It is a place of woeful repute. I would fain have died with sword in hand than such dishonor! Oh, do not speak so, Sire. You find yourself in a most notable prison. A most fearsome jail.

The young woman's eyes quaver, the green seems paler, her gaze hovers above his head or to one side, she keeps her hands tight-clasped. Foulques de Coëx studies her garment with its blackened hem, her soiled apron, her gray bonnet, her clogs, the flowers carved into the clogs. He pictures the slender ankle, the pretty foot, the narrow waist; he proffers a few coins, says thank you for the broth. Oh, but you are most welcome. Most welcome. Then her father the jailer arrive; is the girl simpering still? Cannot she see that it is bootless! They die, all these fine young gentlemen! They die!

The young woman brings a hand to her mouth and stifles a sob that does not come.

The jailer smiles. This e'en perchance ... Or on the morrow ... Cannot our little lord fathom why the prisons stand empty? Foulques painfully observes the pleasure of the boorish commoner, the joy they take in seeing a nobleman suffer. The jailer's harelip flaps to the whims of his curses and imprecations. Coëx feels like a beast whose pain affords pleasure. Like a dog one might watch perish on its straw bed.

We take a hundred, two hundred royalists and lock 'em up on an old barge, says the jailer. We stow 'em away in the hold, all tied up good an' tight. We waits for nightfall ... And we sinks the barge. With first trickle of water come the first screams of terror. We listen as ye struggle, ripping arms and legs off to try to work free, banging your heads against the slats.

We watch the ripples move over the black waters of the Loire, the bubbles burst, and all is over.

The eyes of the jailer's daughter are flooded, flooded with horror. Only a day since, she watched long lines of doomed men roped together and led to the Loire. The moon and its ghastly glow on the river so broad ... The bulbous barge loaded with men drifting toward Trentemoult, stopping midriver past the tip of the island, pitching and reeling, hovering for an instant, then disappearing into the watery darkness.

Foulques imagines himself drowning in the icy dark, hands lashed to his neighbor's, he can scarce contain his tears. The jailer leaves the cell. His daughter follows. They take away the candle. Foulques turns over on the straw mattress, tries to bury himself in it as a rat into the earth.

I shall bring you a fresh dressing, Sire.

Foulques de Coëx sees that day is breaking, a gray dawn that sketches the bars of his cell in shadows on the floor. He finally succumbed to sleep. I thank thee, he says. Bring drink, too, if you please. Food and drink. The jailer's daughter is as graceful as ever, her eyes as green as the Loire, as the waters of the ocean, the color of the countryside. Foulques smiles at her, gazes into her eyes, studies her body, she finds it difficult to hide her chagrin. Demoiselle, might you be so good as to change the lint of this compress? She wavers, I know not ... I shall ask my father ...

I shall pay, of course.

Foulques pulls on the shackle restraining him and hauls himself to his feet. His thigh aches like blazes. There is a heavy chain about his ankle, set into a metal ring. He hobbles a step or two like a young colt on a bridle. The leg does not seem to be broken. The flesh around the dressing is livid purple. A fine saber slash. Ho, my pretty jailer, is there talk of me abroad in the city? What say the Blues? Here, have three sous for the bread.

Foulques stares at the coppers before handing them to her; on the obverse, the scales of justice, on the reverse the motto, "All Men Are Equal before the Law." *Sols* minted by the National Convention. The same convention that drowns the men of the Vendée in the Loire. What falsehood. Men are equal only before God. And even then ...

The young woman wraps the coins in her kerchief. She turns her head, speaks as she walks away. They say ... They say that on the morrow you will die. They say ... they say you will be drowned ...

Foulques remains standing, gripping the ring set into the wall. He feels blood drain from his face. Drowned ... Like a litter of kittens tossed into the Jaunay. Drowned. The young man feels his chest tighten with dread, he thinks on his mother and, softly and unthinkingly, he prays to Christ. From the doorway, the jailer's daughter watches. Longs to comfort him.

Fear not, Sire, I shall fetch the lint and return.

Foulques does not so much sit as slump onto the floor. The Lord knows he has valor enough in arms and battle. That he is willing to defend King and Christ even unto death. The Lord knows, too, that he trembles at the thought that he will perish lashed and bound, drowned in the bottom of a hold.

The young woman reappears with bandages and pail. She steals forward, close enough to touch Foulques. She kneels beside him. He can smell her, a scent of toil and smoke. Slowly, she unbinds the dressing, removes the lint caked black with blood, gently, very gently, she bathes the wound as she might stroke the hair of a babe; Foulques grits his teeth—but not in pain; he runs his hand down the young woman's back, attentive to her breathing, he believes he feels her heart beat through the skin—but it is only his own.

If indeed I am set to die tomorrow... he thinks, then murmurs into her ear, If indeed I am set to die tomorrow...

The jailer's daughter's cheeks are flushed red with the heat. Is it the heat, then? The cold? The prisoner's hand upon her back?

... Would you help me escape?

She recoils as though stung by a bee; she bows her head. How then? How, Sire? How might I help you ... She raises her face to his.

If you could but release this ankle ...

Alas, Sire, I cannot, I have not the skill.

Take pity, for they shall surely drown me.

Youth has a horror of death. The jailer shudders at the word "drowning"; for an instant, she stares out at the Loire, ablaze with steely glints beneath the mackerel sky. The round-bellied barges are headed for Saint-Nazaire. The tip of the island seems close at hand. A hammer and a rod, she knows, would suffice to release the shackle. And then what? The man is wounded, he would not get far. They would surely catch him.

Can't swim, Sire?

Oh, should I need to, I can swim, fear not! My wound will slow me nothing in that regard, I shall swim with my arms.

You must cross the river Loire ... Creep past the coffee store and make southward for Rezé. There you will find friends.

She will know how to remove his leg-iron, to lead him through the tunnel to the river; she pictures the current sweeping him westward, like the barges; she sees him struggle, exhausted from the waters at Trentemoult amidst the fishermen.

This e'en, when night draws in, she said. My father ...

Your father?

When he's sotted, in the tavern ...

And the men-at-arms?

None guard the river crossing.

Foulques feels himself come alive once more; in winter, night falls early—he pulls toward him the young woman whose heart is suddenly pounding fit to burst.

Will you return here?

I will return when we are victorious, this I pledge. He takes her hand in his. She rises too swiftly, too abruptly, and stumbles.

The day is long. The day is hellish long. She wonders whether she has chosen aright, but just the memory of the touch of Foulques's hand, his eyes upon her body put her mind at ease. When night draws in, the jailer, as is his wont, goes to the tavern to wassail. His daughter mounts the steps to the cell, bringing bread and water and, hidden in her pocket, a hammer for the shackles.

She would be hard-pressed to explain her actions.

The young nobleman is a-quiver with impatience.

Eat, while I set you free.

He eats. With a few deft hammer blows, she undoes the fetter. Foulques knows that, before he takes ten paces, his wound will gape, that the bandage will be crimson with blood, that his crossing will be long and arduous. That, in the end, mayhap he will still drown. Or be slaughtered by the sentries. He heaves a sigh. His fate is in God's hands! For God and King!

When you reach Rezé, ask for the Libedan. 'Tis a tavern ... There shall you find ... people who will aid you.

At the end of the tunnel is a slippery light, the reflection of an infirm moon and the smell of silt.

No sooner has his pretty jailer shown him the point that he must reach than the prisoner plunges into the Loire.

Foulques Valère de Coëx feels as though he crossed the river in a single breaststroke—the current bears him onward to the bank, to Rezé.

He has a last thought for the young woman who has just saved his life. He vows that, should he come again to Nantes, it will be to take her to wife—he cannot know that, in but a short time, he will perish, with a republican bullet directly between his eyes.

At the very moment when, for the last time, he pictures the face and the green eyes of the jailer's daughter, by some flawless twist of magic, beyond the mist that shrouds the Loire, like some far-off cry muffled by great distance, the bells of Nantes begin to ring out in chorus.

IV.
THE ANNUAL BANQUET
OF THE GRAVEDIGGERS' GUILD

"Valorous gravediggers and sorry toilers, Grand Master Gnarl-cock, Treasurer Squatchoad, Chamberlain Pizzlebeer, friends and fellow members, another year has rolled around and again we are gathered to celebrate, for the space of three days, the hiatus of our sorrowful travails, the pause accorded to us since the dawn of Time by Fate, three days in which we deliver no bodies to the earth, when Death herself gives us leave to rejoice, to forget that which all men know, that we will end up in her arms, a last lover, the same for one and all. This, then is the Annual Banquet of our Guild, as it has been every year since the beginning of the world, where we shall feast, slake our bellies and our throats. Let us rejoice, brothers in sorrow, and leave off our long faces for roars of laughter! But above all, like our forebears, let us be temperate in drink; let it not be said that a gravedigger can be found 'neath the table before the appointed hour—already, I can see your eyes caress the flagons. So we shall quaff in chorus, in the honorable tradition of the Guild, and before and after drinking, we shall converse, at least on this, the first day; thenceforth we shall place our trust in the bottle divine, the sacred vessel that illumines us with its wisdom; we shall drink until we drop, still struggling to make our gastral gurglings intelligible while in drink, then finally, on the second day, we will scarce speak, but contemplate the nectar in silence and await the miracle of sleep, and when we shall be drowsy, Death will reclaim her rights over life and we, our sorrowful toil, as is written in the Scriptures. This is the Truce! O Death, suspend thy scythe! Take pity on our suffering! Let the Wheel cease from turning!"

The ritual words having been pronounced, Martial Pouvreau drained the contents of a great chalice, drenched his mustache, stained his shirt; the assembled company was a sight to behold, the pockmarked faces, the staring eyes as, trembling, they waited for permission to fall upon the coveted flagon, upon the chat of victuals set out by servants, upon the cornichons and the beasts turning upon the spit in the great hearth.

"A toast to you, my gallant gravediggers! Long live Death!"

There came the gurgle of liquids through gullets, the smack of tongues on lips, the eructations of the more churlish, the sighs of relief from those a-thirst: the Banquet had just begun.

"Long live Death, that big-hearted strumpet!"

And, as one, they chorused "Long live Death, big-hearted strumpet!" in the strangled cry of the convict, the shriek of the furious captive.

"And now … now my brave gravediggers, my beloved crypt keepers, churn-curdled bollock batter, let us live! Let us eat and speak! Let us fork the dead flesh to our lips!"

It was a sight to behold, ninety-nine guests launching their paws toward the pâtés en croûte, the bread, hacking slices, piling them up, several among them choked, spluttered, coughed, and had their neighbors not clapped them on the back, they would have made a mockery of tradition, which decrees that, during the Banquet of the Gravediggers' Guild, nothing dies save poultry, rabbits, pigs, lambs and oxen, in vast numbers, slaughtered ad hoc in preparation for the feast, and, this year, a surfeit of frogs and eels in cast creels; but afore jawbones could gnaw, afore gullets could guzzle, Grand Master Gnarlcock took the floor to give the response to the invitation, and pose the first ritual question:

"I thank thee, Maître Pouvreau. Long life! Thanks for the welcome to this glorious abbey! We who are untouched by calamity, let us here rejoice, for 'tis afforded us but once a year. Let us ruminate, friends, on our sad fate, and extol the doctors, who bake our daily bread." (A general roar of laughter, a splutter of cornichons.) "May our wives bring forth Immortals! We all shall be entombed in turn! So turns the Wheel! Drink, my friends, let us drink, since it is accorded us to disremember and rejoice for these three days, churn-curdled bollock batter!

"The first question I would ask you, my good gravediggers, concerns the lot of women. Thus far, they have found themselves excluded from our Brotherhood. But the twenty-first century commands that we admit them. Are they not equal to men in all respects?"

It was a sound to be heard, the cavernous silence elicited by this daring declaration. They all leave off masticating, some spit their wine to their left-hand side, in disgust, to the grievous displeasure of their neighbor; others prick their earholes wide, full of interest.

"Women? You would have women? I fear you do your thinking with your pizzle, Gnarlcock, that pale and paltry manhood. I'll wager it is him speaking through you." (Muffled laughter.) "You would have women in the Gravediggers' Guild! Would turn this Banquet into an orgy! Why burden ladies with our woeful trade? Why yoke them to our doleful Fate, from which they are excluded? Would you, under pretext of equality, impose our sorrows on them? You live too high on the hog, Gnarlcock. You forget our condition. Let us leave bosoms to the world of beauty."

All roar: "Well said, Pouvreau, well said!" and take advantage of this lull to once more suckle their bottles in a melancholy dream of dugs. It was a sight to see, Gnarlcock's face, as it paled at this affront.

"Wrong, Pouvreau! Wrong! You would toss the babes out with the bathwater, sophist! Here lies my argument: you know fine well why there are no women in this Gravediggers' Guild, why our own wives are not admitted. I say it is an antiquated business. One born of myth. Injustice. Superstition. How can it be that our wives may keep our ledgers, take delivery of our clients, yet not bury them? Do we not see them at the obsequies, veiled in mourning black? Are they not more fitted to consoling the bereaved? To making flesh the renewed desire of the mortified widower? To touching hearts, to staunching tears? And you, Pouvreau, if God forfend that you should die, would you not rather a delicate and gentle hand to assist at your last bath than the hairy hand of an apprentice? Say you that women may beautify and coif the living, but not the dead? Say you that they may do aught but join this Guild? I say: a little balm would aid embalming."

He drained his glass. The whistles of admiration were not long in coming. No more the whispers of discontent. Pouvreau gave a scornful smile; he waited for Gnarlcock to set down his goblet.

"Friend Gnarlcock, that is not the issue. Would you also have women to be torturers, executioners, soldiers? See where modernity has led: the fair sex quite fallen from grace. Is a woman still a beauty when in uniform? And if they be beneath a helmet, are her pretty wits still worth the candle? I say, long may it toot, the old pork flute!"

At these sonorous and well-chosen words, Pouvreau drained his glass—a Beaujolais, a little light, precocious, easy quaffing, so sprightly in the goblets that it dashed off ruby sparks when e'er it met the candles' glow. For to the great weighty blood of Bordeaux, the shadowy deeps of Corbières, the purplish velvet of Languedoc, he secretly preferred the dark Gamays of the Monts du Lyonnais, the Pinots Noirs, the nocturnal Côtes, the Beaunes, the Chalonnais, which he naively believed could be guzzled by the hectoliter without injury, as one might float down the Saône from Auxonne to Dijon, belly thrust into the air, like a whale whose blowhole sent up glorious showers, upwardly micturating the surfeit of nectar. On this particular year, seeing the gathering was to be held in the West, in the refectory of the Abbaye de Maillezais, whole barrels had been brought from Anjou and the Loire, supple, easy-drinking Chinons Les Graviers, ripe with blackberry and licorice, lingering on the palate, high in tannins, with tartar that clings to the teeth and stimulates such thirst that, with a straw that extends from the Devinière hill, he might drink the Vienne, or the great Loire down to the lees, having long since drained the Vendée, Lay and Thouet and each of the Deux Sèvres in turn, dried up the marshes the better to capture eels and frogs, that, well seasoned with garlic and parsley, well sliced and well sautéed, would as nobly adorn dishes as delight palates, so well do butter, garlic and parsley complement all things—the small rubbery bones of the amphibians may be used as toothpicks to rid the front gnashers of the clutter of greenery before public speaking, just as great gulps of rotgut, by sheer dint of force, mask the stench of garlic on the breath, not merely the garlic of snails and frogs, but also the garlic of pâtés and terrines, garlic that is raw or nearly so: the most fearsome, the most powerful.

So it was that this year, after Martial Pouvreau drained a glass of Beaune salvaged from the previous Banquet (Pouvreau was a rich man and hence was dubbed by some tightfisted, by others prudent), and brought back by car from the environs of Cîteaux, which none dares compare to earthly paradise (Pouvreau, ravening from the saliva-producing cornichons, the salt-heavy pâtés, and the sheer habit of the Beaune, was now eyeing the suckling pigs and lambs roasting in the hearth so hard that he all but suffered a detached retina), and after the assembled crowd of gravediggers, earthmovers, monumental masons, cemetery keepers, mortuary makeup artists, cremators and funerary coachmen (only one survived in Europe, an elderly one-eyed Dutchman as blind as a horse bound for the knacker's yard and very drunk) had fallen upon the buffet, after Martial Pouvreau (the master of ceremonies for this year) and Grégoire Gnarlcock (the Grand

Master) had corroborated Montaigne's adage that it is the duty of princes to lead people in battle, had been the first to ingurgitate a goodly quantity of wine, terrines and cornichons, in the midst of this frenzied aperitif, affrighted by the prospect of a famine, while each and every man swiftly endeavored to reach some semblance of inebriation, some glimpse of gluttonous satiety, while mustache streamed red as boxers' nostrils and beards were spangled with crumbs, Gnarlcock once more took the floor, though not before first knocking over two empty bottles to enjoin silence:

"Guildsmen and friends! Morticians and gravediggers! I hereby solemnly declare that the Annual Banquet of the Grave-diggers' Guild has begun! Let us sing!" And, in chorus, everyone spluttered (some spitting crumbs, one—an epicurean—a whole hard-boiled egg, another a frog's thighbone) as they intoned the hymn of the Brotherhood, a March in D Minor, the same grave, solemn air that Mozart bestowed upon Death, which some unknown poetaster had embellished with Latin verses overflowing with plural ablatives ending in *-ibus*, which are, *in infidelium partibus*, the veritable mark of poetic and scholarly language. Hands on hearts, they all took up the refrain, *de poenis inferni et de profundo lacu*, "from the torments of hell and the bottomless abyss," and the Hebrew words *Y'hay Sh'may Raba Mevarakh*, "May His Great Name Be Blessed," gentiles and Jews, Catholics and Muslims, Protestants and atheists, zealous Marxists or members of the Petite Église, whether local men or distant souls, all gave full-throated voice to the hymn, since the founding principle of the Guild of Gravemakers was to check one's beliefs in the cloak-room of common generosity; all professed to enjoy the gefilte fish, for example, even gentiles and those who loathed fish in aspic, whether carp, pike or pike-perch, they would open wide their mouths to gorge on it at the appointed hour, because this was one of the principles of the Banquet, equity in the face of death, and so, for the space of three days, even the most bigoted of undertakers forgot their prejudices: all here exercise the same whoreson profession, by the belly of Sanct Buff, we know—atheists, Christians, Jews and Muslims alike—that we will find our end in the grave's depths or the furnace flames, and that from those flames, good or evil, none escapes: welcome to ashes or to decay.

Martial Pouvreau, as the master of ceremonies, had greeted the delegates of various denominations, received tributes and accolades, offerings and gifts. The monks' refectory of the Abbé de Maillezais was vast enough to contain all ninety-nine members, the poor gravemakers, the burial men, the embalmers, and their animals, the lambs and suckling pigs now roasting in the hearths, the fish and fowl in aspic and in pies, the dogs that lay at their feet beneath the great U-shaped table which was a pleasure to see, so long it was, so long, so broad it was, so broad and laden as it was with wine, victuals and great minds. After the hymn was over, after Mozart had been murdered in a chorus of yelping and chewing, the decidedly dogged Grand Master Gnarlcock once again took the floor and restated his earlier submission:

"Know you, gentle gravediggers, that in the past women were admitted to our Guild? That they had a say in the matter? That they not only buried, washed, embalmed, perfumed, corked and uncorked, and wept, but also wassailed, whistled and lowered the dead? In a word, they banqueted? Did you know this? Moreover, in the words of the poet Venantius Fortunatus *in sexu muliebri celebrat fortes victorias et corpore fragiliores ipsas reddet feminas virtute mentis inclitae gloriosas.*"

One among the Muslim gravediggers, long both of beard and of cloak, hastened to reply:

"In our faith, brothers, women have washed the bodies of the dead since all eternity. Women are needed so we can bury women, this I grant. But to admit them into the Brotherhood? To allow these cackling quidnuncs to perturb our Banquet? To become a Guild of popinjays where all would strut like peacocks to delight them? I can picture you, Patureau, with your tongue lolling and your propeller blade feathered. And what of you, Leborgne? And you, Nadking? And you, Moshe, do you think they would respect your piety?"

"*Bravo*, my friends, *touché*!" said Gnarlcock. "The harpies would surely throw themselves at our feet like insatiable castaways. No woman could resist the splendor of your proboscis, Lebel! Or the angle of your shell-like ears, Séraphin, wide as a mizzenmast, that make all cry: 'Ah, what a conch is Séraphin!' And well 'tis known in divers ports, Dessais, that womenfolk are drawn to your warts. Were they amongst us, e'en Bertheleau would rouse himself from lethargy and turn this Banquet to debauchery! 'Tis plain as the nose on Lebel's face! Your feral masculinity has no measure, nor your great skills in things of pleasure! I near forgot, my friends, 'tis just, that this is how you satiate your lust: good fellows all, you think but when you thrust!"

An outraged clamor rose from cups and plates. An ancient gravedigger suddenly spoke up:

"Forgive me, Master Gnarlcock, but you go too far. What need was there to make so great riposte, or to mock us so. To falsely flatter our virility, sophist! I propose we use a little guile. To equivocate. To litigate. To welcome modernity. Let us put the matter to a vote and leave off talking."

"Friend, you know it is not the custom of this august assembly to vote upon a motion unless it be lengthily discussed, debated and deliberated!"

Indignation swelled: "To the vote! Leave us to stuff our faces, Gnarlcock! Leave us to slake our parched throats! Enough of speechifiers! A plague on prolocutors! Let us eat!"

This was obviously mere provocation, since all were already at table, and eating more than ever. But Gnarlcock, accustomed to these gatherings, realized that stomachs were rumbling and gullets conspiring against him. A modicum of inebriation was required before serious matters could be discussed.

"Be it so! Let us vote! Who here favors a single, mixed Banquet? Who here contends that women should be accepted as full members of this Fraternity?"

"'Twould no longer be a fraternity, but a sorority! Or even a prolixity!"

A few brief laughs rang out.

"Let us vote, comrades! Let us vote! All those in favor, raise your hands!"

It was an unexpected landslide. Some even raised both hands to further manipulate the vote. The result was clear—Gnarlcock had prevailed, male privilege had been defeated.

"The 'Ayes' have it," he drained his glass. "The verdict is foremost, to the devil the hindmost! Now jackanapes, all raise your glasses in toast!"

As ever in such matters, the losers were happy to drown their sorrows and the winners to drink to their victory; and forthwith began flagons to go, gammons to trot, goblets to fly, great bowls to ting, glasses to ring, there was much gurgling and tippling, gullets were irrigated, uvulas soused, glottises flooded; all knew that grave matters would resume and they would discuss the business before the Banquet, but for now they roistered in the Overture, the Incipit, the Flood Tide. Gnarlcock, who considered it high time that women were made full members of the Guild, was delighted that his motion had passed; he celebrated with a tartine spread with rillettes au Vouvray into which he planted a bright-green cornichon, as one might load a cartridge into a shotgun; the crust of the baguette was neither too hard nor too soft, it tickled the incisors and stroked his palate, and then the rich pork fat, illumined by the crisp tartness of the cornichon, triggered a spurt of pleasure in the Grand Master's brain—ah, rillettes like these are a cure for all ills, he thought, the ills of mouth, belly and soul, and this irruption of joy upon his face did not go unnoticed by Pouvreau, his neighbor, who saluted him and poured him a glass of Chinon Les Graviers whose youth, the mayor contended, promised a great future, fruity, fruity yet not coarse, tannic yet not astringent, "a smile in a bottle," as the mayor-cum-undertaker liked to say.

From time to time, the roasters checked the springs of the rotisseries, basted the suckling pigs, the lambs, the hares (the hares were almost cooked) well anointed with fat, daubed generously with a sauce of sorrel and thyme, the hares smelled like an English lawn, like a Corsican grove, like a marshland that has been drained: the power, the sweetness, the madness of Nature. The hares, of course, had been sourced from poachers, since to shoot them in spring was forbidden; a few were allowed to be abstracted, long-eared old does, wearied and wily, plump and libidinous, moon hares and angoras, and jackrabbits would have been snared had they known how to sex them, an impossible task, one that led to the belief that the hare was doubly unclean, as an animal that cheweth the cud but divideth not the hoof, and as an incorrigible sodomite, which was naught but calumny and deep-rooted jealousy—the female hare, as Aristotle noted, can become pregnant before she gives birth to the leveret in her womb: this practice delighted the gravediggers who, of all men, were most attached to life, for they lived among the dead.

The meats were eaten according as they were cooked, in other words by size, and the vegetables only when no meat remained, out of spite; first the hares, then spit-roasted lambs, then veal roasted in quarters; the fish, eels, lampreys, carp, pike-perch and pike, sautéed, in terrines, in quenelles, in aspic or in sauces, following the entrées, soaring pyramids of eggs mimosa, white, yellow and green as a still life, luscious with fresh mayonnaise, speckled with parsley and tarragon; as in ancient Megara, the serving plates were fashioned from bronze, craters overflowed and the amazement kindled by new foodstuffs fired greed in every belly. Each year, the host was tasked with adding a local touch to the banquet: Martial Pouvreau had chosen, in addition to marshland *froggas*, the dried beans known as mogettes, which gurgled deliciously in venerable cauldrons hung at the corners of the thousand-year-old hearths—the gluttonous, who were seated on the floor by the hearth, toasted hunks of black bread on the coals, rubbed them with garlic and spread them with a goodly helping of beans, like schoolboys eating an afternoon snack; they were a sight to behold, slobbering, drooling and burning with impatience, mouths wide as cannon muzzles.

Gnarlcock took a moment to look around at the hubbub of the gravediggers, at the terrines and pâtés being scoffed, at the flames in the vast refectory chimneys. Sage Gnarlcock well knew how to bide his time, and, should he roll 'neath the table like the others, it would not be until late in the night, heaven forfend! So, he sipped rather than swigged his dark Chinon: many's the gravemaker would fall before Banquet's end! Some would pitch forward, foreheads in the mustard, sleeping the sleep of the just, their snores offering a counterpoint to the speeches! But the Grand Master could not permit himself to keel over, his face in the sauce, his eyes insensible; his duty, until the end and except-ing official hiatuses, was to remain ramrod straight as a *poilu* atop the war memorial.

Shuddering with the onset of *agape* (which in Greek means nothing less than "love"), the gravemakers eyed one another like thoroughbreds before a race; they speculated as to who would be first to speak after the officials, and to what purpose, for deep down they were avid for new stories and tales, more partial to emotions than to motions. A gravedigger named Bertheleau was first to take the floor. He had just polished off a bowlful of frogs' legs and was licking fingers glistening with oil and stip-pled with parsley and garlic; on his plate lay a pile of small bones like a matchstick sculpture. His lickings concluded, Bertheleau requested the floor, raising his right hand, as was custom, and Gnarlcock hastily granted his entreaty, eager to break a silence now becoming awkward.

BERTHELEAU'S SPEECH:
HOW LUDIVINE DE LA MOTHE RELIEVED
GARGANTUA OF HEARTSICKNESS

"Gravediggers and friends, to return to the matter of women
which so nettles you, for there can be no good Banquet without
talk of love, and of prick, as it is the practice of this Guild to
say outrageous things, and corporeal pleasures have their rightful place (while you scoff, dig the wax from your ears! Swill the
juice of the vine!), there will be mention made (with no vulgarity) of a form of gigantism of the cunt, of disproportion in the
gash and of vim in the quim." (At these words, the guests sat
stunned, hands raised, elbows frozen.) "We are all familiar with
its interior, dank as a cave, a slimy enclave, its texture like liver,
its lips all a-quiver, its perfume of humus, its mystery a rebus,
its shape like a plow." (The words instantly prompt an outcry:
slime? humus? plow? What swinish pearls of wisdom, these!
You go too far, Bertheleau! Enough of the wine, bring water!
We shall have none of this, by the devil! Bertheleau, you boor,
you insult the fair sex!) "Hold your whisht! I speak as behooves
me of grooves! Of gargantuan asses! Of heavenly lasses! Pro-
digious crevasses: cunts wide as crossbeams, from which flow
great streams. Torrents between mountains! Ah, yes! 'Pon my
word! Remember, fellow gravediggers, where we find ourselves,
the refectory of the abbey of Thélème, from the solar disc the
divine Analemma. Here it was Gargantua was born! Upon
this selfsame spot! Born fully formed, primed and ready. Now
suppose this brave giant knew not where to stick it, where, in
what vessel and by what excipient: for it was so big that no cunt
could contain it. A nanny goat was tried: she ended up a harelip,
cleaved in twain and inside out, her horns on her ass and her
fleece in her guts. A cow was prepared for his Homeric member. The problem, the pressure, as all will remember: though
roped by her shanks and with steel round her flanks, she ex-

ploded. Fearful of taking a woman's cherry, Gargantua essayed a dromedary: her head in the sand the beast prated, while the giant her intestines ablated, resulting in untimely death. Zounds, poor Gargantua, doomed never to wife! O cruel fate! O woeful plight! Condemned to hand-to-glans combat! O how he beat his meat, how he swung his salami! Like the bell ringer of old Notre-Dame, ding dong, ding dong, up down, polishing the snake whose lone eye was blinking. And beware the emission! The cannon fired thunderous salvos wildly, it rained homunculi! All Poitou was knee-deep in cream that pâtissiers piped into éclairs. The semen delighted the fishermen, for in it were oyster pearls and caviar."

(What in Christendom is this horror? Eww, Bertheleau, you churn-curdled bollock batter! Enough! This is vile! Shut the fool up! The comments turned nasty, because the gravediggers were prudish: they wanted no talk of cum while they ate. Bertheleau cared little and carried on.)

"One day, following a colossal bout of bishop bashing, a hiccup from the shameless shaft drowned an alderman in midspeech when he opened his mouth at the wrong moment. Perched atop Poitiers Cathedral, the giant was desolate. 'By Sainte Radegonde! Beware, my friends, for in spite of myself and for want of a cunt for my comet, all parliament is plagued with the vomit: the ministers must reach for their bonnet.' In those days, the debate centered on the price of gas and of rubber bullets, which the gendarmes used with abandon: some (arrant rogues) lost an eye, others (bawds and thugs) lay open-mouthed, their bodies purple with bruises. The common herd had a great urge to grab the president by the ears and unblock his auditory canals so that the great man might once again heed the cries of the Nation. Gargantua, a philosophical soul, observed the protest marches from the roof, one fist beneath his chin, dumbstruck; he daydreamed and finally dozed off; his pizzle, quick to leak, was now pissing—far below, the panic-stricken henchmen raised their shields to protect themselves as best they could from the golden shower. Battle orders! Testudo formation! Let it piss down!

"Gargantua was dreaming. He was dreaming of a magnificent island, where he was urinating against a palm tree. The downpour continued, the waters rose—the copulace were terrified, they remembered the Notre-Dame affair, when, as he doused the fire raging through the roof, Gargantua's powerful stream had drowned a hundred cops playing cards in their cars.

"Warmed by the sun, sprawled upon the smooth slate, the giant went on dreaming. A giantess named Badebec was teasing him. She tickled him, twiddled him, topsy'd him, turvy'd him, tweaked him with a fingernail, thrilled him with her eyelashes (oh rapturous bliss, the flicker of her lashes on his gonads!), charmed him, alarmed him, and in his dream Gargantua crooned, swooned, festooned: he turned over on his roof and slate tiles rained down on the police. Gargantua, moaned Badebec, Badebec, groaned Gargantua, and the gigantic prick stood proud.

"Of a sudden, darkness fell upon the battlefield below.

"'Gendarme, an eclipse! The darkest shadow has surprised our armies!'

"'Not so, Commander, 'tis the giant's schlong that blots out Phoebus! His tumescent pork sword is big as a billboard!'"

(The gravediggers, now won over, grinned at this perilous situation. They shrieked like children. It made a powerful din. Men pawed at the pâtés, fought over the cornichons, slashed hams with huge knives; they fell upon pastramis wreathed in whorls of steam; sides of beef formed a guard of honor, gherkins by their sides like Cossacks' whips. Seeing his listeners gorge themselves, Bertheleau himself took a break. He gobbled an egg mimosa, lapped the mayonnaise from his fingers, rinsed his mustache in his glass of Chinon, fragrant as a spring evening rose. Then, greedily, he grabbed a small goat cheese gougère—to soak up the wine, as he put it. The gravediggers now were all ears, ready for the epic.)

"'O Badebec, my sweeting, my leman, my doxy, my caprice, my codpiece, my pantofle, my panton never shall I see thee,' crooned Gargantua, waking from this perfect dream.

"Badebec's cunt was like the Cave of the Apocalypse: cavernous, numinous and radiant. The place of the Revelations according to Gargantua! Through it flowed a river, the air was sweet-scented with the smell of mushrooms. Saint John of Patmos himself would have swooned! Here it was that the Seven Sleepers of Ephesus spent three hundred years. The people of the cave had a dog, which gleefully poked its tail out of the opening. The walls of Badebec's cunt were smooth and moist, the mucous membrane viscous; press your ear to it and you would hear the gurgle of bubbles: echoes of the neap tide in the cecal colon. Hidden within the folds, Pythia delivered the answers of the oracles; frightened by her voice, the pricks reared and turned like whinnying horses. In the bottomless depths from which the wellspring rises, it is said that a blind people lives and anemones grow, white as asparagus, bloated like purses.

"Gargantua pictured the place as paradise, the perfect cavern, and dreamed that there he might make his bed, pitch his tent, dance the tarantella, found a family.

"Alas, this cavernous cunt, this conch shell of love, this palliasse of pleasure existed only in his dreams.

"Gargantua, up on his rooftop, was sore aggrieved.

"Below him, in the darkness, clashes continued between protesters and police. Each striving to best the other, stones against shields, cudgels against caps, the civilians refusing to cede, the cops redoubling their virile fervor with missiles and grenades. The pitched battle reminded Gargantua of the wars fought by his father, the Great Strife and Debate betwixt the *Fouace* bakers and all that ensued. He was a man of peace, gadzooks! He ripped the cross from atop the campanile to scratch his nose, to clean his nails, to clear his mind: naught to be done, God the Son, he bellowed, I want the lickage and the frolickage, the expulsion, revulsion, impulsion, of carnal love the great convulsion, the melding, the melting, the gelding, the coupling, the cuckolding, the culbatizing, I want the revelation, in short, I want marriage! Alliance, connivance, contrivance. To put beard-splitter to bum-fiddle. To paddle in a cunt of velvet! The sacred union! The *sacrum convivium*! To swive the split fig!

"The more the giant upon his roof lost hope, the more his prick grew proud, and the more the police below cudgeled varlets out in the dark. On a sudden, Gargantua let out a huge roar, the howl of the male rut, of the hot to trot: he hurled the iron cross from the bell tower like a javelin, southward and upward. After a moment's flight, it planted itself i' the ground, outside the House of the Rose Maidens, in La Mothe-Saint-Héray, landing, *thwack*, bolt upright as the Good Lord, a stone's throw from the river. Suddenly, Jesus Himself illumined the countryside! A Miracle! A Monument! A Benediction! The village maidens were chosen from among the indigent and the intelligent who had, since their first Communion, afforded the greatest proofs, in words and deeds, of their devotion to their duties to God, country and King, to their parents and to humanity, they were wise and industrious, neither bawds nor harlots, drabs nor doxies, sirens nor strumpets, madams nor tarts. So much so that, of them, the poet writes:

> Her wimple white, its wings a-quiver
> Her complexion rosy as a velvet peach
> The Maid of Mothe is a pearl beyond reach
> Whose radiance doth make fine ladies shiver.

"These chaste maidens were to be married off, endowered by the village, to some pack mule, some brute boor, who chose but by his eye. The sole hindrance that he could choose but one, and not a basketful of these corporeal roses! But one, and she for life! Ah, those beauteous damsels in their wimples! They were gathered in the House of the Rose Maidens when the crucifix landed, *thwack*. One among them, a pious girl, Ludivine by name, watched the cross fall and fell to her knees in prayer, for she had recognized the sign: Sainte Radegonde was calling to her. A Miracle! A Monument! A Benediction! On to Poitiers, to answer the call. And off she set, in her white wimple, traveling on foot, through Pamproux and Lusignan. She arrived on the morrow, at midday.

"Gargantua was still snoozing, still on his rooftop, his face upturned; protesters and police were still clashing down below. Once again, the giant lay dreaming; his member writhing, twisting and coiling in waves like a serpent. Like a palm tree blustered in a typhoon. His swollen gonads dangled like church bells, then suddenly drew up close against the shaft, as if a-cold—they looked like cartwheels braced against a cannon, or blue planets, drawn to some celestial spear. The writhing of the member, swift and steady, made one fearful of a storm. The police now had protection, having been issued with diving suits.

"Ludivine espied the giant lying on the roof, his head against the bell tower, his feet caught in the rose windows of the great facade, asleep, engrossed in reverie and his piss-proud prick, now and then scratching belly or thigh sending a hail of slate tiles raining down upon the battle between miscreants and militia and police raging below, betwixt the cathedral and the marketplace: the chaste rose all but swoons in grief to see the public square so ill-used—she runs the short distance to the tomb of Sainte Radegonde, there to meditate and pray. 'Tis said it was the saint herself who gave her inspiration: Ludivine, you must save the cathedral! Ludivine, you must sacrifice yourself! Ludivine, you must bring Gargantua his release!

"The chaste rose was of normal size, perchance a little smaller than the average, what could she do? Stealthily hang an iron collar upon the prick? Yoke it to a pair of oxen and have them pull the balls? She was a brave lass and a strong swimmer and therefore unafraid of anything, and so she scaled the stairs of a belfry against which Gargantua had rested his left foot. The giant was asleep once more: his contented snores set the vaulted cathedral trembling and Ludivine all but tumbled. A strong gale came from out his nostrils and nearly whipped the wimple from her head. To steady herself and check her fall, she gripped the *membrum virile*, wrapped her arms about, though they scarce encircled it. Like a deckhand trimming the foresail, she clambered up the mast. She clung to the blue veins that streaked the shaft, her legs full arched about the trunk; like a child on a gnarled tree, she scaled the phallus up to the prepuce and settled upon the balcony, looking for all the world like a muezzin in the minaret! Her wimple blowing in the wind like a turban, Ludivine chided the protesters: 'Peace! Friends, peace! Leave off your quarrels! Let the president hear the people! And God for all!'"

The gravediggers chortled heartily—here is a very singular chaste rose, who dares to call on God and on the president! In the hearth, the men working on the spit to baste the hares brandished the glowing *flambadou* from which molten lard drizzles onto the spit-roasting beasts; the aromas were enough for a man to sell his soul, to throw himself upon the flames and sink his teeth into the steaming saddle of hare, nibble the thighs, suck on the front paws. The two gravediggers turning the spit and larding the beasts drank to avoid succumbing to temptation—and if perchance one strayed too near the skin of a doe, the other splashed him with hot fat and the scalded man brought his fingers to his mouth, and the mingled tastes of salt, of pig, of smoke, calmed him. The meat was basted all the time it cooked, this was the secret; great logs burned in the back of the hearths, their embers were raked toward the front where a complex system of weighted spits turned under the vigilant eyes of two henchmen per hearth, two rustic, sinister gravediggers. A barrel was judiciously placed on a nearby trivet, for cranking the capucin handle was thirsty work. The spit turners and basters drank the best of the best, the rosé de saignée, the rosé of heart's desire, made from grapes plucked from the vines in a single night, a juice the color of the sun glinting from the thighs of a wood nymph, a *coulure* of autumn dawn, and all envied them, the Nadkings, the Gnarlcocks, the Pizzlebeers, the delegations from the Moselle or the Vosges, who sorely missed their gris de Toul and the cheeses of their beloved Lorraine, which were grilled with lard on two slices of black bread—ten pounds of Gros Lorrain, its rind washed and gently rubbed, that went down smoothly as mirabelle brandy! Ah, making raclette from ripe Gros Lorrain, by an open fire! O Welsch of east Lorraine! O sons of Saulnes! O rare ambrosial cheeses!

The gravediggers ate meat but once a year and that only at the Banquet, but, oh, what meats; here they were permitted all things: the remainder of the year was a long mourning, the tail of a comet carried off by Death ... While Bertheleau took a short pause to rinse his palate, the bouillon was served—a beef bouillon swimming with mother-of-thyme and tarragon, a bouillon of simmered oxtail, beef knuckle, parsnips, celery and whole onions—since a place was needed to stick the cloves! A seeing-man's broth, with eyes! The broth steamed and the grave-makers drooled! Some (because, though rare, choice was permitted) preferred a broth of spring mushrooms—woodwaxes, white agarics and wild morels foraged in March. The Grim Reaper is the friend to fungi and molds! Ere long, there came a symphony of sighs and breaths, lips smacking, gullets gobbing and gurgling amid the clink-clank of spoons."

The drunken spit turners basted the hares while slaking their parched throats, meanwhile Bertheleau, having inhaled his scalding bouillon, sensibly decided to allow it to cool and continued with his tale.

"And so Ludivine gripped Gargantua's foreskin with the imperturbable nonchalance of a Damascus barber. Down on the square, fresh reinforcements were piling out of police cars and by sheer number, truncheon blows and tear gas, forcing the eco rabble to retreat.

"It was at this point that Gargantua stirred, aggrieved to find himself not in his dream with his Badebec, but on the roof of Poitiers Cathedral. Filled with great melancholy, and noticing he was prick-proud, he reached down to take matters in hand. He pistoned his prong with a downward force equal to the quantities of flesh compressed by his fat fist and the zephyr thus unleashed sent Ludivine flying ass over tit into the air. She executed three somersaults and landed in the meatus, as welcoming as a gaping mouth, to be swallowed by the urethra. Gargantua felt a not unpleasant tingle, which caused his ballsack to tighten. Like Jonah in the belly of the whale, so Ludivine slid, as on a bobsled, and found herself a feminal vassal of the seminal vesicle. There she struggles. Thrashes about. The tension mounts. Still she flails, clutches and shakes as Gargantua writhes upon the vaulted roof. Uh! Ah! Uh! Ooh! Oooh! Mama! The pent-up profusion of the pulsing prostate! The testicular tightening! The shudder! Gargantua's eyes are wide and bulging fit to burst their sockets, egad! His ass cheeks clench as his cleft contracts—he writhes, wriggles, wrests, wrastles, wrangles in the nick of time, he humpfucks, he springbucks, he flushes and swoons, his body convulses, his bawdy expulses, his quhillielillie quivers: Ah, thinks he, I shoot, I skeet. The sidereal butter doth churn in the dairy! The pilloc spews! The foutre flies!

"And once again Ludivine is in the air, borne aloft on a white foam-flecked cloud, tinged with sal ammoniac, soaring, seething, shimmering, snotty and sticky, that rains down like shellfire and spreads like a swamp.

"And so we come to the end of the acts of the Divine: Ludivine landed in the arms of a gendarme, whom she married. The president emerged from the skirmish pearly white, the glare of the affair now faded. Now that the cotton bud had scoured his shell-like ear, he offered this good-natured intervention: 'You asked that I pay heed and here I hear and heed.' Gargantua had scored a bull's-eye, the eco rabble worshipped him—he clambered down the facade and went into the west, followed by a flock of protesters, there to fight fresh battles."

The gravediggers were filled with dismay. Bertheleau the mischief-maker! Let laughter ward off Death! People of the Camarde, rejoice! And since on this day everything was permitted, rank vulgarity as well as high-minded oration, Bertheleau was castigated no further. It was customary that the opening and closing speeches at the Banquet be devoted to the theme of love—Bertheleau's tale added to this noble subject a whiff of the supernatural that well suited the toothless, parsley-flecked smile (the egg mimosa!) of the gravedigger.

As the ninety-nine guests finished their bouillon, they watched the arrival of the vol-au-vents, so airy one would have sworn they were frothing. Ah, Master Lentenfast himself would not have despised them, thought Gnarlcock, ever the gourmand. He imagined sweetbreads, morels, cream; perhaps even bianchetto truffle, so light, so fruity that it enhanced the flavor of the crayfish tails—from such a distance, Gnarlcock could not divine the contents of the croustades, whether sea or land or even surf and turf; flagons of white began to circulate: a dense, straw-yellow, yet mineral Chenin, the perfect accompaniment, with its faint acidity, like the memory of life itself, thought Gnarlcock, whom feasting made philosophical. It was a pleasure to see and hear the vast table: some were still slurping the last of their bouillon, lifting their bowls with both hands to pour the dregs directly into their mouths, as plumes of steam poured from their nostrils as though they were dragons. Others were still savoring the terrines and the eggs mimosa; some, like Gnarlcock, were eagerly anticipating the next speech.

PIZZLEBEER'S SPEECH, BEING AN INTRODUCTION
TO THE ECOSYSTEM OF THE COFFIN

Chamberlain Pizzlebeer next took the floor; as befitted his venerable name, he hailed from Artois, from a mysterious village called Sainghin-en-Weppes whose inhabitants are (doubtless erroneously) dubbed cat-eaters.

"Gravemakers! Brothers, all! Before distraction once again holds sway, ere the tales of love again assail our ears, ere wine stops them more effectually than beeswax, ere we founder in the pleasures of inebriation and the joys of Lethe, I shall once more evoke our doleful trade. There is no death but it does pass through us! We carry the weight of humanity upon our shoulders!"

Soft-soaped by the terms of this address, the gravediggers turned as one to the speaker; Grand Master Gnarlcock wondered what inexcusable innovation Pizzlebeer was about to advocate: he was wary of the man, knowing him to be unreasonably open-minded.

"Brothers! The time is ripe for change. You have seen that trees are burning the world over, animals endangered, the planet warming, the soil tainted, the skies filled with dark smoke—ere long will come the Great Extermination! Soon there'll be no gravediggers to put the dead in the ground... *Gaudeamus* adieu, the humus will have us!"

(A fearful murmur rippled through the Banquet. All dead? Who then would bury the gravediggers? *Quis sepeliet ipsos fossōrēs?* Who buries the burier? Shall his body sully the earth, and be abandoned to carrion crows, the last man?)

"In the interim, friends and fellow gravemakers, what can we do? How can we, in our doleful trade, succor the planet? By being holistic, by being honest? First and foremost, we should forswear the use of formol. I can hear quibbles and protestations from here. Yet, brothers, it is true! Postmortem injections serve only to pollute! Formol, that vile poison, trickles into the earth... Everything leaks ... What purpose is served by embalming? What reason is there for this biochemical intervention? It is a peculiar practice from a distant time! A ghastly viaticum! Drain life-giving blood and replace it with death-dealing formalin, eight pints of poison that end up in the earth! The time has come to make way for dry ice, for swift burials, for coffins fashioned of unvarnished noble oak and fir! Formol is friend only to leukemia!"

The gravediggers glanced at one another. The gurgling, chomping and uncorking trailed away as each in turn fell silent. All waited for the storm about to break. For the embalmers to mutiny. It was the host, Martial Pouvreau, who spoke:

"Pizzlebeer, you've raised my dander. Your spineless words are naught but slander! 'Tis you that needs a dose of formol! A pint, I think, no! a whole bowlful! That might verily bung up your blowhole! Do you realize how much we'd lose? That formol is not mere perfuse? Embalming's how we earn our keep—ban formol and four boards are cheap! Farewell to suckling pigs on spits! Adieu to boobs and baps and tits!"

"Martial Pouvreau is our host this year," Gnarlcock interrupted, thereby reintroducing Pizzlebeer's challenger for all those who had forgotten since the feminal opening of the Banquet.

"Pouvreau, your words are hollowware. Mere churlish jibes and much hot air!" resumed Pizzlebeer. "You know in Europe formol's banned—to safeguard and protect the land? We needs must make a great decision—sow fear now; we reap division ..."

"But that's just it, no time to lose—it's now we must, inject, infuse! Act now before the legislation—all men here will risk starvation! I say we must be clear and formal: let's formalize the need for formol!"

"Pouvreau, I say to you before this plenum—science is clear, formol is venom! You want something fresh, new and cost-effective? Then ECO® funerals are my corrective. If our trade is to be profitable and stable, this Guild will need an eco label!

Move with the times! The bar is set! But do it cleanly for the planet."

"For the planet, Pizzlebeer, for the planet? Go be an eco warrior if you please! Off you go, fool! Hug some trees! Bask in Greta Thunberg's fame! Tell us all that we're to blame! But let me say this clear as glass: environmentalist activism shall not pass!"

A gravedigger from the South raised his hand; Pizzlebeer, struck dumb by Pouvreau's words willingly ceded the floor. The man's name was Hardhorn. Hardhorn was from Béarn; his booming voice shook with river gravel of the Gave de Pau. One could almost hear the leaping trout.

"Chamberlain Pizzlebeer, Maître Pouvreau, a plague on both your houses: formol is already banned, both for cremations and inhumations. That is a fact—no need to bleat about the ecosystem. Tarnation! Unless you'd have us return to benzoin, to the balsams and bandages of ancient Egypt. But, damn it all, refrigerated tables keep a stiff cool for as long as we need! No need to throw open windows or slash dead skin, no need to tip the entrails in a neighbor's garbage bin ... I've seen men throw human tripe to dogs, God Almighty! And others mine it up to make andouillette!

"But ECO®, that's another can o' worms: ECO® means green cemeteries and wicker baskets, the end of costly marble and expensive caskets! Naught but little plaques of wood, I hear, and what, pray tell, do we make out of that? Small beer!"

"It's true, Hardhorn, that green cemeteries offer scant margins for those of us who wield the chisel," said Pizzlebeer. "No marble, gilding, steles or cenotaphs, no family vault bas-reliefs ... Farewell to angels, cherubs, gilded handles, adieu the velvet purple livery of grief. Goodbye to easeful death! Instead, austerity for eternity! Farewell, the florist's wreath, farewell. But we can push up prices on the digging! Charge exorbitant fees for planting, greening and spring sowing: in a nutshell, go from gravemakers to landscape gardeners!"

"No more gravel paths, no more glyphosate to keep down weeds?" murmured a cemetery keeper who knew his onions. "Though we're hardly likely to give our tenants cancer!"

"Gather ye dandelions while ye may, but only ECO® weeds may stay!" sniggered Pouvreau.

"Mock all you like, Pouvreau, but this is the future," Pizzlebeer said as he sluiced his palate, proving that, with a little practice, it is possible to talk and drink at the same time.

"Not so much the future as the present," said an undertaker from Deux-Sévres. "We've already got our first ECO® cemetery in the area, Souché Natural Cemetery in Niort. It's so bloody green it'd blind you! The graves are marked out by wooden beams. No headstones, just a lump of white limestone carved with a name. And grass, flowers, shrubs as far as the eye can see—and boy, do they grow! What with these newfangled unvarnished biodegradable coffins and all, the corpses rot like no one's business, just watch out for the moss!"

"Sustainable permaculture on mortal remains! That's the future! Hush, it's time for gardener's world!"

The gravediggers all cheered this spirited exchange; Martial Pouvreau muttered vengeful obscenities into his neighbor's ear—he felt that the ECO® party had won the battle. He grabbed the flagon of Touraine Gamay in front of him and poured himself a full weeping glass till it ran over. Then he gently perched his mustache upon the rim, like a tiger prowling a bamboo grove, patiently and stealthily creeping toward a watering hole, breathed in the nectar for a long moment before plunging his upper lip into the glass and, with the sounds of pleasure and suction, quaffed the first centimeter of liquid—then, all perils now avoided, he picked the glass up by the foot (Lift it by the foot, miserable wretch! You'll overheat the wine! Churn-curdled bollock batter, this isn't cognac! Pouvreau would roar when he saw someone break this golden rule, and would have bellowed it in the Élysée Palace or even Buckingham Palace if the president or the Queen of England had the notion of cupping a balloon glass filled with wine) and emptied the contents into his gaping maw, arching both arm and his back, before bringing his head and shoulders to an upright position, swallowing, and unleashing an interminable *aaaaah* of satisfied relief and gazing longingly at the grilled oysters à la Dumas being passed around on trays—careful, they're hot, said the gloved waiter placing white ramekins filled with oysters au gratin in front of those who wanted them. Pouvreau, as the host of the Banquet, had organized the feast; he knew there were yet three or four starters and soups to come before the meats. He was very partial to a grilled oyster with parmesan and champagne, but first he needed to cleanse his palate, so he picked up his water glass, filled it with a Château d'Oiron Chenin, adopting the same approach he had for the Gamay, and drained it in the same way, but for a little sonorous gargling to wash away the memory of tannins from his palate. He signaled to the neophyte serving the mollusks; the poached flesh had the beautiful hue of mother-of-pearl; the oysters had come from the Bay of Aiguillon a few leagues from the Abbaye de Maillezais, where they grew wild in their thousands on the abandoned mussel and oyster beds.

The old refectory crackled with the crunch of ninety-nine sets of mandibles, and the hum of more or less private conversations taking place far from the leading lights of the Guild—the chamberlains, the masters and grand masters who were quick to bicker over proposals and innovations they deemed reprehensible; fortunately, this year, there were no elections and no initiations, this was an intermediate Banquet, a commonplace Banquet, rather than one of the tempestuous affairs that ended with thunderbolts over postprandial coffee—like Zeus the lightning bearer himself—as members brawled and pilfered each other's éclairs.

Pizzlebeer, needless to say, was savoring both his ECO® victory and, more importantly, the langoustines that he peeled and dipped into mayonnaise flavored with a hint of lemon and a dash of olive oil that gave it the green glow of the shoreline at ebb tide. Martial Pouvreau might be a little coarse, a little reactionary, but it had to be admitted that he was a first-class host. Pizzlebeer remembered a disastrous Banquet, a few years earlier, in a large hotel in Vichy, where the gravediggers had all but died of cold and of starvation, where the plonk was scarcely drinkable and wildly disproportionate to the mandatory contribution, as the host that year sought to make the sort of killing from his colleagues that he usually did from the dead—all in all, thought Pizzlebeer, as he reviewed what he had already consumed:

a tartine of rillettes au Vouvray,

a sliverette of duck pâté,

a cask of cornichons to accompany the above,

an egg mimosa, that is to say, two halves,

two tiny goat cheese gougères barely larger than a monkey's gonads,

six thighs, or three frogs,

six or eight large snails, whether from Périgord or Poitevin,

a vol-au-vent à la reine of veal sweetbreads,

a bowl of bouillon with croutons topped with foie gras,

a poached egg en meurette with bacon-wrapped bread,

a croustade of crayfish,

six (he was uncertain of the true number) oysters a là Dumas,

eight—no, sorry, just one more—nine langoustines immersed in mayonnaise,

three small glasses of festive Kir Royale made with sparkling Saumur that tickled his nose,

a flagon of crimson Chinon,

as much again of straw-yellow Chenin d'Oiron,

and was hence enchanted that the Banquet was still in its preliminary stages: though he suspected that Pouvreau would ensure he made a little margin on the affair, this Banquet promised to be among the most glorious of recent years, together with the Banquet organized by Gnarlcock in a chalet in the Vosges, which had been delicious, lengthy and gradual, if perhaps a little high in fat; just at that moment, Pizzlebeer, whose favorite dish was his wife's carbonnade à la bière d'Artois, saw the waiter bring a platter of genuine breaded crab claws with a sauce of the finest herbs, and this sea change, this turning tide (oysters, followed by langoustines, now crab) suggested that the fish course would soon arrive and he was anxious (since there was no thought now of hunger, a sensation forgotten some three or four dishes earlier) to discover what fresh surprises the Banquet had in store.

He noticed that all conversation had ceased, so he looked up from his crab claws to see which of the gravediggers wished to take the floor, and readily identified a young local undertaker, *ding ding*, about to step into the ring.

FIRST NIGHT
THE LADY MELUSINE AND THE LUSIGNANS

The young man, Bellende, hailed from the Vendée. He had a soft, suave voice, clear diction and a pleasing tone. He began by expressing his disappointment that Bertheleau—whom he saluted and thanked, together with Chamberlain Pizzlebeer and Grand Master Gnarlcock, as was the custom—began, then, by expressing his disappointment that Bertheleau had not taken the opportunity to go further in his tale: Gargantua, a figure some ill-educated folk believed to be the invention of François Rabelais, had actually been quite real. Rabelais had undoubtedly supped with him, had him to table, poured out his melancholy, rinsed the glasses, washed the tablecloth, chased the dogs, doused the fire, lit the candle, closed the door, then embroidered those dinners to feed to scandalmongers, this François Rabelais, whose mind, 'tis true, was to be found in books, but his belly in this very refectory, well, gentlemen, this François Rabelais had not invented Gargantua, far from it, Gargantua had been a bona

fide giant whose existence long preceded the aforementioned
Maître Rabelais, αὐτὸς ἔφα, though Bellende's revelation had, i'
faith, a rather limited effect (since most of the gravediggers had
never heard of Rabelais, and only little of Gargantua), and the
guests carried on feasting rather than attending to Bellende's
peroration on François Rabelais, which, for all its erudition on
medicine and theology, on Greek and Latin, was so soft-spoken
and well articulated that it washed over them like a lullaby, a
pleasing piece of music, but one that, played too long, so tran-
quilized its listeners as to pitch them ipso facto face down in their
mayonnaise or bouillon. Nonetheless, Bellende continued his
illuminating orison on the subject of Renaissance philosophy,
on Rabelais and his friend Guillaume Budé until (undertakers
being pranksters, as is well known) Fruits of the Earth began to
rain on the benighted young man, gently at first, a bread roll here,
a cornichon there (Bellende coolly brushed down his shoulders
as though nothing had happened), then more heavily, as though
a thunderstorm were looming: snail shells flicked with soup
spoons from the far side of the table spattered the speaker's bald
spot with butter; langoustines clung as if by magic to the collar
of his jacket while glistening frog bones blossomed in his beard,
and before long he looked like a *tableau vivant* by the artist we so
love because he whets the appetite—what's his name again? Ar-
cimboldo!—so covered was he with every foodstuff that could
be thrown, crumbs, cornichons, even half an egg: this was the
traditional punishment for boring speakers. Traditional though
somewhat unfair since there was nothing boring about Bellende's
speech, it was simply—how to put it?—a little pedantic, that's
it, "Ἓν οἶδα ὅτι οὐδὲν οἶδα," until at length the speaker, pelted
by the avalanche of food detritus from all over the room, and
overwhelmed by the apparent opprobrium, eventually realized
that he had to turn the tables. He dusted himself off, mostly to
give an impression of composure while he racked his brain, then
came out with this maxim:

"Ἡ γλῶττα πολλῶν ἐστιν αἰτία κακῶν. Brothers," he added, "know you not that fairies truly exist?"

The gravediggers pricked up their ears.

"Do you not know that in this land there exists a wondrous creature more powerful even than Gargantua? A fairy of immense beauty."

The gravediggers left off their heckling.

"Did you know that this fairy has built castles, churches and abbeys? That it was she who founded the great family that ruled the isle of Cyprus for many centuries? A family from Poitou, the Lusignans, vassals to Richard the Lionheart? The fairy is known as Melusine, a magical sprite from Caledonia, from Alba, that is to say from Scotland."

Cyprus, Scotland ... The mere mention of such far-flung lands would have caused the gravediggers to salivate had they not already been slavering profusely for other reasons. Their eyes shone, they waited expectantly for a story.

"Not far from here," Bellende continued, now that he was no longer the target of untimely littering, "not far from here lies a mysterious castle, built in the dark and distant times when troubadours and wand'ring minstrels, jugglers and bear handlers traveled from court to court, when all there was to illumine the night was Christ and the drum and the candle, when neighbors warred amongst each other, ravaging crops and killing any fool who did not have time to take cover. Upon a day, King Richard, son of Henri, Richard whom we call 'the Lionheart,' Duke of Aquitaine, Count of Poitou and King of England, for the Plantagenets ruled green Albion from Cornwall to the borders of Caledonia; King Richard then, having traveled to the Holy Land, there to wield the powers of the King of Jerusalem in his fight against Saladin, one day, this same King Richard gifted the isle of Cyprus to the House of Lusignan, the Lusignans; Guy de Lusignan was made King of Cyprus and his brother Geoffroy (known as Geoffroy Great Tooth, for he had a snout like a wild boar and was fantastically fearsome) was made Count of Jaffa and Ascalon, all this to please the fairy Melusine, who protected the family as though all these knights born since she had wed Raymondin, son of the Count of Forez, in times more ancient still, were her children. Melusine is a fairy of rare beauty—a fairy of great power, a magic castle-builder. Unfortunately, fate had decreed that she should be betrayed by her husband Raymondin, despite the pact they had agreed to whereby she forbade him to see her on Saturdays, while she was bathing, a pact that Raymondin respected for many years until his brother, by guile and cunning, sowed mistrust and jealousy in his heart. 'Melusine hides from you a-Saturday the better to betray you,' he told him; 'she takes a foreign knight with her to bath each week, and unbeknownst to you, there revels in the lust and debauchery.' Ἦθος ἀνθρώπῳ δαίμων."

The gravediggers clacked their tongues in chorus, proving that their mouths were empty and they were interested by Bellende's story—though many of them took advantage of this brief pause to rinse their palates and the more gluttonous took a gougère that they used to sop up the remains of the white wine and melted cheese from their oysters au gratin. Rather troubled that no further dishes had appeared since the breaded crab claws, they eagerly pounced on the remnants of the starters, a ruse carefully planned (and rightly so) by the caterers to ensure that all dishes came back to the kitchen as smooth and shiny as pebbles at low tide.

Bellende, feeling a little thirsty, knocked back a tumbler of red wine, for he scorned white wine, considering that it lacked that sense of virility. Wine that, he argued, was denuded of its fleshiness, its muskiness, its ballsiness, was akin to a eunuch, lunar, glabrous, translucent. If one could see through wine, then it held no mystery. And so, the proud man of the Vendée took the flagon of Mareuil he had requested especially out of love of his homeland; his shaven upper lip meant he had no mustache to wipe.

Despite his youthful age and short tenure in the trade, Bellende was among the most prominent cemetery keepers in the Guild—shepherds of the motionless, those who watch over the dead love stars and stories, fairies and will-o'-the-wisps; Bellende knew about such things, and was familiar with the strange phenomena of the fields of eternal repose, the shrill wails of grieving souls, the nocturnal whispers, the subterranean creaks, the strange lights, the many manifestations that issued from the land of the dead.

"And so, breaking the pact he had made with Melusine, one Saturday Raymondin resolved to spy on her while she was at her bath to determine the truth. Alack, what he discovered left him appalled. True, he found Melusine alone at her bath; she was combing her golden hair, which was beautiful as ever; her breasts were milk white, her nipples two brown discs, each surmounted by a red fruit, the very form and image of desire—but her hips and her legs—dear God!—were like the tail of some monstrous snake, the lower part of her body was black and glistening as a salamander! 'Ὕπαγε, Σατανᾶ!' and Raymondin was so affrighted that he screamed, and his scream alerted Melusine, she realized that she had been seen, had been exposed, and instantly she took flight in the form of a dragon, her hair no longer combed gold but celestial fire, and Raymondin, recovering from his shock, realized that he would never more see she who had made him happy, and for all his knightly valor, began to weep inconsolably."

Just as Bellende concluded his description of Melusine's snakelike body—as if by some miracle, as if he were in league with the caterers—there appeared long, narrow serving platters of virginal white porcelain scarcely tinged with a rosy-fingered sauce, on which lay long silver snakes whose segments were so well concealed, so well caulked with buttered oakum that they looked whole and entire, they steamed and glistened as though about to move, as though recently come from hell: eels! These monsters, almost a meter in length, hid their teeth behind their long reptilian faces—the gravemakers shuddered, especially those from the East and the mountains, being ignorant of this noble fish. Bellende was forced to break off his recitation: Melusine was being served on a platter. The chefs had surpassed themselves—a miracle! The eels, boned and stuffed with crab meat and fresh chervil and tarragon and cooked to perfection were served with a hollandaise made of butter from Pamplie and lemons from Valence, tinted pink to bewitch the eyes. The firm, succulent flesh of the eels cried out for wine as a newborn babe might cry for its mother's breast, and even the most landbound of the gravediggers, like Gnarlcock from the Vosges, swooned, first with fright, and then with pleasure.

As host of the Banquet, Martial Pouvreau rejoiced: for once, he had been right not to scrimp and cheesepare, but instead he'd given carte blanche to the chef of an auberge he knew, and he had created a veritable feast!

Bellende had no need to call for silence so that he might continue his tale: the only sounds to be heard were chewing and the groans of gastronomic rapture.

"Μοι ἔννεπε, Μοῦσα: So Raymondin wept that he had thus betrayed Melusine, that she had transformed into a wingèd dragon and vanished into the heavens and was not seen again, save once, some years later, when Raymondin, Lord of Lusignan, breathed his last and offered up his soul to God. On that night, Melusine was seen to fly high above the castle and, for a moment, it rained fat raindrops thick as tears.

Geoffroy Great Tooth, son of Melusine, is numbered among the ancestors of Pantagruel, according to Maître Rabelais himself. Geoffroy Great Tooth, he of the outsize canine like wild boar's tusk, was cruel, vicious and wicked; he and his men ravaged the Abbaye de Maillezais where we now find ourselves, until one day his mother, the fairy, so mortified him that he was changed and instead became protector of the monks of this noble place. One night, as an act of atonement, the fairy decided to build a splendid church for the Abbot of Maillezais—the Cathédrale

Saint-Pierre. She was surprised at her work by a monk named Jean, who thought he saw a bat flitting in the moonless dark, and she left off her travails, though she had built only the north wall and half the transept: the cathedral as you saw it when you arrived. Melusine also built Notre-Dame-la-Grande in Niort, and she helped Richard the Lionheart—whom she loved above all others—to build the famous castle in that same town, the double keep that stands upon the banks of the Sèvre, where Richard liked to sojourn, surrounding himself with jugglers and troubadours, welcoming acrobats from the North and poets from the South, and here there was much singing of the Lionheart's own verses but also the love poems of Jaufré Rudel together with songs from the Crusades. Indeed it is said that, at twilight, the fairy Melusine would fly along the valley of the Sèvre, leaving her forest on certain mild evenings, when breezes bore the perfume of angelica from the river to the castle, and would perch upon a windowsill, hidden by creepers, or the shadow of some gargoyle, would perch upon a windowsill and listen to the love songs, the lament of the hurdy-gurdy, the dirge of the rebec, and there mourn the memory of Raymondin, weeping golden tears which, when they touched the waters of the river, were transformed into the golden-yellow water marigolds that ever since have been called Melusine's tears."

Bellende was so pleased with his beautiful evocation of the fairy moved by the troubadours' songs that he allowed himself a large, quick gulp of Mareuil—Γίγνωσκε καιρόν, as Pittacus of Mytilene would say—which spilled down his chin, before delightedly tucking into his eel, thereby signaling that he had finished his tale—his perplexed audience was on tenterhooks; the gravediggers sat waiting for something. The mythological speeches were certainly exciting, but a certain undefinable *something*, surely, was missing.

Squatchoad, the treasurer, hailed from Lyon; he managed a large number of funeral parlors and had worn the robes of the

Guild with humility and devotion for many years. *Chacun fait gras à sa façon* was his maxim—*each man eats according to his custom*; more than anything, he relished cardons à la moelle, the wines of Chiroubles, and the rue Mercière. He looked around at the gravediggers basting themselves in wine just as the men turning the spits constantly basted the meat and game, their faces sweaty and flushed by proximity to the glowing coals, embers of gnarled and knotted vines that they tended with passion. The grilled hares would soon be ready, their skins had begun to crack despite being larded with bacon; Squatchoad was overjoyed that they had reached the fish course, for that meant that meats would soon be served! *Montjoie! Saint Denis!* Death to the beasts! The treasurer knew the precise order of the dishes being served since it was he—according to a tradition dating back to the Brotherhood's beginnings in the Holy Land—it was he, as treasurer, who told the host the tariff that everyone would pay, and which would be reimbursed to him—"by my whiskers!" as they used to say in the jargon of the gravemakers. Therefore, he had perused the menu. Squatchoad, according to custom, was seated to the left of Pizzlebeer. It was an excellent position; here there was no shortage of anything; the cupbearers kept him as well hydrated as a babe at the beach, he drank endless quantities of the aquiline red that grips the drinker like a lamb in its sharp talons and carries him to its aerie, where all wines become thirst quenchers, for thirst is as unquenchable as life, and Squatchoad knew whereof he spoke, having toiled for almost forty years up to his knees in dirt and death. He had listened distractedly to Bellende's tale as he wolfed down his eels, and regretted—as every year at Banquet time—that it was not the intellectuals who took the floor to speak about Death, but the drunkards who shouted themselves hoarse about love, about everything and nothing. He well knew that the Banquet moved inexorably toward its conclusion as night tends toward the new dawn—the Great Truce granted by Death was short-lived.

Squatchoad considered himself a typical philosophe Lyonnais.

So accustomed was he to these revelries that he wearied even of his own regrets: such was the Banquet, at times sagacious, at times mischievous, he thought as once more his glass was filled, and once more he brought it to his lips, to drain it and to sigh. Squatchoad had in mind these lines by Boethius ...

> *Wouldst thou from thy grapes have wine?*
> *When April wreathes herself in bloom*
> *And vines are filled with buds and brume,*
> *Pluck not the fruit, let nature shine.*
> *Stay your hand till autumn's gloom!*
> *Then see your cellar fill with casks,*
> *As Bacchus makes the wine to flow.*
> *For to each season its own task!*
> *And to each day its share of woe!*
> *Thus God commands, Man's dare not balk,*
> *Since all things have their needful order*
> *That are not Man's to sow disorder*
> *To meddle so with God's great plan*
> *Would rightly bring upon beast and man*
> *Disaster and destruction*

... as fine a verse as any, and Squatchoad watched, a little condescendingly (*For to each season its own task! And to each day its share of woe!*), as waiters whirled about the floor with steaming platters of fish. Discreetly nudging his neighbor, he pointed out that no one was speaking—something that would never happen in the banquets of the Ancient World where philosophers would blather even as they ate eels. Squatchoad was not so much aloof, pretentious and arrogant as he was stoic. Every day, his profession served to remind him that the only important thing in life was to die well. Dignity, above all things, dignity. Courage. He had witnessed countless breakdowns, endless derelictions of duty. His profession served to bolster his stoicism a little more each day. He so revered Seneca that at his place of business—Squatchoad Funeral Parlor, rue du Repos, in Lyon's seventh arrondissement—in the collection of brief texts offered to bereaved families to read aloud at funerals or cremations was not the usual motley collection of threnodies and paraphrases of Victor Hugo, but extracts he had personally copied out from Seneca's letters to Lucilius: *Why do you voluntarily deceive yourself and require to be told now for the first time what fate it is that you have long been laboring under? Heed my words* [insert name of the deceased]: *since the day you were born you were being led thither*, and it grieved Squatchoad that no one chose these texts: *Listen up gramps, since the day you were born you've been marching toward death*, Squatchoad never heard these words spoken in the hypostyle hall of an urban crematorium. Nor did he ever hear his beloved story of Cato's suicide: *Why should I not tell you about Cato, how the great man read Plato's book on his final night, with a sword laid at his pillow? He had provided these two requisites for his last moments—the first, that he might have the will to die, and the second, that he might have the means. So he put his affairs in order— as well as one could put in order that which was ruined and near its end—and thought that he ought to see to it that no one should have the power to slay or the good fortune to save Cato. Drawing the sword—which he had kept unstained from all bloodshed against the final day—he cried: "Fortune, you have accomplished nothing by resisting all my endeavors. I have fought, till now, for my country's freedom, and not for my own, I did not strive so doggedly to be free, but only to live among the free. Now, since the affairs of mankind are beyond hope, let Cato be withdrawn to safety." So saying, he inflicted a mortal wound upon his body. After the physicians had bound it up, Cato had less blood and less strength, but no less courage; angered now not only at Caesar but also at himself, he rallied his unarmed hands against his wound, and expelled, rather than dismissed, that noble soul which had been so defiant of all worldly power.*

Cato rips his soul from his wound with his bare hands! He

puts it out, expels it from his body! Begone, *generosum illum spiritum non emisit sed eiecit*, adieu! What mettle! O Cato, thought Squatchoad as he masticated a piece of stuffed eel, O Seneca! Guide us along the path of courage! Then he drained his glass of red, in homage to the shades of these great men.

Squatchoad, his spirits revived as much by the memory of his heroes as by the Chinon, cloaking himself in all his wisdom, swaddling himself in the armor of his knowledge, solemnly got to his feet, shot Pizzlebeer a haughty glance, and then, looking up, he issued a heartfelt challenge:

"Enough of these folktales, Bellende. We are no longer in the age of myth. The time of legends is long past. Let us hear not more of Gargantua, of Melusine, of Pantagruel! Let us put away childish things, Bellende! The time has come! The time has come to speak of Death."

The gravediggers shuddered at the mention of the Lady in Black. Speak of Death! Bellende recoiled as though he had been hit full in the face by an egg mimosa. This affront could not be allowed to stand! Folktales, legends, childish things? Excuse me? This was Squatchoad blathering! Time to launch the attack! To make the drunk vomit up his words.

"With all due respect, Treasurer Squatchoad, you are mistaken. Gargantua is no mere folktale. Your childish prank's beyond the pale! Wisdom and knowledge befit Gargantua! Not bland quenelles à la Nantua."

Squatchoad took umbrage at the geographical allusion belittling a dish from his native Lyon. True, quenelles are a little soft. A little bland. But they are the epitome of sophistication. This Bellende was a churl.

"Friend Bellende! To speak of Death is noble graciousness! For thought cannot exist without His Dread Highness!

> Oh, let him, who pants for glory's guerdon,
> Deeming glory all in all,

Look and see how wide the heaven expandeth,
Earth's enclosing bounds how small!

Shame it is, if your proud-swelling glory
May not fill this narrow room!
Why, then, strive so vainly, oh, ye proud ones!
To escape your mortal doom?

Though your name, to distant regions bruited,
O'er the earth be widely spread,
Though full many a lofty-sounding title
On your house its luster shed,

Death at all this pomp and glory spurneth
When his hour draweth nigh,
Shrouds alike th' exalted and the humble,
Levels lowest and most high.

Where are now the bones of staunch Fabricius?
Brutus, Cato—where are they?
Lingering fame, with a few graven letters,
Doth their empty name display.

"Listen to the words of Boethius, Bellende. Not Cato or Gargantua's gas. All must die, all must pass."

A flustered Bellende—assuming that Squatchoad was attempting to blame the Guild for Death—hastily improvised:

But such graven letters these, and upon such stone!
Dexterously carved on marble for the tomb
Eternity, with icy hands, beckons from the gloom
Intoning psalms and prayers, great sighs and moans.

Squatchoad continued his quote:

But to know the great dead is not given
From a gilded name alone;

Nay, ye all alike must lie forgotten,
'Tis not you that fame makes known.

Squatchoad was pleased with himself, he felt that, though he had won this skirmish by dint of another's verse, another's thoughts, it might win him some semblance of respect among his brothers, who, in truth, were more given to mastication than to contemplation. But he had not reckoned on the proud man from the Vendée:

"But is man's true body not his thought?" was Bellende's riposte. "You quote Sallust, Boethius, Cato—surely, like Plato, to us they are living still? Is not their presence felt for as long as man still reads their works?"

Squatchoad retorted:

Fondly do ye deem life's little hour
Lengthened by fame's mortal breath;
There but waits you—when this, too, is taken—
At the last a second death.

Squatchoad puffed out his chest and draped the toga of self-satisfaction about his shoulders. Bellende longed to prick this pomposity. The true question was: Does Death exist? Might we not forget it, as we do for the three days of the Banquet? Can we not believe in the perpetuity of existence?

The gravediggers were discomfited. To speak of Death was always a perilous endeavor. True, it was to Death they owed the miracle of the Banquet. True, it was the Reaper's long scythe that kept the Guild alive. Yet every year since the dawn of time, as the dishes were served, glasses emptied, bellies filled, voices were heated and knives sharpened, Death took the floor, or more precisely, the tablecloth.

No one quite understood Bellende's position; they could hear him flail in the face of the arguments from Squatchoad, the stoic Lyonnais. Then, suddenly, a whisper rippled around the table that made the company believe there might be some new contention: some got to their feet, others fell over as they tried to stand, having slipped on God alone knew what discarded greasy scraps and scrapings, the Banquet was seized by a panic. Death! She is present! Those seated at end of the vast U-shaped table rose up, a few gloriously drunken gravediggers made a break for the doors, stuffing their pockets with gougères, flagons, bottles, snifters—*sauve qui peut! sauve qui peut!*—only to find their escape thwarted by waiters carrying trays laden with the next fish dish, lamprey à la nantaise, also known as lamprey à la rochelaise, or lamprey à la bordelaise, that is to say, a fish stew of lamprey stewed in red wine, which the chef had elected to garnish with the creature's misshapen head, with its beady yellow eyes, and the sinister, fanged sucker that serves as its mouth. This ghastly apparition stopped the poor undertakers in their tracks. The shock was terrifying; the thick, dark, scalding sauce left the would-be escapees fugitives screaming with fear and pain; more than one waiter tripped and ended up on the floor with his arm, his belly, his head plunged into the stew; the ensuing eruption was so violent that it catapulted the head of a lamprey—with its horrid suckers, teeth and eyes—some ten meters, where it narrowly missed the plate of a venerable gravedigger and crashed into a pyramid of butter-drenched snails that had yet to find a gullet, scattering the gastropods, which rolled erratically like marbles, eliciting howls of terror, further adding to the shock and confusion.

And there you have it, everyone is drunk, muttered Pizzlebeer. That's it, everyone's sozzled, grumbled Pouvreau, bemoaning all the food as yet untasted. At last, the Banquet had come alive, thought Gnarlcock. The commotion prompted everyone to drink and talk all the more, creating a veritable clamor that curtailed the service of the lamprey and hastening the arrival of the carpes à la juive, glorious carp from Damvix, caught by Pouvreau and his assistants one night when they were at least as drunk as they were today, thought Pouvreau, because in contrast to the hunter's, the angler's drunkenness posed a risk only to himself or—in the case of extreme inebriation—his immediate neighbors. And besides, said Pouvreau to anyone prepared to listen, I can hardly be blamed if fish have a penchant for pastis! Only the Great Architect of the Universe can explain this particular quirk. You soak the bait in a tot of pastis, and it drives the carp wild!

Indeed, it was only the most altruistic of motives that prompted Pouvreau to take a magnum of pastis (smuggled in from Andorra) to the river or the pond, "because the Great Architect of the Universe has bestowed upon the humble carp a truly human trait, a passion for pastis." Gradually, some semblance of order was restored. Bellende and Squatchoad seemed to have taken a break from their philosophical disputation (one was guzzling eels and lampreys as though he were on the brink of death, the other was thoughtfully sipping a glass of Gamay and teasing a piece of fish with his fork); Bellende, now keeping his powder dry in anticipation of the second act—a moment before the general panic and the flying trays of lamprey, he had made one last dig at his well-heeled opponent: "And unless all of you are even drunker than you seem, you'll realize that death is an excellent living!" Barely a soul heard this quip above the din. Like a sharpshooter firing into the fog as his ammunition wanes, Bellende regretted squandering such a well-turned phrase. If hostilities were to resume ...

THE BLACK HOLE
&
DRINKING SONG
(to the tune of lampreys)

Pouvreau signaled to Grand Master Gnarlcock who immediately understood that an entr'acte was required, some entertainment capable of providing order and revivifying hunger. They had arrived at the midpoint of the Banquet, after the fish course and before the meat. It was time for *the hole*—the miraculous shot of liquor that restores strength and rekindles the appetite. All around, the gravediggers, who had sensed the moment was coming, began to roar: "A song! A song! The hole, the hole!"

The common herd foolishly equate the black hole with a shot of Calvados known as "le trou Normand," whereas the practice exists in every region of France after its own fashion, le trou: *le trou de Lorraine*—a shot of mirabelle plum brandy—is the most redoubtable; *le trou antillais*—a flaming shot of rum—the most exotic; *le trou du moine*—Chartreuse—the most Christian; *le trou d'Alsace*—kirsch—the most easterly; *le trou nordiste*—beetroot brandy—the most earthy, and so on: cognacs, Armagnacs, brandies and liqueurs of every stripe and provenance can be consumed *en trou*, i.e., liberally, down in one, in the middle of a meal (the drunkard's *trou*—a dash of Ricqlès® peppermint spirit gargled before going home to the wife—does not qualify, since a "hole" presupposes the existence of solid ground, of surrounding land) to stimulate the flow of gastric juices, which not only whets the appetite for the remainder of the Banquet, but clears the throat in anticipation of the singing, since a characteristic of *the hole*, for those who dug them, was that it be accompanied by songs urging further drinking and divers pleasures often involving the so-called weaker sex—barrack-room anthems, in other words—which was particularly apt in the case of gravediggers, for whom anthems and holes are the core of their profession. Each year, the honor of choosing the ballad and the libation fell to a different delegation—this year, it fell to the gravediggers from Occitania; the *hole* would therefore be celebrated in the tradition of Béziers or Narbonne; the bracer, from the West: an angelica brandy from the Marais, green as Chartreuse, intoxicating as a fairy in the mists, or a moonshine triple-distilled from wild blue plums, a little crude, a little surly, granted, but as fragrant around the edges as the corpses it revives. As one, the Occitan rabble burst into a raucous song, set to a familiar tune so that the other gravediggers could join in the refrain:

> Our heavy hearts have seen us fated
> To fall in love, infatuated
> By wines so dense they're masticated
> And gulped in gallons in Saint-Chinian,
> Vive le Grenache,
>> Vive le Grenache,
>>> Vive le Grenache et le Carignan.

It was a vintners' roundelay, specific to the region of Occitania once known as the Languedoc—the melody was pleasing, and the cheerful lyrics made one thirst for *cinq étoiles*, *supérieur*, for *treize*! For the wines of yesteryear! And while reserving the wine for the meats whose heady aromas—redolent of charred wood and sizzling fat infused with bay leaf and thyme (those manning the spits had ceased their basting, set down their *flambadous* and begun to remove the meats from the skewers)—caused every pair of nostrils to flare with pleasure; those who were not singing were knocking back small snifters of brandy flavored with plum or angelica (*Angelica archangelica*), to perk themselves up.

> The wine's not red, it's purple-black,
> So deep and dense one must attack
> It both with teeth and tongue,
> Poured straight from casks of heft and brawn,
> Vive le Grenache,
>> Vive le Grenache,
>>> Vive le Grenache et le Carignan.

> A gravedigger who sups it might toss off
> Eight bottles in a single quaff
> To slake his thirst in days unsung
> With nectar from the Lézignan
> Vive le Grenache,

Vive le Grenache,
　　Vive le Grenache et le Carignan.

Grapes now a-cluster on the vine
Need swift relief to craft the wine
We tread and knead them while they're young
We press them into demijohns,
Vive le Grenache,
　Vive le Grenache,
　　Vive le Grenache et le Carignan.

We come now to the bawdy part [censors, about your work! The lewdest lines of this bucolic ditty we shall preserve in rhyme alone so as not to shock, as Gnarlcock might say, the fair sex]:

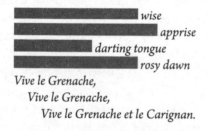

Vive le Grenache,
　Vive le Grenache,
　　Vive le Grenache et le Carignan.

The gravediggers from the Languedoc gleefully launched into the penultimate verse, for it was by far the most vulgar:

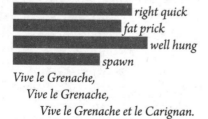

Vive le Grenache,
　Vive le Grenache,
　　Vive le Grenache et le Carignan.

And all in chorus raised their glasses and drained each drop of precious liquor as the waiters prudently brought out the *relevé de trou,* for it was vital to eat something to soak up the spirits, as

the Languedoc contingent bellowed the last verse of their song
to thunderous acclaim:

> *Thy withered charms are not so fair*
> *Thy queenly eyes, thy derriere*
> *Would pay not for a calèche ride*
> *From Rivesaltes to Sérignan*
> *Vive le Grenache,*
> > *Vive le Grenache,*
> > > *Vive le Grenache et le Carignan.*

The *relevé de trou* consisted of a little cocotte filled with coquillettes in a creamy sauce of aged Comté and truffles, malodorous
as mortal remains, reactionary as a film starring Louis de Funès;
a single mortiferous mouthful was sufficient to cleanse the palate
before the serious business, the acme of the Banquet, the meats
once known as *viands*. These melodious libations had allowed
the gravediggers to rewhet their appetite and pursue inebriation;
the Biterrois choristers clapped each other on the back like a
rugby team after a win; those manning the spits had unskewered
the hares and suckling pigs, piling them ad hoc onto huge platters. All that was needed now was to carve the beasts, and slather
them with sauces, a sorrel-butter sauce for the hare, dark chocolate for the suckling pig; spring vegetables were placed upon
the table, a jardiniere of fresh-picked marvels, peas, green asparagus, baby carrots, melting artichokes, La Ratte potatoes from
the Île de Ré, spring onions and green garlic, pumpkin au gratin,
white beans, followed by exquisitely carved lamb, gigot, rack of
lamb, salt-crusted lamb fillets tossed into the flames, lamb shanks
smothered with spices and thinly sliced as in a kebab, and every
mouth began to water, even those of the drunks, having been
perked up by the *trou* and the accompanying *relevé*. Pizzlebeer
mentally rehearsed the litany of everything he had consumed
so far:

> a tiny tartine of rillettes au Vouvray,
> a preposterous smidgen of duck pâté,

a sheaf of cornichons to relive the tedium of the foregoing,

an egg mimosa, that is to say, two halves, just for the taste of parsley,

two cheese gougères,

seven frogs' thighs, being four frogs, including a one-legged amphibian,

eight large snails together with their garlicky butter,

a vol-au-vent à la reine of veal sweetbreads,

a bowl of bouillon with its floating rafts of foie gras,

a poached egg en meurette with bread,

a crayfish croustade,

six (how long ago it now seemed) oysters à la Dumas,

nine langoustines with citrus mayonnaise,

three breaded crab claws,

four thick slices of stuffed eel,

two helpings of lamprey à la rochelaise,

half a fillet of carp in aspic,

a plum brandy *trou,*

a spoonful of coquillettes with Comté and truffle sauce,

an angelica liqueur *trou,*

another spoonful of coquillettes,

a slice of suckling pig in chocolate sauce,

a ramekin of courgette gratin with Tomme de Maillezais cheese,

a haunch of hare in sorrel sauce,

a first slice of leg of lamb with a few white beans,

a too-small portion of veal fillet grilled on the open fire and worth braving the fires of hell,

a scant few petals of the spiced thigh of that same beast,

sauce béarnaise for the sheer pleasures of unctuousness and tarragon,

a jardinière of spring vegetables.

As to drinks, he had lost count, but it seemed to him that he had drunk some Chenin, a little Gamay, and was now relaxing

with a ten-year-old Chinon, deep, deep, so deep that he saw reflected in it his soul entire—his soul and his weariness, for he had
dozed off for a short while—how much time had passed?—the
Banquet seemed less vivid, more distant, somehow muted; with
an absentminded fork he still managed to spear a pea or a baby
carrot, but was unable to swallow a single mouthful of the lamb
méchoui, or the thin slices of roast haunch of veal—the huge
U-shaped table was a vast dumping ground; on the floor, the
canine and feline companions of the cemetery keepers busied
themselves with gnawing on a lamb bone or lapping up eel sauce;
many of the diners had pushed their chairs back from the table
in abject surrender, set their clogs either side of their plates and,
tipping up their chairs, now teetered precariously on two legs, a
glass of Chinon in their left hands, a toothpick in their right; still
others had fallen over and now lay sleeping with a head, an arm,
an elbow in the sauce, while their neighbors used the high winds
of their snores to stage an amateur regatta, sailing small bread-
crumb boats across spilled lakes of soup and wagering on the
outcome; in a corner, four gravediggers were playing jacks with
lamb vertebrae, they were dead-drunk, which was of scant aid to
their playing; all the while ghostly waiters stepped over the pud-
dles and piles of detritus in an attempt to restore order—a pall
of melancholy invariably hung over the interlude between the
meat and cheese courses: the abandoned hearths were content
to glow as the light began to fade and the voices; apart from the
wisest and the youngest, died away, the crapulous ditch dwellers
floated in a congenial state of drunkenness well tempered by the
quantity of victuals consumed. Yet still from here and there came
sounds of chewing and gurgling; a young undertaker, plate in
hand, was asking whether there was any béarnaise left to sauce
his veal; a single-minded man had a hunk of gigot speared on the
end of his fork and a slice of suckling pig on the tip of his knife
and was warming both over the glowing embers: he abhorred
cold meat. Martial Pouvreau was pouring himself a seventh glass

of Chinon to wash down the baby potatoes drizzled with meat juices he so relished; as was his wont, he filled the glass to the ringing brim until the surface of the wine was slightly convex, which he checked, stealthily approaching the glass with the wiles of a Sioux warrior, chin resting on the tablecloth, as though the precious liquid must be caught unawares before it should flee: once again Martial Pouvreau managed to ambush the wine's meniscus; with pursed lips and an inhuman slurping noise, he drank off a good two centimeters of Chinon in a single draft before lifting his glass by the foot, with airy insouciance. Martial Pouvreau sensed that the Banquet was now gliding toward its conclusion, and the more the end seemed inexorable, the more he bestirred himself: in the few remaining hours, it was crucial to ingest as much food and drink as possible before the great Ritual that would put an end to *agape*. Hence did he hail the waiters— Come! Put matters in some order, for God's sake! Shake up the tosspots! Stir up the coals! Bring forth the cheeses! Speak prettily! Drink hideously! Stand up straight! Think swiftly! Lay your boot into the dogs! Bellende, a disquisition!

Hearing his name bellowed from the far end of the table, Bellende looked up from a plate still spilling over with lamb and mogettes, unquestionably one of the finest I have eaten in my life, he thought as he added a twist of black pepper, a fragrant, tender succulent gigot, Bellende who, like many of those present, ate meat and drank wine but once a year during the Banquet, being, for the remainder of the year, a man of exemplary abstemiousness: teetotal, vegetarian and married. Although Bellende practiced his trade in the Vendée, it was not far distant from Pouvreau's fiefdom at La Pierre-Saint-Christophe, which, though it offered no explanation, made it conceivable that the two men were acquainted without actually liking each other. When Bellende heard Pouvreau shout "A disquisition!" he could not help but look to Squatchoad to carry on their earlier verbal joust, cut short by the appearance of the *trou*.

Treasurer Squatchoad was in contemplative mood.

His eyes were closed, his shoulders straight, though it was clear from his air of superiority that he was not sleeping. He found it distressing to be surrounded by so many men wallowing in excess. He had sampled all of the divers meats and accompaniments, of course. But loftily. Soberly. He had drunk, as was fitting during the Banquet, but very little. Inebriation? Not for him! He might perhaps have drunk a little more had there been a Coteaux du Lyonnais, or even a Beaujolais, a Saint-Joseph or a Crozes Hermitage, because the wines of the Loire Valley that they had been served had been startling, disorienting and exotic. In a word, aqueous. That's it. They lack the depth and concentration of wines from Lyons, reflected Squatchoad. They probably contained more water, less grape than at home, thought Squatchoad. A Crozes Hermitage is the blood of a sacrificial bull, rich, revivifying, Roman, thought Squatchoad. To say nothing of a Côte-Rôtie! Zounds! The very sound of the cork being pulled would be enough to wake the dead and have the departed lining up in front of the bottle with their baptismal shells. But a little drop, my lord, and it please you! The dead holding out their goblets! Côte-Rôtie was holy water! But everything is wetter here in the West, thought Squatchoad. They cannot boast our perfect climate, thought Squatchoad. Doubtless it rains here all the time, it is a miracle they can persuade any vine to grow, thought Squatchoad. We should be charitable to those less fortunate, but retain our sense of judgment, thought Squatchoad.

Bellende's interrogative gaze caught Squatchoad unawares. Is this some supplication? Are we to speak again of Death? Elaborate, young man, if you would be so kind. Are we to fear Death? Is that your question? Should we be afeared?

Bellende pushed away the gigot and rubbed his hands. Here was an opportunity to expound upon his theories—as a staunch man of the Vendée, Bellende believed in Christ, and so, to him, Death was but an angel, a force that emanated from the Almighty that led the soul into the presence of the Lord or to eternal damnation according to one's actions here below. Christ had suffused Death with hope, the hope of salvation, of paradise, indeed of resurrection at the end of days. Death was nothing but a proof of God's existence; if we should die, it is also so we might extol the Lord Almighty. Each day, as he buried the dead, Bellende's Christian resolve grew stronger. Christ alone gave a sense to all things. How could one not fear Death, as one fears Judgment? I might be deprived of Heaven, of the presence of the Lord, I might be cast into Hellfire. Will the suffering I have known so well in life not find me in that other world? Squatchoad rose from his seat. He stretched his limbs for a moment. He took a sip of the curious Chinon that tasted of gravel, as deep as the river Acheron.

All this is for dramatic effect, snickered Bellende.

To rouse themselves from their torpor, the gravediggers elbowed one another. Later chroniclers would insist that it was Squatchoad's speech that roused the Guild that night; some would remember the name of Bellende, for, although a Christian, the young man was the future of the profession; in a few short years he would find himself at the head of an illustrious funeral parlor and it would not matter to him that he had envy as his neighbor.

Squatchoad shot a look at Bellende.

"Bellende, listen to what Lucretius has to say."

> Hence, where thou seest a man to grieve because
> When dead he rots with body laid away,
> Or perishes in flames or jaws of beasts,
> Know well: he rings not true, and that beneath
> Still works an unseen sting upon his heart,
> However he deny that he believes.
> His shall be aught of feeling after death.
> For he, I fancy, grants not what he says,
> Nor what that presupposes, and he fails
> To pluck himself with all his roots from life

And cast that self away, quite unawares
Feigning that some remainder's left behind.
For when in life one pictures to oneself
His body dead by beasts and vultures torn,
He pities his state, dividing not himself
Therefrom, removing not the self enough
From the body flung away, imagining
Himself that body, and projecting there
His own sense, as he stands beside it: hence
He grieves that he is mortal born, nor marks
That in true death there is no second self
Alive and able to sorrow for self destroyed,
Or stand lamenting that the self lies there
Mangled or burning. For if it an evil is
Dead to be jerked about by jaw and fang
Of the wild brutes, I see not why 'twere not
Bitter to lie on fires and roast in flames,
Or suffocate in honey, and, reclined
On the smooth oblong of an icy slab,
Grow stiff in cold, or sink with load of earth
Down-crushing from above.
So shalt thou slumber down the rest of time,
Released from every harrying pang.

"I relieve you of this doubt, Bellende," said Squatchoad. "You cannot fear death in such a fashion—the pain of death itself, the coldness of the grave: these are things you cannot suffer, Bellende. This death is not fearful. Why then do we fear it? Do we fear the suffering our absence will cause others? Are we so generous that we fear death only out of a profound altruism? Such a notion would seem more pretentious than noble at first glance, but above all—since every man will one day be absent, departed—absurd. Why fear that which for all is certain sure. Can we regret we shall not know what will become of the world after we depart? Unquestionably. But fear it? No. I leave regret to you, but regret is the privilege of the living, the dead cannot regret not knowing how the movie ends, Bellende, for two reasons: either death is the annihilation of being, and therefore they cannot regret, or else God takes them into His bosom, and it is they who live (as it were) happily ever after. Regret is impossible. There can be no regret, no joy, no sensation, since death is extrinsic to experience, Bellende. It is entirely beyond such things. The great Schopenhauer poses this question, Bellende: you fret and fear some future time when you will no longer be, but what think you of the countless eons during which you were not yet? Do you fret about those? Surely the absence of suffering and experience precedes your birth? Surely it is the first cry or the rustle of a first cell dividing that marks the beginning of existence— could you feel ere you were born? Does your coming into this world so reshuffle the deck, Bellende, that all rules change with your advent? No? Why then, in death you will be as you were before your birth: free of suffering and existence."

> Standing beside whilst on the awful pyre
> Thou wert made ashes; and no day shall take
> For us the eternal sorrow from the breast.
> But ask the mourner what's the bitterness
> That man should waste in an eternal grief,
> If, after all, the thing's but sleep and rest?
> For when the soul and frame together are sunk
> In slumber, no one then demands his self
> Or being. Well, this sleep may be forever,
> Without desire of any selfhood more,
> For all it matters unto us asleep.
> Yet not at all do those primordial germs
> Roam round our members, at that time, afar
> From their own motions that produce our senses—
> Since, when he's startled from his sleep, a man
> Collects his senses. Death is, then, to us
> Much less—if there can be a less than that

Which is itself a nothing: for there comes
Hard upon death a scattering more great
Of the throng of matter, and no man wakes up
On whom once falls the icy pause of life.

Those gravediggers who were fit and able and had both hands free burst into loud applause, those holding a glass or a fork in their paw pounded their fists on the table, in a slightly Teutonic, slightly barbaric gesture; those who, by misfortune, had both hands full with glass or victual, contented themselves with shouting, those who had their hands and mouths full spat, while those who were asleep did nothing. All appreciated great oration.

Squatchoad warily raised his glass of Chinon and drained it. He was thirsty. He was happy.

Bellende met this philosophical evidence with the sanctimonious smile of the believer. He in turn got to his feet, drained his glass, not to be outdone, and propounded one or two axioms such as the immortality of the soul, that which sets in motion the *saccus merdae*, the spark received at birth, the energy bestowed by baptism; he cited the Holy Scriptures, the commentaries, and most especially Saint Thomas Aquinas, whom he revered, in particular his commentary on Aristotle's *De Anima*, wherein it was proved that the soul was not only distinct from the body, but as a substance, separate from its accidental qualities, and contrary to the opinion of Aristotle, immortal. Bellende relied for his eloquence on that of the divine Bossuet:

"*O Soul besmirched with crimes, thou art right to fear the immortality that would make thy death eternal! Yet behold, in the person of Jesus Christ the resurrection and the life: whomsoever believeth in Him shall never die; whomsoever believeth in Him is already imbued with a spiritual and inner life, imbued with the life of grace that heralds the life of glory—natheless the body, perforce, is subject to death—O soul, take comfort: if the divine architect, who hath undertook to mend you, should allow the outworn edifice of thy body to molder piece by piece, it is so that He might return it to you in a worthier state, so that he might rebuild it in better order; for a brief time it will sojourn in the kingdom of the dead, but leave there naught but mortality itself. Be not swayed to see corruption according to the wisdom of medicine, as a natural consequence of composition and concatenation. We must lift our spirits higher and believe, in accordance with Christian doctrine, that what foreordains all flesh to necessary corruption is that it draws evil to itself, it is a font of rank desires, a sinful flesh, as the holy apostle hath said. Such flesh must needs be destroyed, I say unto you, even amongst the chosen, since in this state of sinful flesh, it is unworthy to be reunited with the blessed soul, or to enter into the Kingdom of God."*

For all its beauty and its wisdom, this peroration, which wed Bossuet to Aquinas to Aristotle, had an immediate effect on the gravediggers: mutiny. Once more, Bellende found himself the target of fresh assaults from these fustilarians driven to further drunkenness by the profundity of the debate; they hurled small bones, whistled, sang barrack-room ballads (*Pieds de cochon Marie-Madeleine, Pieds de cochon Marie-Madelon*) and took no heed of the ongoing debate; they did not care about death, it would come back into their lives soon enough. Certainly, it was important to ground it in thought; but the gravediggers were free men and hence allowed themselves to change their minds according to their awareness of the ultimate ends or as and when a glass of red proved more tempting than a homily. During the Banquet, they preferred the forthrightness of Lucretius, Schopenhauer and Squatchoad to the long-winded, abstruse Christian thought of Aquinas and Bellende.

The guests, alas, were more atomists than Thomists.

Bellende instantly came up with a response. Brushing himself down with the back of his hand like Faust in Auerbach's cellar, he bellowed: *The cheeses! The cheeses! The wines!* and everyone knew that cheeses meant unctuous fat, crusty bread and fine wine, and so as one they roused themselves and chorused: *The cheeses, the cheeses! The wines, the wines!*

There were cheeses from all over France, from the France of Switzerland and Italy, the France of England and Holland, la Grande France, with cheeses as French as the cumin-scented Handkäse from Frankfurt am Main, the most venerable old Gouda, smoked sheep's Idiazábal and powerful Somerset cheddar. No sooner did Bellende's cry resound than the apprentices appeared carrying huge wicker trays festooned with vine leaves and spring flowers and piled with dozens of cheeses of every shape, parallelepipeds, cubes, hearts, cones, cone trunks, pyramidions, spheres, half spheres, quarter spheres, cylinders, cylinder sections, and of every hue, white, cream, green, yellow, gold, blue inside, gray, ashen, brown, orange and even a smoke-black and a brick red, inimitable; every hardness on the Mohs' scale was represented: here were the cheeses hard as the heart of an oak, Comtés whose aged wheels had rolled down from the Jura, Têtes de Moines powerful enough to stun a heathen; softer cheeses whose pale fat spread like the belly of a pasha on a divan in the seraglio and melted without need of heat under the effects of time, ripe raw-milk Camemberts, vacherins liquefied by lethargy; the terrifying Époisses which, like the Reblochons, slithered in waves from their washed rinds; the Fourmes d'Ambert and Montbrisons that sweated like great sticks of dynamite; the Roqueforts that smelled of sheep and mold, in short of Aveyron; the Munsters that vied with the Maroilles for the attention of the nostrils, the small goat cheeses paled modestly—though it was they who were kings of the cheese board: the Mothais wrapped in chestnut leaves, the unctuous Chabichous, the Sainte-Maures nestled in straw, the Selles-sur-Cher with their tang of hazelnut, goat cheeses that were ripe and runny, fresh and firm, white and cream, or daubed with ash.

The bread had been carefully selected—what was required was a slightly brown sourdough bread, made of ancient grains, slightly acidic, with a texture that was dense yet not too dense, springy yet melting, and a scored crust baked so that it was almost black in places and redolent of fire, of charcoal, of ovens; the bread circulated in loaves weighing four or five pounds, which waiters carried wedged against their left shoulders like a violin so it could be sliced to order—all thought of sleep was now abandoned, all space for melancholy, the cheeses had arrived!

The gravediggers once again began to sing, this time canticles and antiphons, a Magnificat to the glories of fermentation, to curds, to rennet drawn from the stomachs of calves, glory to all Ruminants, glory! Glory to the Goat, the Ewe! Glory to bacteria, glory to Death! And the wines began to circulate! Damnably fine white wines! White wines to accompany cheese! White wines from every terroir! Pouilly, Sancerre, Chablis as round and plump as the baby Jesus! Enough to make one swoon! Color paired with color! A white Crozes Hermitage with the Comté! A Marsanne or a Roussanne for Beauforts from the upland pastures! Glory to the Cow, glory to the Ewe!

White wine, but not exclusively! Behold, said someone, the effect of this fine port on Roquefort and the aged sheep of the Pyrenees … Dear God! I swoon! The salt within the sugar, the boundlessness of matter, the angels!

Pizzlebeer turned the cheese plane over the Tête de Moine like a damned in torment, opened wide his mouth and delicately savored the gossamer-thin petals, following each mouthful with a goodly glass of Meursault, his right hand never leaving the handle of the girolle for fear it would be taken away from him by force or guile, never ceasing in his turning until the bottle of Meursault was empty and his slice of bread consumed. He considered opening another bottle and cutting himself another slice, but there was no need. Better to broaden the horizons and sample another cheese, like Squatchoad who was rewarding himself for his fine speech by helping himself to a morsel of Arôme de Lyon (in his opinion, the finest cheese in the world, one made from cow's milk and washed with grape brandy) with a drop of Saint-Joseph. Pizzlebeer followed his lead and the melding of cheese and wine was such as might have sent Sainte Blandine straight to hell. It elicited sparks of happiness. Even Gnarlcock, steadfastly loyal to Lorraine, would—God forgive him—almost have renounced the Welsche of the Abbaye de Vergaville and white Moselle for a morsel of Arôme and a dewdrop of this Saint-Joseph.

There were ninety-nine different cheeses at the Gravediggers' Banquet, and the cheeses were worth a thousand speeches: as a result, no words were spoken during the cheese course, the orators and storytellers (rejuvenated, revivified by this enforced hiatus) were sharpening their tongues, for only the desserts were left to shine—dessert was traditionally a time to speak of love, chiefly in tones jocose and waggish, a fact explained by the nature of dessert itself, being hollow and filled with soft matter, like the skulls of all those present.

The plateau phase was drawing to a close; the passion for cheeses had palled. They had reached the darkest hours of night. The only gravemakers not yet drunk were on the wagon. The gold-robed dignitaries, Grand Master Gnarlcock, Chamberlain Pizzlebeer and Treasurer Squatchoad, for whom this was the last Banquet, since their term of office would end the following year, maintained their rank—not one would leave the Banquet standing. Even the abstemious man from Lyon, having rediscovered the wines of the Rhône, was a little tipsy. He was floundering— pish! Fortunately, life-restoring desserts were still to come.

The time had come for the host to take the floor, before the arrival of "platters, salvers and trenchers sundry of sweetmeats, spiced treats and ribald feats" promised by way of dainties.

For his part, Martial Pouvreau was wondering whether he might be about to explode rather than expound, recuse rather than enthuse.

He was shattered, he could take no more.

He was sprawled across the table, cheek pressed against the tablecloth, a filament of bile-tinged drool extending from his gaping mouth; he was not sleeping, he was brooding, he was breathing. It is vital to breathe from time to time. He gazed at his full weeping glass whose madder hue was dappled with orange from the embers' reflected glow, a strawberry in the August sunlight, a garnet transpierced by flames with no depth, whose paleness, even from afar, suggested a Pinot Noir, one of the red Burgundies so rare in these Atlantic regions that they are instantly recognizable; though his gaping mouth was almost a foot from the chalice, Pouvreau was beginning to feel the effects of the Grail without needing to bring his lips to it. What Good Samaritan had poured him this marvel whose beauteous robe evoked the thigh of a nymph, the skin of a newborn babe, a magical elixir in which honeysuckle would vie with blackberry and wild strawberry cleave to black currant? The supple tannins would round out the whole, thought Pouvreau, and the more he gazed at the glass, the more he lost himself in the ruby liquid as in a kaleidoscope of every shade of red, the more he came back to life; with singular effort, he managed to close his mouth; to focus his mind on what was going on around him; his thoughts laboriously gained strength and shook off numbness. Still lying with his head to one side, he succeeded in extending a creeping, desperate hand toward the glass, to draw it to him without spilling the nectar; when the glass was balanced on his face, still pressed against the table, his grasping fingers clenched about the foot and brought it close to his ruddy proboscis, then tilted it toward him slightly—as a little wine flowed down the side of the glass, Pouvreau poked out his tongue to intercept it: oh, what celestial pleasure, it was as though Bacchus had just invented it, he tilted the glass a little more, red wine rinsed his eye, streamed down his nostril only to be slowed by his mustache and trickle toward his mouth—which Pouvreau was forced to horribly contort in order to catch the liquid that had spilled from the glass—with a terrifying gurgling noise. The stain on the damask tablecloth was no longer just drool, O wine of life! You have all but resurrected Martial Pouvreau.

His first feat was to raise his head, then shake it quickly from right to left; in doing so, he sprinkled his neighbors with the drops of Nuits-Saint-Georges embedded in his mustache and, like holy water from an aspergillum, it awakened them in turn. Then he drained the glass with a long draft and a lengthy gargle and, feeling somewhat better, and having overcome his malaise, he took the floor in spite of a slurred, drunken stammer and a voice from beyond the grave:

"Dearest friends! My gallant gravediggers! Allow me to thank you all for your presence here. All too soon, the desserts will be brought in. But before that, let us raise a toast! Let us raise our glasses to Death, divine strumpet, lover to all!

"... To Death, the one and only Mistress!"

The gravediggers raised their glasses, or at least all those who could still do so; those whom the cheeses had not finished off: the great satisfied snore that rose from the Banquet was not yet unanimous. Some were waiting for dessert and for the Ritual before they succumbed to unconsciousness. Others who had been sleeping since the meat course were waking up, fresh as daisies, or almost.

Having gauged the Brotherhood's state of consciousness during the toast, Pouvreau cast around for a speaker who could take the floor before dessert and concluded that Nadking seemed fighting fit. Nadking, a gravedigger from Talmont-sur-Gironde with a terrifying, pockmarked face, a flat nose and rosaceous cheeks, compensated for his preternatural ugliness by his extraordinary good nature: everyone loved Nadking. It was generally felt that at the selections for the Guild officials the following year, Nadking might well become Chamberlain; or Gnarlcock might become Chamberlain and Nadking Grand Master—an arrangement that, admittedly, seemed a little Putinesque, but was permissible according to the bylaws of the Guild, with which Gnarlcock and Nadking were intimately familiar. Just now Nadking, like Martial Pouvreau himself, was draining his glass as he waited for the desserts. So Pouvreau designated him.

NADKING'S SPEECH:
THE STORY OF JAUFRÉ RUDEL'S JOURNEY
AND THE FOUNDING OF THE GRAVEDIGGERS'
GUILD

"Chamberlain, Grand Master, Treasurer, gravediggers, blackmasters, I was eager to recount one last tale before we return to our doleful duties, before Death reasserts her rights. You all know the fortress of Blaye, on the magnificent estuary of the Gironde, Blaye of the exquisite vineyards, Blaye the birthplace of Roland, slain at the Battle of Roncevaux Pass, with Durandal his brand sundered by his side—Blaye, as you all know, was also the fiefdom of Jaufré Rudel, the most handsome of troubadours and the noblest of the princes of Aquitaine; Jaufré loved, loved from afar, he loved love, springtime and the nightingale's song."

> *Quan lo rius de la fontana*
> *S'esclarzis, si cum far sol,*
> *E par la flors aiglentina,*
> *E'l rossinholetz el ram*
> *Volf e refranh ez aplana*
> *Son dous chantar e l'afina,*
> *Be'ys dregz q'ieu lo mieu refranha.*

> *When from the plashing wellspring*
> *The water doth run clear,*
> *And on sweetbriar rose the tender buds appear*
> *When the nightingale upon his bough*
> *Doth trill with dulcet notes enow*

Perfecting his sweet song,
Pray, Lady, scorn not mine.

The gravediggers were of course all familiar with Jaufré Rudel, and the invitation to sing the prince's sweet songs was irresistible: as waiters cleared the table of the remaining clutter of vittles in preparation for the desserts, while candles and candelabras were lit in anticipation of the last Ritual, they began to hum "Quan lo rius de la fontana," that tantalizing evocation of love and springtime.

"Jaufré Rudel was lovesick—he loved a lady he had never seen, but a lady so beautiful, so noble and so devoted that her name had crossed the seas and reached Jaufré's ears—the lady was Princess of Tripoli, in the Holy Land. Jaufré Rudel had heard her name from the pilgrims lately returned from Jerusalem whom he welcomed to his castle; they spoke to him of Antioch, of the land and of the Princess of Tripoli, her face, her soul—and of such beauty were they, that face, that soul, and the songs sung by the pilgrims so moved him that Rudel, the poet lord of Blaye, fell hopelessly in love and sang of his love:

Amors de terra lonhdana,
Per vos totz lo cors mi dol ;
E non puosc trobar meizina,
Si non au vostre reclam
Ab atraich d'amor doussana
Dinz vergier o sotz cortina
Ab desirada companha.

O fair one from far-distant lands,
For you my heart doth flame;
Nor have I cure at my command
But to sing out thy name,
A sweet refrain of love,
In gardens screened by richest drapes,
At one with my beloved.

"He sang his love until he could bear it no longer, and decided to set off for the Holy Land there to find his princess—with a band of other lords, Hugh de Lusignan, Taillefer, Count of Angoulême, he set off overland to Sicily, and there crossed the sea to reach Tripoli."

The gravediggers listened attentively to Nadking's story as they waited for the dessert that promised to arrive soon. The immense table was gradually emptied; wine glasses had been taken and replaced (providing the opportunity to drain them, pressing open mouths to the rims like a hussar kissing a maid) by small translucent phials which, within the Guild, were used both for liqueurs and brandies, phials seven centimeters tall with narrow necks measuring five centimeters whose opening was a finger width. The bellies of these flasks were round and tempting.

The attendants began to arrange the sweets on the tables, the traditional dessert since the founding of the Gravediggers' Guild, choux à la crème—choux pastry, that miracle of the pâtissier's art, where, in the center of the contrivance of flour, butter, water and eggs, in the mysterious heart of the oven, a hollow formed, and this magical hollow could be filled with lightly sweetened Chantilly, the rich cream of spring milk, cream from the pastures of market gardens with their milkmaids all in black and white, incomparable!—and so, as they listened to Nadking's tale, one that they already knew, the gravediggers once more began to drool as they saw pristine, perfectly sized pyramids of choux buns placed upon the table, cream puffs and their close relations, pets-de-nonne, sweetened and lightly flavored with aniseed, chocolate or coffee, éclairs filled with crème pâtissière, religieuses of two choux buns placed one atop the other, and even the fiendish profiteroles, which are no more than vanilla cream puffs dripping with thick, scalding, melted dark chocolate. The gravediggers had a code of conduct, and the Guild was bound by a sense of justice, in which one did not name things as anything but what they were—the gravediggers were also constant, and had a true sense of duty; so they listened to Nadking with an impatience mingled with interest.

"After a protracted journey, having braved tempestuous seas and wild shores, and enfeebled by an illness contracted aboard a ship, Jaufré Rudel reaches the Holy Land. The lovesick troubadour is also a noble warrior. Despite his weakness, he battles the Infidels threatening Tripoli. With a host of gallant barons, he lays siege to the city of Damascus. It is here that he pens many of his songs—never has his beloved, the fair Lady of Tripoli, been so close and yet so far. Jaufré's illness grows worse; he is mortally weakened; he determines at last to see his beloved. The siege is lifted and he travels to Tripoli; the magnificent city is enclosed by high ramparts that encircle an impregnable castle that sits atop a promontory almost a league from the sea and the harbor, among hills blooming with olive trees and those bitter golden apples they call oranges.

"Jaufré Rudel is sick unto death when he arrives in Tripoli, supported by lords and barons; one of whom sends word to the castle: Princess, the Lord of Blaye, Jaufré Rudel, is smitten with love for you, and would fain not die ere he has seen your face. The princess has Jaufré moved to her royal apartments; she embraces, she pities him. And the moment he realizes that he is in the embrace of his beloved, Jaufré Rudel comes to himself; he sees her, hears her, smells her sweet scent, touches her—he gives thanks to God for keeping him alive long enough to see his inamorata, and he dies in her arms."

The gravediggers all knew this story by heart, and yet, by dint of weariness and alcohol, as the first gray shoots of dawn began to streak the night in Marais to the east, behind the great ruined cathedral of Saint-Pierre de Maillezais, the forlorn gravediggers, sensing that the Banquet, like Jaufré Rudel, was swiftly approaching its end, and that, before the last embers of joy died out, they too might find their black princess, the gravediggers could not but weep at the memory of Jaufré Rudel and his faraway love, consoling themselves as their hands reached for the mounds of choux; ate one, whose delicate shell surrendered, as is the wont of choux pastry, thus liberating the sheer white lightness of whipped cream that invaded their mouths, filling them with happiness; and so, they wept a little less—mawkish gravediggers, ever ready to shed a tear!—and Nadking de l'Estuaire resumed his tale:

"So bereft was the princess by the death of Jaufré Rudel that she decreed that he be buried with full honor and ceremony in the church of Saint-Jean atop Mont Pèlerin, the temple of Tripoli, as though, for an instant, he had been her husband, and she, the fair princess, did wed the Lord Jesus, and entered a nunnery so that she might have no other husband but him."

No sooner had he finished this sentence than the gravediggers sobbed louder still. Oh, how they wished that they might have been the ones to carry the bier of Jaufré Rudel to his grave! And it was a close call! The Gravediggers' Guild had been founded by Saladin after he captured Jerusalem, that they might bury Christians, Jews and Muslims with equal rite and ceremony, and sanctioned by Richard the Lionheart after the Battle of Jaffa, when the Brotherhood buried English knights and Saracens alike—Good King Richard, Duke of Normandy, Aquitaine and Gascony, and Count of Poitiers, Anjou, Maine and Nantes, and King of England; and Pouvreau and Bellende, whose forebears had been his subjects, as had those of the gravediggers from Normandy, spared a thought for Éléonore and Henri, poet-king, vanquisher of Saladin, and, as the Guild began to mop up their tears with choux, Bellende recited these final lines by Good King Richard, prisoner of the Germans:

> Or sapchon ben miey hom e miey baron,
> Angles, norman, peytavin e gascon,
> Qu'ieu non ay ja si paure compagnon
> Qu'ieu laissasse, per aver, en preison.
> Non ho dic mia per nulla retraison,

Mas anquar soi ie pres.
Car sai eu ben per ver certament
Qu'hom mort ni pres n'a amic ni parent;
E si'm laissan per aur ni per argent
Mal m'es per mi, mas pieg m'es per ma gent,
Qu'apres ma mort n'auran reprochament
Si sai mi laisson pres.

They know this well, my barons and my men,
Normans, Angles, Gascons and Poitevins
That I had ne'er follower so base
As I would, for mere gold, let languish in a jail.
I say this not for a reproach to them
Yet prisoner I am!
Of this one thing I now am certain sure
That death and prison know nor bond nor kin
Since 'tis for want of gold that they thus do let me lie
Much for myself I grieve; more for my people.
For when I am dead, they will bear the blame
If they should leave me prisoner long.

It was Nadking himself who hurled the first choux bun. A small
one, a chouquette; the projectile of vanilla cream exploded
against Bellende's right temple, tracing opalescent constellations
on the undertaker's face and the shoulder of his sinistral neighbor—Bellende smiled, greedily gobbled the remnants of pastry
and sweet filling and took advantage of the commotion to push
his dextral neighbor face down into a vast choux à la Chantilly
the latter had been foolish enough to eat by bending over: Gnarlcock joyfully crushed a choux in the center of Squatchoad's bald
pate, and the latter, unable to avoid the blow, did not know
whether to laugh or cry at this sacrilege; Martial Pouvreau, the
host of the Banquet, was the target of several salvos of choux and
chouquettes, being unable to sidestep, and even had a vast chocolate religieuse explode against his rubescent schnozzle, sending
a meteor shower of black particles over the faces of his neigh-

bors. Each man took the time to lick himself and savor this shrapnel fire as they gorged on these divine desserts as if they were the last, for the Banquet now was drawing to a close. A waiter carrying in a pyramid of choux slipped on an éclair (unless he was tripped up), unwittingly projecting a shower of cream-filled spheres of pastry backward as he sprawled—despite the rule which states that one does not kick a man when he is down, he was pelted with choux buns and submerged by a torrent of cream and pastry until he pleaded for mercy; and everyone laughed and yawned and slipped and laughed again, enrobed in melted chocolate, whipped cream, vanilla—the myopic could see nothing so blindly fired sweet projectiles like machine guns in order to defend themselves; the cats yowled and cleaned their whiskers when hit by a missile; the dogs, having no idea what was going on, barked long and loud and gobbled the choux buns in their gaping maws; the soused spit turners snoozing by the hearths, roused by a tidal wave of cream, were coming to their senses— those not scrabbling to their feet to launch a counterattack took cover, and this culinary combat carried on until all ammunition had been exhausted and abdominal and zygomatic muscles cramped—what larks, dear God!—then, gradually, they all regained their composure: spectacles were cleaned, the ritual phials polished; faces were scrubbed clean, legs were lifted as apprentices sluiced the floor with buckets of boiling water to intimidate the filth; help was provided to aid Gnarlcock in straightening his Grand Master's robes, Pizzlebeer the Norois his chamberlain's robes, and Squatchoad his treasurer's toga. Behind the ruined cathedral, dawn was beginning to divide white threads from black, and the gravediggers realized that, though some would spend all the following day feasting for the sheer pleasure of it—so that nothing, as they say, would go to waste—the Banquet itself would end with the Ritual, and although they knew that later, to invigorate the gravediggers and clear out their bowels, they would be served onion soup au gratin, the quintessential dish of love and dawn, followed by dozens of large, plump, freshly shucked Marennes oysters to dispel their hangovers, that in spite of this breakfast which, as it were, prolonged the ceremonies, the Banquet ended with the Ritual that Grand Master Gnarlcock was about to perform, though not before mentally revising the list of everything he had managed to ingest so far: "Let's see, I had a tiny tartine of rillettes au Vouvray, which seems almost as long ago as the preposterous slice of duck pâté, with a handful of gherkins to tease the former; an egg mimosa—a scant two halves since parsley aids digestion, followed by two cheese gougères— naught but hot air, a few frogs' legs, which are famous for their diminutive size; snails which deserved no better; a vol-au-vent à la reine of veal sweetbreads—probably the most subtle and delicate dish in the world; a bowl of beef bouillon on which floated thick crunchy croutons topped with a curl of foie gras; an egg in a thick sauce meurette of pink onions with Chinon for the sheer pleasure of dipping the toast with fresh thyme into the perfectly cooked, barely thickening yolk; a vol-au-vent filled with crayfish bathing in pleasure and a cream sauce of white wine and fumet de poisson; six warm oysters à la Dumas, in the manner that the noble Alexandre insists they be cooked, taken from their shells, sprinkled with parmesan and parsley, doused in a rivulet of champagne and grilled; nine langoustines from the pond at Croix-de-Vie, simmered in unadorned brine and accompanied by a simple mayonnaise with just a drop of lemon and a splash of not-too-bitter olive oil; breaded crab claws fried to order and dipped in the selfsame mayonnaise to which has been added a few sprigs of tarragon, chervil and chives; four slices of eel stuffed with the remains of the crab meat in a hollandaise tinted pale pink with tomato puree for the sheer pleasure of the hue; two fillets of lamprey à la nantaise, à la rochelaise or à la bordelaise, a hideous fish cooked in a thick stew of red wine, bacon and its own blood; half a carp filet in aspic à la juive, with a jardinière of baby carrots and vegetables vainly attempting to disguise the silty taste of the carp; one small glass of plum brandy at 55% ABV to open the *trou*, a timbale of coquillettes in a sauce of Comté cheese and truffle to close it up again; a small glass of Angelica at 55% ABV to reopen the *trou*, followed by a ladleful of coquillettes to forget the ghastly medicinal taste and close it up permanently; a slice of suckling pig spit-roasted in the hearth, as smooth and creamy as the accompanying chocolate sauce; a ramekin of pumpkin au gratin with Tomme de Maillezais, exquisite; a fragrant leg of hare roasted over embers of vine stock, with a slightly tart sauce of sorrel, garlic and spring mushrooms; a little gigot of lamb with a few mogettes, white beans from the Marais cooked on the trammel with pork rinds; a diaphanous slice of veal fillet in salt crust thrown onto the flames of the hearth, for which many a man would sell his soul to the devil; a little roasted reconstituted veal shank suffused with spices, carved with a ham knife; green asparagus, peas, baby carrots, pearl onions, green garlic, all accompanied by a hot herby mayonnaise in the béarnaise style but forgoing the vinegar; one third of a small Chaource, a slice of summer Beaufort, an exceptionally rare artisanal mountain Beaufort, a sliver of Fourme de Montbrison, for its unique sweetness, a few petals of Tête de Moine to marry with the white Meursault, because when all is said and done, I am Grand Master; a morsel of Arôme de Lyon to please Squatchoad and to sample the utterly scandalously good white Saint-Joseph; a shaving of ripe Chabichou du Poitou with no chalky aftertaste, to finish off the divine Sancerre; a slice of bread, perhaps the best, an old-fashioned loaf of homemade sourdough made of sumptuous flour with no chemical additives, ground by a millstone turned by the rushing waters of a river mill, kneaded with spring water and baked in a oven heated with charcoal from the ash trees of the Marais; a glass of Chinon to wash it down—which reminds me that I also drank a lot of Chenin, considerable quantities of Gamay from Anjou and Touraine, a few glasses of Mareuil to slake my thirst, and then came the desserts, a choux à la

Chantilly which I ate before smashing another on Squatchoad's
bald pate, followed by a small religieuse, a few profiteroles that
hit me in the face—delectable—and one or two final coffee
éclairs and voilà, now it is all over; let us add a little brandy—
aqua vitae—for the Ritual, an onion soup au gratin with Comté
cheese and nice croutons, a dozen Marennes oysters, plump
number two size oysters, with a well-chosen Muscadet sur Lie,
then off to bed for a few hours before finally heading back to
Lorraine. Because the Poitou is sorely lacking in mountains and
smoked ham hock.

"But now let us begin the Ritual."

LAST RITUAL

LET US DRINK MERRILY WHILE WE AWAIT DEATH

And so, first, Gnarlcock of Lorraine, proud hauler of the timber sled and Grand Master of the Gravediggers' Guild, dropped
into the general silence one simple, solemn and univocal word,
Die, and raised his curious hooch phial filled with spirits-of-wine
and drained it without a shudder; his neighbor picked up the
thread, *perish*, and drained his glass in turn, the next man whispered *expire*, and drank, and the next *pass away*, the man to his
right *decease*, the next one *give up the ghost*, the next man added
depart this life, his neighbor *breathed his last*, all emptied their
phials in good order, *meet one's maker, go the way of all flesh, return
to dust*, one by one the gravediggers gravely offered a verb or an
expression, *meet one's end*, then knocked back a shot of brandy,
snuff it, next, *croak*, always moving to the right—no layman had
ever witnessed this secret ritual, the most arcane of the Gravediggers' Guild, *kick the bucket*, then *shuffle off this mortal coil*, one
after the other, *pass on*, solemnly and without hesitation, *go to
glory*, then *hop the twig*, Bellende offered *cease upon the hour*, and

Pouvreau *succumb*, another proposed *turn up one's toes*, still another *join the choir invisible*, and another *go into the other realm*, and each in turn drank when came his time to pronounce one of the ninety-nine names for Death, *to pass from life to death, to make the great journey, to cross the bar*, from the most simple, *to end one's days, to have lived, to lose one's life, to enter into Eternity*, to the more colorful, *to kick the oxygen habit*, or the hackneyed, *to go to a better place*, each gravedigger proclaimed one of them, and knocked back their spirits-of-wine, *to be called to one's reward, to rest from one's labors, lie in the arms of Jesus, bid adieu to earthly scenes, go to God*, slang terms, *bite the dust, buy the farm, baste the formaldehyde turkey, drink the eleven o'clock broth, cash in one's chips, go into the fertilizer business, file for bankruptcy*, the unusual *pick turnips with a stepladder*, the natural *be laid to rest*, the simple *snuff out the candle*, the optimistic *depart this life in hope of a better*, the realist *pay a debt to nature*, the military *to have fought the good fight*, the practical *pack up one's tools*, the elegant *put on the wooden overcoat*, the current *to drift away*, the descriptive *to go out feetfirst*, and each member of the Most Noble Gravediggers' Guild, whose privileges dated back to the Crusades and to Saladin's capture of Jerusalem, drank a little glass as a sign of grief and being thus forced to carry upon their shoulders all the misfortunes and the sorrows of the world, they drank as, one by one, they intoned the names of death, one of the expressions that means to die, *to buy a pine condo, to blow one's camoufle*, and one continued, glass after glass, expression after expression, *to visit the moles, feed the worms, push up the daisies, eat dandelions by the root*, and the names of the angels of Death, Azrael, Samael, Thanatos, and all the esoteric words, those that cannot be written, or even read, without Death appearing, without Death appearing in person, and the hundredth name, the true name of Death, that which no human mouth has ever uttered, because the phonemes are the secret of humanity, our secret because we alone must die.

And they drank a final glass, just for the sake of it.

THE GRAVEDIGGERS NEVER SHALL GO HOME
EMPTY-HANDED:
LET US BURY ALL THE BODIES
THEN BURY DEATH ITSELF,
CHURN-CURDLED BOLLOCK BATTER!

SONG

Esther was weeping. She tried to stifle her sobs.

In late November 1951, seven years later, when she finally found the strength to make the journey, she visited the churches of Melle: Saint-Hilaire with its beautiful horseman, Saint-Pierre with its twin apse, and the more modest Saint-Savinien, and in each of the three she prayed, she prayed to Christ, prayed to the Virgin, prayed to the saints that she might find some cure for her grief; Esther was not a Christian, but she found brief moments of consolation in these presences, these images, these accounts of miracles. Esther headed south to Tillou, the place where the three children had been hidden, the place where they had spent three years of the war. The names of the villages were strange and ominous: Paizay-le-Tort, Sompt, Gournay-Loizé; the countryside seemed suddenly to lurch into winter; hilltops crowned with leafless trees, barren meadows. The road slashed deep into the flesh of the hills. The farmhouse was an old mill that stood on the banks of a river called the Somptueuse; there was a shed, a byre, some ducks; she was greeted by a man with a flowing beard and pale eyes whose wife was sitting in the farmyard with a duck in her lap; she was force-feeding the animal using a funnel whose endless, threaded tube was stuffed into the bird's beak; she was massaging the duck's throat to push the food down; Esther averted her eyes.

The man said, We didn't touch anything. He showed her an attic room with three small beds and Esther collapsed, the breath drained from her. Warily and respectfully, the man lifted her up like some fragile object; she thought she saw his pale eyes quiver slightly, a tear trickling down his black beard. Esther could not breathe, an overwhelming pain obstructed the cycle of air in her lungs, she longed for death to take her here and now, for the Everlasting to abjure his pity and destroy her in an instant, as a house is wiped out by a bomb, as the three children had been shot at point-blank range.

The man led her back out to the yard where the woman had just caught another duck and was stuffing the feeding tube down its throat.

We only do it in winter, the man said seemingly inadvertently. Come summer, it's too hot, the ducks croak if you feed 'em in summer. Esther's mind was blank, she stared down at her patent leather shoes spattered with the white mud of the farmyard; it looked to her like white blood, she shook her feet absurdly to shake it off.

It's only juice from a stone. It ain't nothing.

The man was trying to reassure her. He too was staring at the ground.

Offer the lady a cup of chicory, said the woman with the duck.

Would you ... Would you like a cup of hot chicory? With milk?

Esther glanced around; here the river split in two, circling the farm with water. A weeping willow dipped its mane into the water. She pictured the children playing by the stream and started to shudder.

Or a verbena, maybe? It's not all that warm, is it?

She had no need to answer.

She could feel the children's hands, their cheeks against her belly. Seven years and still the presence persisted. She could not consign them to the past. Make them disappear. As she stared at the woman with the ducks, she wondered why she had made the long journey back to Tillou in Poitou. In 1941 the demarcation line was just a few kilometers south, in the Charente. In 1944, Nazi troops moving northward looted and murdered as they retreated. That was seven years ago. For a moment, Esther wondered why these people had never touched the attic room. They had returned the suitcase to her. In it, she had found a photograph of herself—an image that had forever sundered her heart. What the children had written on the back of their mother's portrait. To keep her close to them while she was absent. Now there was no one close to her, excepting this image of herself. Esther once again began to sob. The woman released the duck, which waddled away as though drunk, and grabbed another.

The man looked at Esther, not knowing what to say.

D'you … D'you want to go see the spot?

She had to go and see the place. After all, this was why she had come. To see the place, to see death. The man was not used to cars.

An' you really drive that thing yerself?

Esther started the engine of the Peugeot 203. The farmer was reluctant to get in but eventually sat down next to Esther. They left the valley and headed toward the village; Esther noticed an isolated four-square chapel like an ancient temple. The line of houses ran parallel to the river. The farmer told Esther to take the road toward Brioux—he found it hard to believe that she had no idea which direction he meant. He jabbed his finger; there, that way. They drove between hedgerows on a narrow, flinty road like the one by which she had come. Esther tried to concentrate— had the landscape changed in seven years? The fields were tilled; the slightly orange soil, it seemed to her, was lined with furrows, scattered here and there with clods; she asked her passenger if it was the sowing season; the farmer gaped at her as though she were an American, or someone from another world. Nope, red lands like this, you got to till the ground early. Winter plowing. If there's too much rain or there's a hard frost, you can't, you needs a tractor. You don't sow 'til February.

The red lands. Esther felt a sudden wave of nausea and tears once again rolled down her cheeks. You can't be driving while you're crying. The road's too narrow. Suddenly, Esther panics, swerves, a great chestnut tree like a giant almost catches the car, the farmer screams, he screams, Esther's mind goes blank, she is absent, but she rights the vehicle and shifts down a gear; in spite of everything the Peugeot 203 continues on its way.

It's over there. There on the right. The farmer's voice is suddenly hoarse.

Esther flips down the right indicator and stops. It's a flagstone courtyard with a brick building to the rear. The farmer looks relieved to be getting out. He is very pale.

'Tis the old slaughterhouse, he says.

The place is every bit as grim as she imagined. Cracked red bricks, rusty metal gates; rotting wooden crates and an abandoned cistern cluttering up the yard. She wonders whether she will have the courage.

A young man wearing a cloak and cassock appears as if by magic from a house to the left of the gate. He is wearing a clerical collar whose whiteness sharply contrasts with the black of his clothes, the gray of the sky, the red brick of the building. Esther nods at him. He shakes the farmer's hand. Nicholas, he says. I'm the parish priest. I'm the one who wrote to you.

Esther wipes away her tears with her coat sleeve. She does not want to go inside this building. She does not want to know another thing. Coming here was a terrible mistake. She is cold—shivering. Nicholas warms her a little with his smile. He has a strong, reassuring voice, a priestly voice, she thinks. Come in. Come in.

Esther cannot help but follow the young man into the slaughterhouse. Old, grimy tiles, a sloping concrete floor inset with drainage channels and a low railing. Metal railings, like the barriers you might find at a circus or in a stadium. She has seen enough. She wants to leave. She feels herself choking. There is no air. No light. Nothing but children's cries. Not cries of pain. Cries of joy. Howls of joy, Mama, Mama, and suddenly her body is being kneaded by six hands, six arms, three faces are pressed against her, the suffocating warmth of happiness, the simple pleasure of the impossible in the evidence of the miracle, the first child says, I had a good sleep, Mama, the second adds, Me too, the third whispers, I thought I was in heaven, and they are so beautiful, and Esther cries, she cries with joy, her whole being cries out with joy in this slaughterhouse transfigured by the presence of Nicholas, by the dazzling light of the present. Of course, she hears nothing else, she no longer hears the outside world, she does not hear the gendarme, she does not hear the doctor, her head was slammed so hard against the chestnut tree that she died instantly, she does not hear the gendarme, you were lucky you landed up in the long grass, she does not hear the farmer, all torn up by the windshield, stammering, yes, I was lucky, she cannot hear, she cannot speak; in the pocket of her blouse they found a small scallop-edged photograph about two inches square, with writing on the back scrawled by childish hands. No one ever dies instantly.

V.

GALLIA EST OMNIS DIVISA
IN PARTES TRES

Lucie was reveling in the sheer joys of nature, though the land was made bleak by winter; the gentle wind blowing through the branches of the silver poplars around the field trilled a leafless melody; the low January afternoon sun would quickly veer to pink, the moisture rising from the nearby marshlands would soon turn to mist—despite the fact that Lucie's garden was on higher ground, outside the marsh itself, in particularly wet years, her cabbages, lettuces and chard would be submerged under twenty inches of water and the high tunnels turned into indoor swimming pools: but this is increasingly rare, as recent years have been quite dry. She knew that she would soon be forced to leave this place—her separation was all too real, everything had been divided: Franck got to keep the lands and the greenhouses while she kept the calluses on her hands and the clay under her fingernails. She looked around; of course, all this belonged to Franck, he'd inherited it from his parents; all she had ever done was live with him, helped with the farm and sold the vegetables at market. Franck was not a rich man, but then again what did *she* have? Two pairs of boots and a crappy car. Had they been married or civil partners, things would have been different. Franck would've owed her a solatium in recompense for all the years they had toiled together. She liked the word *solatium* because it had a historic, almost medieval ring. You could tell that it was an ancient right. Or perhaps not. These things are complicated. Lucie felt that women were always the losers in these stories. Shares and Limited-Liability Companies, Common Agricultural Operating Groups; the modern world had a talent for eye-catching acronyms like EARL, GAEC, yet still the inequality persisted. Don't get married, that way you're both still free, bullshit. Lucie did not feel free. She had been duped—not by Franck, no, by something older and more entrenched like entitlement, something as ancient as *solatium*. Something that had been crushing rural women for centuries.

She was lucky that she could live with her grandfather. To have a roof over her head meant she could leave Franck. Well, "lucky" was a stretch. The house was a dump. The old man disgusted her. Fortunately, she loved Arnaud. He was completely insane but he made her laugh. And he was a gentle soul. His astonishing memory for dates was both unsettling and miraculous. Lucie had had little contact with Arnaud's mother, her father's sister, who had died five years earlier of a terrifying illness, an illness that could be called sadness, abandonment, the sheer burden of life; at the time, Franck and Lucie were living a few kilometers away, on the other side of the road to the Vendée, near the fields and the greenhouses, so, naturally, Lucie had looked after her cousin and the repulsive grandfather who had terrified her as a child; although now retired, her father seldom visited: all he had inherited from his own father were a fearful respect and various scars made by a belt buckle.

Lucie very much wanted to move out, to get back to life, a home that might be considered "normal." But where? And with what money? Lucie's mother owned a little land in the fertile area of the marshlands between Secondigny and Bressuire, land that was planted with apple trees, next to which was a little house that Lucie dreamed of moving into, a place where she could set up a few high tunnels and grow organic vegetables, it would be paradise—it wasn't huge, but it was well irrigated and the soil was rich; unfortunately, for decades now the whole thing had been rented for a pittance to a local farmer. And even if Lucie managed to recover the property, the place would need at least €80,000 to €100,000 in order to be viable. Franck had offered to help out, to lend her farm machinery on condition that it was within reasonable distance. But Lucie didn't want to set eyes on him again. Not since he had demanded €50,000 from her to remain a partner in the business. It felt to her as though Franck were putting a price tag on their separation. Fifty thousand euros to acquire the right to continue working now that she would no longer be sleeping with him. For almost a decade she had slogged and sweated on this land, in these greenhouses—and now that they were separating Franck was demanding €50,000. Which meant that, to him, her company, both physical and sentimental, was worth €50,000. In a nutshell. She had felt terribly hurt. So, she carried on working for Franck on a temporary basis for a little cash up front plus commission on the market sales that she generated. Just enough so that, with her social security benefits, she could make ends meet. Or almost. But every time she found herself out here in the fields, every time she was caught unawares by dusk, saw humidity rise as a mist from the marshes and eddy in the twilight, every time the air was pervaded by the cool of the Marais and she could just make out the last flutterings of thrushes in the half-light, she felt a pang of melancholy, a peal of bells, like a death knell, at the thought that soon she would have to leave this life, this place—the thick golden straw mulch on the plant beds reflected the last glow of the evening, Lucie shivered, why think about cash, dough, shekels, moola, scratch, like a parched dry summer, lack of money had desiccated her whole life, blessed are those who win their freedom by giving up everything, she was dirt poor, yet still the weeds kept growing, it was getting chilly, she pulled up two leeks, picked a savoy cabbage that was too small to sell and went to the storeroom to get some carrots

and potatoes. The prospect of eating the soup she would make
by the fire, in that stinking shack, made her depression complete.
She took her phone from her pocket for a second (telling herself
she was checking the time, though from the twilight she could
tell it quite precisely). She glanced around to make sure she had
not left any tools lying about, whistled for the dog slinking behind the poplars looking to flush out a water rat, took off her
gloves, took off her mud-spattered black fleece and pulled on a
blue padded coat, opened the tailgate of the van so the dog could
hop up, climbed behind the steering wheel and, as she did every
evening, looked at her face in the rearview mirror for a second:
nothing to worry about, it was still her: the incipient crow's-feet
around the corners of the eyes, the frown lines on the forehead,
the dimple on the chin, the bright-red lips, everything is fine, no
dirty streaks on her cheeks, no straw in the hair; the dog poked
its muzzle between the seats and gently nudged her arm as if
to say, come on old girl, let's go, you can look at yourself in the
mirror later: Lucie smiled, patted the dog's head and keyed the
ignition. It was 6:15 p.m. but already the treetops of the poplars
had disappeared, devoured by the darkness.

*

Whenever Father Largeau had one too many, he did not sink
into unconsciousness but rather the brandy or cheap wine banished his sorrows and brought him a nebulous joy; he no longer
thought about Christ or his crisis of faith, but allowed his imagination to focus on some commonplace object and gaze at a plant
or observe some animal—one of Mathilde's cats for example;
from his chair, he would watch the little feline creep into his garden and scamper about, rub itself against the trunk of the tall
catalpa tree, attempt to catch a fly or a butterfly with a swipe of
its paw, roll in the grass, and this contemplation allowed Father
Largeau to think of nothing else, to remain utterly motionless
behind the window, his elbows propped on the red-and-white

checked tablecloth; he longed for nothing more than this brief respite, this hiatus in his thoughts. Then, as questions once again began to swirl, as doubts and morbid images returned, he would quickly grow irritable and, grabbing his cap, he would pull on a jacket and go out. He all but raced through the village until he reached open country; he could not believe that these vast expanses were suddenly shorn of God, that the spiritual breath had abandoned the countryside, that the river of faith no longer irrigated these lands—walking was his way of meditating. He would tramp through the fields, heading southeast; he would cross the Sèvre at Saint-Maxire, past the magnificent Beaulieu farm, then, leaving the road, would head down to Mursay and continue toward the wayside crucifix at the junction of the roads leading to Chauray and Échiré: the calvary tree was the only one that the process of land consolidation had thoughtfully allowed to remain in place in this bare, undulating landscape of desolate ground strewn with white pebbles cast up by the tractor's blade, and what significance did He have here, this poor man's Jesus, crucified at a forgotten crossroads, who served only to prevent motorists from being able to see whether there was a car coming from right or left? Largeau tried to pray, he mumbled as he walked a few hundred meters then gave up. He preferred to focus on his walk, on his breathing, on the surrounding landscape—when he reached the top of the hill, the wind would try to whip off his biretta. In the distance, he could see the valley of the Sèvre, with Siecq and Surimeau to one side and Saint-Maxire and Échiré to the other; beyond Saint-Maxire, he could see the turning blades of a cluster of wind turbines that marked the border between Saint-Rémy and the village—from here, Largeau could just make out the bell tower of his own church. The next day, he had a baptism in Faye-sur-Ardin over there, a few kilometers away, followed by a wedding in Villiers-en-Plaine; and the day after that, he had to officiate at a funeral in Béceleuf; his parishes were countless, and not a month passed without some new mission being conferred on him—what if he truly were the last? The Archbishop of Poitiers would soon reorganize the twenty-five existing parishes to the north of Niort into a single area, to be named after a local saint; there would be no more deaneries, only a single parish, a flock of forty thousand souls presided over by one or two priests, helped by a few deacons and himself, he hoped, for many years even after his retirement—in these regions, spirituality had begun to die out; it had become a blanket of mist that whirled and whirled and disappeared. Father Largeau felt that the past forty years had turned everything on its head; he felt as though he were waking up, at the age of sixty-five, to a world where everything was unfamiliar; groping his way through the shadows of time, a black and poisonous morass.

He readjusted his biretta and continued on his way; of course he knew that no bridge crossed the Sèvre between here and Surimeau—to press on to Surimeau, then to Siecq via Sainte-Pezenne and from there back to the village was a good two hours' walk, four or five in total. The priest glanced up at the clouds: the early spring sun was like Largeau himself, hale and hearty, yet capable of wavering at any moment. At Mursay, he headed back down into the valley and walked along the river, between the trees and the horses—thankfully the ground here was reasonably dry, his feet did not sink too deeply. The air smelled of grass and putrefaction; high in the treetops, for as far as the eye could see, only mistletoe brightened the leafless branches of the willows and poplars. The Château de Mursay was a piteous ruin—the ramparts were long gone and the roof of the main building had collapsed; great gaps opened in the towers whose former nobility had been ripped away by years of neglect. Brambles and ivy were devouring everything, invading the windows, tickling the loopholes, the tentacles of a noxious creature that, sooner or later, would fell the vast stone edifice, the mullioned windows, the groin vaults, even the little second-floor balcony that overlooked the river—only the three swans and two ducks seemed unconcerned by the devastation that loomed over their ripples in the water.

Largeau had not prayed for weeks, perhaps months—he had simply mechanically reeled off words which, if his heart was not in them, were devoid of meaning and effect. He celebrated mass by rote, feeling as though a recording were speaking and singing in his stead. At weddings and funerals, he was increasingly conscious that no one knew the hymns; no one knew that they should stand for the reading of the Gospel. Largeau blamed himself; his anxiety mounted as evening drew in and he knew that as soon as he arrived home, having taken off his muddy shoes, put on his wool slippers, removed his clerical collar and traded his sweater for a dressing gown, he would have to pour himself several small glasses of white wine, followed by as many small glasses of red and a few thimbles of brandy in order to regain a state of torpor, to stifle the mounting dread while he waited to see whether Mathilde would drop by as she often did—he both feared and longed for these visits, knowing that Mathilde would inflame his desire as though the Evil One himself were blowing on the embers of his heart. Largeau knew all too well that his carnal desires were merely a symptom, a mark of dereliction; the more he was abandoned by the spirit, the more his demon body took over; the very flesh that he had mortified for so many years now reemerged as he was entering old age, and this left him feeling so helpless, so alone, that despite himself, he could not help but sink further into that spiritual sloth that monks call accidie.

*

As Gary headed home through the worsening storm after seeing the wild boar frolicking in the snow, he was completely unaware that, in the course of early rebirths, he had been the strong-minded landlady of a bar in Lezay; a leatherworker in a factory in Niort who died in childbirth; a bombardier from La Chapelle-Bâton who died in 1918 of Spanish flu in a Reims field hospital; a one-eyed well-digger from Rouvre who died in 1896 aged one hundred; and a gray she-wolf from the forests of Hermitain between Aigonnay and La Mothe-Saint-Héray, where wolves can be heard howling in the winter twilight as they approach villages of drystone houses on the edge of groves of chestnut trees or oaks; where, in spring, they can be seen on moonlit nights drinking from the stream near the Devil's Rock—people hunt them for the thrill or for a bounty, they set powerful steel-toothed traps that slice cats in half and amputate the limbs of foxes, and when, from time to time, they catch a wolf, they cut off its ears and its tail to claim the bounty from the town hall, which sends the accounts to the prefecture in Niort. As is well known, the wolf attacks humans only if it has rabies, at which point it is dangerous, as much for the disease itself as for the wounds it inflicts—in 1894 the département paid out bounties for thirteen wolves; in 1895, seven; in 1896, six, in 1898 only four and in 1901 only a single wolf, and that was that; there would be no more of the Canidae that prey on sheep and children in fairy tales.

On 23 Frimaire, year V, on the eve of the well-digger's birth in the commune of La Couarde in Deux-Sèvres, a recently created département from which the fires of war were slowly retreating, leaving the countryside deserted, fields ravaged and livestock decimated, on what is now called December 13, 1796, an official named Proust, acting on behalf of the widow Marie-Jeanne Landron Bouchet, who is illiterate, signs "a petition to the members of the municipal council imploring the citizen administrators to request a pecuniary recompense from the département for the noble actions of her late husband Jean-Pierre Bouchet who, while repairing a paddock fence, was attacked by a rabid wolf which gashed his hand and inflicted a minor wound to his thigh; realizing that he was injured, Jean-Pierre Bouchet threw himself on the savage beast, crying: 'Willingly I sacrifice my days on earth to deliver my country from the depredations this rabid wolf might bring about. Happy am I if my death should spare the lives of my neighbors.' Thence he proceeded to engage the beast in singular combat: though gored and bloodied, he found the strength to lop off the head of the animal with the axe he was using to defend himself. Jean-Pierre Bouchet perished of his wounds, and in so doing, left a widow and a large family whose only means of subsistence had been the fruits of her doomed husband's labors."

The gray she-wolf, who will later be a well-digger, then a bombardier, then an innkeeper, caught the infection from the urine and saliva of a red fox; the disease gives her an irrational fear of water accompanied by an unquenchable thirst, her jaws lock onto whatever they find—a branch, a stone, a fence; a slobbery foam trails from her lips and clings to her teeth; her howl is strange, a piercing yowl of pain. She does not know that she is doomed; the virus slowly incubated in her body has reached her brain and eaten away at her nerves; she has bitten one of her cubs on the neck, not realizing that she was passing the disease on to him; for days, she has wandered aimless, plagued by a thirst so intense she would drink the very stones—but the pain triggered as soon as she ingests a drop of water is so intense, so excruciating, that the she-wolf even fears the dew that forms on blades of grass and the trail left by slugs on the leaves, everything serves to aggravate the disease, everything pushes her toward exhaustion. She no longer fears the open country or the smell of man, which she has avoided since birth; she heads for the edge of the forest, her eyes filled with mortal fire, she howls, her coat ripples in bluish waves, bristles with sweat.

The she-wolf sees a man moving—she breaks into a run, attacks him as wolves do more powerful opponents such as deer and cattle, sinking their teeth into the leg, forcing their adversary to bend to gain access to the throat. This is the first time the she-wolf has smelled humans at such close quarters, a smell of smoke, wool, blood and onions. The she-wolf snaps at the hand gripping the wooden fence, rips it with her fangs; the farmer screams—it frightens her, this sound so unlike the bleating of sheep, the yelp of foxes or the bellowing of a doe as her fawn is slaughtered. The she-wolf is trying to take the man down, but she also has the urge to bite the wooden fence to relieve the tension in her jaws, quell the excruciating pain in her throat, she growls, she cannot lap up the blood dripping from the mutilated hand, she leaps for the man's throat, her jaws wide. Instinctively, the man protects himself, the two fall to the ground, the she-wolf sinks her teeth as hard as she can into the arm, the chest, the thigh—the man is swinging something hard and brutal, the she-wolf tries to catch it, the man pulls back and stuns her with his axe, she staggers and pants, she is disoriented, panicked by the blood in her mouth, she is afraid, very afraid, the glinting metallic shadow comes down on her, the darkness falls, a black thunderbolt, a veil of darkness falls over the she-wolf's eyes as, dumbstruck by his own pain, the farmer stares at the severed head lying on the grass, the blood-smeared fur and his own wounds before fainting from fear and exhaustion while the soul of the she-wolf moves through the Bardo to the little village of Rouvre, near the church of Saint-Médard, where for almost a hundred years, she will be a well-digger, later a bombardier, later still a bar owner in Beauvoir-sur-Niort and, lastly, Gary, who was heading home that morning after having glimpsed the wild boar that had once been Father Largeau, a few meters from the hedgerow, rolling in the light dusting of snow.

When he got back to the farm, Gary hugged Mathilde and told her about sighting what seemed to be a wild pig on the outskirts of the village, told her about the mobile hairdresser visiting tubby Thomas, and the appearance of the gendarmes; Mathilde knew Lynn slightly and liked her, though she preferred to go to the salon in the shopping center which, in addition to the same services, offered the additional distractions of getting out of the house, going for a walk and doing some shopping.

Mathilde was enjoying the last days of Advent and preparing to celebrate the birth of the Savior. She always looked forward to Christmas Eve: since childhood, she had attended midnight mass—walking home in the cold and dark after the service then eating a sweet juicy clementine and drinking a mug of hot chocolate before going to bed. The following day, all the family would gather. The patriarch René, Mathilde's father, at the head of the table surrounded by uncles, aunts, cousins, brothers and sisters; the fresh oysters, the terrines, the poultry, the chestnuts, the log known in the local dialect as a "cosse de na," whether referring to the log that burned in the hearth or the log of cream and sugar set down on the table. Mathilde thought back to the things they had used back then, the stoneware pickle jar, the oyster dishes shaped like shells, the enameled container on the table for shells and bones, the knife holders—all the things she associated with the 1970s and which had long since disappeared together with the electric-orange can opener screwed to the wall, the engraved napkin rings and midnight mass itself, which was now celebrated at ten o'clock some twenty kilometers from home. Before Christmas, she would always buy a couple of the magazines you find near supermarket checkouts filled with ideas for decorating (flowers, vases, candles, napkins, silver pine cones, mistletoe, holly), for the tree (baubles, tinsel, gold cherubs, spray cans of white snowflakes) or even the yard (a lighted Santa, an outdoor Christmas tree, a lighted doghouse), and it filled her with joy, because the significance of all these preparations (beyond the Savior's coming into the world) was that the children would be home, the whole family would be together, loving and hugging and giving each other presents. This ritual kindness was particularly important to her; she preferred it when Christmas gifts were attributed to the baby Jesus rather than to the slightly preposterous red-faced man with a beard who, though likable enough, meant nothing to her and whose reindeer symbolized absolutely nothing. In fact, she found it difficult to remember when this so-called Father Christmas had asserted himself as a benevolent figure in this region—elsewhere people anticipated a visit from

Saint Nicholas or from the Three Wise Men, but here, between the Loire and the Dordogne, the baby Jesus—perhaps because he was a newborn—had been completely supplanted, to the point where Jesus had all but been erased from Christmas cards. Mathilde was the secretary to the Association of the Faithful; there were still some people who tried to keep the flame of faith alive, to remember that a church had a greater meaning beyond being an additional expense when it needed a new roof.

Mathilde watched as Gary walked with his dog through the swirling snow toward the northern edge of the village on the brow of the hill, next to the little copse known as Le Luc with the stone that Mathilde refused to call the Devil's Rock—the Rock was quite sufficient. Mathilde was oblivious of her previous lives, of the endless turnings of the Wheel that had lugged her soul hither and yon, of the fact that she had been a raven-haired witch dreaming of the Great Goat, a dray horse that died on the job, a farmyard cat, various farmers, farmers' wives and laborers, a golden oriole, an oak tree uprooted by a storm that had ended up beneath the woodcutter's axe at the time when a boundless forest had stretched away from the village, a vast forest that extended to the foothills of Brittany: the Marais protected the forest, and the forest protected the Marais—the marshlands were a lacework of islands surrounded by brackish water, the Gulf of the Pictones, which Strabon refers to as the Two Crows, white-winged and black-winged: at the far end of this lagoon, near the ocean, there had been an island exclusively populated by women long before the legions of Caesar first visited the region, women who were possessed by a dark god, to whom they made sacrifices, a god they appeased with rituals and libations. No man was allowed on the island; when the women wished to talk to men or mate with them, it was they who went ashore; they were priestesses of a secret temple who dedicated their days to the upkeep of the temple building lashed by winter storms. Nothing is known of the deity they worshipped—likely a crazed, drunken, outrageous

Dionysian figure—before he was tamed by the druids, or by the daughter of Zeus and Demeter, before she became queen of the underworld; no one knows, just as Mathilde did not know that near the Standing Stone she could not bring herself to call "the Devil's Rock," thereby uttering the name of the Evil One, there was once a sanctuary that welcomed the druids, those godless priests who believed in the transmigration of souls from body to body and for all eternity, the flesh could be cremated, the soul was reborn; Julius Caesar saw it as a font of courage, the warriors of Gaul did not fear death, they knew that if they had the honor of dying in battle, they would be reborn: they feared only defeat and cowardice, failure and spinelessness. "Happy are those whom no fear penetrates," wrote Lucan in his *Pharsalia*, "Happy the peoples 'neath the Northern Star / In this their false belief; for them no fear / Of that which frights all others: they with hands / And hearts undaunted rush upon the foe / And scorn to spare the life that shall return." Bards with their songs guided the souls toward reincarnation and druids were like those shepherds keeping a watchful eye on their flock. Not far from the village was a sacred wood, long inviolate, whose tangled branches blocked out the rays of daylight, creating a cold, shadowy gloom beneath the dense canopy. This was not a place inhabited by rustic Pans, by sylphs and wood nymphs. Instead, it veiled a barbaric cult and gruesome sacrifices. Altars and trees dripped with human blood; and, to believe the superstitions of antiquity, it was a place where the birds dared not perch on the branches, nor the wild beasts make their lair; thunderbolts hurled down by the clouds would not land here, the very winds feared to touch it. No breath stirs their leaves; the trees quiver of their own accord. Dark springs disgorge foul waters; somber rough-hewn statues of gods are fashioned from shapeless trunks; the pale worm-eaten wood stirs terror. Man does not tremble so before familiar gods. The more unknown the object of his worship, the more formidable it is. It was said that great roars came from the depths of the forest;

the uprooted trees that lay on the ground rose up of their own accord; the forest offered the image of a vast conflagration yet was never consumed; here dragons embraced oaks within their long folds. People never dared approach these woods. They fled these gods. Whether Phoebus stood at midday in his course or dark night shrouded the sky, the priest himself feared this place, afraid that he might surprise its dread master.

This was the forest that Caesar ordered to be felled; it was close to his encampment, and having been spared by war, it alone stood, thick and bushy, amid the barren hills. At this command, the bravest men trembled. The majesty of the forest had filled all with a pious reverence, and no sooner did they strike these sacred trees than it seemed as though their avenging axes turned against them.

Seeing his troops tremble and their hands shackled by terror, Caesar was the first to dare seize an axe, hold it aloft and strike, driving it into the trunk of an oak that soared into the heavens. Then, showing them the steel plunged into the violated wood: "If any man among you believes it a crime to cut down the forest, then I am guilty," he said. "The responsibility falls to me." On an instant, every man obeyed, not because they were comforted by his example, but because their fear of Caesar surpassed that of the gods. For the first time, the ancient elms, the gnarled oaks, the water-loving alders and the cypresses saw their long locks fall, and between the treetops there appeared a passage that gave way to daylight. The forest whole and entire falls in upon itself, but in its fall, supports itself, the sheer density defies gravity. The tree is loath to die, the oak holds all together and the miraculous wonders of the druid come to pass—branches fall in sheaves of fresh-cut spears, ivy transforms itself into the net of the retiarius, the bay laurel forgets not its divine essence and Nature's warriors now wage battle against Rome; by rights, the forest should break, but it is Rome that bends and retreats, leaving behind weapons and breastplates, men and firebrands. Your dark light will not invade these trees—their mystery remains pristine.

In the village, the druids and the bards were long forgotten, the forest had been gradually disappearing since ancient times; only two small woodlands now darkened the plain, Le Luc and the Ajasses, two beauty spots on porcelain skin—people vaguely remembered that Le Luc owed its name to a Gaulish god, but of the peaceful Pictones there was no trace and, had anyone asked Mathilde, she would have been hard-pressed to say what tribe of Gauls had once lived here, whereas she could have reeled off numerous Roman monuments and Latin quotations. She had forgotten that the Yule log was formerly used during the long night of the solstice to fill the darkness with sparks, by striking the red-hot log with a sword, as one might slay a dragon—on this, the darkest night, people read these flaming wisps as one might interpret constellations in a summer sky, as one might listen to the future on the wind, or discern it in the flight of birds. The sparks traced crimson tori around starry clusters, in the smoky December cold, and all the villagers gathered to watch swords beating on the glowing trunks—childhood is pagan; and though the custom had been lost centuries earlier, because priests love no gods but their own, the name and the shape of that log endured in every pastry shop of Europe.

Mathilde watched the snow fall for a long moment, as though hypnotized, then set about cooking, since it was almost noon.

When he had almost reached the top of the slope covered in snow, struggling against the fierce wind and the snowflakes like needles stinging his cheeks and nose, Gary finally persuaded himself that the dog would not be able to pick up a scent in this storm, so there was no point in watching the hedgerows for a phantom boar that he was not about to try and shoot in any case; out here on his own, with little visibility, he was more likely to put a bullet in anything but the boar—a gendarme, for example, like the ones he had seen prowling around their police van in the middle of the fields, blue shadows on a carpet of white.

He approached the spot where, barely an hour earlier, he had glimpsed the *Sus scrofa*; the dog flushed out a pheasant that had survived the previous week's release—the bird hopped to the other side of the hedgerow without quite taking flight, its red cheeks seeming to streak the snow with blood. Instinctively, Gary shouldered his rifle, but did not fire; he had loaded the gun with bullets rather than buckshot. The dog was preventing the pheasant from taking cover; the bird was an unmistakable stain of ocher, green and red on the field of white. Farmed pheasants made for very poor game; Gary realized that he had more than enough time to reload the shotgun, but he gave up. He felt vaguely sorry for the bird and whistled at the dog, which glanced at him, then back at the pheasant with a look of bewilderment. Gary gently patted the dog and told him he had done a fine job, but his master was not in the mood. And just as he glanced over at the two gendarmes bustling around their Renault Trafic near the soaring pylons of the electrical substation, he clearly saw the boar run across the field at full speed, making for the deep cover of the hedgerow on the other side and the Ajasses. Once again, Gary shouldered his rifle, realized that the gendarmes were in the line of fire and that, even if it was a safe shot, they might reasonably feel that they were being fired on: he lowered the rifle for the second time and watched as the boar that had been Father Largeau took cover right under the noses of the two cops who were still circling their vehicle, though given the distance and the fact that visibility was poor because of the snow, Gary could not quite make out what the hell they were doing in the middle of a land consolidation path in this weather.

*

When Lucie's cousin, Arnaud, came home that noon, happy and excited by the heavy snowfall, he greeted his grandfather who was sitting in his armchair in front of the fire, prepared a quick lunch (Knorr® Cup-a-Soup Creamy Mushroom, a can of Dieux® sardines "The gods feast upon sardines and ambrosia, *Iliad cantus XXV*" in tomato sauce, with a La Festive™ baguette), the most entertaining part of which consisted of meticulously lifting out the sardine fillets before spreading them on the baguette to make himself a sandwich. Arnaud wiped his mouth on the sleeve of his overalls, grease against grease, then cleared his plate and, one by one, gathered up the bread crumbs on the tablecloth, which he deposited outside in the little garden on a plate set there for that purpose, where titmice and finches would come to peck at them; he made the most of this to play with the dog, catching snowflakes like fireflies, before going back inside shivering, and changing his clothes (draping his overalls on a chair, putting on a tracksuit) and settling down in front of the fireplace and the Christmas lights, only to realize that, while the gas was working (he had been able to boil water for the soup), there was no electricity, since the lights refused to twinkle. He shared this concern with the grandfather who simply dragged his slippers across the blackened floor and tossed a log back into the fireplace without bothering to respond—but that was no problem; Arnaud sat in his armchair next to the old man, and, convinced that Lucie would be home soon, he dozed off: with sleep came visions. For a moment, he was a pollarded ash tree on the banks of a pond, its surface frozen with a thin film of soft, crackling frost; he left the tree for another time, far, far back in the past, when he had been a badger with a deep sett—this life had ended in the jaws of a red fox, and Arnaud saw his soul return to the deep-hued Bardo for forty days before choosing to be reincarnated as a human, a nobleman in a fortress, a powerful regional king who delighted in war, travel, song and poesy—this life was thrilling and opulent, the king's court was dazzling; his name was Guillaume. Arnaud listened as the king sang a long bawdy ballad for his friends, delighting the assembled company; Comte Guillaume was witty, skilled in the arts of *trobar*—he invented language as he sang. The mistress of Comte Guillaume de Poitiers was a ravishing lady called Dangereuse, known as La Maubergeonne; Arnaud dreamed his way through time like a bird through the air—he followed the Comte de Poitiers as he set off on the Crusades, to the thrice holy city of Jerusalem which smoldered with incense; he watched the Comte de Poitiers grow old, and then sing as he felt death looming,

> Toz mos amics prec a la mort
> Que vengan tut e m'ornen fort,
> Qu'eu avut joi e deport
> Loing e pres et e mon aizi.
> Aissi guerpisc joi e deport
> E vair e grey e sembeli.

"All my friends, I ask that after my death you come and pay tribute to me, for I have known joy and pleasure—today I leave behind joy and pleasure, I cast off the vair, the ermine and the sable," and Arnaud found the song deeply moving. In dreams, he could perceive the vast spider's web of souls, the wool ball of existences interleaved in time, and he could follow a single life as one might pull on a thread, jump from one moment to another and, from the infinite heavens, even observe the forces that cause the stars to move, immense dark flows like streams of nothingness. In his sleep, Arnaud had access to untrammeled knowledge—he was aware of the myriad living creatures around him, the countless rebirths of the dog, of his grandfather, of spiders, of gnats, all the way down to the terrifyingly invisible levels, bacilli, paramecia, those microscopic beings that are a sightless multitude, that live and die in the terrible agony of ignorance, and Arnaud felt compassion for all these creatures whose torments he understood, although this insight, too, was a form of pain: often, when he woke from dreams, he felt a heavy sadness that he had to shake off, as one might shake off a flurry of ashes.

When he opened his eyes, his grandfather was still next to him and had just put another log on the fire. Arnaud scratched his forearm and sniffed it, as a way of retaking possession of his body; the light was beginning to wane, the glow of the flames spread like contagion to everything, the walls, the table, even the grandfather's face, which suddenly seemed immense, Papi, can you fish for crayfish in the snow?

Arnaud was considering taking his bike to hunt for crayfish; he loved to fish for Louisiana crayfish with a ring net. Arnaud lured the decapods with dog food stuffed inside an onion net that he placed inside the metal mesh and it was wonderful to see how, at dusk, within minutes of immersing the ring net, dozens of crustaceans were fighting each other for access to the meager bait; Arnaud delightedly watched them swarming in the bottom of the net as he lifted the rod—he loved to play with these hideous little creatures, poking at their red-spotted claws; they were the most voracious of creatures, capable even of eating each other when food was scarce.

The old man, as usual, did not answer his question, he simply laughed: the idea of fishing for anything in the snow seemed highly comical—and in fact, in freezing weather, Louisiana crayfish hide in huge burrows dug into the banks and seldom emerge.

Arnaud could read other people like a book—he alone knew that his grandfather had been—in no particular order—tenant farmers (male and female), farm girls, an itinerant poacher, a number of deer, a dog, several starlings, or that he himself owed his technical knowledge to the fact that he was the reincarnation of a mechanic from Villiers, whose skills he had retained—he could explore these experiences, these memories of other lives, stroll through them, as one might follow the line of fate on a friendly palm. Arnaud could see the sufferings and sorrows, the violence and joy that marked a soul like the wrinkles of a face and, to him, such a miracle seemed entirely ordinary; he listened to his grandfather's lives as one might listen to a spring babbling over pebbles, much of the time not troubling to heed the sound made by the pebbles rocked by the current, but if he had a mind to, he could prick up his ears for a moment the better to enjoy an incident; Arnaud loved the distant echoes of battles, the clash of steel and swords; he himself had met his death (one of his innumerable deaths) in a long-ago battle, near the banks of the Clain, on the Roman road that leads to Tours, during the hundred and fourteenth Ramadan since the Hijra, barely a century after the death of the bearded Prophet who, in distant Araby, had founded a faith that became a kingdom and a way of life, in which former slaves became warlords and now were slaves only to Allah. Thousands of warriors with their caravansary of wives, tents and horses, thousands of soldiers arrived from the new kingdom of al-Andalus under the command of its governor, Abd al-Rahman ibn Abd Allah al-Ghafiqi—whether these warriors from Moorish Spain came to plunder the territories beyond the Pyrenees or to conquer them in the name of the Umayyad Caliphate, it is impossible to say. All Arnaud had to do was say, October 14, 732, Battle of Tours, and instantly he would hear horses snorting amid the clang of scimitars, arrows whistling through the autumn sky and the howls of the wounded and the dying, turning the Roman roads crimson with the blood of martyrs, and to feel himself perish, in the icy cold of the river; Arnaud did not witness the outcome of the battle, which would become one of the most celebrated battles in France even though it was unclear whether it had ended in victory or defeat, despite the fact that Eudon son of Loup, Duke of Aquitaine, managed to save his duchy, and Charles Martel earned his place in the annals of history. Arnaud dreamed that the Saracens had left their arrows, their scimitars and their tents scattered around his home (between the poplar grove and the marshlands, between the rivers Autize and Sèvre, between the ash trees and the dog roses), something of their music, something of their memory, and that a few years later, during the reign of Charlemagne, they returned, commanded by the legendary King Agolant, after the capture of Agen; in the west, Saracens, Moors, Moabites, Ethiopians, Turks and Persians regrouped and Charlemagne engaged them in battle at Taillebourg near Saintes, whose castle was occupied by the Moors. On the eve of the great battle a miracle occurred; having stacked their arms outside their tents for the night, the Franks woke to discover that their wooden lances had taken root, that they were covered with bark and leaves: these were the lances of those who would find martyrdom in battle for the love of Christ Jesus. The imminent martyrs hurled themselves into the fray with all the strength bestowed on them by the Almighty—they slew many Saracens before they perished: four thousand were martyred in a single day, and Charlemagne himself was sorely wounded, his horse slaughtered beneath him. Finally, King Agolant fled down the river known as the Charente, and it was there that the King of Béjaïa met his end, drowned together with his steed, and was buried on a nearby hill, facing Mecca as a valiant knight of Muhammad, before Agolant passed the ports and retreated to Pamplona.

Arnaud saw all this and more as he sat next to his grandfather and stared into the flickering flames of the hearth, and if he did not enjoy watching television, it was because the images on the screen replaced his inner narratives with images that were less beautiful, less vivid, less alive than the shimmering reflections on the Sèvre or the Charente when in the scarlet winter sunsets they seem to burn; the flames showed him the Rochefort ferry bridge, the estuary and its mud snakes at ebb tide, the jet fighters at the nearby air base playing tag across the island like sparrows, the arsenal where once the dexterous strands of ropes were braided, the dry docks in which ships were harbored while the hulls were caulked or their quickworks completed, before they put out; he saw the imposing ruins of the naval hospital, where men had died of exotic fevers and piteous gangrene, where it was said that, despite the scents of resinous balms and sundry medications, the

stench of the vast wards was more distressing than the groans of
the dying; Arnaud averted his eyes from the prison in which so
many men had suffered under the whip as they hauled ships from
the dry dock to the sea—he also shunned the horrific floating
prisons in which the troublesome priests the Republic wished to
forget died of typhus and the dead were piled up like the vermin
that swarmed over their cassocks, and whose bones whitened
the sea spray on the Île d'Aix or the Île Madame; he tarried on
the Place Colbert, allowing his eyes to linger on the magnificent
fountain in whose carved limestone ocean the waters of the Atlantic mingle with the green waters of the Charente—then he
wandered the classical grid of perpendicular streets, low streets
with low-roofed houses, until he reached the solemn facade
that concealed the madness of Julien Viaud, an adventurer and
naval officer who became a writer under the pen name Pierre
Loti, a son of some of the rare Protestants in the West to escape
persecution—Arnaud knew nothing of Pierre Loti, the author
who had stirred the imaginations of the ladies of his time with
dreams of exotic marriages and forbidden love behind Persian
blinds; he knew only the Pierre Loti given to excess, who had
transformed his austere Rochefort home into an outrageous op-
ulence of marble staircases, tall Gothic arched windows, a vast
fireplace, carved wood paneling, heavy draperies, and Arnaud's
glacial childhood had been fascinated by this place, this theater, a
stage for Loti's costumed dinner parties in the 1880s, homages to
Charles VII and Louis XI, at which diners were obliged to speak
Old French, ladies wore tall headdresses and veils, and the men
wore doublet and hose, had ermine around their shoulders and
greyhounds lying at their feet while they ate with their hands, fi-
lets of hedgehog or squirrel, or carved the breast of a swan whose
long white neck raised sullied feathers to the sound of lutes and
bagpipes.

On the first floor, after the late Middle Ages and the Renaissance, came the Orient, and the most beautiful mosque in all of

France: the carved cedar ceiling from Damascus towered over six rose-veined marble columns which supported Cordovan arches, the mihrab with its scalloped dome carved from precious woods and the dazzling qibla niche tiled with green and blue ceramics imported from Persia and Turkey, the walls alternating between painted doors from the Cham and tiles from Iznik—the mosque was cluttered with candelabras, prayer mats, tall catafalques empty of imaginary saints and memories of old loves: the Ottoman stele to the memory of Hatice, the true name of his fictional Aziyadé, gave the viewer the unsettling impression of suddenly being out in the open air, on a hill rising from the Golden Horn; of suddenly stepping from a mausoleum to stroll through a cemetery. A hypnotized Arnaud watched Julien "Pierre Loti" Viaud stroll around Eyüp Sultan Cemetery in Constantinople, his soul in torment, his eyes turned toward the Golden Horn below as rough Bosphorus winds battered clusters of black cypresses that soared like minarets; Julien Viaud wanders between the tombs, searching for the stele of the woman he loved ten years earlier, the young Circassian girl with the skin like milk, a voice like honey, with eyes like poppies, Hatice, the woman that he garlanded in his novel *Aziyadé* with all the silks of the Orient, the young woman who, he learned, died of grief, loneliness and abandonment. Loti does not read Ottoman Turkish; a guide reads to him the inscriptions on the steles, those ears of corn that flourish in the fields of the dead—in the distance, the lights of Stamboul, a city he knows well, are reflected even in the clouds. When the tomb is found, Julien Viaud is moved to tears; the guide reads out the name of the young woman, and the Fatiha, the brief sura that opens and closes all lives. To the girl who sleeps beneath this stone, Loti says, as though to himself: "I will come alone to visit you, my little girl, I will spend tomorrow morning here with you, in your desert; you already know how much I love you, since I have made this whole long journey to find you ..." In 1905, almost twenty years after his first visit to Aziyadé's grave, Pierre

Loti has her headstone replaced with a replica and the original stele shipped to his home in Rochefort: he steals it. He steals it in a fit of melancholic passion, the writer-traveler becomes a grave robber; in his private mosque on rue Chanzy the stele has lost none of its beautiful color; for Loti it holds the illusion of time, the illusion of remembered love, and before it he prostrates himself, dressed as a Turk or a Bedouin, for there is nothing he loves more than the magic of artifice, and in this house that so enthralls Arnaud the half-wit, this house that is a treasure chest of falsehoods and illusions, Loti amasses images, objects, stage sets for the theater that is his life—where does he sit down to write? In front of the mummified Egyptian cats in the Chambre des Momies, mummies that could serve as a warning to all the overly conceited cats still living? Or on the cushions of the Arabic salon, the Turkish salon, perhaps lying on the prayer rugs of the mosque, reclining in a caftan like an Egyptian dancing girl with a turban badly tied around his brow? What does he read? In this house there are no books except his own. No library—or almost none; no shelves, only an escritoire whose drawers are empty—there are pictures, pictures, everywhere except in the last room, his bedroom, the spartan room of the Protestant naval officer from Rochefort, which contains two fencing foils, a fencing mask, an iron bedstead, a trunk, a dressing table, a razor, a bottle of cologne and four bare whitewashed walls.

*

Tubby Thomas slapped his dishcloth on the bar, the game of belote was over, Paco and the others had returned to their homes or gone about their business, the café was deserted at this hour; smiling, Thomas tidied a few glasses: the god of the cards was unquestionably wild and unpredictable, as he should be. A small, repulsive, horned god, that would happily bite the hand that fed it, thought tubby Thomas, and the man who would later be a bedbug of the species *Cimex lectularius* was just finishing tidying the bar when Hervé Nicoleau, the doctor from Villiers-en-Plaine, pushed open the door of the Café-Pêche, an event rare enough to worry Thomas—Doctor Nicoleau was what one might call a fine man, almost excessively devoted to his practice and his patients; he was approaching sixty and, though retirement was still some way off—thank God—people could not help but wonder what would become of the region when Nicoleau (round spectacles, round face, forthright handshake) no longer made house calls. Thomas draped the dishrag over his right shoulder and greeted the doctor respectfully, all the while worrying about what had brought him to La Pierre-Saint-Christophe—and fearing he had come to see *him*; that suddenly, with the angel of death, the doctor had discerned some secret ailment, some invisible and malignant tumor, whose distinctive odor tickled the nostrils of medical professionals. Tubby Thomas was as stout a hypochondriac as he was a rogue. Dr. Nicoleau replied, cryptically, the cold, and ordered a mug of Viandox®; Thomas remembered this old-fashioned broth and wondered whether he still had a bottle somewhere in the back of his kitchen. It's been a long time since anyone ordered Viandox®, he thought, and the brand name brought back memories of the egg stand that used to sit on the bar and the fishermen who would come in at dawn, swallow an egg with their black coffee before disappearing into the marshland mists. Thomas fetched the bottle from the kitchen and poured some of the ominous tarry liquid into a cup, which he filled with hot water from the percolator. Dr. Nicoleau eagerly followed his actions, rubbing his hands in delight. Outside, the snowstorm was worsening; the doctor had a difficult visit to make to a dying patient and wanted to warm himself first. Nicoleau loved his job. He loved his patients, his surgery in Villiers, his home visits; he was sober and friendly; he had studied medicine in Poitiers, his whole family came from the region: his uncle, the late Monsieur Marchesseau, the Petrochristophorian vet, had practiced for nearly forty years, tending to the local livestock, treating Equidae, Bovidae, Caprinae, Canidae and even—in distant times and only in cases of extreme urgency—Hominidae, though without ever boasting of this fact to his nephew or his colleagues; his genitor, Germain Nicoleau *père*, still going strong despite old age and a passion for cognac, had for his part treated generations of farmers and notables in the region of Coulonges-sur-l'Autize; he enjoyed lunching with a notary public at an inn after a christening as much as standing in a farmyard in the depths of winter, when the pig was being slaughtered and the air smelled of charred bristles—neither father nor son had grown rich; as tribute for the miracle of healing, they had often been given chickens, ducks, eggs, rabbits, plenty of wine, hooch, cognac, whiskey and, once, a warning shot fired in the air in a thorny affair that was eventually settled out of court. Dr. Nicoleau *fils* lived comfortably, he was well off, he wore out cars as though they were slippers and knew the region like the back of his hand: he knew the names of the villages, the localities and their inhabitants by heart—there was not a copse of trees whose name he did not know, nor a single remote farmhouse where he did not know the inhabitants, and whether they still lived cheek by jowl with the animals on beaten earth floors.

On this particular day, Dr. Nicoleau gazed out through the window at the heavy snowfall, this winter monsoon, sipping his Viandox® and enjoying the gentle glow of the woodstove. Tubby Thomas was watching the doctor, but from the safe distance of the kitchen, as one might watch a dangerous animal, a tiger that could put you on a starvation diet or send you to the hospital with a click of its fingers. Nicoleau was marshaling his strength for a visit to the old poet-teacher Marcel Gendreau who had left his home in Échiré for a room in his daughter's house, coming back to La Pierre-Saint-Christophe, where he had taught for so many years, a homecoming Nicoleau knew would be permanent: this visit might well be his last, old Gendreau was at death's door, his lungs croaked like crows with every breath, he had been in a coma for two days, his arms swollen with edema, his heart rate was er-

ratic, and all this filled the doctor with sadness—everything was
being done to ease his final hours, and Dr. Nicoleau knocked back
his Viandox® as though it were a thimbleful of mint julep, thanked
tubby Thomas who, having retreated to the back kitchen for fear
of contagion, was prompted by avarice to reappear behind the
bar just in time to collect the two euros (he had pegged the price
of Viandox® to the price of a cup of tea, which he thought seemed
fair) that the doctor owed him, limply shook his hand and gave a
flick of the tea towel as Nicoleau walked through the door. The
swirling snow cloaked the doctor in an icy, fairy-tale shroud that
accompanied him as far as the house of Magali, the daughter of
old Marcel Gendreau, the writer-teacher whose long-forgotten
novel *Nature oblige . . .*, published nearly sixty years earlier, had
caused him to be banished, so to speak, from the village where
he taught and where his daughter, now retired, had been living
for donkey's years. Old age had forced Marcel Gendreau to leave
his Chalusson refuge near Échiré, leave the banks of the Sèvre,
the roach, and the Château de la Taillée, built by Agrippa d'Aubigné's great-granddaughter, one of the *post quem* reincarnations
of Jérémie the hanged man, adoptive father of Lucie Moreau's
grandfather and her cousin Arnaud who was still staring into the
flames and dreaming, and at the very instant when Dr. Nicoleau
rings the doorbell of Magali Belloir *née* Gendreau, her father—in
the hush of ragged breathing, a long continuous death rattle, accompanied by the *sotto* hum of the oxygen machine, to the *largo*
rhythm of the wall clock—is still battling certain death, a death
whose presence the doctor can feel the moment he steps into
the room, he can feel it in the softness of the hand he takes, in
the indentation his finger leaves on the forearm, in the thready,
irregular pulse, in the face turned toward the pillow supporting
it, the closed eyes, the cheeks drooping from the effects of the
morphine, the mouth forced slightly open by the weight of the
chin; the body weighs heavily, thinks Nicoleau, and he glances
at Magali, the dark circles round her eyes from sitting vigil all
night, seemingly distraught in anticipation of the inevitable, her

hands clasped over her mouth, her quavering eyes—is Marcel Gendreau dreaming of Virgil, *Omnia vincit amor: et nos cedamus amori*, is he thinking about his pastoral poems, about the silvery reflections on the backs of a perch, about red winter skies, about the story of Jérémie and Louise, as bleak as the dead season, or is he thinking about the tenderness of his daughter, who has been with him through these last months when, shrunken by age and illness, he has lain curled up in this bed, gradually absorbed into the cotton of the mattress, dissolving into the feathers of the pillow, it is impossible to say, and Magali and Nicoleau sense that a full stop will soon put an end to this sentence, that the voice will fall silent as the utterance ends, that the breath, increasingly unsupported by commas, is running down in the spirals of sibilants, the frequency of fricatives, after the long lyrical flight of nasals, and it suddenly dies away. It is as though Marcel Gendreau has been waiting for the reassuring presence of Dr. Nicoleau so as not to hear him say it's over, not to feel him place his fingers on his carotid one last time, not to listen to the thunderous silence of his heart, he whose soul is embarking on its sojourn in the Bardo, he for whom the Clear Light is breaking like a dawn of hope—Marcel Gendreau, the poet-teacher, novelist of the misfortunes of Jérémie, is no more, Nicoleau has just confirmed as much on the blue death certificate, whose confidential section he folds away while Magali pours out every tear of her body—just as the old tree on the cliff edge can be toppled into the abyss by the brush of a sparrow's foot or wing, so Magali's grief held out until the end, and now poured forth months of stifled sobs.

She took her father's hand one last time.

She stammered out a kind of prayer between her tears.

She closed the door of the room behind her and found Dr. Nicoleau filling in the administrative section of the death certificate.

She said, sobbing, He was waiting for you, Doctor. He was waiting for you.

She said, sobbing, Surely, you'll have a drink, Doctor?

To which Nicoleau replied, a little hoarsely, I wouldn't say no, Madame Belloir. I wouldn't say no.

And while Dr. Nicoleau drained his tot of brandy, Magali picked up the phone to call Martial Pouvreau and the long-faced gravediggers.

SONG

Exile is a viscous sap that streams over your eyes and ends up entering your throat, your nostrils and suffocating you. Pierre Baliveau moves between the red oaks with their long, shiny, palmate leaves, the white cedars, the horsetails and the spindle trees; despite the months of running, he constantly finds himself surprised by this New England forest, its numberless trees, its strange species, its teeming wildlife. The freedom he finds there. The Refuge. It is early June and the late spring is very warm. Insects hum in the shadows, graceful water boatmen move delicately across the surface of the pond. The air is scented by flowers and moss. Pierre sets down his pack and sits by the water's edge. He takes off his smock; the scar is there, on his belly; it reminds him, as it does every time he undresses, of what happened a year earlier, a thousand leagues from here, when the dragoons arrived in his native village of Mauzé—Pierre had never been afraid of anyone. The Edict of Fontainebleau revoking the Edict of Nantes had not yet been promulgated; there seemed no reason to fear the terrible dragoons sent by the King. And yet. Tens of thousands of Huguenots were forcibly converted. Tens of thousands more fled into exile. Hundreds were killed.

Naked, Pierre immerses himself in the cold, clear water, startling the dragonflies and crane flies. It is an exquisite pleasure. The coolness invades and he begins to shiver. Motionless, he allows his body to sink—all around, the teeming silence of the forest answers the infinite echo of the mountains. With his head under the water, he hears his heart beating. He exhales, watching the bubbles of air. He tries to hold out for as long as possible; plays at drowning before finally breaking the surface and taking a long deep breath. For a few minutes Pierre swims, almost treading water in the tiny pool—a well, a natural washtub. He can easily picture animals coming to drink here in the evening— moose, perhaps lynx, definitely wolves. He has spent the past three months traveling the country, setting and retrieving traps, mostly on his own. The beavers are chubby and their greasy fur leaves a goatlike smell on his hands.

Pierre hauls himself out of the watering hole and lies beneath an oak tree to dry off. The Refuge. He knows he will never again see accursed Poitou, nor the France of death and injustice. Adieu. Pierre allows himself to be caressed by his memories and by the warm breeze. From a treetop, a nightingale dispatches its melodious trills. The bird seems so cheerful, in the sunshine and the spring. The sheer joyfulness of its song suddenly fills Pierre with a deep melancholy. He runs a finger over the scar. He pictures his wife again, her tenderness, her beauty, her solemnity, the long hands she used to pick the roses she would give to him.

She would have enjoyed the solitude of this New World, these vast new landscapes peopled by disconcerting savages, with no churches, no villages, no cemeteries. Pierre squeezes his eyes shut, squeezes them with such force that two fleeing tears trickle from the corners of his eyes.

Il y a longtemps que je t'aime, jamais je ne t'oublierai.

VI.
PÉLAGIE READS THE FUTURE
ON THE BARK OF CHERRY TREES

Leaving the village and heading north toward Coulonges-sur-
l'Autize, before crossing the highway to Nantes—the great river
in these parts—you come upon the Standing Stone that gives
its name to La Pierre-Saint-Christophe. In the center of the
little forest called Le Luc, in a nameless glade, the remains of
a dolmen—a fairy table whose central section, several tons of
moss-covered granite marbled with ivy roots resembling wrinkles fallen forward like a closed mouth, is known more specifically as "La Pierre au Diable"—the Devil's Rock. Martial Pouvreau, mayor of Saint-Christophe and undertaker-in-chief, had
a sign erected at the end of the hiking trail used by precisely no
one, excepting a few red squirrels in the spring, explaining that
this huge useless slab of granite was quarried—miraculously—
some twenty kilometers north of here, since the substrata of the
village is limestone; that what is likely a Neolithic burial chamber, known since antiquity, was first excavated in 1886 by Father
de La Croix, a Jesuit member of the Society of Antiquarians: the
excavation work yielded scant results (though the tourist plaque
does not admit as much), with the curious exception of rooster
or chicken bones in the various interstices between the fallen table and the immense supporting stones, piles of coins and, when
the rear of the dolmen was finally cleared of the mound of earth

and gravel, rather than ancient tools of flint and bone, they found contemporary textiles, scraps of bedsheets, dresses, twill trousers, cotton handkerchiefs and even locks of hair which the good Jesuit somewhat disdainfully explained as "coarse commonplace practices among country folk." If a fresh dig were conducted today, aside from a few broken beer bottles, excavators would find fragments of photographs, braided necklaces and bracelets, and names, names, names carved into the rock itself and into the tawdry keepsakes—in short, miniature souls, and only the men and women who came by night to cast these spells could say whether the root of these hexes was some inconsolable yearning or an overweening jealousy exacting terrible revenge, may your oxen perish, may your trees wither, may your daughter be so hideous that she can find no spouse, may your name be lost in the mists of times to come.

Jérémie Moreau, panting for no reason, trembling with both hatred and guilt, reveling in the pleasure of the punishment yet suffering in equal measure, Jérémie took the path back to his shack in the marshlands, still burdened by the mortal stench of the foul package, the unbearable sweetness of the memory of Louise's body, and the scent carried on the breeze that billowed about his face black with hatred and with night when she opened the window, the lascivious sweat of this woman who had been dancing, the salacious scent of this woman who had been to a ball, scents of rose and rosemary, they hit him full in the face, these perfumes of the past, of pleasure and love, and they tortured him as he stumbled deep into the marshes, he conjured the smell of them with a guilt as pleasurable as it was loathsome, he had embarked on his vengeance, so to expunge these scents of past sweetness, in a fit of frenzy, he rolled around in the leaves; in an altered state, beside himself, in the grip of a madness, a remorseful joy, a pleasurable shame, an utter unraveling of his being, he was seized by terrifying convulsions outside his hut, in the first rays of dawn, he buried himself in the mud and dry leaves, sinking his teeth into the soil, filling his mouth with it, flailing with his legs, his feet, burrowing with his hands like a mole or a griffin, slamming his pelvis against the ground, chewing the withered late summer humus that he softened with tears of rage, grinding the acarids, the scarabs, the phasmids between his molars, spewing his pain, coughing up his misfortune, and then suddenly, all at once, he was seized by a terrible cramp that transformed him into a stiff, gnarled stick, and he screamed; he howled and sobbed, images of explosions, of dismembered corpses flashed before his eyes, his ears were filled with hideous rending sounds, and all around him vile beasts seeking to devour him.

He doubled up, everything sore, against a tree, like a feral child, sweating and panting for breath, the taste of copper in his mouth, daubed with earth, his face streaked with tears and mud, his palms ripped by his own fingernails, his tongue mutilated by his own teeth—he spat, took a breath, spat again; the sky, blue now, rose above the thicket; the sun stained the water of the nearby pool with brilliant tears.

After a time, Jérémie's heart seemed inclined to slow, as did his breathing. Disbelieving, he stretched his stiff, aching legs. Again, he thought about Louise, unsettled by Louise's power, by the hold she had over him, by the state she could plunge him into, even at a distance, simply by her smell; not for an instant did he imagine that this terrible pain, this fierce, uncontrollable crisis could have some other cause than the vision of Louise—horrified, he thought back to the episode five days earlier that had followed his sacrifice of the young cow so he could take her calf; the convulsions had been so powerful, the uncontrollable twitches so intense that he had seen himself, as in a dream, plunging his head into the cursed belly of the beast—blood, shit, piss, the taste of fear—right up to his shoulders, his thighs beating against the ground before he lost consciousness only to come to himself, God knows how long later, blistered with dried blood, smeared with excrement, fifty meters from the carcass, his hands still clutching pieces of intestine, hugging the dead calf to him like a doll, with a single image (without knowing whether it was real or a figment of his imagination), of a panicked farmer running through the darkness as though he had seen the devil himself.

This time Jérémie somehow managed to drag himself into the hut, he took off his clothes, lay down on the straw mattress, naked and exhausted, and fell asleep. When he woke, his body ached, but he was still quivering with hatred—he had dreamed of war, of dark waves suddenly ablaze with diesel, of flaming seas, of comrades dying horribly, drowning and burning at the same time, shadows amid the fiery flashes, before being engulfed by the waters; he had the taste of fuel oil and salt in his mouth, as he often did in the morning. Again and again, he wanted to take revenge, each time more terrible; he had had his revenge on Louise, but not on the village, or Louise's parents, or Longjumeau the café owner, or Marchesseau the vet, or the blacksmith, or the mayor, all those who had humiliated him; every night he would go to the Devil's Rock to gain strength and dance naked under the moon, smeared with animal blood, so people would see and fear him, and as he danced he had visions of war and violent death, of shells exploding in his ears, interspersed with images of Louise naked, Louise beaten and bloodied, Louise with her throat slit, Louise's belly blackened by a bullet or a bayonet, and every morning, if the convulsions and the seizures permitted, he would go back to his hut, eat mushrooms, roots, rip animals apart with his teeth, feel their nourishing hot blood run down his throat, and Jérémie wallowed in his revenge, as he took pleasure in the whistling shells and explosions in his ears stopping, the fear, the panic and the pain draining away. Each morning he felt more beleaguered, more invaded, more devoured.

*

When the wild boar that had been Abbé Largeau, who had been a ferryman, a storm and a frog, reached the cover of the hedgerow right under the noses of Gary and his dog, without either of them thinking of flushing him out, the former because he was cold, the latter because he was well trained, the boar happened on a wild sow that had strayed from the herd of females he had mounted while in rut some weeks earlier, a sounder of wild sows with whom he had the hope of starting a herd and the desire of establishing himself, if hope, memory and future exist in the animal world; just now, the boar was rubbing himself against the sow he had bested only after much struggle and was trying to mount her, since it was December, the month of coitus—the sow would carry the young for three months, three weeks and three days before whelping the piglets in a nest of branches, and soon the shoats would be trotting through the woods walking behind her, foraging for food. Boars engage in lengthy copulation with their sows; in the meantime the gendarmes who had driven into the unreported trench had been helped; the new-model blue van did not seem to have suffered, and the cops were chatting in the snowstorm; they were convinced (or had finally convinced themselves) that they had seen a suspicious man running in the direction of the EDF substation, which justified their presence on this dirt road, in the middle of the large sloping field on which the snow was falling, bordered a little to the east by the Ajasses, where the boar was finishing his coitus, his trotters against the sow's ribs; he rolled in the mud, the sow pushed him with her snout, then, seeing a handful of acorns left by a squirrel, ate them up, showing considerably more passion than she had during mating, if passion exists in the animal world.

The second police car, which had towed the first out of the fatal rut, was driven by two young gendarmes—all four were now standing in the snow discussing what to do about this incident; they decided to report this curious trench to the appropriate person, then each pair climbed back into their vehicle and went about their business, two of them admittedly somewhat upset at having fallen into a bizarre trap that they were now convinced had been deliberately set for them. One consoled the other by saying that every cop was bound to crash a car at least once before retiring, to which the other retorted that he hadn't crashed a car, proof being that they were in the car driving home, and both had a point, but still, what a strange idea. The hole in question had been the work of the local water company searching for a major leak, who had stupidly dug a trench where there was no pipe, a trench that they had further widened when they could not find the aforementioned pipe; they eventually realized their mistake but, given the urgency of finding the leak and the stresses of the job, they'd postponed filling in the trench and had forgotten to signal the unsightly hole to any (unlikely) motorists who passed this way.

The sky was a deep, dense gray, the snow was falling less heavily now; evening was drawing in; the wild sow, bored with foraging, was keen to rejoin the sounder a little closer to Ajasses; she trotted up the field and, coming upon the smell of diesel and rubber left by the gendarmes, took fright and raced for the cover of the trees to the north, on the other side of the village; she slipped under a fence; she happened on a small building from which came a continual crackling sound that terrified her—she tried to hide in what looked to her like a shadowy corner, the pervasive smell of ozone frightened her; she felt a jolt of pain, her eyes clouded over: she was instantly charred, the force of the electric shock catapulted her body several meters into the power lines and insulators, where the mass of burning flesh caused the short circuit, causing the tank to overheat and explode, and the resulting fireball and the shock wave to vaporize what remained of her body. The soul of the wild sow returned to the Bardo at the moment of death, then passed through the Bright Light before being reincarnated, some hours later and many years in the future, at the end of this Dharma, in the mid-twenty-first century of the Great Extinction, as a badger; a badger who, with the last of his fellow creatures, burned to death in the great conflagration that put an end to the existence of his species and that of hundreds of others, birds, mammals, reptiles, at a time when all hominids had long since been swept away by floods, hatred and disease, and the boar that had once been Father Largeau, a crow and a monk, watched as the explosion set the winter ablaze, smelled the terrible stench of fire and, seized by panic, ran for as long as he was able into the heart of the little wood and hid, trembling with fear, in an impenetrable bramble where, almost instantly, he forgot the danger and decided he would gladly set out to find a new female to cover.

*

JUDGE: Calm yourself, mademoiselle—Gendarme, get her to calm down and bring her to the witness box.

PÉLAGIE: *Weel, is thon no juist braw, a puckle o pudgie pompus pricks wi thair crannies up thair erses* [fat pompous bastards with their fingers up their asses, translated the clerk of the court, I believe she is insulting the judge], *Ah'll gie ye a penny-geggie for a bawbee.*

JUDGE: What? What's that? What's that she's saying? What is she saying? Who is she talking to? Do you understand this woman? Speak French! Clerk, tell the woman to speak French. Counsel, do something. Gendarme, unhand her and sit down. This is not a market. This is a case of murder! My learned friend, have you anything to say? If not, let her continue.

DEFENSE LAWYER: Nothing, Your Honor. Apart from her age …

JUDGE: Thank you. Monsieur Prosecutor, your turn. We will resume. Incident closed.

PROSECUTOR: So what did your mother say? Before?

PÉLAGIE: *Ma mither warnisht me, dinnae gang near him, dinnae gang near him lass, she telt me …*

CLERK OF THE COURT: Her mother advised her not to go near the victim.

DEFENSE LAWYER: Yes, yes, I understood that part.

CLERK OF THE COURT: She is making an effort to speak French.

DEFENSE LAWYER: An effort? Are you kidding?

PÉLAGIE: A*n he beltit me black an blue—black as a craw in the lea* [She looked like what?—Like a crow in the field—that's what she said], *Ah wis a daft besom tae be wi him, dottle lik, thick as parritch, dippit as a heidless chucken* [She was foolish to be with him, stupid as a headless chicken, a naive young woman, that's what she said], *An the pine, awfy pine, Ah wis greetin a watterfaw, an ma chowks riggit and furrt wi tears* [the pain was so intense that tears plowed her cheeks like a fallow field], *Ma een are wizzen frae greetin, men'll mak ye greet an no juist wi thair belts* [her eyes are dry from so much weeping, men make you cry, and not just with their belts], *The ill-gien bastart cried me a hoor an pit his hauns oan ma erse, skelp* [the victim put his hand on the defendant's buttocks], *He wis smirkin oan yin side o his puss, lik he'd bin hangit, the gansh. He wis strappin lik, gey braw, wi his white sark an his bonnie gravat, but he wis nae bard, he'd nae poetry in his saul, the fuckwit!* [What?—The victim was no poet—Yes, I can well imagine.] *He's chowin … an spittin the hale while.* [He chews … and spits all the time—Yes, yes, I understood that part.] *An it's aw barlic an radge, he's shuved me aginst the wa, dusht me that haird that he's rived ma lug frae ma heid* [he hit her, slapped her and tore off her ear]—*he's gruntin lik a beast an pits his haun up ma kirtle* [he made an animal grunt, he put his hand up her skirt], *Ah coudnae mudge* [she couldn't move anymore]; *Ah coudnae shift at aw an A'm near bowkin frae the reek o his breith* [She almost vomited because of the stench of his breath, she said], *a reek lik a dug wi his tongue hingin oot* [a smell like a dog with its tongue hanging out] *… He wis graipin me wi his haun, an the sair pine* [he hurt her with his hand under her skirt] *sae I bit him, an I bit him, an the bluid, the bluid!* [and she bit him until he bled!] *He taks his neive an skelps me ower an ower, an he's got his clarty hauns aw aboot me, he*

*bit mah breists an he was pechin lik a dug, and he cries, "Ye limmer!
Ye hoor! Ye'r gantin oan it, ye'r giein me a stauner!"* [With his other
hand he … he groped her breasts, he was panting like a dog, he
insulted her, he told her that she was asking for it and that he …
That he what? That he had an erection, I believe, Your Honor.]
He flung me tae the grund lik a deid chucken [he threw her on the
ground like a dead chicken]. *He spelders ma hochs wi his hauns
oan ma knees, Ah skraiched as lood as Ah coud!* [he spread her
thighs with his hands on her knees, she screamed as much as she
could]. *Ah wis sabbin, ah wis feart, a wis fuckin frichtent, sin he wis
skaithin me mind, an Ah grip this stane, a muckle shairp stane, Ah
wis in that much pain, an Ah ding it doon oan his heid as fell Ah coud*
[she grabbed a large stone, a sharp heavy stone, and she smashed
his skull as hard as she could, she said], *He rowt lik a cuddie an
thare's aw this bluid lik whan ye slauchter a sou, an Ah wis kivert wi
bluid, aw claggie wi bluid* [he brayed like a donkey, and there was
blood, like from a slaughtered pig, she was covered in it, all sticky
with blood]—then *he clytit doon, deid as a mauk, richt oan tap o
me, ma face aw bluidy, an Ah didnae ken whit tae dae, he didnae
jee, he leukit lik he was deid* [and then he fell against her, limp as a
worm, and he looked as though he was dead, he didn't move, his
nose in his shirt], *Ah was that feart, Ah shuved him aff o me* [I was
afraid, I pushed him away], *an ah boltit awa skirlin lik a banshee*
[and she ran away, screaming like a madwoman, she says].

PROSECUTOR: Is she finished?

DEFENSE LAWYER: Yes.

JUDGE: Did the jurors understand what the defendant said?

CLERK OF THE COURT: Yes.

JUDGE: How fortunate for them.

*

When the terrified gravediggers laid the head and young body
of Marseil Sabourin in the ground after he had been executed at
the Place de la Brèche in Niort, they placed his head between

his legs in the short ash coffin without troubling to remove
the gray convict's tunic dark with blood, with scant care or
ceremony; they were aware of the heinous crime for which he
had lost his head, a crime so incomprehensible that it greatly
affrighted them: had they dared, they would have explored the
fetid meninges of this man Sabourin in an attempt to fathom
the reasons for this appalling crime—greatly vexed, once they
had buried the casket, they simply headed back to the Fief des
Justices—the hill in the area of Niort now known as Brizeaux,
which was then part of the district of Sainte-Pezenne, the saint
with the seashell—to the place where the Fourches Patibulaires
stood, the gibbet where criminals were hanged by the neck, the
gallows from which their corpses were left to swing as a warning to others, and the gravediggers felt that this mournful place
where black crows gouged out the eyes of some poor wretch,
where witches gathered mandrake root at midnight at the feet
of the hanged men, where wolves howled in anguish like men
being tortured, that this mournful place was fated to receive the
dead: it was here, beneath a pile of stones, that Marseil Sabourin
had concealed the body of his sister. Hélène Sabourin had died
on August 2, 1893, aged twenty-four: the gravediggers had tears in
their eyes as they buried her, so terribly mutilated was her young
corpse, her skull caved in, her belly slashed open, ravaged by the
August heat and the postmortem. Hélène's soul had been reincarnated as a newborn girl near Parthenay, to a family of tenant
farmers who welcomed her with joy; Marseil, her brother, after
he was guillotined, was predestined to continue his exploration
of suffering, being reborn for hundreds of generations as a blind
annelid, which the ethnologist David Mazon, bemused as to the
origin of these strange, unfamiliar creatures that populated his
bathroom, had just unwittingly sent back into the Wheel with a
spray of domestic bleach, and as he attempted to hide the hideous nuisance with a final wipe of the sponge, he hoped, from
the young woman now lying in his bed, a young woman who

he anticipated would wish to make use of the aforementioned bathroom—so he finished his panicked, surreptitious cleaning of the shower, micturated, considered washing his crotch, then, still naked, and tiptoeing because the tiles were cold, he rejoined the sleeping woman in the bedroom. Half-hypnotized by her beauty, he stared for a long moment at her shoulder blades, at the birthmark beneath her right shoulder, his eyes moving slowly down her back to the muscular buttocks, her spine, the closed thighs that ill-concealed the pinkish, slightly clammy labia, the long bony legs bent at the knee, and on down to her ankles, her ankle bracelets, and the feet half-hidden by the sheet: Lucie was asleep, her wild gray eyes hidden behind their lids, her face buried in the pillow, her hair splayed across the white cotton, and David stood, gazing at her, a little incredulous, yet filled with tenderness, surprised by the perfection of this body that molded itself so perfectly to his being that it seemed like a plastic star set into a child's toy. He was not thinking of Marseil Sabourin or his curious first name, since he did not even know of the man's existence, Marseil Sabourin whose crime was born of concupiscence and the mysteries of women's bodies—brother and sister, Marseil and Hélène Sabourin, had grown up in poverty; when their father was imprisoned in Rochefort jail for thieving and pilfering, Marseil had been sent to Chizé reformatory and his sister to the Carmelite convent in Niort until she came of age. Marseil oozes brute fury; the blows and later the corpses (a murdered warden, a teenage girl raped and strangled) swirl around him, dark clouds of ill omen. Marseil is locked up, justice is ineffectual and he is released; he leads a wild, indigent and savage existence, alternately working as a farm laborer or a handyman; he sees little of Hélène. Marseil burns with passion—whenever a girl passes, his words, his hands reach for her, and every girl flees, desperate to escape him. Every one of them. All but his sister, who has just moved into his hut on the outskirts of Sainte-Pezenne; Hélène is ill, she requires treatment; Marseil sleeps on the floor—his sister is outraged when he suggests sleeping with her; girls, he feels, are too easily outraged; Marseil Sabourin likes to watch his sister undress—why does she hide herself? Marseil Sabourin steals money from her; Hélène confides in a friend; she no longer wants to live with her brother, whom she considers a monster, which he undoubtedly is—then, one day, at the height of summer, as July heat shatters in August storms, Hélène secretly packs her trunk, she hopes to leave while Marseil is still at work, but Marseil found no work that morning—returning home, he sees she is about to leave, he grabs her, tugs at her skirt, tries to slip his hand beneath, she pushes him away, she wants to leave, he wants her to stay, his sister wishes to leave and he wants only to possess her, so he grabs a heavy tool and brings it down on her skull; she crumples and exsanguinates. Hélène Sabourin, sister of Marseil, is dead; already her soul is elsewhere but her body remains, so her brother strips her, undresses her as though she were a living woman, a sleeping woman, though her hair is matted with blood, finally, Marseil finally penetrates her, he finally has carnal knowledge of a woman and he takes pleasure in her, he takes pleasure in his dead sister.

He wants to understand. He gazes at the woman's body, the mons veneris, the pubic hair, the thighs, the hips, the breasts that spill out of her torn dress, he needs to understand what it is about women that makes him so wild, so potent, so filled of desire, he needs to know what women have inside, what they are made of, so he takes his knife; he takes his knife, shoves it between his sister's labia and moves upward; he cuts through the pubic symphysis, opens the belly, searches, becomes aroused, drives himself insane—he removes the womb, becomes aroused again; he carries on all day: no one knows whether Marseil Sabourin pierced the mystery of his own desire, but toward evening, he takes a photograph of his sister at her first Communion and slips it into the secret sex he has profaned, perhaps in an attempt to heal it, or to forget that she was his sister, to forget altogether, before wrapping the body in a sheet, carrying it over his shoulder, and hiding it in a quarry near the road to Saint-Gelais, in the Fief des Justices, beneath a pile of stones.

Hélène Sabourin had been countless birds, many farmers, beggars, brigands, men, women, more women, more men and even a fierce warrior, in 1373, when the English occupied Poitou and its environs, where everything was the same but English soldiers manned the ramparts and the royal arms of King Edward of England and France—gules three lions passant guardant in pale or, armed and langued azure, quartered with azure, fleurs-de-lis or—fluttered atop the battlements. Much renowned was the name of Henry of Lancaster, whose campaign caused great clamor and greater harm; famed too was the name of the Black Prince, and the great name of the Black Death, which hurled many souls into the Wheel, whose deadly miasma pervaded the air and settled upon Christians, whether they be French or English, and the people of Niort, whether English or French, were sore afflicted to see their lands ravaged by war and their towns by disease, and all the while the governor of Niort watched from high atop his keep, behind his battlements, as the armies of Bertrand du Guesclin, Constable of France, passed with their bombards, their trebuchets and their mangonels; the warrior who will later be Hélène Sabourin is a freelance, a mercenary in the pay of the English, who are in sore need of henchmen to do their bidding; a vicious, battle-scarred soldier inured to rape, murder and pillage—Bertrand du Guesclin has just laid siege to Chizé and the Constable of France seems loath to surrender, despite the relief troops sent from Niort: three hundred Poitevin mercenaries and seven hundred English soldiers are marching on for Chizé when they happen on horse carts heading for the city town, carts loaded with casks of good wine, which they are quick to commandeer and, as Cuvelier the troubadour sings in his "Chanson de Bertrand," *needful of wine þey did break ope' þē casks, and in-to þē wyn did plunge theyr coifs, theyr caps, theyr spangenhelms and lustily did drink vntil the wyn theyr minds did addle,* and the warrior who will later be Hélène Sabourin, who will be numberless women and men, is also very drunk, since all have filled their helmets like great pewter tankards, and, the song tells us, are *aslosh with the heady wines of Montreuil-Bellay*; hence, the English are drunk during the battle, while the braying Poitevins, the mercenaries, whose brains are addled by the wine, consort with the troops of Bertrand du Guesclin, since they speak the same language and know the same towns and villages: when battle is engaged between the English relief army and the troops of the Constable of France on a lea outside Chizé, the English swap lances for halberds—drunk as they are, they hack and stun untold Bretons and Poitevins while, from up on the ramparts, longbows slaughtered men and horses; only by dint of great effort and fearsome blows did Bertrand du Guesclin succeed in capturing the castle.

> *At once a fearsome battle raged and roiled*
> *But brief it was, the castle soon despoiled.*

Once the Chizé castle had been captured, the blowhard Bretons and roughneck Poitevin rabble marched on Niort—they donned the armor and clothes of the vanquished English, they even marched beneath their banners so that the drawbridge was opened without resistance, and so it proved:

> *On, on they marched till Nyort did once appear*
> *And, drawing near the gates, as one did cheer:*
> *Saint George! and when the Englishmen did hear,*
> *They ope'd the gates and bid the French draw near,*
> *Yet once inside, Death came swift and clear,*
> *The wildered English quailed in dread and fear;*
> *Of those who offered ransom all were spared,*

All those who fought, by blood and Death besmeared;
Thusways the French did conquer Nyort.

And the looter, who would later be Hélène Sabourin, retook his
hometown of Niort, though fighting alongside the French, and
became a wealthy burgher—he survived until the year of grace
1380, when his feet became infected with a fungus causing ergo-
tism, or Saint Anthony's Fire; he was reborn as a female child
who died of hemorrhage shortly after being delivered, then a
man who would be an alderman of Niort, before dying in a terrible fire caused when a torch fell on a tapestry, and so on from
woman to man, man to woman, until he was reborn as Hélène
Sabourin, the martyr felled by the blows of her vicious brother
Marseil, who, after a trial lasting a scant few days, is sentenced
to public decollation by the guillotine which, so that all might
witness the event, is set up on the Place de la Brèche, the largest
square in Niort, next to the Avenue de Paris, where the horse
market was held; the public executioner, Louis Deibler, arrives
by the eleven o'clock train one Thursday, bringing with him his
guillotine and his son Anatole. Anatole serves as his assistant,
and a few years later will succeed him in the role. The local newspaper, *Le mémorial des Deux-Sèvres*, makes much of every detail
pertaining directly or indirectly to the death machine and the
Lord High Executioner's mustache: it is known that he was put
up at the Hôtel des Étrangers, now the Hôtel de France, located
at 8 rue des Cordeliers; that, as soon as he arrived, he dined there
on Marennes oysters, rillettes de Tours, cold meats and fish sautéed in butter, all washed down with wine from Anjou; that the
executioners took to their beds early and were awoken at 4 a.m.
on Friday, February 16, 1894; that the Seventh Hussar Regiment
came down from the du Guesclin barracks at the top of Saint-An-
dré hill and took up positions on the Place de la Brèche where
they were responsible for keeping the public from the square

while the guillotine was erected—work began at 4 a.m. and two
hours later, while all was still pitch-dark, everything was in readiness. Twice, Deibler *père* tested the deadly blade, which, swift
and smooth, slid home into its groove, drawing gasps of terror
from the crowd. All that was lacking now was Marseil Sabourin.
From the Procureur de la République Renault we learn that,
shortly before 6 a.m., Sabourin's appeal for clemency is rejected
by President Sadi Carnot. Sabourin asks to see a priest and to be
allowed to attend mass. Sabourin takes communion. Then finally
the tumbril. The condemned man arrives. The crowd begins to
sing a ballad:

> *Pay heed, ye lads and lasses all*
> *From Niort town and fair Souché*
> *And hearken burghers to my call*
> *In Saint-Maxire and Échiré*
> *Give ear, good folk of Sainte-Pezenne,*
> *Staunch peoples of the Marsh and Plains*
> *This crime doth turn the hearts of men*
> *And every mortal soul doth stain*
> *The brother here condemn'd to die,*
> *Did leave his own fair sister dead.*
> *While she in slumber's arms did lie,*
> *Took up an axe and crushed her head*
> *And thus snuffed out a young girl's life.*
> *Ere any man could take to wife.*
> *All honor to the magistrate*
> *Who fairly judg'd this crime obscene*
> *And sent him, for his foul offense,*
> *To meet Madame la Guillotine.*

The milling crowd on the square is so thick the Hussars can
scarcely contain it; all have come to see the supreme moment
when the monstrous head is severed from the common trunk,
thus putting an end to the tragedy; all long to see the wheels
of justice at their work; dozens of onlookers are perched in the

branches of the plane trees the better to enjoy the show; the executioner come lately from Paris, in bowler hat and elegant suit,
looks like a clerk, a scribe—as Sabourin's limbs are lashed, he
loudly wails; he is laid upon the pillory and the lunette closed
around his neck; one of Deibler's assistants tugs his ears so that
his neck is straight—the executioner operates the release handle; a hush falls over the Place de la Brèche, the silence so complete that it is possible to hear the sibilant hiss of the heavy blade
in the grooves, the dull thud as the steel slices though the neck
of the condemned man, the rustle of the head as it falls into the
wicker basket; so, Sabourin the rapist, Sabourin who slaughtered
his own sister, is dispatched to join the ranks of worms and the
crawling creatures, in endless reincarnations from which he will
never escape, but where, unbeknownst to him, he will encounter Deibler the Lord High Executioner, the state-sanctioned
murderer of three hundred and ninety-five people—while the
sempiternal gravediggers carry Sabourin's still-warm body to
Bellune cemetery to bury it with the head between the legs,
and before taking the afternoon train home to Paris, even as his
assistants are cleaning and dismantling the Widow, Deibler, in
company with Renault, the public prosecutor, takes luncheon
at the Auberge de la Bonne Foi des Gens, run by a man named
Texier, which was—according to the public prosecutor—the
best restaurant in town.

The train was punctual, and Deibler left Niort station at 4 p.m.,
after a leisurely lunch whose bill of fare is lamentably unknown.

It was not Deibler who executed the younger of the Chaigneau
brothers almost fifty years later, but Henri Desfourneaux, then
chief executioner; public executions having been banned since
1939, the younger of the Chaigneau brothers was quietly guillotined in the paved prison yard, by the same blade and on the same
plank as Sabourin, the blade and plank having been transported
on the same train, or as near as makes no difference—Desfourneaux was just as genial as Deibler, and at least as efficient; young

Chaigneau did not wail, he roared, insulted those present, their mothers, their daughters, viciously attempted to bite the hand of Desfourneaux's assistant and succeeded in scratching the man's face as he was being bound; he continued to roar until the beveled blade whistled down and deftly truncated him: many of those present looked away, especially the gendarmes, as timorous as gravediggers—Chaigneau was a right bastard, commented a militiaman in a black beret to a young gendarme whose throat was dry, gunned down two gendarmes with a rifle; a poacher, he was, skinny as a rail, but a vicious bastard, beat up a lot of the old cons while he was locked up here! They'd have done better to send him to the Eastern Front—the upshot would've been the same, but at least he'd 'ave had his chance ... An' he'd have massacred a few Reds, let me tell you! The gendarme did not share the militiaman's matutinal excitement; he was feeling a little queasy; the sight of so much blood at five in the morning may be fitting on the Eastern Front, but mostly it seemed inhuman—the militiaman carried on prattling while Chaigneau's body tumbled into a trunk where, it seemed, it would keep oozing until drained of all its blood; the assistant executioner casually upended the wicker basket, tipping the head into the same trunk—together with a goodly liter of grape juice—it was utterly unspeakable, thought the gendarme, makes you want to join the Resistance, to take to the maquis (though, being a civil execution, this had absolutely nothing to do with the Occupation, the Resistance, or anything else—Chaigneau had slaughtered two cops, and whether in peacetime or in war, this feat of arms would have earned him the Widow, everyone knew that, but taking to the maquis would have spared the young officer from having to witness this execution which, not being public, was particularly gruesome in terms of bloodshed, since the executioners were taking their ease). Morin, one of the executioners, suddenly grabbed a hose and sprayed the tarmac, causing a torrent of blood and water to stream down the slope toward the shoes of the bureaucrats (the prosecutor, the judge, the prison governor) who hopped and pirouetted like ballerinas to avoid having their shoes stained along with their consciences—this prompted the cop to snigger and the governor to roar, Morin, what the hell d'you think you're doing; Morin, remembering that he had once worked slaughtering pigs in an abattoir, knew that blood had to be hosed down otherwise it congealed, and became thick and viscous as oil: If'n you don't spray it down, it gets very slippery, M'sieur le Directeur, an' you wouldn't slither an' land ass-first in it, Indeed not, said the judge with a laugh, indeed not, and the prison governor roared, Have a little respect, Morin, this isn't a butcher's shop, as the bureaucrats kept prancing on tiptoe like burlesque dancers to escape the reddish flow, since there was no exit on their side of the yard, only the huge prison gates, now closed, through which the dismantled Madame la Guillotine had made her entrance; the blood-tinged waters streamed under the gates, down the hill to the rue du Sanitat, and down the rue de l'Abreuvoir to the Quai de la Préfecture and the river Sèvre where Chaigneau's blood mingled with the waters of the Sèvre, which bore him on, through the Marais to the ocean, while his soul was reincarnated as a skinny red worm next to Marseil Sabourin, a worm almost instantly dissolved by bleach and by David Mazon, who could not understand where these horrible creatures were coming from.

As for the body of the younger Chaigneau brother, it was inhumed by the sempiternal gravediggers: placed in a coffin immediately after the execution and discreetly transported in a gray van to an anonymous grave in the cemetery on the rue de Bellune—by the time he was visited by his elder brother, recently released from a stalag, and Chaudanceau the postman, he had completely rotted away (all that remained were his bones, dull and gray amid cobwebs and tattered clothes); the visitors asked the cemetery keeper where the headless Chaigneau had been buried, and the caretaker, who had been present when the gravediggers arrived with the little ash coffin, kindly told them, and the elder Chaigneau brother shed an incredulous tear for his little brother before striding across the town to the market to get drunk on small glasses of white wine in the company of the postman, who was masterful when it came to drinking and, though passably plastered, the two men managed to meet up with Patarin, the butcher, and get a lift back to La Pierre-Saint-Christophe in his truck—the elder Chaigneau brother died in a car crash some years later; he was reborn in the egg of a great tit in the heart of the Marais, an egg where he would remain for several weeks before painfully piercing his shell to cheep and beg for food; if the chick was not devoured by a predator or killed by some parasite despite all the care of its mother, it would grow to be a magnificent bird with a plumage of yellow, white, black and gray; Chaudanceau went on to reach retirement age and reluctantly hung up his postman's bag, no more rounds, no more cycling, no more coffees, no more little glasses of wine or hooch every time he brought a money order, no more beautiful crisp new bills crackling under his fingers—he died many years later, in the era of the Renault 12 and Case International tractors; he was reincarnated as a newborn in the maternity ward at Niort hospital, a baby girl who would grow up to be a respected professor of ancient Greek, a specialist in Homer, at a university in Paris.

The elder Chaigneau and Chaudanceau, like Poupelain the blacksmith and Marchesseau the vet, all bore witness to the madness of Jérémie Moreau—the first two were playing cards at Longjumeau's when they heard poor Louise had died, her eyes still open, her jaw still clenched, after a month of catatonia, a month of silence and starvation, having uttered not a word since the fatal night.

Lucie's future grandfather was devastated. The boy clung to his mother's lifeless body; he did not want to leave her in the hands of the gravemakers; Louise was reincarnated as a baby girl about to be born to a good family in Parthenay; she would grow up to be a seamstress.

Grief spread through the whole village, the gravediggers wept as they laid her in the earth, the priest gave a deeply emotional funeral service, everyone in the village of La Pierre-Saint-Christophe walked behind the coffin—everyone in the village except-ing Jérémie, of course, Jérémie was cursed: Louise's father had said nothing about the circumstances in which he found his daughter that fateful morning, but all sensed that Jérémie the madman had been responsible for this death; old mother Pélagie told anyone who would listen that she had seen him, daubed with mud or blood, dancing upon the Rock and contorting himself, as though possessed, beneath the trees of Le Luc; a terrified Longjumeau said Pélagie was a witch herself and could not be trusted, because he had once happened on her while she was lustfully, lasciviously fondling the bark of his old cherry tree—and, despite the gravity of the moment, his story made the assembled company laugh: a cherry tree is a lovely thing to fondle, Longjumeau, the bark is smooth and wrinkled, like your wife's ass, and Longjumeau hurled a dishrag in the face of Chaudanceau, who had made this crude remark, since it was universally agreed that no one could comment, positively or otherwise, about the body of another man's wife. The image of Pélagie, a virginal old maid with tow-colored hair and a hooked nose, making love to a cherry tree tick-led those present. A thought suddenly occurred to Chaudanceau:

"Now that I think of it, Pélagie wasn't at poor Louise's funeral, was she?"

"Of course she was there, you bloody fool."

He hadn't noticed her; Chaudanceau hadn't noticed her, but Pélagie had been there, dressed from head to toe in black; this last remark made the surviving Chaigneau brother double up, and he roared:

"Hah! Always dressed in black, that one!"

He clutched his sides and chortled, and as they thought about it, the other men realized that they had never seen Pélagie wearing anything but, and Longjumeau said solemnly:

"I told you she's a witch, I saw her molesting my cherry tree."

"The issue is whether what she said about Jérémie Moreau is true."

A silence descended, since it is one thing to believe a healer is more or less a witch who fondles cherry trees, and another to decide that a man has made a pact with Death, a deal with the Devil no one believed was real yet everyone feared.

"If Jérémie is responsible for poor Louise's death, why aren't the gendarmes out there looking for him?"

At the word "gendarmes," the elder Chaigneau brother stiffened. Though, out of tact, no one ever mentioned his brother, he felt defensive.

"She died of a fatal illness."

"Well, maybe Jérémie cast a spell on her!"

They had all heard of spells that could curdle cow's milk, cause apple trees to die, infest good wheat with weevils, make people fall in love or out of love, but they had never heard of spells that could cause death.

Chaudanceau was the most naive:

"But that's impossible, surely, I mean, what about the Good Lord?"

At the words "the Good Lord," they all felt reassured, for though they were not devout Catholics, simply to call upon "the Good Lord" was to invoke the very nature of things, the rules governing life and death, and nothing in those rules allowed for someone to call upon death, still less for such words to be effectual.

Therefore, poor Louise had died of an illness, and Jérémie had been crazy since he came back from the war; this was the conclusion they came to.

Meanwhile, Pélagie remained harmless yet mysterious; the villagers needed her to heal sprains, rheumatisms and dislocated shoulders; they suspected that she might have other arcane or forbidden skills, but since she said little, and then in a dialect no one fully understood, not much was known about her, except that she was not a native of the Deux-Sèvres. She came from a little hamlet in the remote farmlands deep in the Vendée, and no one remembered how she had come to live in the village, because she was unmarried, perhaps she had not always been so, no one knew, and only a couple of elderly women remembered her arrival, shortly after the Great War, at the unveiling of the church memorial plaque commemorating all those who had fallen in defense of France: the Pouvreaus, the Moreaus, the Goudeaus, the Chaigneaus, etc.: this was the moment when Pélagie appeared in the village, she wove baskets, helped out with the milking, she knew how to heal broken limbs, sprained wrists, twisted ankles; even the doctor in Coulonges and Marchesseau the vet agreed she had a gift; Pélagie, who was not yet called the Witch since she was still too young, but already dressed all in black, eternally a widow. No one ever asked her where she came from; she had spent time in an institution, a convent in La Roche-sur-Yon, before she came to the village, but everyone associated the word "convent" with religion, with religious education rather than the abject misery of prison. Twenty-five years later, Pélagie could fondle the cherry tree in Longjumeau's orchard, visit the Standing Stone, the woodlands of Le Luc or Ajasses, she belonged to this world, to La Pierre-Saint-Christophe and to no other.

Nothing is known of how Pélagie drove Jérémie into an early grave: it is not known what dark, mysterious spell, what shadowy enchantment she used to dispatch him to the gravediggers, a rope about his neck, his boots lying in the straw, to be discovered by Louise's son, whom she must also have bewitched, since he had no memory of the corpse swinging from the rafters of his grandfather's barn, of the accusatory toe protruding from his sock—all that is known is that, in the clearing in the woodlands of Le Luc, near the Standing Stone, Pélagie bent over Jérémie as he recovered from one of his fits, while he was still gasping for breath, his vacant eyes filled with images of the war, the Ardennes, the English Channel, the fire on the water, the roar of the planes, and images of Louise, the pleasure of forcibly taking Louise, trying to make her pregnant, the madness of the knife he used to slit open the young heifer and tear her calf from her as Louise had torn Jérémie's child from him; old mother Pélagie had whispered sweet words in Jérémie's ear, phonemes no mortal ear had ever heard, she told him the story of her own life, and Jérémie's own life story, told him of the stars and the seasons and the impending end of all things; to him she uttered words of truth, of refuge and consolation, and his convulsions were stilled, as were his moans, by Pélagie's breath, by her secret tongue—she stroked Jérémie's brow, mopped his sweat, gave him herbs to chew to ease the pain of the spasms, herbs gathered from mysterious plants, and Jérémie, his cheeks streaked with painless tears, and Pélagie's words like a balm to the soul, recovered the strength to walk, forgot about his vengeance, forgot about life, and in the noble and desperate gesture of the schoolboy who with the stroke of the eraser rubs out what he has spent weeks drawing and considers a failure, Jérémie set off to that old house where he had known some semblance of happiness; for a moment, he surreptitiously watched the boy whom, in his stupidity and pride, he had failed to take as his own—then, a little mechanically, a little awkwardly, a little slowly, he retreated into the barn and into himself one last time, forever.

*

For two long years, Father Largeau's watch continued to tick inside the grave, marking the hours with a muffled click that frightened only the moles and voles, for the village cemetery had no caretaker and its gates were always open so that Mathilde had only to cross the road to lay flowers on the graves, and the municipal gardener could go in and rid the paved paths of couch grass the old-fashioned way, so the weeds would leave the dead

in peace, he said. Shortly before his death, Largeau appeared to
overcome his spiritual crisis; he spent his days reading Bossuet
and the Holy Scriptures when he was not taking long walks in the
country; he felt that God's Adversary was retreating. That he had
found a means to appease him in exchange for peace and serenity
and, though it was a high price to pay, such was the meaning of
existence, that the Faith was One, that it held the possibility of
mysteries, and the sure and certain hope of salvation. Mathilde
still came by every evening, and even she sensed a difference
in the elderly priest (aside from the fact that he now abstained
from drinking wine and brandy); he no longer looked at her the
same way—he was more at peace, serious yet at peace, and one
day she naively asked how he had managed to recover hope,
and Largeau said that hope and faith were one and the same,
and that he had recovered the former by regaining the latter, or
vice versa, for he had seen through Satan's wiles. And Mathilde
was astonished, for he never spoke in such precise or solemn
terms; she did not react, but simply asked Largeau to suggest a
reading on which she might meditate that evening, and the old
priest thought for a moment and said, Luke, chapter four, verses
1 to 13: Christ's Temptation in the Desert. Mathilde smiled and
thanked him. Temptation. She wondered whether the century
that had just begun would be that of the End Times and of Last
Judgment; she wondered where Largeau found the strength, in
this world filled with illusions, with stones turned into bread,
to repudiate the easy familiarity of desire; she did not ask the
question—she knew the passage about the Temptation of Jesus,
the temptation of material desires, of powers and of miracles.
But she had understood the priest's meaning. Largeau put on
his overcoat to go out, it was early spring, the air was still chilly.
As usual, he hid his Roman collar behind a scarf and put on a
beret. He walked over to Mathilde, who was also about to leave
the presbytery, and kissed her on the forehead—something he
had never done before; Mathilde suddenly felt like a little girl;

profoundly moved, she stammered something as she watched Largeau head toward the woods of Le Luc and the Standing Stone. When he reached the edge of the little wood, he turned left as usual toward Saint-Maxire, headed down into the valley, then followed the banks of the Sèvre as far as the Château de Mursay, where Agrippa d'Aubigné had once lived, and which was falling further into ruin with each passing day; he crossed the Sèvre by the mill, and headed back up to the plains (hedgerows of blooming blackthorn, rowan trees with their pinnate leaves, field maples) where birds flocked above the plowed furrows: he had been walking for two hours without realizing. From this hillock he could look down on the river, taking in the sweeping panorama of Villiers and beyond—just beyond—the village of La Pierre-Saint-Christophe, invisible but for the distant flickering movement of wind turbines.

Mathilde had gone home, intent on doing some gardening; there was serious spring cleaning to be done; it was time for the potted seedlings to be bedded out, for the vegetable garden to be weeded and fertilized; the protective winter covers could now be taken off (Mathilde was always afraid to remove them too early), and bare areas covered with mulch; then, toward evening, as the low sun began to sink into the Marais, she packed away her tools, took off her gardening gloves and her plastic boots, washed her hands and made herself a cup of tea; then she took down her Bible and opened it to the Gospel of Saint Luke—a long slim card fell out of the book, on the yellowing card was a poem:

> As the church bell sings out for evensong
> and softly tarries in the mossy dale
> beside a turtledove, gray-pink and pale,
> so does my humble soul sing out to you.
>
> As the white lily feeds upon spring rain
> and scents itself with essence of the dew,

so your sweetness, like a soft refrain,
lights on my soul and perfumes it anew.

Yet now the bell, the bloom, the rains, the dove
remind you of a boy of common stock
who, passing, left poor tribute to his love
his soul laid at your feet like hollyhocks.

The poem was decorated with a drawing of a hollyhock—like an old-fashioned postcard. The poem was signed Francis Jammes, a name Mathilde did not recognize. Mathilde was unfamiliar with poetry, she reread the poem a second, then a third time, wondering how this card that she had never seen had come to be in her Bible, precisely at the chapter of Luke's Gospel she wanted to reread—she was suddenly extremely moved, her eyes welled, she felt a wave of emotion course from her feet through her stomach, she felt her chest tighten, felt as though her heart might stop, and burst into tears; she wept over this passage in Luke's Gospel, then, suddenly seized by a terrible premonition, she dabbed her eyes on her coat sleeves and ran across the street and round the church to the presbytery, all the while whispering Holy Mary Mother of God; it couldn't be true, couldn't be true; she opened the door almost without troubling to knock—and instantly clapped her hand over her mouth, sobbing louder as she fell to her knees.

*

"I'm telling you, these stories of wild boars waking up in the trunk of a car are bullshit, it's a rural myth, it just doesn't happen—have you seen the state of my bumper? He got what was coming to him."

But tubby Thomas refused to concede. Ever since the men had wrestled the mammal into the back of the van a few seconds after the accident on a bend in the little wood of Le Luc that had left the boar lying stiffly on the pavement, he had been retelling the story of a distant cousin who been involved in a similar accident, except that in his case, it had resulted in various problems, not least the fact that the two rear seats had been completely destroyed.

"What do we do if the fucker wakes up in an hour, in the back of the van, or in Patarin's kitchen? Has anything like this ever happened to you?"

Martial sighed.

"No, never."

Tubby Thomas was neither the smartest nor the shrewdest man in the village, but he was definitely among the most brutal.

"Why don't we put a bullet in him just in case."

"You'll spoil the meat," the mayor protested.

"No, I'm talking about a bullet in the head. Who cares about the head? It's not like we're going to hang it over the fireplace. Okay, so you won't get to have pig's snout in aspic! Just give me two minutes to get the gun, open the tailgate, and I'll put lead in his snout. No need for buckshot at this distance."

Martial realized that the idea that the beast might wake up was just a ruse, that Thomas simply wanted to fire a bullet into the animal at point-blank range for the thrill of it: to someone who had never hunted big game, only partridges and hares, the notion of a wild boar thrilled him; perhaps he felt that the bumper of a Renault was not a noble weapon for dispatching such an animal; and perhaps Thomas's disturbing desire to possess women, his warped desire for power, force and pleasure fed into his desire to shoot this feral, dying animal.

Martial sighed, this time resignedly.

"Alright, fine, we'll head over to your place, finish the beast off just in case, then take the carcass to Patarin so he can butcher it for us. Can't help but think it's bad timing though; ten days later and we would have eaten it for New Year's Eve."

"Hey, at least we got him," said Thomas. "It's going to be delicious. Roast haunch of boar, fillets, sausages, terrines ... How much do you think he weighs?"

"A couple of bags of cement at a rough guess. Say, fifty kilos, give or take."

"A good day's hunting, I call it!"

Thomas's remark reminded Martial of his duties and responsibilities; a worried frown flickered across his face as he considered the risks, deemed them to be negligible and smiled:

"Actually, it's called poaching."

"Poaching? It's hardly our fault that the animal wound up on my bumper. Right on a bend, too. The beast could have wrecked the van."

"In cases like this, you're supposed to hand the carcass to the gendarmes or the local council. That's the law."

"You're the law, may I remind you. And we've both got hunting licenses and it's open season, as far as I'm aware. Okay, granted, we're not allowed to hunt with a car. That's why we need to put a bullet in the boar. That way, it's all legit."

At this line of reasoning, the mayor—whose rank had given him a veneer of legal authority—winced.

"Here..." said Thomas, jumping out and running through the gates into his yard. "... I'll just get the gun."

He had left the headlights on and the engine idling; the mayor listened to the stillness of the night, there was no sound except for the muffled chatter of the TV in Thomas's house. The sound of a gunshot would wake the whole village, he thought; he glanced at his watch, it was just after 11 p.m. Oh well, they'll just go back to sleep; besides, it was too late to change the barman's mind.

Red-faced from running or perhaps from the excitement, Thomas had already reappeared with the gun; clumsily, he loaded it; as agreed, Martial opened the tailgate and took cover behind it. The bartender slipped a fat finger into the trigger guard, a double blast set the night quiver and sent the shooter's beaming smile reflecting off the stars. Fucking moron, pulling both triggers together, thought the mayor, his ears still ringing, and using a buckshot shell, the round pellets barely have room to spread out after they emerge from the muzzle; at a range of five feet, still tightly grouped, they blasted away the snout and the muzzle, shattered the left tusk, the jawbone, burst the eyeballs, smashed through the parietal bone, cut a path through the brain, thrusting it, together with a piece of the right ear, deep into the driver's seat. The other pellets ricocheted at their own speed and ended up embedded in the plastic of the dashboard and the glove compartment. One last heartbeat instantly spilled the blood of the magnificent boar all over the diamond plate steel truck bed and brought death to the wild hog that had been Father Largeau, who had been a frog, a water rat and a ferryman on the dark marshes; who had relished a half hour spent mounting a wild sow, had croaked in the summer twilight, had swum until he could swim no more, had played with fireflies, listened to the liquid song of the boat, the gurgling of the punt as he steered; the one who had flitted between the ruins, who had been a resplendent crow, a highwayman, a monk, a peasant, an indomitable oak, a pebble collected by a pilgrim and, once, even a storm, a terrible storm capable of uprooting trees; he who had desired Mathilde more than life itself now lay dying on the steel truck bed; he who would later be a woodsman, a Moorish warrior, a mud-blackened serf, a sheepdog, a ravening fox, a weeping willow, a lawyer, a wealthy merchant, yet eternally himself, according to the merits his blind soul managed to accrue, as do all of us who shimmer for a time in the boundless night, before being hurled back into the Wheel, thrust over and over into suffering and pain, which is here on Earth and nowhere else.

SONG

Heed me in this, 'tis not land taxes that has caused them to revolt. Speak not of tailles and taxes, 'pon my word, only a callow mooncalf would credit such a notion. That they are indigent, I grant, and sore troublesome it is for us to make a sou from their labors—as you know, I am well placed to speak to the matter, having had the good fortune (hark you, good fortune! ...) to know these luckless Jacques Bonhommes as well as any man alive—take that poor wretch up there upon the cross—'twas I that had him put there. Tailles and taxes ... S'blood, these wretched Jacques-a-napes who brandish pitchforks at the slightest quiddity. Foul creatures of the mud and mire! What know these clodpolls of taxes and tariffs, of the Spanish menace, of New World gold, of trade or crops or creed ... ? They needs must be subdued. Gruel! Soup! In sooth, these are the only words known to savages! Hast read the travelers? Monsieur de Montaigne has written of savages, the noble youthful savage humanity of the New World! While here, Sweet Lord, we are faced with choleric brigands! It warms my soul to see him on the rack. We can but hope these troubles will abate, that France can recover some semblance of order. Know you that they almost razed the castle? Our troops arrived from Béarn in the nick of opportunity. O what a splendid massacre. O exquisite butchery! Run through with muskets, hacked down with halberds! These Gascon soldiers are superlative. The villainous rabble was cut to pieces—

Ha! Ha!—pray excuse my laughter while I do find my kerchief.
No, no, 'tis not tailles and taxes that has them so inflamed, the
Jacques, their rancor and resentment are directed at us. At us. At
beauty. At wisdom. Starvation? Pish! These creatures scrabble
in the dirt for three meager cabbages and a bushel of wheat ...
Starve them, and they toil the harder, 'tis common knowledge.
Give them riches and they wallow in filth and lust like swine ...

Peace, the henchmen are about to start. Hark to the silence,
hear the dread that courses through the mob. Dread and diver-
tissement in equal measure, for all appreciate a trial by ordeal.
Look you, does he tremble? Verily, I say he is all atremble. Where
is your overweening vanity, vile Jacques? Lashed to Saint Andrew's cross! See the executioner? And the iron bar? List and
you shall hear the crack of bones! Such brute strength—yon
that executioner is like unto Goliath. Oh! Holy Mother! A foot!
Dear God, Dear God. Didst thou see? The broken bone piercing
through the flesh? One can almost glimpse the marrow ... Mer-
ciful God. *Beati qui ambulant in lege Domini.* The hand, oh horrid sight, those crook'd broken fingers dripping blood. Both feet
now, and there the thigh, Sweet Lord, what barbarous spectacle
... *Et peribunt a facie tua.* That blood streaming down the cross,
miserere nobis! He is about to deal a last final blow to the chest
... to shatter the ribs ... Canst see his face? O fearful rictus! As
if he would fain die, but is roused from death by the rod of iron!
He stirs still. Onward, for the King of France! His every bone is
broken, poor wretch, what agony. Look now, they shall lash him
to the wheel ... Conceive the pain as your broken body is carried
and your shattered limbs bound to the wheel. Ever and anon,
they take pity on the condemned man and throttle him—if the
judge be moved to clemency! See, the rope about his neck—a
henchman beneath the platform need only pull and the deed is
done upon the moment. But no, our Jacques Bonhomme still
lives ... I heard once of a Jacques tortured in Limoges who lived
for two long days and, broken as he was, did plead for water. He

was whimpering still when, finally, the provost marshal had him garroted. And it please you, let us wait awhile until the crowd grows bored before approaching. O the ordeal, *O tempora, O mores*! Mine eyes revel in the sight. Sweet Mary and Joseph, what thrills! See, his finger doth wag still. Come, let us move closer afore the sudden hand of Death close up his eye!

VII.

THE LOVERS OF VERONA

I long to see old Syracuse
Fair Kairouan and Easter Isle
See great birds soar into the blue
Uplifted by the winds awhile.
Glimpse the source of Amazona
And the Palace of the Lama
Dream of the lovers of Verona
Atop the peak of Fujiyama.
      —Bernard Dimey & Henri Salvador,
            "Syracuse"

January 15

At last! I've finally got my car, my Argo! The registration papers
are in my name and the address, thanks to the lease signed by
Mathilde, is the Savage Mind. The advantage of living near Niort,
world capital of insurance companies, is that you don't have to go
far to find a broker. On the other hand, the bastards took me for
a fortune on the pretext that I've never had a policy in my own
name. But the guy was decent enough. He was trying to sell me a
Comprehensive Insurance Policy covering windshield breakage,
theft, etc., but when he saw that the car was more than twenty
years old, he said, Look, third-party should cover you, yeah? And
since it's a two-seater, that makes it slightly cheaper. That said,
the cost of the insurance is three times what I paid for the car. So
I went back to the garage, washed it, checked the pressure of the

tires, bought a can of oil and a chamois leather. A hi-vis jacket. An emergency warning triangle. Bliss. Thirty years old and this is my first car; not exactly precocious. Bonus: an old issue of *Playboy* in the glove compartment (October 2003, "*Koh-Lanta*: Steaming Hot," with the centerfold missing). Curious thing: there are two small metal pellets embedded in the plastic of the dashboard and three more in the glove box. Wonder whether this has anything to do with the porn mag. What the actual fuck did Thomas do in this thing?

After two liters of superconcentrated bleach, it still stinks, but the stench is different—sort of like a rotting corpse in a chlorinated swimming pool. To make matters worse, blowflies have taken up residence in some holes in the backs of the seats. But it's no big deal, I'm sure they'll go away.

So, I drove the Argo back from Niort, easily managed 80 kph on the motorway, windows rolled down because of the smell: an amazing feeling of freedom.

Extra bonus: it's got Deux-Sèvres registration plates, so I can travel incognito.

Finally, the great rural idyll is within my grasp!

January 16

Went for a spin just for the thrill of having the car: La Rochelle–Châtelaillon–Rochefort and back. Really beautiful. La Rochelle harbor is lovely, even in the rain—had coffee on the (heated) terrace, a bar called La Grand Rive. Remembered that in *The Three Musketeers*, d'Artagnan and the others take part in the siege of La Rochelle. Now that's an idea: reread *The Three Musketeers*. Should be easy to find a copy. The seaside town of Châtelaillon is pleasantly deserted (which on a weekday in January is par for the course) and it has one curious strange feature: at low tide, the sea goes out several kilometers, leaving vast expanses of mud. I had planned to take a paddle, but I would have had to wait three hours for the tide to come in again. Then again, the place must be heaven for people gathering shellfish— you can't have everything.

Saw the Corderie Royale in Rochefort, a very imposing building. Pierre Loti's house is also here, but I don't know anything about Loti, who, for some reason, I tend to associate with the Basque country. Thinking about it, I could buy a couple of books by Loti while I'm getting a copy of *The Three Musketeers*, then come back in a few months and visit his house. Otherwise, Rochefort, with its rectilinear streets and squat identical houses, is a little mournful. But maybe that had something to do with the weather. I thought of *Les demoiselles de Rochefort*, but I didn't see a single pretty girl. Being a weekday morning in the dead of winter, this is hardly surprising: they're all at the gym.

The Argo runs a little hot when we're stuck in traffic, but otherwise, she's fine.

January 18

Ended up breaking the passenger side window from constantly opening and closing it to counteract the smell of rotting flesh— now, the window drops into the "half open" position the minute you touch the door, or at the slightest bump in the road. Had to jam it shut with a red-handled screwdriver that sticks out—which makes for a steampunk vibe. Went to the garage just outside the village where Arnaud works—his initial surprise at seeing me gave way to delight. Jucheau, the owner, is a squat, mustachioed little man in his fifties who wears the same overalls as his eternal apprentice. He looked at the car, looked at the screwdriver and then pulled it out, leaving the window dangling

352

pathetically, then said, I think you've found the ideal solution. I must have looked bewildered, because he explained this cryptic phrase—the screwdriver isn't a bad solution to the problem. I ventured an, Oh? You mean it can't be fixed? which he followed with an, Oh, it can be fixed. Anything can be fixed. I'm just not sure you want to pay €150 to repair a heap of junk like this. A heap of junk, the Argo? Bastard. But I suppose he had a point. Couldn't we consider something more aesthetically pleasing than a screwdriver? Hmmm, the advantage of the screwdriver is that it has a handle, so can be easily removed if you want to open the window. Or replaced if it falls out. I'd stick to the screwdriver. If you're passing a scrapyard, you could try buying a door, but I doubt they'd let you have it for less than €60. If you do find one, buy it and they'll fit it for you. It's a pain in the ass to do it by yourself. So, there you go, for the moment, I just have to get used to the screwdriver.

I've noticed that the events and impressions recorded in this field diary have less and less to do with my thesis. The science/holiday-in-the-country ratio has been subtly reversed over the past weeks and the car has further added to a difficult start to the year. Read my horoscope in *La Nouvelle République*: "Gemini First Decan: Prepare for turmoil, tweak your plan." Can't wait.

January 21

Found this on the web: "The position of Neptune means that those born under the sign of Gemini are keenly intuitive and have great potential to inspire, which is why they naturally gravitate toward humanism and the social sciences. Gemini First Decan: Chiefly guided by instinct as a primary motivating force ... Intelligent and perceptive, possessed of a deep innate sensitivity that facilitates the building of lasting relationships." So an all-around great guy, then.

This morning, I'm back at work and on top of the world.

January 25

Right, that's it: I've written fifteen new pages for the *Questions* chapter. Olé, olé olé olé. It's more than a text: it's an irrefutable block. I tell you, the laptop keys were smoking here at the Savage Mind!!! The cats couldn't believe their eyes: David hasn't played Tetris or done anything but write for three days solid. I haven't seen anyone, chatted with anyone online or touched a drop of alcohol. Granted, I've guzzled six cans of baked beans, two frozen lasagnas and a family-size pizza, and at this rate, by the time I've written four hundred pages I'll be a beached whale: a brilliant PhD graduate, but clinically obese.

What a difference between what I've just written and my pathetic earlier attempts! Now I understand how important it is to work in the field. My intuition is honed, my ideas are stronger, my arguments clearer. Woo-hoo!!!!! I wonder what Calvet will think of it. If he has an iota of integrity, he'll let me have his chair immediately.

It's 1 p.m., it's not raining, I'm going to take the Argo out for a spin, get some fresh air.

David Mazon, you're back in the game!

February 2

It occurs to me that it's been almost ten days since I last talked to Lara. She hasn't called me either, which is strange. Just a few text messages back and forth. Seems like we've found our rhythm with this long-distance relationship thing.

+ 2 pages for the *Questions* chapter. Need it to be watertight.

February 5

Found this on the website for the winter issue of *Elle*: "Geminis: Whether you're single or in a relationship, you will gain new perspectives on your love life and, thanks to your intuition, will succeed in finding the right balance while preserving the freedoms you hold so dear." That's me to a T. (Why this sudden passion for astrology? Could it have something to do with the magic of the countryside? Absolutely must reread Jeanne Favret-Saada, it'll serve as a talisman against bad luck.)

Feeling a little tense, time to get some fresh air. And eat more green vegetables and salad, anything other than this processed shit: I'm horribly constipated.

October 17

Can an old love simply fall away like an old scab on a knee or elbow, giving way to healthy pink skin? Can something we believed was rooted in our very being simply flake away like dead skin, ripped away by time after a fall from a bicycle? Have I simply fallen off my bike? These questions haunt me. For a long time, I was hesitant to reread this diary, or to continue writing it; now I think it's necessary. While I have a keen intuition and tend to act on instinct, there are times when reflection is necessary. The last entry was in early February;[1] I left the Savage Mind in early summer. The whole thing about my constipation is typi-

1. February 5, to be precise. I will continue to add footnotes, it's something I've really missed.

cal of someone who refuses to listen to his body. It reminds me of Max. Anyway. Madness in the countryside can assume very different faces.[1] I was struggling to write pages of problematics that were of no interest to anyone, while Max was steadily photographing the same shit for months on end.

Vegetables! Vegetables! Lao-tzu said: you must find the way. I've found it … It's quite easy, I'm going to chop off your head.[2]

Five portions of fruits and vegetables a day: one little spliff and I'm clearly extremely lucid. Well, I suppose, weed is an herb. Two apples, three spliffs and there you go—that's your five a day.[3]

Can old loves fall away like scabs from a grazed knee?[4]

I'm going to take things in chronological order starting with February 6: at the time I didn't know it, but the war had already started between the supporters and opponents of the construction of ancillary reservoirs.[5] The first violent clash of the "Pond War" in December earned Lucie twenty-four hours in police custody and a whole heap of trouble afterward. I had paid no attention to the reasons for the protest, only its consequences, which just shows that, by burying myself in the writing of my thesis, I was actually distancing myself from its subject matter. It was all very well learning to make vegetable soup from online recipes, but if I could not truly experience the issues at stake

1. Mazon, David, *Sayings & Maxims*, Plon, Paris, "Terre humaine," Volume I, Axiom 1, Proposition C.
2. Hergé, *The Blue Lotus*, p. 57, Casterman, Tournai, 1948; English edition, Methuen, London, 1983, translated by Leslie Lonsdale-Cooper and Michael Turner.
3. *Fruits and Vegetables—Your Five a Day*, Ministry of Health brochure, Paris, 2012.
4. Mazon, David, *Complete Poems*, vol. 1, "Ballades," p. 857, Bibliothèque de la Pléiade, Paris.
5. *Ancillary reservoirs*, hereinafter referred to as "ponds"—these vast artificial lakes containing millions of cubic meters of water are used for irrigation. The "Pond War" was among the highlights of the activist year.

in the territory my thesis was supposed to illuminate, I was not likely to produce any observation worthy of the name.

By February, I was making great strides in my knowledge of mechanics and cooking, but little headway in the sciences. Calvet had emailed to congratulate me on the *Questions* chapter, but reminded me that I still lacked the necessary groundwork to begin answering the questions in question. I had made little headway on the *Answers* chapters. Though it pained me to admit it, he was completely right. Granted, I had formulated a number of objectives, but in the very process of formulating them, I had put a distance between me and those objectives.

So, I devoted my time to gastronomy and market gardening.

Well, when I say gastronomy, it wasn't exactly rural *Master-Chef*; Mathilde had lent me an old first-generation Thermomix™ multicooker she no longer used, and I was slowly hacking my way through the online recipe jungle. I was venturing into unknown territory unarmed and defenseless, "with nothing but my cock and my potato peeler," to put it crudely. Clearly, Lucie's vegetables were of the highest quality, since before long I was not only making complex and sophisticated soups,[1] but also intricate dishes, like vegetarian pot-au-feu. From the end of February, I was heading out to the fields with Lucie every day and she seemed happy to have company (my incompetence and my neophyte ineptness greatly amused her). I even became quite friendly with the dog, always ready to play; in fact, I spent more time playing with the dog than I did hoeing, though this didn't seem to bother Lucie. She often asked me how my work was progressing, and I began to realize that I was lying to her for no real reason, out of sheer habit; I'd tell her, it's going fine, I'm making good progress, when in fact I'd already given up on doing interviews. I had told myself, look, I've sorted out the problematics, I can afford to take a few days off, but a month later there I was,

---

1. Soupe à l'oignon gratinée, cabbage soup, garbure.

bent double, feet in the straw, sowing rows of peas. It's a bit of a risk, Lucie said, but we'll take it—if we start out with the high tunnels, global warming and a little bit of luck means we could earn an extra thousand euros in May. If there's a hard frost, or if the weather stays cold … all we'll have wasted is our time, the seeds cost next to nothing.[1]

The only progress I was making was in watching vegetables grow.

Throwing the ball for the dog.

Pulling up weeds.

Watching leaves appear on the branches of the poplars and listening to the gradually swelling rustle of birds in the Marais.

We were lucky; there was no late frost; the peas grew vigorously (in fact, they were magnificent, a "prime early crop" like those of yesteryear) and Lucie made an extra couple of hundred euros—her customers were thrilled, they clamored for the sweet little spheres that Mother Nature beautifully packaged in such splendidly green pods.

Lucie was ecstatic. In the mild, early spring, the whole region looked magical. The perfect season! But I am straying from the point. I need to get back on track. The winter had been simultaneously quiet and eventful.

I gave up trying to be Nimrod,[2] I wasn't really interested in applying for a hunting license, though legally it would mean I could do some "supervised hunting," a bit like a student driver—I'm not convinced that Gary was thrilled at the prospect. Besides, I was a bit discouraged by the cost (to say nothing about the fact that the equipment—rifles, etc.—is a substantial investment, and that doesn't even include a hunting dog; in a nutshell:

1. Lucie is referring to the inherent risks of late frost on early sowing, and the potential of losing an entire crop. Cf. "Interview with Lucie Moreau," Appendix III, *Interviews*.

2. Cf. Genesis 10, Chronicles 1: "a mighty hunter before the Lord [and] … began to be mighty in the earth."

not everyone is cut out to be Jack London). In June, I managed to take an interest in angling and even took part in "a thrilling adventure weekend in the wild depths of the Marais,"[1] but I said I'd start by relating what happened during the winter, so let's go back to February.

So, in early February, around the tenth, I got an email from Calvet asking me (in rather more well-chosen terms) what the fuck I was doing pissing about in the ass end of nowhere, encouraging me to get a move on, as this was the third year of my thesis, and informing me that my application for a position as Teaching and Research Assistant for the coming academic year had been rejected, which was a bitter blow. My grant for the fieldwork and my allowance would both run out in June, and I had been hoping to get my first job at the university in autumn, because, although I had some savings, Paris isn't cheap. Going back to live with my mother at the age of thirty was not an option. So, I sank into a depression, and depression meant holing up at home, forgoing my visits to the Café-Pêche and a concomitant increase in the consumption of frozen pizza and other crap.

I spent a good week playing Tetris and reading Rabelais.[2]

I was out of circulation for so long that Max, worried that I no longer showed up at the bar for aperitif, paid me an impromptu visit—he was concerned to find me sitting in the dark with my shutters closed, deathly pale and with dark circles around my eyes; according to him, the Savage Mind reeked of cat piss,[3] in short, he said, I was dying, "of a wasting disease worthy of a love-sick virgin."[4] He generously undertook to take me out to, he said, "take my mind off things";[5] not only did he invite me to lunch,

1. See pp. 393–403. We had a wild time—one of the best moments of my life.
2. Fouaces! Fouaces and King Picrochole's wars!
3. I still find it hard to believe.
4. See below, "Interview with Maximilien Rouvre," February 12, Appendix III, *Interviews.*
5. Ibid.

he also suggested I take part in a number of other activities—activities that, as we shall see, were not without consequences. The first of these—which I have to say I could well have done without—was a guided tour of Maximilien's studio, most especially its secret part: the unveiling of the Magnum Opus, as yet unseen by anyone, which he had completed on the morning of January 2. After several weeks spent making arrangements, everything was in readiness and, according to Max, I was about to be the first human being to see it: "Such an unfurling of aesthetic power will instantly revive you, my boy. Inspired by this masterpiece, you will be utterly galvanized and raring to get back to work. Think of it as a beacon in the darkness. This is why I have decided to show it to you. So that you can recover your faith. So that you can once again find hope."[1]

I was overwhelmed by the grandiloquence of his claim.

Max said all this as he stood outside the studio, his hand on the door handle; we had just had lunch.[2] I felt a little intimidated, but proud that he trusted me. I hoped my artistic judgment would be up to scratch.

The old barn is a long, narrow building with a windowless wall to one side, and large windows overlooking the farmyard. When Max ushered me inside, the long red drapes like theater curtains were drawn and the vast room was steeped in darkness; I could just make out a desk, a drawing table, a stepladder and the lofty ghosts of easels beneath dust sheets.

Are you ready? said Max. It's called *The Bristol Scale: Autobiographical Droppings.*

He switched on the light.

No, I wasn't ready.

The wall facing the courtyard was covered by dozens of photographic prints, illuminated by powerful spotlights; the edges of

1. Ibid.
2. Roast chicken and homemade fries, bottle of Haut-Médoc "La Paroisse," from the Saint-Seurin-de-Cadourne cooperative.

each photograph were pale white or bluish, the center dark, black, dark green, brown or tobacco colored. I was dumbfounded: hundreds of images of feces, turds, of every shape and size; small, medium, large, hard, lumpy, smooth, soft blobs, ragged-edged, liquid, etc., etc., in short, interminable variations on the theme of poo.

Yuck.

I was knocked on my ass.

I could not formulate a single word.

"Admit it, it takes your breath away," said Max.

" ..."

"Are you familiar with the Bristol scale?" said Max. "The Bristol scale is to defecation what the Richter scale is to seismology." Then, sounding concerned, "You're not saying anything?"

I still could not bring myself to speak, I wondered how an artist like Max could have forsaken beauty and plunged into abjectness. Some kind of depression, no doubt. Weltschmerz. The horrors of the world that plunge you deeper and deeper into excrement every day. This was not some subtly ironic game for art cognoscenti, nor a conceptual piece by Manzoni, an inside joke for the happy few, but an almost pathological immersion, a way of *being in the shit*, which to me seemed both borderline psychotic and very much part of the zeitgeist. The effect was so disturbing that it caught in the throat like a noisome stench. As though one had glimpsed the depths of a desolate soul.

Thinking about it now, I realize this impression was probably due to the absence of a mediating element—a museum, a gallery, an exhibition space; the crudeness of the barn, the presence of the artist next to me, his impatience. He looked at me, bewildered—we were both struck dumb. Max was suddenly ashamed; I think he was truly seeing his work through my eyes, through my discomfited silence: he could glimpse his own breakdown and the fragility of these obstinate copromaniacal fragments, the crassest form of autobiography.

(I have to admit that Max is a genuine artist, endlessly resourceful: when he realized that this gigantic oeuvre was a "failure," he immediately transformed it into a "minimalist diary," with few photos, and rather amusing pencil sketches, with each day bearing a number corresponding to the Bristol scale; a pastiche of travel diaries, with watercolor highlights, a small thirty-page book of lithographs, wildly funny and bursting with energy, whose first print run sold out almost immediately).[1]

So, there I was in Max's studio, feeling somewhat revived by the Médoc we had had with lunch, silently contemplating piles of bluish shit and the first phrase that popped into my head was one I had seen on gardening websites: "Liberally add thoroughly decomposed manure." After I walked to the far end of the barn-cum-studio, I finally found something inane to say:

"Very powerful. Thoroughly decomp ... deconstructed."

Max was not fooled. Gave a heavy sigh and stared at the long wall.

"Yeah, I think maybe I've let myself go a little ..."

"And ... you're planning on exhibiting all the images together?"

"That's the idea, yes, though I don't really know what form it'll take."

I tried to replace my apparent lack of enthusiasm with heartfelt theorization:

"I think it is very much a work *of its time*. It's a reflection on the immediate, and on the infinite yet frustrating materiality of *homo faber*, who is capable of *simultaneously producing* art and excrement. This is not about sublimation, about the artist transforming shit into art. We live in the era of *and*, of *conjunction*. Art that is simultaneously this *and* that. The sublime *and* the shit. The impossibility of escaping from the mire, you know? Perhaps it's the anthropologist in me, but I see this as a state-of-the-world

1. Rouvre, Maximilien, *The Journey to Bristol: a Defecation Diary*, Franck Bordas Éditeur, Paris.

piece—not simply a linguistic metaphor, but a profound reflection. Of course, it's brutal. But it's this very brutality that might eventually lead to a fresh awareness of the relationship between man and nature. An *ars cagandi* in much the same vein as *ars moriendi*."[1]

I was astounded by my own pedantry.

Max stared at me as though I were talking about someone else. "Deranged."

"A little crazy, yes, but you were conscious of that while you were working on it, right?"

"Not really. For me it's something immediate, like an expression of revolt."

Max looked at me with a slightly wounded pride.

"What are you up to this afternoon?"

"I think I'll go help Lucie out. It'll do me good after so many weeks working on my thesis," I lied.

"See you at the Café-Pêche later?"

"Yeah, go on, I'll pop in for a quick one. And it'll be on me, to celebrate the end of your long sojourn in Bristol."

This made him howl with laughter.

Back at the Savage Mind and inspired by Max's work, I felt like writing a note to my thesis director, scrawled in shit on the back of a postcard from the Marais depicting a cow on a barge. His reaction when I asked him about the appeal in *Libération* had been beneath contempt. It's impossible to overstate the cowardice of people.[2]

I phoned Lucie to ask whether she was working; it had been ten days since we last spoke, she seemed happy to hear from me, and, truth be told, I was happy too. She was out in the fields—the weather was gray, gray and warm, a typical twenty-first-century

1. Mazon, David, *Saccus merdae, Petitions and Repetitions*, L'Harmattan, Paris.
2. Cf. p. 381

muggy late winter day. I'll drive over and give you a hand, I said. The fresh air will do me good.

The Argo was running as smoothly as a Rolls-Royce, she cleaved the air, within twenty minutes I had crossed the plains, through Villiers, avoiding the wind turbines, crossed the highway to Nantes and plunged down toward the Marais, where channels and rivulets ran westward to the ocean. When I reached Benet, the first village in the Vendée, I had to take the road toward Bouillé-Courdault (it's a name I've always found particularly pleasing, Bouillé-Courdault) and five minutes later I came to the sign indicating Maupas and Bee & Bean Ltd. Damn—Franck's car was parked outside the gate, which meant the atmosphere would be tense... Franck is quite a pleasant, polite guy when not in the presence of his ex, Lucie; the corollary is equally, perhaps even more viciously, true. I greeted them both; each was working on a vegetable patch a hundred meters apart. Lucie wore the permanent scowl that was a sure sign this was one of her bad days; Franck had the same effect on Lucie as kryptonite on Superman.

I briefly told her about the lunch with Max, my visit to the studio, the "Magnum Opus"—Lucie was dumbfounded—she told me that one of her friends, Lynn the home hairdresser, had been having an affair with Max, one that some weeks ago had ended in disaster (to the apparent sadness of both parties) because of "a series of depraved and terrifying photographs Max hid on the wall of the barn." She understood now how her friend could have mistaken art for perversion. Lucie said she would call Lynn and explain things. Explain what, I said. Y'know, tell her that it's just art, nothing pervy, no big deal, she said. It's funny how the labels we attach to things change their reality, I said, pulling up a young weed threatening to invade the fragile pea plants in spite of the mulch. It's sow thistle, Lucie said, don't put it in the compost, it infects everything else with powdery mildew... But you can add it to salads. That one looks tasty, spring's almost here!

A salad of weeds—now there's something I've never tried.

Then I said, Why don't you come over to the Savage Mind for dinner tonight? Lucie looked up at me, a little puzzled; you mean you can *cook*? she said. Aha, you'll see … mostly I just cook your vegetables … So is that a yes or a no? Suddenly I remembered I had agreed to have a drink with Max at the Café-Pêche. Or we can do it tomorrow if you're busy tonight? No, no, I've got nothing planned tonight. Shit, I thought, now I'm in a bit of a bind—let me think … That's great—why don't you come around at about half past eight, that'll give me time to cook. Whatever suits you, she said, if you want I'll come earlier and help out—she said this with a note of gentle irony, implying that she did not rate my culinary skills, which I thought was a bit unfair. No, no, you wait and see, I'm a candidate for *MasterChef*.

My first thought was that a bit of sow thistle in a salad would not a banquet make—pop over to Super U, do the shopping and the cooking, get everything ready, then go for a drink, roll home drunk at 8:15 p.m., fuck up the whole dinner—bad idea. Plan B: meet Max for a drink, insist on Orangina®—bad idea. Plan C: give up on the idea of going for a drink—not a viable solution. Plan D: invite Max over, have drinks and dinner.

I asked Lucie if she minded me inviting Max for dinner, and she said no. I had an idea about what I would cook. I relieved Franck of a kilo of carrots, two turnips and a head of lettuce, sent a text message to Maximilien, drove hell-for-leather to Super U, bought wine, beef and a red tablecloth; cleaned, scrubbed and polished the Savage Mind, then rinsed, peeled, chopped, sliced, trimmed, blanched, sautéed (cooking is like sailing: it's mostly a question of vocabulary) and chucked everything in the Thermomix™, added water and the white wine, forgot to add the thyme and the spices, borrowed some wine glasses from Mathilde, laid the table, lit some candles. 8:20 p.m., they'll be here soon.

I think it's fair to say that the dinner was a roaring success. Sow thistle is delicious.

The boeuf aux carottes was precisely that: beef with carrots, the meat was a little chewy, but edible if cut into tiny pieces, and the carrots were meltingly soft—practically liquid.

The conversation was very pleasant.

Max seemed a little absent, dreamy or perhaps melancholy; Lucie was careful not to mention Lynn. Lucie recognized my candles as being the same as the pilfered ones she'd found at her grandfather's house after the power outage; we asked her about her arrest and her night in the cells—it's nothing very exciting, she muttered and looked away (I can picture her now, her slender face, that half smile); she was trying to sound modest as she told us how, as everyone was chanting "ZAD: GIVE THE PLANET A CHANCE," "ZAD ACTIVISTS ARE EVERYWHERE," "NO MAN-MADE RESERVOIRS," "SAVE OUR COUNTRYSIDE," Lucie and the other "activists" found themselves being charged by the police, who—to go by her account—had suddenly decided to give them a hard time: Lucie was tear-gassed, beaten, arrested; she had been grabbed by the hair and thrown to the ground by two cops—who "accidentally" stamped on her hand for shits and giggles before tossing her into the police van. This was followed by hours of falsehoods, spitefulness and suspicion during which she feared for the very fabric of democracy, had feared the power of the officers in blue behind the desks, their military-sounding titles, lieutenant, captain; captain, lieutenant, because they had not accused her of anything, had not told her anything, they had kept her in custody by a flagrant abuse of the law that means that, in practice, anyone could be beaten up, banged up and sent home without apology or explanation, with only their cuts and bruises, their shame and the last shreds of their principles. They're destroying the very idea of the Republic, said Lucie. Before this, I was never afraid of arbitrary arrest or a miscarriage of justice. Now I know anything is possible, that violence is deeply rooted in the system, that only the strong survive.

Max (we were on our third bottle, counting the aperitif) quickly saddled his high horse:

"These bastards are paving the way for a future dictatorship! We must mobilize the resistance! I'll start hoarding canned food and shotguns in the cellar!"

"It's perfectly possible that as the pressures of climate change increase, as we're faced with more devastating storms and hurricanes, the cops will just crack down harder. The government has to look like it's doing something…"

"What's crazy," Max said, pouring fuel to the fire, "is that when the farmers' unions burn piles of tractor tires, set fire to roundabouts and spray police stations with shit, no one seems to want them arrested."

"That's true, no one ever does anything to them," added Lucie.

"That's because the Ministry of Agriculture and the Ministry of the Environment are separate entities, and they don't share the same goals or the same means."

"C'mon guys, let's not spoil the evening talking about those fuckwits."

It was Lucie's turn now to sink into mournful silence, while Max was suddenly fighting fit.

"I suggest we listen to military music. David, for dessert, why don't you put on 'The Farewell of the Cavalry of the Imperial Guard to the Brave Polish Lancers'? And bring out a bottle of vodka."

He had started to bellow like a calf over the oompahing brass:

> And when France celebrates its brave
> Our thoughts fly to the valiant Polish lancers!
> Their honor and glory we vouchsafe
> Three cheers for the valiant Polish lancers!

We couldn't help but wonder why—but there was no reason, Napoleonic military songs made him happy. I asked whether he had been named Maximilien in homage to Robespierre, which made him laugh—Why do you think I moved to the ass end of the Vendée? To root out the counterrevolutionaries!

His bombast and his madness made Lucie laugh.

It was a wonderful evening; we stayed up until all hours.

Max was the first to leave, and Lucie, well, she never left.

It just happened, the way a plant sprouts; you're not paying attention and then, suddenly, there it is right in front of you.

I didn't want her to leave; she didn't want to go home.

That was the sum total of our thinking.

I googled "Gemini man—Aries woman": Sparks will fly. Deep relationship despite the innate duplicity of the Gemini (my duality). So, nothing to worry about. Might sound stupid, but it cheered me up.

It was February 19 (not long after Valentine's Day) and Lara was due to visit the following weekend.

The scab had not quite fallen off yet; I felt a little lost—happy to have Lucie in bed with me at the Savage Mind, but unable to admit what this really meant, i.e., the end of my relationship with Lara.

The next few days were somewhat complicated—spending my days and nights with Lucie meant I didn't find the time or the inclination to talk to Lara; and as the weekend and her arrival drew closer (I was supposed to pick her up at Niort station on Friday at 9 p.m.) my anxiety grew. I dreaded telling Lucie, I didn't want my indecisiveness to scare her off. O how hopeless lovers are. Mine was a twofold cowardice: I was not prepared to admit the truth to Lucie (who assumed we were exclusive) or to Lara (who assumed likewise). The horns of a dilemma!

But Lucie's presence was a revelation!

I never imagined I could be so passionate—physically and mentally. I wanted to know everything about her life. I couldn't help but wonder what she could possibly see in me ...

I decided on a particularly spineless solution with Lara—I'm a coward, what can you do? On Thursday I sent a text message: "Sorry—this weekend is looking pretty complicated work-wise, any chance you can change your train ticket?" I wasn't exactly proud of myself. Her response, in the form of three missed calls, was swift (I deliberately put my phone on silent), followed by a text message that read something like:

> Are you out of your mind? What the fuck's wrong with you?

Lucie was asleep, lying naked beside me, while I texted Lara; the shame of it. I summoned all my courage and typed:

> It's for the best if you don't come.

I turned off my phone and, with gentle caresses, woke Lucie.
Right, now I'm going back to bed, to her: see you tomorrow.

October 18

> Item: to Monsieur Calvet I send
> A loathsome and most horrid pox
> His trouble-gusset to distend
> And fructify his shrivel'd cox.[1]

I write quatrains in the style of Villon's *Testament* to entertain myself—it took a few months before I finally abandoned my thesis, enough time for all things to ripen, the vegetables and my desires for the future. I won't say that it was an easy decision, it's never easy to change your life, but it is always possible. I spent hours in front of the computer writing satirical poems before I finally realized what they meant—that Calvet, the poor bastard, had nothing to do with it. Sometimes you just have to act. But let's go back to February. Lucie spent most of her time at the Savage Mind: exploring each other's bodies was a revelation!

1. Mazon, David, *Complete Poems*, vol. 2, "Quatrains," p. 112, Bibliothèque de la Pléiade, Paris.

The alchemy of desire, the conjuring of lust! I'm sorry, but I'm convinced that people fuck better in the country than the city. They feel freer; they're inspired by the orgiastic nature, the wanton mating of insects, chickens, rabbits, deer, the coppice and climbing plants. Constant copulations in their billions pervade all things. By contrast, in the city, our experience of sexuality is either that of the succulent plant or the fire engine. In Paris, you either indulge in Haussmannian coitus or copulate while honking your horn like an Uber® driver. I mentioned this hypothesis to Lucie, who told me it was a stupid Parisian idea, then laughed and jokingly jumped on me. But still.

Sioux-like precautions were necessary to ensure that Mathilde (whom Lucie did not want to find out—which, I told her, was a waste of time) did not notice Lucie's presence. Nigel and Barley seemed to like her, and rubbed up against her legs the moment she came through the front door. Strangely, Gary's dog never barked when she walked across the farmyard. Don't forget, he's known me longer than he's known you, said Lucie. I learned a lot about Mathilde's family from her, including how Lucie's great-grandfather's land came to be commandeered in the most bizarre circumstances, everyone having died during the war—village gossip, where under every stone there lurks some hideous tale of jealousy and resentment. Lucie confessed that, had she not been compelled by circumstance, she would never have come back to live in this godforsaken hole. For Lucie, La Pierre-Saint-Christophe was like a millstone around her neck.[1]

Of course, I regularly passed by Lucie's house: her ghoulish forebear was slowly continuing to decline, while Arnaud carried on reciting his litanies (*February 16, Feasts of Sainte Julienne and Saint Jérémie; February 16, 1831, birth of Nikolai Leskov; February 16, 1899, death of Félix Faure; February 16, 1723, coronation of Louis XV*) and building things out of Lego™—forklift trucks, trains—

---

1. Mathilde was no fool; she later told me she'd known about Lucie and me, and I quote, "from day one." Which I think is possible, even probable.

when he was not napping with his mouth hanging open. I enjoyed seeing them together, with Lucie; they played or bickered like brothers despite the vast age difference—sorry, what I just wrote was miserable: actually there's no difference at all in their ages, and yet it steadily grows year after year. I remember, one evening at the Café-Pêche in late winter, while Paco the truck driver was trying (vainly, I admit) to teach me how to play belote, Arnaud suddenly appeared and the whole bar greeted him (he had not been there for several weeks) like the prodigal son returned, with genuine warmth; everyone was eager to give him a coin to hear him recite his ephemera, and it occurred to me (I realized) that this had probably been happening for more than twenty years, since Arnaud was a child. Needless to say, the Basket of Deplorables, as I've nicknamed Martial the gravedigger and Thomas, did their usual trick of trying to get Arnaud drunk, one Ricard™, two Ricards™, three Ricards™ until the poor bastard was completely out of his mind, but Paco and some unfamiliar guy with a swollen ruddy face and a monumental honker shot through with more veins than Roman marble angrily called them out, proving that attitudes to getting vulnerable people drunk were changing. Arnaud had only been able to drink two shots of pastis, he was certainly a little tipsy, he was joyfully sniffing his forearm, but had lost neither his memory nor his use of speech: he carried on exuberantly reeling off his dates.

(I have to say that those present were intrigued by his particular fondness for me—he would constantly call out, David, David! and tug at my sleeve and recite February 19, Feast of Saint-Gabin, February 20, Feast of Sainte-Aimée, etc.; they probably wondered how we had come to be so close. I suppose some even guessed the answer to this riddle.)

The one person I really could not stand (God rest his soul!) was the grandfather—fortunately no one will ever read these lines, but I feel a little to blame for his death: he died in April, Lucie found him sprawled on the floor in a coma having just guzzled a box of Jeff de Bruges™ chocolates and knocked back a whole bottle of plum brandy (the chocolates and the plum brandy came from a weekend I had spent in Nancy with Maman) that I had given to Lucie (among other things) for her birthday and which she'd left on the dining room table. Not that I miss the pervy old bastard, he gave me the creeps, but what a way to go! "Yo-ho-ho and a bottle of rum," like *Treasure Island*, and *whack*, face down on the floor.

Martial the mayor-cum-undertaker informed Lucie and her parents, I'm afraid you've picked a bad time for it, just before the Easter weekend ... So, the old man had to spend a week in the freezer (like the great and the good of this world) before being buried the following Tuesday—the gravedigger-in-chief and his Three Graces looked very strange: they were sallow, with dark circles around their eyes, and they moved as in slow motion, as though they had all been victims of a bilious attack; they probably had too many Easter eggs.

It was my first trip to the village cemetery—obviously, I walked at the very back of the cortege, with Max, whom I asked to come with me; he looked extremely dapper, in a sleek purple-black suit, and, though it was overcast, a pair of Ray-Bans™ (*always wear sunglasses to funerals, kiddo*, he said with a knowing look, impersonating Alain Delon or God knows what film star of the silent screen). Lucie walked at the head of the procession with her parents, her elder brother Julien—whom I hadn't yet met—and, inevitably, Franck, who still acted like he was her husband, which must have tickled Lucie; Arnaud was there dressed like I'd never seen him before, in his Sunday best, with a red bow tie. The village was out in force: Thomas—!!!—Mathilde and Gary, the regulars at the Café-Pêche, the hunting fraternity—basically everyone who had been able to get time off on a Tuesday afternoon. It was a brief funeral service; the priest knew nothing about the deceased, and no one else got up to speak—there probably wasn't much to say about his life. "We pay tribute to a

372

son, a farmer and a father," said the priest, which sounded curious. "His children, his grandchildren, his friends ..." and so on. The bells did not toll.

I eyed Lucie's parents from a distance, they looked a bit like Mathilde and Gary, same age, same kind of noble, dignified demeanor, same reverential air.

I hadn't set foot inside the church since my act of petty larceny; I couldn't help but smile at the weird shit we do in this life, pilfering candles from a church to provide light for an old geezer who was now lying in a wooden box in the middle of the transept of that same church—it's pretty wild.

After a few meters of tramping gravel behind the coffin, which was being transported on a hand-drawn bier, I was unceremoniously abandoned by Max and his Ray-Bans™ as he went off to join Lynn, Lucie's hairdresser friend, who was walking a few meters ahead.

I watched from afar the Three Graces and their ropes as they lowered the coffin into the ground; Martial gave a short speech, and then we all dispersed, *sic transit gloria mundi*.

> *Great Lords as any Serf yet may;*
> *Be blown from life and gutter out:*
> *So much the wind doth bear away.*[1]

A little reception (of a lugubrious kind) was held at the grandfather's house, or rather Lucie and Arnaud's house—Max came, as did Lynn; I remember wandering alone through the village, feeling a little melancholy, wondering where this new life would lead me. I felt as though I were hovering between twin fates; science was falling away like the shades of the underworld, yet I felt the quest for knowledge more keenly than ever. I studied the drystone walls, the blooming lilacs and bignonias, the hollyhocks thrusting up through the pavements, the wooden shutters

1. François Villon, "Ballade on the Foregoing Theme in Old French" (Ballade, à ce propos, en vieil langage françoys), *Œuvres complètes*, Gallimard.

of the houses, the verdant arbors, the tractors in the farmyards, the rotavators next to the tractors, the gleaming plows, the neatly stacked hay bales, the empty byres and the cows—dark distant shapes out in the meadows.

I was thinking, life is just time spent waiting for death.

I was thinking, one day, *oops*, you knock back a bottle of brandy and *bam*, you cross the bar with no hope of return. We are all part of the great circle of life. It's beautiful, at once beautiful and sad.

I turned right and headed to Lucie's house, strange to see all the cars and Max's motorbike parked in this narrow lane where no one ever came.

The guests were mostly standing, the grandfather's chair stood empty; Lucie had pushed the table back against the wall, there was fruit juice, white wine, a bottle of cassis and another of pastis, I just grabbed a peanut; Lucie was talking to some people I didn't know. Max was chatting to Lynn and drinking pastis; he had pushed his sunglasses up so they looked like a headband; Arnaud came over to me, I said "December 2" and off he went, *December 2, Feast of Sainte-Viviane; December 2, 1804, coronation of Napoleon; December 2, 1805, Battle of Austerlitz; December 2, 1993, death of Pablo Escobar; December 2, 1852, proclamation of the Second Empire*, proud as a peacock. Then I asked if he felt sad and he came out with a phrase I will never forget, "I don't know what to do with my sadness." I wanted to hug him, but didn't dare. Max had taken a large notebook from his pocket and was sketching a quick portrait of the deceased from a photo Lucie had placed on the mantelpiece, at first, a few lines with a fine felt-tip pen, then shading and contouring using a pen with a brush tip—something I did not know existed. He's actually really good. Needless to say, as soon as he'd finished the portrait of the old geezer and given it to Lucie, he set about drawing Lynn's portrait—amazing, two sinuous black lines for her hair, features lightly sketched yet completely recognizable—what an artist: he doodled a heart at the bottom of the portrait before handing it to Lynn; I think she blushed. Maximilien Rouvre at his (lofty) work.

I have to confess that when I picture myself twenty years from now, I'd like to be Max.

After half an hour of sketches and flirting, Max and Lynn headed off for lunch by the riverbank somewhere in the Marais— without inviting me to join them, it goes without saying. People had gradually begun to drift away; Lucie came and introduced me to her parents, Christian and Françoise; her father had a handsome face, a shock of white hair and a firm handshake; her mother had a very sweet smile and almond-shaped eyes. She smelled of detergent and roses. Lucie introduced me as "David, a Parisian who's recently moved here to Saint-Christophe," which I thought sounded unfair, it always sounds unfair when people say Parisian—I know the word trips off the tongue, but there's a huge difference between the Paris of fourteenth and fifteenth arrondissements on the one hand and Montmartre or the Porte Dorée on the other; even in Paris we have our distinctions. And besides, the noun "Parisian" makes it sound absolute, irrevocable, incapable of integrating—a Parisian can never become a Provincial. Over time, a Provincial can eventually become a Parisian, of course, but the converse is impossible. Now, several months later, I'm still there, about thirty kilometers farther away: a Parisian in the country, a Parisian who has gone "back to nature," a cartoon, a caricature. If I were from Tours, Bordeaux or Nantes, I'd be just as urban, but the label would be different. But, thankfully, here in the West my accent doesn't stand out as much as it did in Ariège. I pass unnoticed. Well, most of the time. Sometimes I wonder if I'm not a bit like Thomson and Thompson when they're in disguise: nice suits, but not very effective. Actually, next February we're planning on going to the International Agricultural Show; it'll be the first time I take Lucie to Paris—I'm a little apprehensive, to be honest. I wonder whether

I'll stay calm if she doesn't know how to put a Métro ticket in the machine like a Japanese tourist. Never mind, Porte Brancion to Porte de Versailles, we can always walk, no need to panic.

But I digress: I was talking about meeting Lucie's parents. Christian almost immediately asked me this question:

"I heard you recorded an interview with my father? That he told you his life story?"

I couldn't admit that I'd never listened to the recording because I was pretty sure I wouldn't be able to understand a word; I said, yes, yes, I did, if you like, I'll send you a copy. Later, needless to say, I was embarrassed by the puerile questions I had asked and I thought, uh-oh, it's going to take some creative editing to cut that out; and that night, while Lucie had stayed at her house to keep her cousin company on this night of mourning, I put on my headphones and listened to the three-hour recording. *What a roller coaster.* I was fascinated. It was like listening to a program on France Culture or reading a book in the Terre Humaine series—a long, arduous yet ultimately unique experience. Bloody idiot that I am, at the time *I hadn't listened to a word the old man was saying.* It's unbelievable, it's as though I was *resistant,* as psychoanalysts say. The recording relates an extraordinary story. The death of his mother, his father's suicide, the fact that he was illegitimate, cast out by his family, forced to work in the fields, robbed by his cousins of his rightful inheritance, forced to earn a living as a tractor driver, a knife grinder, sometimes a lumberjack—"two weeks we'd spend out yonder, camp'd out in the swamps, hackin' down trees, hewing elms, buckin' the poplars, endin' up sky west and crook'd." Oh, he had a regional accent and an old-fashioned turn of phrase, but he was perfectly intelligible. It's strange to think that during the recording session I was both present and absent. Place-names I didn't know at the time now sounded like incantations—the Devil's Rock (actually another name for the Standing Stone, according to Lucie), the washhouse, the river, Le Luc, his whole life revolved around La Pierre-Saint-Christophe, Villiers, Faye, Benet, a life lived in a space the size of a handkerchief. A trip to Niort was an occasion. When people said "the city" they meant Coulonges-sur-l'Autize, with its few thousand inhabitants.

Completely demoralized by my tin-eared, perfunctory questions, I edited them all out. How could I have failed to react to the story of the schoolmaster, for example? It defies belief. The grandfather tells me that the village schoolmaster wrote a book about his mother, and I don't ask a single question, not one. I don't seem to give a shit. Anyway. I asked Lucie about it the following morning but she didn't know anything. She asked her father, but he didn't know anything about it either. A book—but what *kind* of book? I did a quick search of the Bibliothèque nationale de France database, nothing on "La Pierre-Saint-Christophe," apart from two postcards of the Standing Stone and the church. It was like looking for a needle in a haystack. The least I could have done was ask the name of the schoolmaster, that would have made things a little easier. But I hadn't bothered.

October 19

A pox on it, I hate bureaucracy. Deeply depressed today: my application to transfer my academic credits to a degree in agriculture has been rejected. Fucking bastards. The letter from the agricultural college is crystal clear: *Despite the undoubted skills implicit in studying for a Master's degree and beginning a thesis in anthropology, we do not feel that these are transferable skills, nor are they among the qualifications required to become an agronomist or a farmer.*[1] *We therefore unequivocally suggest, per our advice during your com-*

---

1. The fat fuckers.

petency assessment, that you enroll in one of our courses in order to
obtain a Graduate Certificate in Agriculture. Competency assessment, the most humiliating thing I've ever done: Gontrand, my
adviser at the agricultural college, bluntly told me that I had only
one skill. But it was an important one: I had the skill to acquire
new skills.[1] I hope he winds up being beaten to death by tofu, as
they say in Japan.

Which means we're up shit creek at the moment because, in
theory, Lucie is the only one allowed to farm; which generates
endless problems for me in my role, which we've called "management, administration, trade and development."[2] Applying for
grants, subsidies, etc. for our farm without the fucking diploma
complicates everything. I'll just have to go back to Niort, set up
yet another appointment with Gontrand, who's going to glower
at me with his beady eyes when I explain our situation yet again
(*I'm afraid I don't quite understand, if you are not a farmer by pro-*
fession and you are currently working on a thesis in anthropology,
why do you want to transfer into market gardening?), and, look, it's
true that this whole thing is very sudden, the decision to set up
a farm, but you only live once, Monsieur Gontrand, you know I
have some savings from my late father, that I plan to invest them
here, in French soil, in the fertile loam of the Deux-Sèvres, to
grow French vegetables in the soil of the Deux-Sèvres, the very
soil in which our country's dead lie rotting, providing the carbon, nitrates and trace elements as fertilizer for cabbages, carrots, corn and wheat, all these crops sanctified by the Common
Agricultural Policy, the greatest politico-industrial-environmen-
tal-agricultural scandal in history, which sees billions of euros of
investment detrimental to the planet, detrimental to consumers,

1. Cf. Agricultural College, *Handbook for Personal Tutors*, chapter 2: "Assessing
the competency of those who have none," p. 7.
2. Minutes of the first general meeting of the GAEC Noble Savage Holdings,
p. 2, "roles and responsibilities."

to animals, to farmers themselves, detrimental to everyone and beneficial to no one simply because of poor governance—and I know these things because I'm doing a thesis, Monsieur Gontrand. But, whatever. Nothing in life is simple. All we're trying to do is save the planet, Monsieur Gontrand. If everyone saves a single hectare, that's it, that's all it takes, Monsieur Gontrand, and we can keep living happily, stroking our dogs and enjoying sorting out our recycling.

Where was I? What was I writing about in this journal? Oh, yes. So, a little over six months ago, in April, after Lucie's grandfather's funeral, long before officialdom started fucking up my life, when, obviously, nothing had yet been decided about moving here, Lucie and I had only been together for a couple of months, and though our romantic idyll was at its height I was still stubbornly pursuing this thesis that would catapult me to fame; in my recording of the grandfather's interview from the previous autumn, to which I had paid scant attention at the time, I'd heard about this book that the village schoolmaster had written about Lucie's great-grandparents at some point somewhere in the 1950s. Wild. Naturally, my first instinct had been to find out what the family knew—neither Lucie nor her father had ever heard of it. How many schoolmasters could there have been in La Pierre-Saint-Christophe back then? How could I find their names and track down the book, assuming it actually existed? The following day, I went to see the mayor, Martial Pouvreau, to sound him out, and within two days I had my answer: the schoolmaster's name was Marcel Gendreau, his daughter, a certain Madame Belloir, still lives in the village—Pouvreau, the mayor, knew all this because he had been the one to bury Gendreau the previous December.

It was easy enough to get in touch with Madame Belloir, talk to her about her father and ask her whether she had a copy of the book. She lent me a slim volume of poems entitled *Muses of the Marshlands*, which mentioned a genre hitherto unfamiliar to me, the eclogue, which sounded amusing but mysterious, and which I immediately looked up in the Le Robert®:

ECLOGUE [ˈɛklɒg] n.—1375; Lat. ecloga, Gr. ἐκλογή (eklogē, "selection"). ◆ A short poem, especially a pastoral dialogue. ▸ **bucolic, idyllic, pastoral.** *Virgil's eclogues, Ronsard's eclogues.*

(It's handy having a dictionary at home).

I found the poems quite beautiful, I have to say—evocations of rivers and marshes, of loves lost, lost in the fog, of the waters that flood the fields in winter; descriptions of Chalusson, a village on the brow of a hill overlooking the valley of the Sèvre:

> *Chalusson, O storm-tossed beacon illum'd above the plain*
> *When Phoebus's radiant lifeblood did the heavens stain*
> *With susurrating nets, rash Icarus you did save*
> *With open arms, and narrow paths that fain would ramparts brave.*

But the most extraordinary thing, without a doubt, was the novel *Nature Compels . . . ,* as written, with its tantalizing ellipsis.

It was a novella bound in gray livery, without no publisher's colophon, printed in Niort by Chiron in 1956. The opening sentence deftly set the tone:

Nature is possessed of a power for rebirth and renewal so forceful that it can sometimes break us. Whether one calls such powers fate, chance or divine will, what is certain is that once the first inadvertent step has set them in motion, they are inexorable.

What followed was quite unexpected: it recounts the tragic story of Lucie's great-grandmother, Louise; how she came to be with a child out of wedlock after an affair, a child who would be Lucie's grandfather; how Louise's parents had married off their daughter to a brutish, indigent farmhand called Jérémie, for some reason; how, after several years of marriage, Louise had once again apparently fallen pregnant, something that greatly pleased Jérémie; how, unfortunately, while Jérémie was fighting in the Ardennes in 1940, she lost the child and dared not write to let him know; how, when he came home in the summer of 1940,

Jérémie realized his wife was no longer pregnant and suspected her of cuckolding him with a young man from the village; how Jérémie went into a self-imposed exile in the Marais where he became a warlock, poacher and woodcutter, and did not return to La Pierre-Saint-Christophe until the end of the war when he sought to take his revenge on the night of the Liberation Ball; how his vengeance was so brutal that it led to Louise dying of a mysterious ailment two weeks later; how, before he took his own life, wracked by guilt and grief, Jérémie found the strength to terrorize and humiliate the villagers, wreaking his revenge on those who deemed him a savage, a half-wit, a fool, a bastard.

But, the most moving thing about *Nature Compels*... was the descriptions of daily village life: cultivating crops, raising cattle, growing fruits and vegetables, the farmyards, the shops that still existed in the village, the bakery, the greengrocers, the cafés; the butcher's van that made its rounds once a week, on Monday or Wednesday, when there was no market; the schoolmaster's writing betrayed a passion for description, a desire to produce an *ethnographic* document that might serve future generations, though not without a certain paternalistic tone; when he wrote about the "people of the land" he said "they": *they are like this, they are like that*; it was a tender form of paternalism—these were simple people, perhaps brutish, but honest and endearing. His tone was characteristic of his time, of the 1950s, of the superiority conferred by education, of the power wielded by the elite over the great unwashed.

I skim-read both books, the poems and the novella, and gave them to Lucie to give to her father, together with a copy of my interview with her grandfather.

Lucie read the history of her ancestors eagerly, in a single sitting; from time to time she would comment as she read, as though we were watching a TV series—what a scumbag, what a bastard—at times she thought she recognized certain characters and events, and then realized that it was all too long ago,

Louise and Jérémie's generation had long since disappeared and the next generation (represented by her grandfather with his oversize ears) was gradually dying out. Even the village was unrecognizable: time was, it had a heart, a center almost like a town, with four cafés, a grocer's, a bakery, a post office, a doctor's office, a veterinary clinic, a blacksmith's forge, laborers, farmers, landlords, a wine merchant, an undertaker—it was a completely different place. For the five hundred villagers in the 1950s (much the same population as today), there were ten times as many services. It was possible to live in La Pierre-Saint-Christophe and visit Coulonges only occasionally to go to the market, the general stores or the notary public. Now . . . there was almost nothing. In fact, it's possible that when Thomas retires, the Café-Pêche, the last remaining business in the village, will close its door and all that will be left is the vending machine selling baguettes in front of the town hall.[1] Everything is going to hell in a handbasket.

Lucie was simultaneously glad to know more about her grandfather's life and sad that it turned out to be so tragic. She imagined, perhaps rightly, that her father and her brother would have mixed feelings about the book.

I have included Gendreau's work in my database, after all, it's important to cite previous research on one's terrain—especially when there is very little. I could easily add it to the *Questions* chapter—it'd really fit in.

Well, assuming I ever finish this fucking thesis. Right now, it's not going well.

Here, I feel I should mention the response of Calvet—that peerless authority on all matters rural—while the "Pond Wars"

---

1. A nonexhaustive list of items and commodities sold in vending machines throughout the world: milk, oysters, bread, pizzas, marijuana, condoms, toothpaste and toothbrushes, pens, cigarettes, newspapers, fishing weights, roast chicken, orange juice, foie gras, chips, women's underwear, tinned sardines, mobile phones, champagne.

were raging; to do so, I have to recount, however briefly, the history of the "pond wars."

Back in the spring, some weeks after the grandfather's funeral, in late April, the month of precipitation and deception, a ripple of anxiety coursed through right-thinking circles worried about the environment: government proposals for man-made reservoirs (millions of cubic meters of water stored in large artificial open-air ponds, pumped underground in winter and used for irrigation in summer) in the Deux-Sèvres entailed the creation of sixteen "ponds" with a total capacity of eight million cubic meters of water, pumped up from the water table during the winter at a cost of fifty million euros (a trifling sum). In both the medium and the long term, the project is absurd for several reasons—first and foremost, such a policy in the Deux-Sèvres would be tantamount to promoting livestock farming, which is responsible for 14.5 percent of global greenhouse gases, over a sector that is already in crisis, while the "road sprayers" familiar to motorists are mostly used to irrigate maize. Even if it could be proved that draining millions of cubic meters from the water table (the Marais, the Sèvre valley, etc.) had no appreciable impact—which is far from true—deciding to increase production of methane and carbon dioxide in the teeth of climate change is utterly absurd. The same millions of euros could be used to reduce livestock farming, which predominates in the southern region of the département. But no. So, these investments are clearly based on environmental bad faith and partisan short-term goals. In the twenty-first century, the utterly delusional idea that human activity exists without consequence is astounding. The phrase "we plan to extract billions of liters of water from the rivers (a mere eight billion liters, to be precise) but, don't worry, we're pretty sure that this won't change anything," used by the Chambre d'agriculture and the prefecture, is beyond a joke. Eight billion liters of water is *just a little* more than the contents of a toothbrush glass suggested by the prefecture of Deux-Sèvres.

Anyway. Even the corollary "we plan to extract eight billion liters of water during the winter months so there will be no need to extract water over the summer" is equally preposterous—painstakingly planning a crime does not make it any less criminal. Given that it is generally accepted that temperatures are soaring and summer droughts are worsening, the solution is not to suck every drop of water from the land over the winter; what is needed is a radical transformation of how we exploit the land, adapting to new climatic conditions while attempting to combat global warming and the impact of anthropogenic activity.

Yeah, well given what's happened with the reservoirs, I wouldn't exactly hold my breath.

The problem is that all decisions being made are short-termist—based on election cycles, or to use a hackneyed phrase, *après moi le déluge*. The scrabble for reelection is the great tragedy of democracy. Stories like this demonstrate why we'd be better off having "representatives of the people" picked by random ballot … There is a press photo that made Lucie and I laugh a lot during the "Pond War," a photo in which the agreement to construct the aforementioned reservoirs was signed—believe it or not— on a large oval table in a cattle shed (corrugated iron roof, hay bales in the background) by the Minister for Ecological Affairs, a regional préfet in full regalia (golden officer's stripes, headgear of the same ilk [which the government officially refers to as an *embroidered tricorne*, which looks as if an eighteenth-century sailor's tricorne was swallowed by a Stetson hat and sprayed with golden shit by a magical dove]; my bad—in bureaucratic terms this is *operational clothing*), while fourteen people, twelve men, all of them bald, all of them weathered by the years, all of them over sixty, look on. Two women matched against twelve men all of whom are leaving by life's back door, and whose youthful decisions one can only imagine.

What was needed was a *protocolian* war, a hulking benevolent giant, guardian of environmental thought, who would march in, overturn this table, sweep away the agreement, and rain down the bales of hay on the bad faith of these "local actors," a hay bale for the minister, one each for the ecofriendly politicians, a hay bale for the government, one for the farmers, another for the elected representatives: Gargantua would probably have done a lot worse, he would have rammed the delegates, one by one, up a cow's ass, there to contemplate the meaning of life and methane production in the bovine *saccus merdae* for a few days.

Unfortunately, there is no Gargantua to save the planet or even the Deux-Sèvres from absurd decisions. Let us, as Panurge would say, return to our sheep. Lucie was deeply invested in the fight against these artificial reservoirs; she took part in all the protest marches, the leafleting, the meetings—I took a back seat, a position that I felt suited the University, but then I had the idea of writing an article for *Libération*: Paris and the whole of France needed to be informed of these noble battles. So, I wrote a little article, which I tried to disseminate; I asked for Calvet's help— and I cannot resist the temptation to quote his reply:

I can't advise you strongly enough to focus on your thesis—I feel that you have lost your way. Get your act together! Be master and navigator of your life! Do not let your subject consume you!

That really stung.

My subject, it seemed, had already devoured me.

I gazed into the gray eyes of Lucie beside me, her tenderness, her energy, her wisdom; I needed to make a decision. I felt lost. I remember going for a long walk through the Marais, strolling for several hours along by the water between Magné and Coulon. So, what now? I couldn't imagine myself going back to Paris at the end of the year, leaving Lucie, leaving this place. I remember at one point, standing on the towpath with my feet in the mud, I said to myself, you've been consumed by your thesis. The terrain has swallowed you whole... In front of me, I could see green waters, a line of poplars, a field bounded by irrigation channels; some guy was drifting past in a black boat with a dog (a Newfoundland?)

calmly sitting in the prow, tongue lolling, watching the water and the banks flash past. The man nodded to me without pausing. Sitting at the stern, he rowed powerfully and steadily, always on the same side. The weather was grayish and slightly chilly. Behind me, and behind their fence, two horses stood next to each other, grazing. From the distance came the sound of a chainsaw or a Weedwhacker. I had been here for five months. I was getting to know the place, to understand it. My Insta was teeming with photos of marshlands and vegetables. I loved the people, the landscape, my life at the Savage Mind. I think that, at some point, every ethnographer or anthropologist has wondered whether they belong to the environment they chronicle. Maybe not Malinowski, who spent his time bitching about the long nights he spent under canvas; then again, deciding whether to make a life for yourself in the remote Pacific or in an equatorial rainforest with tribespeople who shrink heads is more complicated than it is in the Deux-Sèvres. *Paris by Train—Only Two and a Half Hours,* as the tourist office and the SNCF proclaim.

NEW TIMETABLES! MORE DEPARTURES! FASTER JOURNEY TIMES!

I suddenly felt that I needed to talk to Lara. Something was unresolved. I needed to see her again, to bid a symbolic farewell to Paris, and I also needed to spend some time with my mother, who is a font of good advice.

I beckoned the horses behind the fence; they shambled over, looking at me curiously. I slipped my hand through the wire mesh—luckily it wasn't an electric fence. I thought, if they let me stroke them and don't bite, I'll stay and become a market gardener, I'll settle down with Lucie. It was the first time I consciously formulated this thought.

The horses craned their long heads toward my hand, I stroked one soft brown muzzle; the other licked my fingers, perhaps thinking they contained a treat.

I took out my phone and jotted down the following ideas:

Learn to row.

Learn to ride a horse.

And I finished my walk, thinking about my upcoming trip to Paris.

October 20

On my way back to the Savage Mind, having bought a TGV ticket to Paris for the following week (in exchange for an arm and a leg, or a kidney, or a three-figure sum, may God strike them down), I composed a little poem in the style of Villon:

> *Item: great Calvet, I decree,*
> *Shall fashion eclogues pure as glass,*
> *Right good manure for field and lea,*
> *The twelve-month product of my ass.*[1]

In gratitude to my distinguished mentor for all his help, I wrote this quatrain on the back of a postcard of a cow on a barge in the Marais with the intention of sending it to Paris, but compassion (or cowardice, let's face it) prevented me from doing so.

Somewhere online, I read that *item* is a legacy or bequest in a will. I'm really enjoying this François Villon.

To celebrate, as it were, I took Lucie for a spin in the Argo to visit Saint-Maixent. My sudden desire to see this little village made Lucie laugh. Most of the people there are soldiers, she said. There's a military school for noncommissioned officers. Not so many poets from the Middle Ages. From *the late* Middle Ages, if you don't mind, I said.

> *Item: my body now deceased*
> *To grandame earth I do consign;*

1. Mazon, David, *Complete Poems*, vol. 2, "Quatrains," p. 111, Bibliothèque de la Pléiade, Paris. For the meaning of the word *eclogue*, see p. 379.

Though worms will think it meager feast
So much hath I made hunger mine.[1]

Although I know Villon spent his last days in Saint-Maixent under the protection of the local abbot, it is only because Rabelais mentions it in his fourth book. (Rabelais also tells the story of how Maître François managed to rid himself of a monk named Tappecoue in a fantastical and gruesomely bloody episode in which Niort and Saint-Liguaire are mentioned.) This whole region is full of great forgotten men. I'm sure that if people looked hard enough, they'd find some more recent ones too. In a few years there will be a plaque: "The French writer and ruralist David Mazon, author of … and …, a leading figure in the reform of food culture, visited Saint-Maixent and graced this humble tavern with his presence on April 17."

So it was that, in a restaurant with a pretty timber-fronted facade near the abbey of Saint-Maixent (an impressive site, much ruined during the Wars of Religion, a forgotten period of history, I feel—a little research is required), that I proposed to Lucie, not a marital union but a business partnership. I said to her, Listen, you know your mother's land, the farm in Gâtine? Well, I was wondering if you would take me as your partner. I've got a little money that my father left me, you provide the land, we borrow the rest and we set up in business. Fruits, berries and vegetables. What do you think?

And then came the brutal slap in the face:

"Ha! Ha! that's very sweet, David, but you don't know shit, you can't tell a pea from a dandelion. And I'm sorry, but I promised myself I'd never work with a boyfriend again. I'm really sorry. Besides, this land is leased …"

I was furious. WTF? Did no one appreciate my skills? Did no one want my money? Was I being made to pay for Franck's mis-

1. François Villon, *The Great Testament*, LXXXVI.

takes? This was a terrible injustice. I can put up with anything, except injustice.

I ostentatiously paid the bill to show her how much she had humiliated me and didn't open my mouth—or almost—on the way home. And God knows it takes a hell of a lot to shut David Mazon up.

I felt desolate as a swath of alfalfa.

Fortunately, the rumble of the Argo's engine filled the silence.

"But I'm glad you brought up the subject, I need to have another talk with my mother about the land."

I said nothing. I dropped her off at her house and drove back to the Savage Mind feeling heartsick. I spent the whole afternoon lying on the bed with a cat in each arm staring at the ceiling. That night I played Tetris to try and take my mind off things, but it was futile. I thought long and hard about whether my desire to move here could survive a breakup with Lucie. During our weekend in Nancy, Maman had told me not to let myself get too carried away. I could always move to Nancy, I thought. As provincial towns go, it's a serious step up from Niort, I can't deny it. Nancy can boast a baroque cathedral. And the Dukes of Lorraine, the Grand Siècle, the Macaron sisters, art nouveau. Otherwise, it's like being between Scylla and Charybdis, if Scylla were slightly bigger than Charybdis. But there would be no Lucie, no Marais. No ocean. Only Germany, with Metz and Strasbourg close by, the Vosges, Champagne, Alsace . . . A center-right bourgeoisie, a streetcar line. Mirabelle plum brandy. A streetcar line. Bergamot oranges. A streetcar line. Saint-Epvre cakes. A streetcar line.

I spent the whole day and the following night holed up in the dark with the cats, then drove the Argo to Niort station and left her in the long-term parking lot; I remember sleeping like a log on the train and waking up just as the TGV® was pulling into the Gare Montparnasse. I hope I didn't snore—the shame of it.

My first steps in Paris, with my rucksack slung on my shoulder: I felt as though I had emerged from a tunnel. When I left

Montparnasse, I felt so happy that I decided to go home on foot, a half-hour stroll heading south; the square Georges-Brassens hadn't changed, nor the rue de Danzig, and Maman even less.

*

I stayed three days. I was happy to be at home (well, at Maman's place). Lara was an unavoidable mistake. Tears, heartbreak, fury. I don't think we'll ever see each other again. No matter how often I apologized, it didn't help. I was pretty sad myself as I left the Bassin de l'Arsenal, despite the glorious sunshine that Paris alone seems to be able to sometimes produce in spring; the weather was warm, the Seine beneath the Pont d'Austerlitz gleamed, the Jardin des Plantes rustling with burgeoning buds.

"Did you know the botanical garden in Niort city center is also called the Jardin des Plantes? It's exactly the same, set on the banks of the river, and built in the same era?"

Lara looked at me as if I were a half-wit. I'd arranged to meet her on the corner of rue Cuvier and rue Linné, at the majestic entrance to the gardens, thinking that we might walk to Bastille—a walk seemed less intimidating than sitting face-to-face on a café terrace. Lara was glacial. It reminded me of *Doctor Zhivago*.

Even the monumental gates of the Jardin des Plantes in Niort look just like these, I added. Though obviously, they're not on the same scale; and another thing, the cathedral in Niort is called Notre-Dame. And people often confuse the Sèvre and the Seine in conversation.

Lara gave precisely zero fucks. She alternated between hot tears and black fury. Her cheeks, usually so diaphanous, were flushed with a rage she could not put into words.

"You're a complete fucking bastard. Say one more thing about how Paris is like Niort and I'll kick you in the balls and walk away. Is your little whore from Niort?"

Her face was contorted by her ugly words.

Lara had been transformed into a hideous Gorgon, whose

frustration, sadly, I could completely understand. I had said nothing to her about Lucie; I wondered how she had guessed. I opted for a facile answer:

"There's no whore, you don't have to worry about me."

"You really are a first-rate asshole. I've supported you all these years, I've encouraged you, we've built our worlds around each other and now you're leaving me to move to a shithole with some whore."

I didn't know what to say, so I lied:

"I never said I was leaving you."

"That's brave of you—you're a complete asshole."

We had passed the Jardin des Plantes and were walking by the Muséum d'Histoire Naturelle.

I thought about plants, about apes, about animals that became human. She was right, I was a coward and a bastard.

"You're right, I'm a coward and a bastard."

"Are you fucking with me? Fucking scumbag. Why did you even ask to meet? So you'd have a clear conscience?"

I could no longer remember the reason I had come to Paris. I had a lump in my throat. The silence dragged. Icy tears tricked down Lara's cheeks. All around, there was a complex ballet of strollers and nannies; it had to be five o'clock. Don't be so fucking spineless, David! Use a little psychology! I wanted to hug Lara, to comfort her—bad idea, she would have sent me packing. I was completely at a loss.

"I'm thinking of moving to the country," I said. "And becoming a farmer."

At this, Lara burst out laughing. A spontaneous, genuine, uncontrollable laugh; she was laughing and crying at the same time, she would laugh for a moment, pause for a few seconds and say "farmer," then laugh again. She was still laughing when we reached the Seine.

"Hey, look—it's the Sèvre!!"

October 21

Finally, there's been some good news about the farm: the Crédit
Agricole has officially agreed to lend us the money as soon as we
have legally registered Noble Savage Holdings as a Common Agricultural Operating Group. Mathilde and Gary gave me a lot of
help filling out applications for subsidies; we'll see if it all works
out. Farmers of the world, unite!

So, to get back to the story I was telling yesterday—Lara continued to ridicule me until we finally went our separate ways,
I was sad and upset, we didn't know whether to kiss or shake
hands, so in the end we just stood two meters apart and gave a
little wave goodbye—it was pathetic. I trudged back to Maman's
house in the fifteenth arrondissement, like a loser.

As I was walking back through the Jardin des Plantes, I told
myself that regardless of what happened with my relationship
with Lucie, I was better off away from Paris, in the Bas-Poitou,
which seemed to attract only natives and Englishmen.

I canceled my meeting with Calvet, I had nothing to say to
him.

I told my mother I was going to try and find some way to
stay on in Marais Poitevin, to settle down there. So, you want to
grow old in the marshes, as Duplessis-Mornay said to Henri IV,
she said with a smile. I didn't dare mention the idea of farming.

Two days later I was back at the Savage Mind, filled with a
sense of renewal, with that powerful zeal for reform that inhabits
a man or woman from the capital when he or she ends up in the
provinces. I had recharged the batteries that powered my pride
and arrogance. When I got off the train, I remember stopping at
the market, it was Thursday; it was difficult to find a place to park
on the banks of the Sèvre, opposite the covered market and the
castle. Okay, so it's not the Seine, far from it—despite a couple
of bookstalls on the quay outside the eyesore of a library—but

it's beautiful all the same, the medieval castle worthy of Robin Hood, the verdant river, the vast covered market with its fretwork roof of glass and wrought iron, the neo-Renaissance town hall: there were numerous local vendors (fruits and vegetables, goat cheese, flowers) on the forecourt, and quite a large crowd despite the sudden shower of fat raindrops. I took refuge in a bookshop opposite the market and leafed through local history books, finally decided to buy the volume of Michelet's *Histoire de France* devoted to the Wars of Religion, for my research, which started well: *My heart had been transfixed by the grandeur of the religious revolution, moved by the martyrs, whom I have been compelled to lead from their tender cribs, through their heroic deeds, thence to the stake there to witness their execution. In the face of such acts, books no longer mean anything. Each of these saints was a book in which humanity will read for all eternity.* Go, Michelet! This is going to be a blast, that's a brilliant opening. I also purchased a pocket guide to the flora and fauna of the Marais, with a special foldout waterproof map which would be handy for canoeing accidents, as well as walking tours—an excellent book, from which I have benefited greatly.

Bookshops are the soul of a country, embracing as they do local and foreign, childlike wonder and wisdom, backlist and new arrivals.

The bookseller rang up the two books and said that if I was planning to go for a walk in the Marais, the weather should be nice this weekend, it's usually very pleasant in the spring—an affable lady; if bookshops are the soul, then booksellers are the arms and legs of the nation. Right now, the weather is far from clement, more the kind that makes you think of buying a K-Way™ jacket; I half ran back to the Argo (I noticed she's taking in a bit of water—rain seeps through the rusty edge of the roof and ends up as a puddle beneath the pedals that moves and shifts as I accelerate and brake—it could be dangerous, I've no idea) and took the Coulonges road back to the Savage Mind, resisting the temptation to stop off on the way at Plaisirs Fermiers™ to buy an organic artisanal treat, and, proud of my strength of will, by one o'clock I was back at the Savage Mind, hungry, I opened a can of mackerel in tomato sauce, ate the mackerel in tomato sauce, thought of Arnaud, sent a text message to Lucie, "just back, what are you doing?" (I think the interrogative proposition "what are you doing?" is, together with "where are you?" the most widely shared on the planet, at least by text message), the answer came almost immediately, "having lunch. you?" to which I immediately replied "just polished off a can of mackerel, I want you," she typed back ":-) leek and potato soup here, hardly the same effect :-)," we agreed to meet up in the late afternoon, I was happy. The cats appeared almost immediately; I'd missed them too.

I went over to Mathilde and Gary's to tell them I was back; it had stopped raining; unsurprisingly Mathilde invited me to lunch the following day, so I could tell them everything; So, how was Paris?

Glad to be back, I said. Glad to be back.

October 22

Autumn is particularly rainy this year. In a single month, it's rained twenty-eight days, everything is soaked. It's not cold, it's warm and it's raining—like a monsoon. So, it's quite nice to be able to stay indoors and do paperwork and tell my life story to the computer. Lucie's not so lucky, she's out supervising the building of a glass greenhouse—greenhouse number one—she is going to be soaked as soup. Thinking about it, I could make her some soup for lunch, I have some delicious fish soup from the Île de Ré in a jar, and some leftover bread I can use to make croutons, and I promised her a tarte tatin for dessert—my cooking is improving by the day; tarte tatin made from our delicious Gâtine apples, lovingly handcrafted at Noble Savage Holdings using supermarket shortcrust pastry is divine. I must be hungry to be thinking of that. Anyway.

So, last spring when I came back from Paris, the weather was nice and warm, Franck's market garden was producing a bumper crop, Lucie was breaking sales records at the market, membership of the local AMAP farmers association was increasing daily. I don't remember who had the idea of spending a weekend in the Marais, Max I think, when he saw the guidebook with the waterproof map at the Savage Mind. One way or another, an expedition to the Marais was duly organized, with two boats, Max's, which was "parked" in Coulon, and Franck's friend's, moored a little upstream on the Sèvre. At first neither Lynn nor Lucie seemed taken by the idea, which they found a little bizarre—getting lost in the Marais, pitching a tent in a field to enjoy the wildlife, like the hide hunters of yesteryear—spotting herons, bluethroats, bluebirds, dragonflies, otters and the big bats known as Rhinolophidae, which I wasn't sure I wanted to see, to say nothing of the ubiquitous roe deer, foxes, owls and water rats that made up the fauna of the marshlands. Spring was certainly the most likely season to see all these animals and more, and I was very excited about the adventure, as was Max. Convincing Lynn and Lucie was not so difficult in the end; both knew the Marais well, having grown up nearby, and they weren't scared of a little camping.

Needless to say, this wild camping in the middle of the nettle fields was illegal but, as Max pointed out, it posed no risk, either to nature, to the owners of the fields, or to us. All we had to do, said Maximilien, was not behave like pigs. I took care of the logistics and our "equipage," as Hugo would say in *Ninety-Three*. Here is the list I drew up, for Lucie and me:

A Decathlon® express two-person tent

Two ultralight duvets for use at temperatures down to 3°C, by the same brand

Two down pillows borrowed from the Savage Mind

Two hand towels

Organic soap and shampoo just in case

A toiletry bag

A small first aid kit with Aspivenin® and insect repellent cream

A battery-operated radio, in case the world ended

A Bluetooth® speaker

A dinner set comprising two plates, two sets of cutlery and two metal tumblers

Fire starters

A windproof lighter

A bag of charcoal

A metal teapot

Two plastic cups

A cast-iron griddle

An icebox

Ice packs for the icebox

A round plastic basin to use as a washbasin

A twenty-liter jerrican of drinking water

Four rolls of toilet paper

A roll of tinfoil

A roll of string

A roll of trash bags

A flashlight + spare batteries

A compass

A pair of binoculars

Maps & charts

A foldable solar mobile phone charger

A Swiss Army knife

A travel salt shaker

Instant coffee

Sugar cubes

Oil, vinegar and a pepper grinder

A twenty-four-pack of Kronenbourg™ beers

Two bottles of Bordeaux

A couple of disposable rain ponchos just in case

A Frisbee and a set of Obut® pétanque balls—the latter in case we happened on a level field out in the Marais, which was unlikely. It was a lot of stuff, and I'm not even including the tons of food Max planned to bring: bags of chips, cans of olives, jars of rillettes, bread, meat for barbecues—enough to withstand a siege. The *equipage* was packed into two supposedly waterproof blue containers intended to protect our gear if we capsized. Of course, we didn't use half of it—except for the beers and the chips. The pétanque balls never left their natural habitat, the trunk of the car; the rain ponchos, fortunately, never needed to be unfolded. The compass, that magical contraption, was not used either—it's funny just how useless Waze™ and Google Maps™ are when you're traveling by boat, though GPS is still useful for locating yourself on the map. We certainly got lost in the labyrinth of channels and gullies, lost but not *lost*: there is a very real difference. The only obstacles we encountered were brambles, nettles and canal locks, which are not always designed to allow boats through without a lockkeeper. But anyway, let me take this in chronological order.

We set off in two cars, to rejoin the two boats; I was wearing khaki fatigues recently bought from Emmaüs, an army jacket from the same source, a headband like in *Apocalypse Now*, a pair of Ray-Bans™—the photos are hysterical, LOL, it looks like a redneck reunion in the Louisiana bayou. Lucie was just wearing a sweatshirt and tracksuit pants. Now I have to confess a horrible truth: I'm a shitty rower. It's hard to admit, but Lucie is much better than I am. When she's at the helm, sitting in the stern, everything's fine, the boat glides straight down the river; when I'm rowing, there's a lot of bumping and bashing and we weave all over the canal; right stroke—whack! into the bank, left stroke—whack! into a tree trunk, and so on.

The expedition was not doing much for my sense of manhood. It was eight in the morning, the sky was clear blue, we pushed off from the pier, heading for La Garette where we were to meet Lynn and Max, who would set off an hour later, I had a Spotify "Swamp Bangers" playlist blaring on the Bluetooth® speaker, the river was glorious, Instagram® worthy. In the middle of the boat sat the blue containers containing all the essentials, and a small suitcase with all the stuff I hadn't been able to fit into the blue containers. I looked at the map, calculated our position by the sun, and said, It's that way, which made Lucie roar with laughter, Of course it's that way, where else would it be? I started rowing, and that's how I found out that it's not as easy as it looks. After ten minutes spent arguing and running aground twice, I was demoted to cabin boy and forced to give up my place at the tiller. Life is tough, but I have to admit that with Lucie rowing we were moving twice as fast and—more importantly—in a straight line. So, I sat in the prow and provided potential energy.

Obviously, we could have taken one boat, they were large enough to accommodate four of us and our belongings, but Max and I felt that a boat for two was more stylish, more luxurious— and more in keeping with a scientific expedition, just as the Niña and the Pinta had sailed together in the past: we had decided to embark upon this expedition flying the flag of science, of the naturalists of yesteryear. Max played along, and even brought a magnificent folding easel of varnished wood, which, he claimed, with immense joy, had traveled to Algeria with Delacroix and seen the women of Algiers! He also brought his box of watercolors: I genuinely hoped that our adventure would afford him time to paint from life, like the explorers.

For me, the biggest revelation of the weekend, aside from the wonders of the marshlands and the Rousseauean pleasures of the wild, was Lynn. Not only was she cheerful and bursting with energy, but (and this was a surprise!) she knew the Marais like the back of her hand: in her teens, she had spent several summers piloting a tourist boat, she had piloted hundreds of tourists through the conches and the channels, had told them about the pollarded ash trees, the dragonflies, the otters, etc.; had told them about daily life in the Marais, standing on a boat with a large chestnut punt known as a *pigouille*, etc.; for our expedition she had taken both a paddle for deep waters and the long wooden punt—when we met up, it was such a surprise to see her standing in the stern of the *plate*,[1] maneuvering easily in the traditional fashion by planting the punt into the mud: this was how boats had been propelled around the Marais for generations. Max had settled himself and was half-lying in the prow sketching—clearly, he had no intention of rowing, except, he said, when his *favorite engine* got tired, which, judging by the aforesaid engine's athletic physique, looking impossibly elegant with her hair tied up in a scarf like a 1950s tourist advertisement for Israel, would not happen anytime soon.

So off we went. Traveling through villages by waterway is a lot of fun, seeing the backs of the houses, discovering a whole world that is invisible from the street; the vegetable gardens, the stacks of firewood, the sheds, the swings, all along the banks. So quiet and so leisurely. I had turned off the Swamp Bangers playlist, preferring to save the speaker battery and enjoy the silence. We chatted—Lucie told me a little about the flora; Until a few years ago, she said, there were duckweeds everywhere. We would set off walking and the boat would cut a swathe through the duckweed, and it felt like you were walking on water. Now it's all gone. The water temperature has risen, there has been an increase in water treatment plants and the fragile balance of the flora has been completely transformed. These days, it's difficult to imagine that these unending canals (several thousand kilometers, according to Lynn) were once completely green; a footpath for insects. Max lay daydreaming, his hands behind his head; soon we left the main branch of the Sèvre and ventured into the meandering

---

1. The name given to the flat-bottomed boats of the Marais.

tributaries. I followed our route on the map as best I could, it was no easy feat; we were now gliding beneath the ash trees and the poplars whose budding bright-green leaves reflected the sun; at times, rays of blinding light pierced some gap in the canopy and played upon the muddy waters. I was completely exhilarated by the beauty of the journey. I couldn't help but shout Yeehaw!!! like a circus cowboy. It was a beautiful day, a little cool in the shade, but the rowing kept us warm. Max sat facing the stern, sketching Lynn as she steadily dug her *pigouille* into the mud, pushed to propel the boat forward, then deftly withdrew it in a series of quick strokes—I've lost my touch a bit, she said.

Needless to say, we did not see a single wild animal all morning—perhaps because we were too noisy—a few birds fluttered away as we approached, some of them quite large, but we (or, at least, I) could not identify them; this bird-watching lark is complicated, you can't say to a little egret, Hang on a second, little egret, I'm just looking through my guide, don't fly away just yet, when you know that there's nothing more skittish (or swift) than a bird. So, despite my binoculars, I quickly gave up trying to identify the birds. Every now and then Max would mock me, shouting, David! David! Look, a crab-footed heron! or, a dancing loon! and some equally comical aberrations. But, on such a beautiful day in such marvelous company, nothing could annoy me: not my ignorance of the animal kingdom, nor my inability to navigate in a straight line, they can make fun all they like, I'll shut them all up with my fire-starting skills: I've read the book, I've got the *Apocalypse Now* headband, the sunglasses, the Zippo™, I'll be fine.

Lucie rowed with metronomic rhythm, she was happy, smiling, telling me stories about growing up in the country. Since it would soon be lunch, I set about making sandwiches for everyone. Lynn and Lucie clearly knew where they were headed, a field that belonged to someone they knew, with a kind of natural harbor where we could tie up and a picnic table where we could eat: heaven. The ground was not too marshy, just a little muddy; it was a square field fifty meters wide completely surrounded by water; the sides of the quadrilateral were planted with tall poplars (old enough to be sold, according to Lucie. Poplars are sold to sawmills while still in the ground, lumberjacks come to cut them down and take away the timber—in autumn or winter, if the area isn't flooded, otherwise in spring; and as it happens, in the distance, we could hear what sounded like chainsaws); the middle of the field was a wild meadow, with tall nettles and an old hayrick in one corner. We put in on a slope provided for this purpose (I managed to get stuck in the mud up to my socks—nice one, David). A wooden picnic table (untreated planks, rusty nails and benches) was set in a corner near the hayrick.

"How does your friend transport his cows here, by the way," I asked naively.

"He waits for a fine day to helicopter them in," said Lynn. "Come back in a month's time, you'll see flocks of helicopters coming and going with cows dangling underneath. Then they set them down in the meadow and come back to collect them in late autumn."

I almost believed her.

"By boat, of course," laughed Lucie.

I suddenly realized that the postcard of the cow in the punt I'd intended to send Calvet wasn't just some piece of folklore.

"The practice is dying out. Hardly anyone grazes cattle on the inaccessible fields anymore, it's too complicated. But a few breeders still do."

There was no risk of our being disturbed, obviously. One side of the field opened onto a slightly narrower gully, spanned by a small wooden bridge; the bridge led to another field, shielded by a tall bramble hedgerow; aside from this narrow passageway, our campsite was inaccessible. We unloaded our stuff, I put my

Swamp Bangers playlist back on and explained that it was Louisiana beats from the boglands.

"We don't have alligators here yet," said Max, "though if the temperature of the water keeps rising, it could happen. And the water rats will have something to worry about."

I imagined huge sluggish, sharp-toothed reptiles eating beavers and gnawing on a tourist's leg from time to time—a strange prospect. Though the prospect seemed to me to be quite remote.

So, to the demonic rhythms of Jamie Bergeron, Sal Melancon and their Kickin' Cajuns, we pitched camp. We put the tents up in a sheltered area where the ground was not so muddy. I unfolded the oilcloth and we had lunch: sandwiches, hard-boiled eggs, tomatoes, a salad Lucie had made. The temperature was perfect, we were in the sun, but not too much; insects buzzed around us, birds fluttered to the rhythm of the Cajun accordion, the beer from the icebox was exquisitely chilled, I was sitting next to Lucie; sheer bliss.

Max spent the whole weekend painting, mostly abstract watercolors, the surface of the waters, grasses, reflections, and beautiful portraits of Lynn, Lucie and even me as a bayou or Vietnam War–style "swamp soldier"—pretty funny.

In the afternoon we separated; Max and Lynn stayed at the camp, while Lucie and I took a little trip in the boat. It was romantic, being alone together in a punt—even if said punt was neither comfortable nor exactly designed for erotic activities, though it has to be said that the prospect that tourists and guides might appear at the bend of a waterway added a little spice to the proceedings, while the risk of capsizing, all too real in the case of such gymnastic contortions, required great caution.

Toward nightfall, Max and I went hunting: in the absence of otters, I was hoping to spot some ragondins, which are usually active during twilight. And there they were: large and skittish, with long tubular tails and long tinted incisors (I didn't believe it, but it turned out to be true), which turned out to be orange colored. The moment we came within ten meters, they leapt into the water. They have a dark coat that, to me, looks like beaver fur.

Lucie told me that once, many years earlier, Franck had shot several with a .22, butchered one and put it on the barbecue. Apparently it was pretty disgusting—maybe they need to be marinated in Cajun spices for two or three days to be halfway edible.

The ragondins are the only animals we saw—but we heard dozens more. At night in the tent, separated from the wild by a meager millimeter of fabric—my God!—you hear all manner of creatures, twigs cracking and some loud breathing (I was scared shitless): apparently, wild boars are famous for their heavy breathing. (It's also possible that it was Max snoring, although he vehemently denied it the following morning and—probably out of compassion—Lynn didn't comment.)

That night, I was in charge of the fire—I didn't do too badly; no snowdrifts fell from the poplars to extinguish it (there was no bitter cold to freeze our feet, no churlish dog:[1] Lucie had left it at home). Of course, I cheated—I had fire starters and charcoal—but I grilled ribs like a pro thanks to a metal griddle placed directly on the embers.[2] Everyone agreed it was a wonderful dinner; the potatoes in tinfoil were perfectly charred; the claret was acceptable (thankfully I'd remembered my Swiss Army knife with its corkscrew) and warmed us up—with the glowing embers and Lucie's arm around my shoulder I wasn't cold. Luckily, in a corner of the field, I had stumbled across a pile of firewood that wasn't too damp; from time to time I tossed a branch onto the glowing coals and it burst into flames, casting an orange glow on the faces of Max and Lynn, frozen in an embrace before us. Gradually the night became chilly and wet, and there was noth-

1. Cf. London, Jack, *To Build a Fire*, 1908.
2. Mazon, David, *The Swamp Pot: Cajun Survival Cooking*, Éditions de la Grenouille Empalée, Niort.

ing but a crescent moon to light our way: when the flames had died down, we couldn't see a thing. Eventually we began to shiver and retired to the tents; it was nearly ten o'clock. Max, unsurprisingly, had thought to bring an air mattress—Lucie and I had to sleep on the hard Marais ground, and despite the supposed telluric and initiatory benefits of such a practice, by morning, what with the humidity (the tent was dripping condensation) and the lack of vegetation beneath the groundsheet, I was aching all over—my hips felt dislocated, my lumbar region ached. While Max and Lynn allowed themselves to sleep in, Lucie and I just wanted to get up, get some fresh air and stretch our legs.

At dawn, the Marais was spellbinding—trails of fog skittered across the water like dragons, the woods rustled with unfamiliar birdsong, while the dawn light stained everything it touched with red. I had difficulty relighting the fire but managed to boil enough water for a cup of instant coffee. Then Lucie and I rowed the boat to Coulon to buy fresh bread—it's funny, rowing to the nearest bakery, and parking your craft as though it were a bicycle. Lynn and Max were amazed when they finally emerged from their tent to find croissants—Lucie really is brilliant and resourceful, something our weekend in the marshes only served to confirm.

October 24

I remember that I felt a little melancholy when we got back to the Savage Mind; returning is tough when you fall from verdant paradise to murky civilization. In spite of this magnificent communion in the Marais (where, among other things, I discovered that Lucie had skills other than being handy with an oar), I felt very frustrated by her refusal to accept my proposal that we set up a farm; I thought that in the intimacy of nature we might make progress on this subject, but this proved not to be the case: I tried subtly broaching the topic, but to no avail. All I discovered was that she had talked to her mother and asked what was happening with the land. Which might be the breakthrough...

Unfortunately, it was precisely during this slough of despond (hence, some weeks after our muggy, rodent-infested nirvana) that we had our first real argument. It was all the more heartbreaking because the only things to blame were me, my delusions of adequacy in farming matters, the hurt I had felt in the restaurant in Saint-Maixent and my desire for revenge.

Like all arguments, the inciting incident was trivial, indeed insignificant. I hereby set down my version of events.

The Lovers of Verona
A pastoral drama in one act
Scene I

A quiet afternoon at the Savage Mind. It is raining outside. (Laughter from the audience.)

DAVID (turning up the volume on Radio Nostalgie®): Do you like Henri Salvador? I love this song.

(*Sound off: "I long to see old Syracuse..."*)

LUCIE (*half-sprawled on the bed, gestures toward the ceiling, grabs a passing cat and hums*): Fair Rouen and Easter Isle...

DAVID (*sitting on the bed, dressed as Eve*): *Kai-rou-an,* not Rouen—ha!—that's not funny.

LUCIE (*genuinely surprised*): I was thinking that Rouen didn't sound very exotic.

DAVID: I know, right?

LUCIE: So, where exactly is Kairouan?

DAVID: I'm not sure, probably somewhere near Easter Island.

LUCIE: And who are the lovers of Verona?

DAVID: The lovers of Verona, that really doesn't ring a bell? You're completely unschooled, my love.

LUCIE: That's a horrible thing to say. Why?

DAVID (*falsely ironic*): Honestly, only a complete moron who grew up in the ass end of nowhere wouldn't know who the lovers of Verona are.

LUCIE (*deeply offended*): Stop that, what's the matter with you?

DAVID (*hammering the point home*): No shit, you really don't know anything—didn't you go to school like everyone else?

LUCIE (*hurt*): Are you making fun of me? Of course I went to school—everyone does. Besides, who gives a shit about the lovers of Verona?

DAVID (*spitefully pretentious*): Anyone who doesn't recognize *Romeo and Juliet* didn't go to school. And no, it's not a Netflix series. It's Shakespeare.

Lucie pulls on her clothes, storms out, slamming the door.

Five minutes after she left, I was still buzzing and thinking I was in the right; I was yelling at the cats, I mean—how can anyone not know Shakespeare? and the more I took my rage out on the cats the worse I felt. What was wrong with me? What was this sudden rage? Where had this sudden spurt of anger come from? After an hour, despite several text messages, she hadn't come back, so I decided to take the car (it was still raining cats and dogs, it had been raining like an incontinent cow for the two weeks since we came back from our weekend in the marshlands, and all this rain rotted your brain, turned it into a sponge) and drive to her house to apologize. Her car wasn't there. I parked at the end of her street and waited; I didn't want see Arnaud, who would insist that we play something, I didn't want Lucie to come home and find me in the middle of a game of dominoes with her cousin, since a three-way conversation would be awkward; so I stayed in my car and texted her; when, after an hour, she hadn't come back, I went home.

That night, there was no news, and I went to bed with a heavy heart.

The following day at noon, I'd still had no news, so I sent Lucie a voice message—a poem I'd found online ...

> *And when I thus espy these melons that await your care,*
> *And wilting blossoms wondering whither thou dost err*
> *Perchance art at some village fete, beguiling some man's daughter*
> *While here today they wane and wilt, and all for lack of water.*[1]

... shamelessly plagiarized from some guy called Nicolas Boileau, who seems to have been a gardening blogger, in the hope that it would make her laugh and come back here to do some watering, although it's been raining for weeks. And then I thought this was just another way of crushing her with my erudite sophistication, another piece of David-fucking-Mazon pedantry, poetry, even if it is cribbed from the internet—so I deleted the voice message before she listened to it.

I felt completely helpless.

Incredibly sad, and hurt that I had hurt her.

I eschewed leguminous poetry and recorded another message, one that was heartfelt and utterly desperate, *I'm so sorry Lucie, please come back, I feel terrible that I hurt you. Please.* And, while I waited, I brooded; I wondered where I'd come by this bullshit sense of superiority, I mean, yeah, I'd been to college, but I'd never studied Shakespeare, never read a single line, I was ignorant, completely ignorant and my erudition was like a haze of insecticide sprayed from a can: erratic, toxic and quick to disperse. Wisdom is the only thing that matters, actual knowledge, not names learned by heart tossed out like the advertising slogans you remember from your teens, the lovers of Verona, the Prince of Denmark, the daughter of Minos and Pasiphaë.

I had to get down on my knees with a bunch of flowers to

1. Nicolas Boileau, *Epistles*, XI, "To my gardener."

Lucie to persuade her to accept my apology. I even broke open my piggy bank and invited her to come to Italy with me for four days in June, Verona, Padua, Venice, a proper honeymoon, and she agreed. Verona is really beautiful, even if the crowds of tourists outside the balcony at Juliet's house are like those at the Eiffel Tower every Sunday—and that's not much of an exaggeration.

Thinking back on it today—now that Lucie and I are settled into Noble Savage Holdings in the Gâtine, and things between us are going well, now that we have a hundred apple trees and land enough for five hectares of fruits and vegetables (Lucie) and aromatics and medicinal herbs (David), a number of high tunnels and greenhouses under construction, a local farmers' association that's growing by the day, four restaurants that buy up the bulk of what we're producing, and plans to invest in a microfactory producing homemade soups—"DocSavage" Cajun Soup® (mock–swamp alligator), Pumpkinhead® (squash and chestnut); with several more varieties to come, including Not All Weed Is Smoked® (spinach and sow thistle); all recipes devised by the great David Mazon and his trusty friend the Thermomix™—now that Lucie has finally come to an arrangement with Franck allowing her to sell part of her production for the next two years while our own vegetables bed in—all our Shakespearean melodramatics seem so trivial.

But I think it helped me to realize not only how much I cared about Lucie, but how much I cared about my new life—anyway, right now, I need to open up my spreadsheet and sort out the budget for the soup laboratory; I've just gotten a quote for etching the glass bottles. The autoclave sterilizer has already cost an arm and a leg ... I'm really going to need to think the whole thing through. I've got a meeting with the manager of the local Super U next door, a really nice guy, and he's going to give me a quick intro to pricing and distribution.

Get cracking, David!

October 24 (contd.)

Read an article in *La Nouvelle République* about the arrest of the
marauding goat-strangling zoophile, how a militia of breeders
and farmers tracked him down, spending days and nights view-
ing live footage from strategically placed webcams until they
caught him in flagrante delicto. I can only imagine his shame.
There's going to be a public trial, unless the judge orders it to be
heard *in camera* because of the potential danger to public morals.

Poor bastard. Poor goats. It inspired me to write another little
poem for Calvet:

> *Item: on Calvet I bestow*
> *This she-goat's fleece, this pelt ornate*
> *His fair Amalthea to know*
> *And biblically to fornicate.*[1]

Ha ha! A charming tale of the mythological goat who suckled
the mighty Zeus. That's where we get the star sign Capricorn:
Zeus is said to have transformed his beloved she-goat Amalthea
into a constellation of stars. Speaking of which, what does my
horoscope say?

Gemini: Your positive attitude will once again help you to
overcome a potentially difficult situation.

Luckily, I have a positive attitude.

The real change in our circumstances took place some weeks
later, when we finally had the opportunity to take over the lands
owned by Lucie's mother Françoise in the Gâtine, about twenty
kilometers north of La Pierre-Saint-Christophe and the Savage
Mind, close to the little town of Secondigny. A middle ground
between desolate plains and small enclosed fields, between limestone and hard granite; the Gâtine Vendéenne is primarily a land
of orchards and livestock, a wooded, hilly country, crisscrossed

1. Mazon, David, *Complete Poems*, vol. 1, "Ballads," p. 641, Bibliothèque de la
Pléiade, Paris.

by hedgerows. A pretty landscape. Lucie hadn't been there for years, so we took the Argo and paid a little visit to the farmer then leasing the Mill Farm, between the river Thouet and the Sèvre, halfway between Secondigny and Vernoux-en-Gâtine. Needless to say, we'd hardly gotten into the car when Lucie started moaning, "What's the deal with your car—it reeks of Thomas! It's absolutely putrid. Have you noticed there are blowfly larvae in the trunk? And in case it slipped your attention, it's raining inside your Rolls-Royce! It's unbelievable, there's a puddle under my feet! Are you trying to learn to row while you drive? Is the screwdriver in the window frame in case of a zombie attack? Stab them in the eye like *The Walking Dead*?"

In short, I was subjected to specious attacks about how my car stank, wasn't watertight, had no working heater and the AC was on the fritz—all of which I'll happily admit, okay? But I'm a perfectly decent driver, I drive in a straight line and not, as Lucie sneered, "all over the road and back again"—a sarcastic reference to my rowing skills that was totally uncalled for.

Together, the Argo and I transported the princess-of-the-pea to safe harbor.

The farm made a real impression on us. A beautiful, gently sloping orchard; fields sheltered from the wind; a small path of woodland, a fine, not-too-crumbling stone farmhouse, various sheds and outbuildings; the river at the bottom of the hill, and, according to the farmer leasing the land, deep, well-drained soil ideal for market gardening.

On the drive back, having spent half a day visiting the fields and the buildings, inspecting almost every individual tree, not wanting to get our hopes up about taking over the land, shouting to be heard over the roar of the Argo's engine as we drove via Scillé, Le Busseau and Coulonges back to La Pierre-Saint-Christophe, we began to make our first tentative plans. We had both fallen in love with the place. It's huge, Lucie kept saying. Much bigger than I remember. And very sheltered, ideal for greenhouses, well oriented—on the right side of the hill, south-facing, over-looking the valley. The slope is good, not too steep. But what are we going to do with all the apple trees ... ? Fruit is hard work. You have to spray it, wage a constant war against worms, all kinds of crap, pick up windfalls twice a week, and so on. Then you have to find somewhere to store the apples so you can sell them until spring. And do people even buy apples?

"Yeah, well if they're good, sure, otherwise, we juice them, we have loads of room to store bottles."

And that's how, gradually, thanks in part to the apple trees, the ideas came.

Lucie would grow her own vegetables, that would be her thing—ten thousand square meters of organic, progressive per-maculture, with the rest of the land being used for other crops (potatoes, which take up a huge amount of space, especially if they're organic) to help with crop rotation. I would only help out as necessary (weeding, picking, gathering, etc.). I would be responsible for apples, general marketing and distribution (farm-ers' markets, new outlets, AMAP, etc.) and especially, processing the surplus: juices, preserves.

David Mazon had a farm. E-I-E-I-O.

This separation of roles allowed Lucie to envisage working with an idiot like me; she could picture working with an idiot whose positive qualities she nonetheless acknowledged: enthu-siasm, a positive attitude, an expertise in written and oral presen-tations, a thirst for knowledge and passion for all things new, and above all, brute strength.

To quote my adviser Gontrand: the skill set of someone who has only one.

But most importantly, the essential: by preserving the hedge-rows, caring for the soil, minimizing chemical inputs, creating spaces for foragers and birds, reducing our need for irrigation, we could save a few hectares of the planet—a few planted hectares that would suck tons of CO_2 from the atmosphere, provide shade, promote the condensation of dew, etc. Lowering temperatures a few degrees in summer; a straw in the wheel of the Apocalypse.

A glorious plan.

We decided that we two would be the only livestock on the farm.

We were so enthusiastic that we loved each other like rutting deer, except in spring. Lucie's uncertainties about working with me gradually faded; the winds of passion dispelled the clouds of worry. Very soon, much sooner than we anticipated, and with a large sum of money from us, the current tenant farmer (a distant cousin of Lucie's) retired and moved to Marennes, "where he dipped his wick" (Lucie's mother's version).

It was at this point that I discovered the Chambre d'agriculture, that Monsieur Gontrand entered my life and all my administrative problems began.

Meanwhile Lucie had to deal with the headaches of converting the farm (selling and replacing outdated equipment, tilling and planting crops [potatoes, alfalfa, onions] that we didn't know what to do with, forecasting rotations, finding new sales networks. In short, so many questions to which M. Gontrand was—finally—able to provide sound answers); my headaches involved pruning the apple trees, spraying the crop, hours spent reading incomprehensible articles about the breeding habits of pests, codling moths and other nasty creepy-crawlies that I was only too happy to dispatch to kingdom come or to the neighboring farm: tenderfoot, go lay your eggs elsewhere.

By mid-May, the legal front lines had been manned and the banking wars were raging.

I found the perfect name: *Among the Noble Savages*, thereby joining Montaigne, Rousseau, Lévi-Strauss and the gentle art of *brand recognition* so beloved of marketing experts.

There is a connection between Hellenic studies and agriculture: the amount of investment required to earn a meager salary after five years is *colossal*.

All this without even renovating the farmhouse, apart from a lick of paint, four kitchen units from IKEA™ and some furniture from Emmaüs.

August, the month of omens and shooting stars, the second month of our time there, was magical. It was sweltering, but we were fine. We were harvesting apples; Lucie was making great progress with her plans and her first growing beds; we ate the vegetables planted by our predecessor; we managed to sell half the crop of onions cheaply and stored a couple of hundred kilos in the cellar; we threw a potato-sorting party, which was lots of fun; we'd pretty much given up tending the potatoes, so had to throw away a third of them because they were green—we had fairground music and disco lights, there were barbecued sausages and fifteen kilos of homemade fries, we invited everyone for miles around—all the way to Secondigny and everyone from La Pierre-Saint-Christophe; Max and Lynn, Mathilde, Gary, Arnaud of course, even Martial, the undertaker-in-chief, Paco and his friends from the Café-Pêche, Franck, not forgetting Kate and James, my London friends, and they all lent a hand sorting the potatoes, before dancing and partying into the wee small hours.

Max, the sneaky bastard, gave me a present: two little black-and-white long-eared pigs, a breed from the Basque country called Euskal Txerria, that he had driven all the way to the deepest darkest Pyrenees to fetch. He said to me, They'll eat all the windfall apples and the green potatoes, it's the perfect solution, you just let them trot around—and he was right; they get on pretty well with the dog, we named them Romeo and Juliet. Over time, Juliet has grown a lot bigger than Romeo, but I'm sure that trend will reverse.

The population of Noble Savage farm is therefore as follows:
two cats,
an old dog,
two pigs,
a few field mice,
a family of hedgehogs,

millions of more or less noxious invisible bugs
and two adult hominids.

October 25

Max has just left—he came by for lunch and made the most of
a break in the weather to get the rust off the bike. He brought all
the news from the village: everyone is fine. Arnaud has adapted
to living at the Savage Mind, he's happy there, and Mathilde is
happy taking care of him a bit. We were afraid that he might be
confused when the grandfather's house was sold, but no. He
comes by quite often to help fix some of the farm machinery, in
fact he's here most weekends, though Max obviously knew that.

The regulars at the Café-Pêche still have their drunken happy
hour every night from 6 to 8 p.m.; Maximilien doesn't go as
often these days, he says; he spends more time at home with
Lynn. Thomas is unbearable, apparently, he's constantly in a foul
mood, and he's in a lot of pain from an inguinal hernia that he's
too terrified to have surgically repaired.

Max is doing a lot better; he's stopped photographing his
stools every morning and has started to paint again. I think Lynn
is a good influence.

When the weather improves, we'll have to go for another
weekend in the Marais.

So on June 30, after a month's notice, a trip to Italy, and dozens of
hours of work getting our future home at Noble Savage Holdings
more or less in order, I left the Savage Mind for the last time.

I was sad and I wasn't.

I went to take my leave, kissed Mathilde goodbye, shook
Gary's hand, Lucie was waiting by the car. I took one last tour
of my demesne—well, my former demesne. The cats watched
me, mewling softly in their carrier; it was joyous and sad; a ray
of sunshine I'd never noticed warmed the bed now stripped of

sheets, for no one. I grabbed my bags, and the carrier containing Nigel and Barley, walked out and left the door open.

Farewell savages, farewell voyages! I yelled.

Lucie gave me a strange look, her gray eyes shining, magical.

I tossed the suitcases into the back, settled the cats, the van reeked of death, but, hey, you can't have everything.

I fleetingly thought about Lara, it was better this way. *And seek upon the earth some far-flung place* ... what comes next?

"I'll do the driving, otherwise you'll be weaving like a drunk all over the road again," said Lucie.

"Yeah, right, that's all we need," I said, "that's all we need."

She tossed me the keys and laughed, I felt myself sprayed by the mist of her laugh, then it suddenly came to me: *Where man is free to till the soil in peace.*

Lucie climbed into the passenger seat and, despite the screwdriver, the window slid down ten centimeters as she slammed the door.

I waved to Gary, blew Mathilde a kiss.

"Come on, we don't have our whole lives," said Lucie.

"Well, actually, we do," I said.

I started the engine, put the car into first gear and we set off to save the planet.

CLARIFICATIONS

This novel was conceived and first begun in June 2009 at La Pensée Sauvage, a writing residency in Rochesson in the Vosges run by my friend Olivier Dautrey. I would like to extend my thanks to the Centre national du livre for the funds awarded me for this residency.

The poems that appear on p. 168 are by Yves Rabault (1911–1990), a singer and poet from Deux-Sèvres, known as "the Poitevin bard," who penned—among other things—the hit song "La Sauce aux lumas" to music by Vincent Scotto.

The verses in honor of the Rose Maidens of La Mothe-Saint-Héray on p. 220 are by Auguste Gaud (1857–1924).

Lucan's description of the forest of Gaul in *Pharsalia* on pp. 295–96 (which is near Marseille, rather than in the west of France) is taken from Jean-François Marmontel's translation.

Bossuet's sermon on death, of which Bellende recites an excerpt (pp. 258–59), was delivered for the fourth week of Lent, 1662, in the Louvre, in the presence of the King, when its author was a thirty-five-year-old parish priest.

The verses of Boethius on p. 240 are taken from book 1, chapter 11 of *The Consolation of Philosophy*, and those on pp. 242–44 from book 2, chapter 14.

The quotation from Seneca is from his fourth letter to Lucilius. The account of Cato's suicide is from letter 24.

The lines quoted on pp. 255–56 are from Lucretius's *De rerum natura* (verses 900–930).

In a bar in Berlin, in autumn 2009, the painter Juan Miguel Pozo told me that he had met a madman in Havana who recited interminable ephemera in exchange for small change—I immediately imagined the man as both a scholar and an omniscient shaman.

Particular thanks to Michel Bertaud de Béceleuf, historian of the Plaine, to whom I owe the novel by the schoolmaster Marcel Barbaud (whom I have called Marcel Gendreau), the real title of which is *Nature exige…* and which is very different from the terrible story of Lucie and Jérémie, which I invented out of whole cloth. The *mirliton* verses I attribute to Gendreau do scant justice to those of the "real" Marcel Barbaud, who (like Marcel Gendreau) concluded in Échiré the career as a schoolmaster he had begun in Faye-sur-Ardin.

Daniel Chotard liked to tell stories of his youth. I liked to listen to his stories of village life, of drunken postmen napping behind drystone walls on payday, of road workers spending weeks on end on farms in exchange for enough pavement to cover the farmyard, of drunken trade unionists doing a barrel roll in a Simca in downtown Niort after an all too boozy celebration of a left-wing election victory.

Many of the stories in this book are true; Daniel told them to me. May he rest in peace.

During one of our last conversations, my father confided that the thing that had given him the most pleasure in life was angling. On December 30, 2019, the gravediggers carried his body to the flames; his soul was sent back to the Wheel.

This book is dedicated to him, and to all those who people the memories of a childhood spent in the Deux-Sèvres.

TRANSLATOR'S ACKNOWLEDGMENTS

In a sense, all translation, all writing is a palimpsest. In finding words and phrases we use, in summoning voices to reflect the music that we hear draws, we draw on all the writers and translators we have read, all the plays and films we have seen, all the chance conversations overheard that left a phonological shard buried in our minds.

In *The Annual Banquet of the Gravediggers' Guild*, Mathias Énard consciously interlaces the veins of history, robing and overlaying them with centuries of linguistic change. In playfully evoking a twenty-first-century Rabelaisian bacchanal, he draws not only on *Gargantua and Pantagruel*, but on the half-remembered, half-forgotten language that underpins modern French. He quotes liberally—from Seneca, Lucilius and Boethius, but also from poets and bards of Poitevin and Poitevin-Saintongeais, dialects and languages all but lost now. His danse macabre is as much an ode to language as it is a hymn to death ... and to life.

I am indebted to a number of translators and writers (some living, others sent back to the Wheel) who have helped or inspired me in rescoring Mathias's glorious polyphonic motet:

Charlotte Mandell, peerless translator of Énard's other novels; it was she who suggested entrusting me with what has been one of the most challenging and exhilarating texts it has been my pleasure to translate.

Sir Thomas Urquhart of Cromarty and *Peter Anthony Motteux,* for the incomparable first translation of *Gargantua and Pantagruel* (Books I and II, 1653; Book III, posthumously in 1693). On occasion, Urquhart (and, later, Motteux) deviates wildly from Rabelais's original—but does so with all the spirit, the brio and the élan of the master and, in doing so, liquefies and refashions language itself.

Divers other translators of Rabelais, to wit *William Francis Smith* (1893), *Jacques Leclercq* (1936), *Donald M. Frame* (1991) and *Michael Andrew Screech* (2006), whose translations I reveled in reading.

Charles J. Stivale for translations of Deleuze.

H. R. James for his 1897 translation of Boethius's *De consolatione philosophiae,* which I have freely adapted to correspond to the French translation used here (which plays fast and loose with the original Latin).

Richard M. Gummere for his translation of Seneca's letters to Lucilius (published 1927).

William Ellery Leonard for the 1916 translation of Lucretius's *De rerum natura.*

Sir Edward Ridley, whose translation of Lucan's *Pharsalia* I have adapted to coincide with the French translation quoted here.

The countless translators who contributed to the King James Bible, and *William Tyndale* on whose herculean work they based theirs.

Beram Saklatvala, translator of the poems of François Villon, which have inspired and informed my parodic verses.

I owe a particular debt of gratitude to Matt Mackie. When Pélagie is cross-examined in court on pp. 321–23, she answers the (French) questions of the barristers in Poitevin-Saintongeais, a *langue d'oïl* that still survives in the Pays de la Loire and Nouvelle-Aquitaine. To preserve the original effect of understanding "through a glass darkly," I elected to translate her responses into

Scots, which is still widely spoken. It was Matt Mackie, a Scots translator, who revised and hugely improved on my efforts. My thanks also to Lawrence Schimel, Josephine Murray and Mariona Miret.

This translation is dedicated to all translators, everywhere, at all times.

—FRANK WYNNE